MÉLISA RYUN

Create Mode Media LLC

7925 W. Russell Road #401103

Las Vegas, NV 89140

eBook Edition ISBN-13: 9781947775145

Paperback Edition ISBN-13: 9781947775152

For permission requests contact:

info@melisaryun.com

www.melisaryun.com

TRIGGER WARNING: This book contains explicit sexual content, cyber bullying, a toxic relationship, and a small storyline about survivors of a natural disaster.

DEDICATION

To the helpers, the givers, the ones who show up when no one's watching—your kindness sends ripples through the universe. Keep making waves with that big, beautiful heart.

CHAPTER ONE

CAM

"Oh shit! *¡Mierda!*" I curse, smacking my head on an oversized flower arrangement. I'm crouched upside down with one leg out, awkwardly wedged between a gaudy vase full of plastic white roses and a candelabra that's begging to catch fire.

The GoPro camera nearly slips from my hands as I fumble to mount it to the floral monstrosity. "Go ahead and fall. I dare you. I'll edit you into Reece's blooper reel."

I rub the sore spot—my forehead crying out in pain as I scan the empty church. Thank God no one heard me cursing in Spanish. The last thing I need is to be struck by lightning before I get these cameras set up.

I bet God himself couldn't find me in this glitter-pocalypse.

"Lord, in case I die here, it's me, Camila Morales. I apologize in advance for how many times I will be taking your name in vain today."

Seriously. Every surface of this historic church has been bedazzled within an inch of its holy life—which tracks since it's the Super Bowl of influencer weddings starring YouTube's crown prince Reece Dare and Astrid Montclair, the "Queen of Extra."

With this much sparkle, as soon as we start filming, the collective glare might just set the whole place on fire.

But hey, if that happens, at least we'll go viral.

One hundred and fifty million subscribers are waiting to watch this train wre—I mean, beautiful union of two content creators whose entire relationship has been scripted, filtered, and presented in 8K resolution.

And I am the lucky videographer who's capturing every moment of this *totally authentic* love story. Two years of filming their staged kisses and manufactured "spontaneous" moments.

"Come on, you sparkly bastard," I mutter, fighting a zip tie to anchor the GoPro to this nightmare bouquet *(because naturally, Astrid made me spray glitter glue on them to "match her aesthetic").*

My cargo pants swish as I grab gaffer's tape to secure the camera. These babies are my pride and joy—twelve pockets of pure organizational heaven. Right thigh: battery packs organized like a SWAT team on standby. Left thigh: emergency ring lights because God forbid we have subpar lighting during a crisis. Front pockets: enough caffeine shots to make a med student jealous.

The utility belt on my waist should have its own documentary series. If these pouches could talk... well, they'd need their own NDAs. I've got more equipment strapped to my body than Batman, except instead of fighting crime, I'm battling nip slips and influencer breakdowns.

I step away to assess my handiwork, but I'm blinded by the over-the-top iridescent sea of decorations. Everything shimmers in here like a mermaid's ass—no, a radioactive jellyfish. Either way, the church walls shift between lavender, gold, and hot pink—it's a highlighter palette on steroids.

Still, my GoPro stands proud and defiant amid the expensive holographic chaos. *Victory!* But at what cost? My cargo pants, which usually act as my fortress of practicality, are now covered in silver glitter. I look like I got down on my knees and serviced a unicorn.

Pulling out my phone, I open the video monitor app and check my framing. Wide shot from the back? *Check.*

Side cameras positioned to record the audience's staged reactions? *Check.*

Roaming close-ups that'll catch important moments like Astrid's spray tan streaking? *All Me.*

Because the money shots can't be trusted with stationary equipment. Still, something's missing.

I need one more angle, a God's-eye view of the wedding march. My gaze travels up the massive stone pillars—ornately carved bases that are wider than my apartment's bathroom—and I see a perfect ledge for my camera. Scaling these architectural masterpieces is all but impossible. Every. Single. Inch of them... is smothered in twinkly lights and crystal garlands.

"Okay, Cam, think." I reach up, fingers grasping at the nearest pillar's base. Nope. Not even close. Unless I magically sprout six more feet, this isn't happening. If I had a ladder, I could rig a selfie stick and zip tie the lens then monitor the shot from my phone.

Hmm. Gotta get creative. These cameras aren't going to mount themselves, and I'm capturing the wedding of the century. Or at least the wedding of the week. The internet has the attention span of a TikTok goldfish, so who knows?

I've filmed Reece jumping between rooftops, swimming with sharks, and once, memorably, provoking a troop of monkeys while dressed as a giant banana. But *this*? This might be my greatest challenge yet.

"Hey, God, quick question. You cool with me doing parkour in your house?"

I shoot a swift glance. Coast is clear. This is why I showed up hours before call time—to put out fires before they become full-blown infernos. Gripping the side of a clear acrylic chair, I drag it across the church floor.

SCCCRREEEECH!

Jesus, Mary, and Influencer Joseph, that was loud. The sound ricochets off the stained-glass windows that have probably witnessed centuries of better decisions than the one I'm about to make. My hands hesitate on the chair back, evaluating the towering pillar.

Deep breaths. Let's do this. I grab the scrunchie off my wrist. There is always, ALWAYS a scrunchie on standby. I have three backup options nestled in my cargo pockets this very second. Because after you've had your hair tangled in a drone mid-flight while dangling off the side of a mountain, you come prepared.

That, and well... I learned in college that a hand job can accidentally double as a hair appointment. Who knew magical man juice could pass for premium hair gel? I won't be sharing that life hack in Astrid's next *Beauty Secrets Revealed* video.

I gather my long chestnut waves into a high ponytail, the familiar motion centering me like meditation. My fingers glide through my strands, catching the faint coconut scent from this morning's shower. The way I'm sweating, I better savor whatever's left of that fresh feeling.

My gaze drifts up the column again, mentally calculating angles and handholds as if I'm a stunt double. This shouldn't even register on my danger scale. I've literally hung off helicopters—one time to get the perfect shot of Reece bungee jumping into an active volcano. *Okay, fine, it was dormant, but still... my brain has a point.*

"Another day at the office," I mutter, testing the seat's stability. The plastic creaks ominously under my Converse. *This is why I wore cargo pants with reinforced knees today. You know, for occasional pillar climbing and other normal wedding videographer to-dos.*

Teenage me would be losing her shit right now. Back then, I was just another film nerd with a borrowed camera and a dream, watching Reece's uploads as if they were sacred teachings. While other girls were freeze-framing his abs *(which, okay, fair)*, I was pausing videos frame by frame, studying his innovative cinematography and groundbreaking editing techniques.

"And now look at me." I snort-laugh, pulling my body up onto the ledge.

Twenty-five-year-old me gets to film with Reece *rebranded (featuring twenty percent more disappointment)*. My one-time idol now does "authentic" morning routines that take longer to shoot than most feature films. Here's a secret: nobody does their skincare routine while gazing soulfully out floor-to-ceiling windows from their mega mansion at sunrise. Nobody.

The worst part isn't even that he's traded storytelling for brand deals. It's who he is in real life. That charming, adventurous guy who inspired me to pick up a camera? Turns out, the guy is as phony as Astrid's platinum blonde hair and double D-cups. The actual Reece Dare has two modes: brooding silence and cutting criticism. The only way I see that famous million-dollar smile directed at me is when I'm watching it through my viewfinder.

"¡Mierda!" My foot slips. I lunge, my arms gripping the rhinestone-covered support beam, cheeks pressed into the cold stone, gemstones scratching my skin.

"Okay. Not dead. That's good."

But hanging on to this pillar like a sequined koala? Less good.

A fall from this height would put me in a full-body cast for sure. Reece's voice plays in my head, all gruff and judgmental: *Maybe next time, plan better, Morales.* I can already picture myself strapped to a hospital bed and him barking: *Edit with your toes if you have to.*

"Not helpful, imaginary Reece."

I glance at the camera dangling from my belt. Almost there. I just need to zip-tie it to the top. Totally doable.

My foot scrapes against the pillar. Glitter showers down like I've taken out a piñata. I tiptoe higher, legs shaking, fingers cramping. One arm holds the GoPro, while the other clings to the pole. It's a delicate balancing act that reminds me of those carnival games that are rigged so you never win. But I refuse to lose.

Up. Up. Up. I stretch, forcing my camera higher.

One more inch.

One more tug.

Pull it tight.

Got it!

My thighs burn. My arms scream. But before I can figure out a plan to climb down, my phone blares in my pocket.

BRRRING! BRRRING!

"Oh, come on."

My toe manages to find the edge of the ledge, still dangling precariously as I fumble for my cell. The caller ID reads: *CPK Forever.*

Katie and Petra. My girls. My lifelines. The name is a tribute to our college obsession with California Pizza Kitchen. Also, our initials: Cam, Petra, Katie.

I swipe to answer, my free hand gripping the pillar. "*¡Hola,* besties!" I say, holding the phone at an awkward angle to keep my face in frame. "Don't mind me. Just hanging on by a thread. Or a pole. Take your pick."

Katie appears first, glowing in soft blonde waves, her green eyes sparkling. Petra pops up next—jet-black hair in a messy bun—looking every bit the punk rock troublemaker she is.

"Cam, babe, what's with the sparkly forehead?" Petra squints at me, grinning. "Is this a special wedding request from your boss, or did you headbutt a stripper's chest?"

Katie tilts her head, eyes narrowing. "More importantly, why does it look like you're one bad decision away from another ER visit?"

"Because I am," I deadpan, tilting my phone down to reveal the tiny ledge beneath my feet. "Welcome to influencer hell. It's glamorous—no, really."

"There you go again, being all brave and shit." Petra smirks through the screen, her red lipstick impeccable as she leans back in her office chair. "You should've quit after that skydiving proposal video. Gone out on a literal high note."

"She's right," Katie adds. The scenic vineyards of Tuscany behind her are a postcard come to life. "If I've learning anything on my spontaneous trip to Italy, it's that there is no time like the present to pursue what you want."

"Buckle up, here it comes." Petra rolls her heavily lined eyes. "Kidding. I usually ignore Katie's cheerleading, but she's right. You gotta chase those documentary dreams. Face it, you're now the reckless friend while I'm stuck here optimizing synergy or whatever corporate BS I'm supposed to care about."

"I know, I know," I say, adjusting my grip. "Soon. I promise."

The lie sits heavy in my chest next to the two-weeks'-notice email I sent Reece's manager, Gordon Thorne, this morning. It's probably burning a hole through his perfectly gelled mid-life hair right now. But I can't tell them. Not yet. Not when my big dreams feel about as stable as my current position on this bedazzled pillar of doom.

My stomach churns as I think about what I'm planning: A documentary YouTube channel. Something real. Something important. Not another I SURVIVED 24 HOURS LIVING LIKE A HAMSTER video.

Ugh. I can still smell the cedar wood shavings from that shoot.

The dream's been lurking in my Notes app for months. Story ideas. Shot lists. Production contacts. Everything I need except the one thing that matters—courage.

When I was in college, I won an award for a short film I did on after-school meals and underprivileged children. It was in my hometown of New York City, and my sister Aria snuck me into the kitchen where she volunteered. I'll never forget the way those kids' faces lit up at their first hot meal of the day—it was pure, unfiltered joy. Not influencer weddings or rich people pretending to be in love for brand deals—real moments, genuine lives, and actual impact. Those are the stories I want to tell.

But success on YouTube isn't simply talent and good ideas. It's algorithms and analytics and convincing the internet that your content has more value than videos of cats knocking things off tables. Which, let's be honest, is a tough sell.

And, I'd never say this out loud, but I'm not exactly comfortable in front of the camera.

This is why I need Reece. A single mention from him—a mere thirty seconds of that stupidly gorgeous face telling his followers to check out my channel—and boom. Instant audience.

But asking Reece for favors? Might as well ask a grizzly bear to share his salmon.

While he's hibernating.

After you've just woken him up.

Still, a couple weeks of honeymooning in Hawaii has to soften him up, right? Nothing says "help a girl out" like mai tais and newlywed coital bliss. Assuming he doesn't murder me when he finds out I'm quitting.

Petra's voice is a whip snapping through my thoughts. "Cam! Are you frozen? This is what I get for being so poor I had to switch to Budget Wireless."

"Yeah, no, sorry."

I blink, the ache in my thighs dragging me back to reality. My legs are trembling under the strain of this ridiculous position.

"We need details," Katie pleads. "Tell us about the wedding. The honeymoon."

"Hard pass," I groan. "Let's talk about you and the Italian Stallion tour guide. Your thirst traps are killing me but not *giving* enough. Spill it."

"Same," Petra chimes in. "My Instagram feed needs more spicy pics of you two."

Katie's cheeks flame red. "It's not what you think. Matteo's my tour guide. He's just... helping me make Jared jealous. You know, so I can win him back."

My heart crumples like a discarded storyboard. It hurts to see my friend in denial. Katie's fiancé just dumped her, but is she moving on? Not a chance. Instead of having revenge sex with hot Italian guys, she's trying to get back together. After bailing on their engagement, Jared is forever on my shit list.

"I'd be climbing that Italian eggplant," I say. "Sorry, ya girl has been in a major sex drought. The most action I've seen lately is my camera's 'low battery' vibration."

"PETRA!" a man's voice booms off-screen. "I need that TPS report on the Johson account, and I need it now."

She blinks like she's counting to ten. "It's coming, jeez! Keep your shirt on, bro!" Petra promptly dives under her desk and whispers like the walls are bugged and she knows too much. "Speaking of droughts, what's your hottie boss wearing for the wedding? A tux jacket minus the shirt? Maybe a bow tie and board shorts? Can we talk about his lickable abs?"

I'd ask Petra how her new job's going, but she's hiding under the desk, so... I think that answers that. Working at her brother's company was meant to be a fresh start, a chance to show her family she's not a screw-up. Her pile of problems goes beyond her massive crush on co-CEO Bryce Sterling *(AKA her brother's billionaire best friend)*, there's also the nonstop tension with her big bro. Yeah, her whole adulting comeback might be circling the drain.

I groan. "My prickwad douchecanoe boss can wear a banana hammock around his schlong. All I care about is surviving this day, flying to Hawaii, and getting my lady bits some much-needed attention on my workcation."

Katie's eyes go wide. "Um, aren't you filming your boss at a couples-only honeymoon resort? How are you getting laid?"

"There has to be at least one Hawaiian hottie willing to show me his—"

"Tiki torch?" Petra finishes for me.

"Exactly!"

"Are you planning to seduce lifeguards with your tactical cargo pants?" Katie snickers. "Although my Aunt Deb would probably suggest using those zip ties as kinky handcuffs."

"Hell no. I've got five sizzling bikinis packed and ready to hit the beach. And my sexy sleepwear collection is so skimpy, it's one step away from imaginary."

"Hunt down that Hawaiian D!" Petra cheers.

"Oh, I plan to go full predator mode. I'm gonna climb every cabana boy at that resort like a coconut tree. I want the entire Hawaiian buffet—appetizer, main course, dessert. Any guy who wants a piece of this curvy Latina ass better grab a number, because mama's got six months of pent-up—"

"Mm-hmm." A familiar throat clears below me.

It's a deep, disapproving rumble. *Uh-oh.*

There he is... Reece fucking Dare.

"*¡Ay, Dios mío!*" The Spanish flies out, and I let go of the support beam as if it's suddenly on fire.

WHAM!

I slam into Reece's chest in the world's most unexpected trust fall. His arms wrap around me like steel cables, strong and unyielding. For a man who spends most of his time laughing in the face of gravity, Reece Dare unexpectedly cradles me as if I'm... *fragile?* No, that can't be right.

My cell is still clutched in a death grip, and Katie and Petra are frozen in perfect *oh shit* expressions. I slam the *End Call* button so hard I probably crack my screen.

His steel-blue eyes lock on to mine...

with the intensity of a shark...

who just saw me double dipping...

and then caught me peeing in his section of the ocean.

And if he wasn't already gorgeous enough, a beam of sunlight—on cue—shines through the stained glass, hitting his jawline as if God himself is his personal lighting director.

His dark, tousled hair slightly covers the scar above his right eyebrow—earned from one of my favorite videos, *Will It Bounce? Trampoline Edition*—and it only adds to his whole brooding-but-fuck-I'm-sexy vibe.

For just a millisecond, I forget how to breathe. Maybe it's the rush of cheating death, or maybe his scent—a heady combination of ocean saltwater and spicy ginger—has hijacked my senses. My cheek grazes his shoulder, and yep, that's pure muscle under the thin layer of fabric.

He'd be absolutely perfect if—

"Is scaling church property while discussing your sexual conquests part of your normal pre-wedding routine?"

—if he never opened his mouth.

"Oh definitely," I say, ignoring how his arms flex as I try to wriggle loose. "Jesus and I were just having a heart-to-heart about my upcoming romance-cation."

His darkening expression is an incoming storm. "About that conversation—"

"My personal itinerary?" I say, breaking free and immediately missing his warmth. *Disloyal body.* "Don't worry, I'll schedule all my Hawaiian hookups around your content calendar. I won't be the third wheel crashing your honeymoon vibes. I'm nothing if not professional!"

There's a fleeting spark of surprise in his gaze before he's back to his default perma-scowl.

"If you're done cosplaying as a holy acrobat," he growls, jabbing a finger toward my camera, "maybe fix that disaster of an angle. You're going to miss half the processional."

Oh no he didn't. I risked my life for that shot. I thrust my cell at him. "Prepare to eat your words with a side of 'I was wrong' sauce."

His fingers brush mine as he takes the phone—a quick, incidental touch, but it sends goosebumps skittering up my arm.

Double shit.

There on my lock screen, in all their glistening glory, is my collage of Hawaiian beach hotties. Surfboards optional, abs mandatory. My finger flies to the sensor, but it's too late—Reece has already gotten an eyeful of my tropical thirst board.

Reece's eyebrow performs its signature judgmental arch. "Location research?"

"Not that it's any of your business, but yes, I fully intend to enjoy my workcation after this circus of a wedding. Umbrella drinks. Beach views. Might even do a hula lesson."

"Don't forget the cabana boys," he says, the sarcasm dripping from every word.

"Trust me, I won't." I shoot him a pointed look, ignoring the heat crawling up my neck. "Now, are you going to admit my shot is perfect, or are we still pretending you know more about wide angles than I do?"

Reece glances at the monitor app open on my phone, his jaw tightening as he studies the feed. He simply stares like he's looking for something to criticize.

Finally, he grunts. "It's... acceptable."

"*Acceptable?*" I gasp, palm to my heart. "Whoa, thanks. That's a standing ovation coming from you. I better bust out my victory dance before you ruin it."

"Don't push it, Morales," he says, handing the phone back. For a split second, a grudging—maybe even amused—look flickers across his face. But it's gone just as fast, and he turns on his heel without another word.

For a guy about to marry the *love of his life*, he's carrying enough storm clouds to cancel a Hawaiian luau. I guess he's nervous? Whatever. Not my problem. I've got a job to do.

"There's my star! Who's camera ready for his big day?"

The shout reverberates through the once peaceful church like a megaphone, and I instinctively cringe. Gordon Thorne, Reece's manager and self-proclaimed *starmaker*. He strides in, a human hurricane of ego, carrying a tray of coffees in one hand and shopping bags in the other. His smile gleams as if it's superglued in place—glossy, lifeless, and weirdly off-putting.

From his obviously fresh Botox to his over-plugged hairline, everything about Gordon screams "fifty-year-old trying to pass for a Gen-Z-years-old." Today he's decked out in a lavender tuxedo—an attempt to complement Astrid's iridescent aesthetic. Honestly, he resembles the missing friend from *Dumb and Dumber* who got lost on his way to prom in 1995.

"Hey, camera girl!" he calls out. "Why aren't you filming?"

"Gordon, man, we talked about this," Reece cuts in. "She has a name."

"Yeah, that's how I remember her—Cam, camera girl! It's our nickname. Right?" He flashes me a we're-on-the-same-page smile. *Newsflash: we're not.*

"Sure?" I answer, though it comes out more as a question.

"Here." Gordon dumps some goodie bags in my arms then whips out a sage green shirt and tosses it to Reece. "Put this on for the intro. The color is everything. That chartreuse monstrosity? Disaster."

"I'm not convinced starting over with designers was worth the cost," Reece says, but his fingers are already working down his shirt buttons.

Sweet mother of manual focus. I should look away. I really should. But my eyes have a mind of their own, sneaking peeks at abs I can never get enough of. Which is completely inappropriate since he's getting married in—I check my screen—one and half hours.

"Take it from someone who knows the game," Gordon says, oozing with I-know-best confidence. "One wrong move, and you're sunk. That's why we kicked off with clothes. Come next month, when your shoe line launches—your income's gonna skyrocket, mark my words."

He spins toward me. "Camera girl, we need DareFuel cans everywhere. New Caffeine Tsunami Coconut for the honeymoon content, but Hyperdrive Honeydew and Orange Eruption are still our money makers."

I stuff energy drink cans into my pockets while my brain short-circuits. *Maybe Gordon doesn't know my full name. What if he doesn't realize that it was me who sent him the resignation email?*

Fuck.

My heart starts racing against my ribs. I haven't thought this through. The email only went out this morning. Even worse, what if Gordon does know and then he tells Reece about my two-weeks' notice right here, right now? My entire plan of breaking the news in Hawaii *(after Reece has consumed his body weight in piña coladas)* will be ruined.

"Let's go over the wedding sponsors real quick—" Gordon unfurls a list so long it could double as a bridal train.

Reece emits a guttural groan that sounds as if his soul is attempting to escape.

"Hey, who got you a private jet to Maui?" Gordon preens. "G-Thorne, that's who!"

I bite back a laugh at Gordon's self-given nickname. The truth is, he's not wrong. It's influencer economics 101. YouTube views might pay for some fancy dinners, but the real money? That's in products and sponsorship deals. Reece isn't just a person; he's an all-out brand. DareWear. DareFuel. DareProductions. It's a giant empire with employees, offices, and overhead. And Gordon? That guy's been running the show for five years, calling himself the "architect of Reece Dare."

"Woo-hoo! Bro wifey'd up!" The shout echoes off the vaulted ceilings.

I look up to see the internet's second favorite prankster zooming down the mirrored aisle like it's his own personal Slip 'N Slide.

THWUMP.

He crashes into Reece at the end, nearly taking them both out. "Bro! Hug tackle!" Blaze says, popping up as if nothing happened, "We gotta do that again for the fans—straight fire!"

And there it is—Reece's smile appears like magic. The one that's launched a gazillion thirst posts and convinced millions of subscribers that he's sunshine incarnate instead of a daily black hole of joy.

Blake "Blaze" Tate is Reece's best friend and perpetual partner-in-chaos. Girls love his bleach blonde hair, blue eyes, surfer bod, and sleeve of random tattoos *(seriously, a fire-breathing gremlin riding a pizza?)*. I imagine he's what would happen if you asked AI to design a dudebro. Sure, the man's got muscles for days and a grin that causes pregnancy scares, but he's no Reece Dare.

The thing about Blaze? Not the sharpest tool in the shed. But he's harmless and perpetually excited about everything. More importantly, he is the only one who can get Mr. Grumpy Pants to laugh.

"Blaze, my man!" Gordon holds his hand up for a high-five.

"G-Thorne! Looking shiny, my dude!" He smacks his hand so hard that Gordon winces.

"Camera girl! Let's shoot the intro like he said. Set it up."

Blaze drags Reece back down the aisle, shouting, "Cam! Get low. For a sick crash angle!"

"That's too risky—" Reece starts.

"Cam's chill, right?" Blaze asks me.

And there I am, once again choosing between common sense and the shot. "Yup." I drop into position. "Anything for the content."

Reece's scowl could frighten a demon back to hell.

"Action!" Gordon shouts.

They take off running. "It's my wedding day!" Reece yells as they hit the shiny runway.

When Astrid proposed a center aisle made entirely of mirrors, I knew it was going to be a filming nightmare. But not gonna lie, this is a fucking epic shot. The boys running, their reflections filling the frame in an echoing blur.

I hold tight as they slide closer, closer, closer—

WHAM.

Suddenly I'm flat on my back with six feet of pure muscle crushing me into the floor. But my footage? Steady as a surgeon. I didn't spend two years filming parkour stunts to fumble the shot.

Reece's weight pins me to the ground, our eyes lock, and for a moment, we freeze. His heart hammers against mine, and I see the flecks of darker blue in his gaze. I can feel his breath on my lips—

"Cut!" Gordon breaks the spell. "Perfect! Now let's get some product placement in there. I want DareFuel cans front and center on the altar. Make Jesus proud!"

I scramble up, refusing to acknowledge my buzzing skin. Through my viewfinder, I watch Reece transform into the charming goofball. It's a magic trick worthy of Vegas—the way he can flip that switch and become the guy everyone thinks they know.

"Hey, DareSquad!" he says with a grin. "Smash that *Like* button if you're pumped to see me get married today!"

"That's right, fam!" Blaze says, beaming. "DareDuo's gettin' married. I mean, we're not, but my boy is. He's gonna be Mr. Astrid."

He looks at Reece, blinking like it just hit him.

"Bro... we still buds after you're married? I can come over, right?"

"Always, bro." Reece throws an arm around him. "This is only the start of our next epic adventure—"

"Hellooo! The bride is here, people! Why are there no cameras on me?"

And just like that, the circus gets its ringleader. Astrid Montclair storms in, one hand on her hip, the other clutching her phone as if her life depends on it.

"Camera girl! What are you doing? Get Astrid in the shot! It's her big day!"

I fight the urge to roll my eyes and focus my lens on the bride. *Here we go.*

Astrid is... a lot. Platinum-blonde extensions run down her back in perfectly styled waves—so shiny I swear they're reflecting the rhinestones on the church walls. Her makeup is an exercise in excess: cheekbones carved with industrial-strength contour, lashes long enough to generate wind gusts, and lips plumped to cartoonish proportions. The neon pink dress she's wearing clings to her surgically enhanced curves like it's afraid to let go, while her teetering glittery stilettos are screaming, *Look at me bitches!*

Nothing about her is genuine. Not her hair, not her smile, and definitely not the green eyes she flaunts for her Instagram followers *(those babies are tinted contacts).* Over the last twenty-four months, I have had a front-row seat to the Astrid Montclair Diva Show. Let's just say I've learned to pack snacks.

"Oh my fucking God, forget the whole damn thing!" She throws her hands up, her flashy acrylics resembling daggers. "And why the hell is Reece here? He can't see me yet! Isn't that, like, bad wedding voodoo or something?"

Right on cue, the waterworks start. Gotta hand it to her—she's perfected the art of crying without smudging her makeup. Must be all that practice from her apology videos.

Reece pinches the bridge of his nose. "Astrid, can we not—"

"Oh my God, Reece, do you *hate* happiness?" She wails, stomping her stiletto on the mirrored floor. "Because that's what it feels like! You are ruining *my* ceremony with your bad vibes. This happily-ever-after kickoff was supposed to be *iconic*! Like, TMZ-wedding-spread iconic! And now? Now it's giving *dumpster fire energy!*"

She flips her hair, turns, and power walks out of the church like someone who just rage-quit a video game. For a moment, nobody moves. The only sound is Blaze's muffled snicker. This is Astrid Playbook 101. She'll be back.

Gordon claps his hands together. "I got this, Reece. No worries." He turns to me, his eyes narrowing. "And you—keep that camera rolling, no matter what. Got it?"

Gordon rushes after Astrid, and I glance at Reece, who looks to be seconds away from breaking something expensive.

I exhale slowly, adjusting my filming rig. *A few more hours,* I remind myself. One last stretch of chaos, glitter, and diva tantrums, then I'm on a plane to Maui.

Paradise is waiting. And it can't come soon enough.

CHAPTER TWO

REECE

"HERE COME THE VULTURES," I grumble, peeking out from behind the church stage.

The sanctuary is filling up faster than Blaze can shotgun a beer. Row after row fill with human peacocks, each more desperate for attention than the last. Astrid's crew of beauty gurus claim the front seats, their faces so contoured and plumped their own mothers wouldn't recognize them. The second row features the usual suspects: gaming nerds who've never touched grass, prank channels that peaked in 2020, and fitness creators who definitely skip leg day but never skip a chance to flex.

It's not a wedding. It's a viral content factory.

I scan the sea of ring lights and selfie sticks—over 500 people who'd sell their firstborn for followers. These are all "special guests" who would never show up without Wi-Fi and an active Instagram audience. I search for a single person I would consider a friend...

Zero.

The number hits harder than the time I jumped off a building into a trampoline of LEGOS for views.

These are influencers: a select group of who's who—people who treat friends as networking opportunities and use social media engagement as currency. They're not here to celebrate love—they're here to be *seen* celebrating love. It brings up that philosophical question: if an influencer attends a marriage ceremony but doesn't post about it, did it even happen?

Every single one of them wants something. A sponsorship deal. A shoutout. A collab. A paycheck. These favor-fishing parasites slide requests into my DMs like desperate ex-girlfriends. "Sup, bestie, let me catch you up on my new hydrating, oat-milk-infused collagen powder." And a recent favorite: "Hey hottie, totally random, but do you want to promote my gluten-free, non-toxic moon water?"

In this whole cathedral, I can count the people who actually give a shit about me with four fingers: Blaze *(when he's not being an idiot)*, my mothers, and Gordon *(though his caring comes with a fifteen percent management fee)*.

They say it's lonely at the top. What they don't tell you is that the view is a sea of faces, all waiting—phones in hand—to capture your fall for their next viral clip.

"Oh em gee. The chandeliers are literally everything!" a blonde in row three squeals. "Wait till my followers see this!"

I'm glad she's impressed; she should be. Last time I checked, the wedding bills were up to three million dollars. Three. Fucking. Million. And that's not counting the "surprise" musical performances Astrid's planned for the after-party, featuring influencers who think autotune is a personality trait.

I glance at my phone. Thirty minutes until I sign away my life for views, trade my happiness for the security of others, and my integrity for a prenup that reads like a brand deal contract.

"G-Thorne has entered the building!" Gordon booms, strutting down the aisle in his lavender tux. *He's eye-catching... in an aging Velvet Elvis kind of way.* Content creators are scrambling over each other to get a handshake from my "starmaker" manager.

I still remember two years ago, sitting in Gordon's chrome and leather office. His new hair plugs caught the fluorescent light as he slid those devastating analytics across his desk.

"Adventure content is dead, kid. The numbers don't lie," he'd said, tapping a graph that resembled a ski slope. "But I've got your golden ticket—Astrid Montclair. She's the queen of beauty; you're the king of stunts. It's a match made in algorithm heaven!"

I'd laughed. Actually fucking laughed. Because surely this was a joke, right? Fake dating the high priestess of overdrawn lips and underwhelming content?

But then he mentioned the staff cuts we'd have to make. The families that would be affected. The healthcare packages that would vanish—including the one covering my mom's treatments.

Funny how fast principles disappear when reality comes knocking.

Keep smiling. Stay relevant. Don't let them see you crack.

That mantra's been my soundtrack ever since.

At first, it wasn't so bad. A few staged dates, some couples' challenges, pretending to care about skincare routines or whatever. Other influencers do it all the time. But weeks bled into months, months into years. Each video more plastic than before, until I forgot what *real* felt like.

Every time I tried to pull the plug, Gordon would play his trump card. "Consider your employees, Reece. The families depending on you. Your mother's medications." Each word was another brick in the prison I'd built myself.

And he was right. I couldn't. Still can't.

Then Astrid proposed the engagement as if she was launching a new product line. "Think of the numbers! We'll break the internet!"

I had just nodded, already dead inside, wondering if this was what my life was meant to be—a walking, talking sponsorship opportunity with trust issues.

"This is literally iconic!" a teenager in an aisle seat squeals as she films the mirrored floor, which shimmers like a river of glass. "I can't believe I'm at Reece Dare's wedding! He's such relationship goals!"

Yup, that's me. About to marry somebody I don't even like, much less love. All for the sake of a channel I secretly wish would disappear.

Keep smiling. Stay relevant. Don't let them see you crack.

***

ALL I WANT IS a moment of peace before this shitshow begins. I glance hopefully at my green room door… It's vibrating, I mean actually pulsating with thumping bass sounds. I pause, hand hovering over the knob, bracing myself. Because either I'm having a stroke, or that's my mother rapping about WAP *(that's right, wet ass pussy).*

I open the door.

My mothers, Vera—better known as Mama V—and Helen, who we affectionately call Mom Hawk, are singing out explicit lyrics about the female anatomy like they're pop stars on a comeback tour. Their voices harmonize in a way that makes it so much worse.

Blaze coined those nicknames back in the day when we were two teenage idiots with a camera and a death wish, long before verification badges and brand deals made everything so damn complicated.

Mama V—my brunette, curly haired mother—is a free-spirited, former drama teacher. She's spitting Cardi B lines like she's been recruited in an underground rap battle. She's perched on her mobility scooter, lips mouthing every graphic syllable.

The dramatic pauses? Unnecessary. The overly expressive hand gestures? Deeply concerning. And now Mama V is twerking. WHILE. SEATED.

I make direct eye contact with my mom Helen, pleading for her to be the adult here. But my normally reserved, gray-haired, architect-to-the-stars parent *(who once grounded me for saying "crap" at the dinner table)* dismisses my frown gently. She's having a blast in full raunch-mode, belting out traumatizing lyrics about buckets, mops, creams, and screams. I start actively dissociating, staring at the ceiling as if it holds the answers to why my wedding day has turned into this.

Kill me. Kill me now.

Blaze is doubled over, his eyes wet with tears, that infectious laugh of his filling the room. The same laugh I've heard through a thousand stupid stunts, bad decisions, and when I got my first million subscribers.

And then there's Camila.

Fucking hell.

She's got her camera up, but for once, she's not the rock-steady pro I'm used to seeing. Her body shakes with laughter, sending glitter from her cargo pants raining down like confetti. Those damn pants are hugging her curves just right, and it's making my mind yearn to go places it shouldn't. Especially not twenty minutes before I'm supposed to say "I do" to someone else.

"Yo, Reece!" Blaze manages between gasps. "Mama V's got bars. We should post this video as *Moms' WAP Remix.* She's dropping lines so dirty. She's got flow, man. I'm scared for society."

My chest tightens. This is my real content. Not the manufactured, pre-planned bullshit waiting in that crystal-covered cathedral. Here's Mama, who sees her Parkinson's diagnosis as just another act in her ongoing performance of life. And Mom, our family rock, who cheers us on with genuine enthusiasm, no matter what.

Every view, every like, every viral moment—they all started because of one trembling hand and a stack of medical bills that were taller than the Washington monument.

When I was fifteen, I found a beat-up camera at a yard sale. Ten bucks and a prayer. I started filming increasingly wild stunts—anything to make people click, share, subscribe. That first viral video—me backflipping off the garage roof into a baby pool of Jell-O—paid for four months of Mama's medications. The second covered half a year of physical therapy. By the tenth trending video, we could afford the specialist Mom had been researching.

And my best friend Blaze has been my rock through everything—the good times, the bad times, and even the *let's car surf in LA traffic* fiasco that had Mom Hawk threatening military school.

His phone buzzes. "Aw, dang. G-Thorne's callin'. Best man stuff, probably, like... folding napkins or, I dunno, holding the rings." He moonwalks toward the door—shouldn't work, totally does. Because he's Blaze and he's never given a single fuck about looking cool.

For a brief, beautiful moment, everything feels normal. No trending hashtags. No analytics. No Gordon breathing down my neck about engagement metrics. Just my wonderfully weird family, my goofball best friend, and Cam...

But as soon as Blaze leaves, anxiety and impending doom creep back in. I do what I always do when I need a distraction—antagonize Camila Morales. Because watching her transform from sunshine to sass is like mainlining dopamine—better than any energy drink.

I lean against the long dining table in the middle of the room, its polished surface reflecting the scattered DareFuel cans and DareWear clothing. Cam is crouched nearby, digging through her cargos, probably searching for a backup battery.

She's muttering in Spanish—a melody of frustration directed at her equipment. Or maybe me. Hopefully me.

"Hand over the camera, Morales," I say, letting my voice carry the slightest edge of a challenge. "I want to check your footage."

"What's wrong, Dare? Don't trust my artistic vision? And here I thought we had something special."

"Your artistic vision gave me three double chins in last week's thumbnail."

"That wasn't the camera angle." She grins, completely unfazed by my scowl. "That was your *Cam's doing everything wrong* face. You know, the face you're making right now?"

Christ, her smile should come with a background check and a waiting period. It's like staring directly into the sun—brilliant and probably causes permanent damage.

"The footage, Morales."

Cam clutches her precious Sony as if I've asked to juggle her firstborn. "This is the new A7S IV. It has a different setup."

"I've been filming for a decade. I can handle pressing play."

"You haven't touched a camera in two years," she says but surrenders it anyway.

I fumble with the buttons, each click making my jaw clench tighter. The screen menu might as well be quantum physics. My fingers, which used to dance across camera controls as if they were extensions of my body, feel clumsy and foreign.

"Having trouble there, boss?" Cam says, eyes dancing with glee.

"Where's the fucking playback?"

"¡Ay, Dios! Watching you right now is like watching a grandpa discover Instagram filters." Cam's lips twitch, fighting a smile. She steps closer, coconut-scented hair brushing my arm as she reaches for the controls. "Time for Film School 101. And don't worry, I'll use small words."

She leans in, her fingers lightly touching mine, and my heart sings.

"This magical circle thing? It's called a control wheel. Con-trol-wheel."

"You're supposed to be my videographer, not a one-woman comedy show."

"And yet, I'm excelling at both," she replies, her grin unapologetic.

"Well played, Camila!" Mama says.

"Way to give it to him," Mom adds.

I give them both a betrayed expression. "Seriously? You're taking her side?"

"Sweetheart," Mom says, "anyone who can make you this delightfully flustered deserves our full support."

"I still know what I'm doing behind a camera," I growl.

"Sure you do." Cam pats my arm with mock sympathy. "And I'm sure somewhere, buried under all that grump and hair product, is the guy who once inspired me to pick up a camera. You know, back when you made cool content that didn't have to be sponsored."

The words slam into me, a wrecking ball to my ego, mainly because they're true.

"Oh snap!" Mama clutches her chest dramatically. "Helen, our son just got served!"

"Indeed." Mom's finger taps thoughtfully against her chin. "Though I'd rate it more of a gentle roasting than a full serving."

Cam's smile widens.

Time to switch tactics. I lift the camera, pointing it directly at her. The reaction is immediate—and fascinating. Cam's usual confidence falters, replaced by something softer, almost vulnerable. The girl who once hung off a helicopter to get the perfect shot suddenly can't meet the lens.

"Now this is interesting." I adjust the focus, watching her squirm.

"What are you doing?" she says, her voice uncharacteristically shy. "Reece, no—"

"Moms, break out the questions. We need answers."

"Reece," Mom warns.

"It's my wedding day. Pretty sure there's some universal law about everyone doing whatever the groom wants."

My mothers exchange their patented "our son is stressed" look—the same skeptical squint they shot me when I dropped the engagement bomb. It's no secret they're not thrilled with who I'm marrying today.

"The phrase is bridezilla, not groomzilla, dear," Mama corrects with a theatrical sigh. "But we'll play along. Sorry, Camila."

Through the viewfinder, I watch a blush climb up her neck until pink is flooding her cheeks. Then she bites her lower lip. *Is she nervous?*

"Mom Hawk, you go first," I say. "What should we ask her?"

"Let's start with family, dear," Mom says with a troubling grin. "Who do we thank for that impressive ability to handle difficult men?"

I make an offended noise. "Me? I'm a delight."

"Oh really?" Cam suddenly forgets about the camera, and her body relaxes. "Is *delightful* something I should feel more of when you criticize my camerawork or when you tell me I dress like a dad on a Home Depot run?"

The wit. The attitude. The way she comes alive the second she's calling me out. It's as if I'm watching a completely different person.

"Umm... Born and raised in New York," she continues, shifting back to shy when she remembers she's being filmed. "My parents immigrated from Puerto Rico before I was born. And my sister Aria is trying to make it as a chef. She's incredible. In her spare time, she volunteers at different food kitchens for the homeless and underprivileged kids."

Wait—sister? Two years of watching her risk life and limb for my content, and I didn't know she had a sister?

My brain flashes back to when Gordon dragged her into my office like she was a shiny new toy he was delighted to show off. "Fresh out of film school," he said.

I was overwhelmed with filming, editing, running multiple companies, and in the fresh hell of my fake relationship with Astrid. My channel needed help, and Gordon decided the solution was a videographer.

Worst. Idea. Ever.

Cam's portfolio was as stacked as she was—artistic shots, perfect framing, and this award-winning documentary that had Gordon salivating. She was brimming with talent and ambition, and, to my immediate dismay, drop-dead gorgeous. The instant she walked in, I knew hiring her was a bad idea.

Because Cam? She's the kind of woman who makes guys forget things. Important things. Like professionalism. And personal space. And that it's my fucking wedding day.

Gordon hired her before I could process what was happening. Just clapped her on the back as if they were old friends and declared, "Welcome to the team!"

The second I forced out "Congratulations," my brain slammed the emergency brakes and threw up a list of survival rules.

Rule one—don't stare at her ass. Yes, that thing is round and curvy, but do not memorize how it bounces, shifts, and taunts you.

Rule number two—keep your eyes on the camera. Whatever you do, don't drown in those fuck-me hazel eyes.

Rule three—her lips. Don't look. Don't wonder. And for the love of God, don't fucking fantasize about how they'd taste.

I've failed at all three. Spectacularly.

So I went with plan B: become the grumpiest boss in YouTube history. Keep her at arm's length with criticism and complaints. Make her think I'm a demanding jerk who lives to nitpick her camera work. It's easier than the alternative—admitting how extraordinarily beautiful and talented she is or how badly I want to kiss that sassy mouth, how I would lick every curve and...

Nope.

I'm her boss. Her BOSS!

Hard stop.

The end.

Get the memo, brain-between-my-legs.

"And what's your dream job, sweetheart?" Mama V asks.

I watch Cam's entire body language shift through the lens.

"Oh! Working for Reece is—"

"The truth, dear." Mom's tone could slice through bullshit at fifty paces.

"Um, well..." Cam swallows hard. "Someday, a long time from now, I hope to make documentaries. Real ones, you know? Help people who need their stories told. The ones society pretends don't exist."

Well, shit.

"Oh!" Mama clasps her palms together. "What a beautiful heart you have."

"So noble," Mom says, shooting me a look that I steadfastly ignore.

Something possessive stirs as I remember Cam's phone conversation from earlier. "Speaking of hearts, tell them about your vacation plans. You said something about treating cabana boys like coconut trees... sampling everything on the Hawaiian buffet."

Her eyes promise slow, painful death, but I can't help myself. The thought of her with random island douchebags makes me want to punch things. Which is ridiculous because I'm on the verge of getting married and—

"REECE!" Gordon shrieks, his designer loafers squeaking against the floor as he storms over. "What are you doing with that camera? You're the talent, not the help!" He snatches it from my hands, throwing it at Cam. "I've been texting you!"

"*Gordon*, c'mon now. This is our son's wedding day." Mom Hawk delivers his name like a warning shot.

"Why, hello ladies. Your front-row seats await. It's showtime!"

I clear my throat. "Hey... ya know, I'm having reserva—"

"Camera girl! Front and center with Reece and Blaze. Now!"

Cam catches my eye, and for a moment that sass disappears. "You good?"

"Absolutely," I lie. "Let's get this circus started."

***

THIS IS MY FUNERAL. It seems like a wedding, but trust me, my will to live is DOA.

Every surface of this church sparkles with an unholy amount of glitter. Each guest is more concerned with their ring light positioning than the actual ceremony. The traditional wooden pews have been replaced with clear acrylic chairs—because God forbid anything come across as naturally beautiful. It's as if Astrid handed Pinterest a blank check and said, "Do your worst."

"This place is extra as fuck," Blaze whispers beside me. His bowtie is crooked, and there's a suspicious flask-shaped bulge in his pocket. "How's the stomach, man? You look like you're about to yartz."

"I'm fine."

"Nah, man, that's your ghost pepper challenge face. Same one you made right before you cried on camera. Remember, dude? And your butthole ghosted you for three days."

"That video got fifty-six million views, so my ass forgives us."

Blaze drops a couple of TUMS into my palm like he's dealing drugs at a rave.

"You promise these aren't... laced with something?"

He wiggles his eyebrows. "Only love, my guy."

I pop them into my mouth. Just TUMS. *Damn.* The chalky tablets aren't nearly strong enough to settle the acid churning in my gut.

Running a global brand has pretty much shot the lining of my stomach. Every damn day there's another crisis—DareFuel sales dropping, DareWear's new shoe line delayed, sponsors threatening to pull out because my "authentic" relationship content isn't hitting their metrics. It's a yacht party with a busted engine and no life vests, and somehow, I'm solely responsible.

My eyes drift to Cam, who's setting up her shot. Her tongue's caught between her teeth in concentration—hazel eyes locked on her viewfinder like nothing else exists. She has no idea how much she's impacted me. I'm about to vow forever to someone, and all I can think about is how fucking wrong it feels.

Pulling out my phone, I tap the camera app and wince at my reflection. I'm only twenty-eight but feel ancient, as if I've aged in dog years since Gordon strong-armed me into this influencer power couple nightmare. The bags under my eyes could carry all of Astrid's emotional baggage—and that's saying something.

I pose for my obligatory pre-wedding post. My Armani tux can't distract from my smile, which resembles more *hostage negotiation* than *expression of joy*.

"Aww yeah, get that money shot!" Blaze launches himself into frame.

I post it with the caption: *Almost time #DareSquad.*

"Bro." Blaze nods with the profound wisdom of someone who once tried to teach a ferret to skateboard. "That's one set of boobs. For *life*. Or until the prenup expires. This is gonna be the longest brand deal ever."

Christ. The prenup. Thirty pages of legally binding bullshit that basically translates to "thou shalt create content until death or irrelevance do us part." My lawyer actually laughed when he read it. Then charged me $500 an hour for the consultation.

"Dude, this isn't one of our usual prank videos," I remind him. "So no fake priest, no trained animals, no surprise dance mobs."

"I know! I know! I cancelled the llamas in bowties. Mama V already yelled at me. Twice."

The lights dim and the DJ unleashes a dubstep version of the wedding march that sounds like the Transformers having sex with a church organ. Because apparently, we haven't destroyed tradition enough today. The bass thunders so hard, the crystal chandeliers above us are having a full-blown seizure. Jesus himself is probably filing a noise complaint with God right now.

Well. This is it. Time to take one for Team Dare. Three hundred and forty-seven employees, two energy drink factories, four clothing warehouses, one production studio soundstage, and my mother's entire medical team are counting on me *not* to pull a runaway groom. Even if every cell in my body is screaming, *RUN!*

And then—holy mother of desperation.

"Queen Astrid has arrived!" she announces as she begins her processional while livestreaming. "Your girl is literally about to become Mrs. Dare! Can we just"—she fans her face with perfectly manicured talons—"take a moment to appreciate this aesthetic?"

Appreciate is not the word I'd use.

"Swipe up for my Wedding Day Glow tutorial! And don't forget to check out my Pre-Ceremony Cleanse juice collab. It detoxes negativity, resets your DNA—plus, it's like, sparkly!"

Astrid's gaze sweeps the room, zeroing in on the digital darlings in attendance. "Helloooooo. Where are my spotlights? It was on the invitation!"

The content creators snap to attention as if their follower count depends on it. Five hundred phones rise in perfect unison, flashlights bathing Astrid in an artificial glow. Every surface reflects light until we're suddenly all trapped inside a disco ball. *My poor retinas.*

"Wedding day fit check!" She stops and poses, popping her hip. "Who's living for this bridal slay? We've got LED strips imported from Milan, crystals blessed by a fortune teller on TikTok, and my sheer MVP thong, which stands for Men's Vagina Parking. Customized by me and for sale online. That's right, bitches. My vajay-jay's an influencer too!"

Blaze coughs violently beside me, his palm clamping over his mouth to stifle his laugh.

I glare at him. "Don't encourage her."

I see Cam, who's already adjusting the camera for the near impossible shot.

"Can we talk about this iconic aisle situation?" She squeals into her phone. "The mirrors? They are metaphors. For reflection. For truth. For showing off my fresh vajazzling—swipe up now and use code HOLYHOLE for twenty percent off your own coochie crystals!"

Blaze wheezes so loudly that even the DJ gives him a side-eye.

I jab him in the ribs. "Pull it together."

"I can't," he gasps, tears streaming down his face. "Holy hole. HOLY. HOLE. Bro, that's poetry."

"Let's work together to get this wedding to hit a billion views!"

The influencers in the pews nod and murmur like they've just been blessed by the Pope of Social Media. Phones all recording, angles adjusted, and hashtags are flying. My eye twitches as I scan the attendees' ridiculous, over-the-top outfits. Metallic suits, feathery gowns, and... a dude wearing what seems to be a functioning aquarium on his head. Yep, there are fish in there. Swimming.

Astrid finally high heels it to the altar, but not before pausing to shoot a slow-motion hair flip that sends her platinum extensions cascading in waves. The DJ drops the bass for dramatic effect. *Subtle.*

The rambunctious crowd eats it up while the pastor, clearing his throat, seems to already be drafting new rules for church weddings in his head. "Dearly beloved—"

Astrid, still streaming, takes my hand and we both inch closer. To the altar. To our future. To our shared lives together. *Oh boy.*

"WAIT!" Astrid screeches. "We have a PROBLEM."

"What. Are. You. Doing?" I manage through gritted teeth.

She dramatically turns with her streaming phone to face the audience, now in full Kardashian ugly cry mode. "Reece, baby... I CAN'T marry you. The universe is sending me signs! My crystals did a TikTok reading. Mercury is in Gatorade! Venus just texted—'Time to level up, babe!' Also, my spirit guide—who's my collab partner for crystal-infused vape pens—says I shouldn't settle. I'm meant to be with someone else."

The masses gasp. Somebody yells, "Oh my God, we're going viral!"

"Astrid," I grit out, "we're in a church. You can't pull pranks in church."

"This isn't a prank, Reece!" And there they are—the waterworks. Perfect teardrops that don't disturb her triple-stack lashes. "I'm so sorry!"

She sprints down the aisle, her LED dress strobing, still narrating: "Besties! Sometimes the universe has other plans. Like my new breakup bundle, featuring tear-proof mascara, use code DUMPED for fifty percent off. And bitches, you better smash that subscribe button. New video tomorrow: I Left Him At The Altar And My Skin Is Literally Glowing! Link in bio for my breakup skincare routine!"

What.

The.

Algorithm exploding.

Fuck.

CHAPTER THREE

CAM

SO MUCH FOR PARADISE.

Every single one of my plans has gone to shit in the last few hours.

No boss's honeymoon workcation. No island hotties to wreck my shores. No sipping piña coladas while eye-fucking a shirtless beefcake bartender. And certainly no asking newly dumped Reece Dare to endorse my dream documentary channel.

Instead, I'm trapped in a limo that smells like desperation and Gordon's extra musky cologne, circling Los Angeles as if we're waiting for clearance to land. I'm editing footage of the most viral wedding disaster since Kim Kardashian's seventy-two-day marriage speedrun. The air conditioning is cranked so high my fingers are numb against my laptop keyboard. And the tension? Thick enough to choke on.

Three hours. That's how long we've been driving aimlessly in this rolling pressure cooker of emotions. Gordon's been glued to his phone the entire time, shouting into it like he's auditioning for *The Wolf of Wall Street 2*. Reece has said nothing, which is actually scarier than his constant nitpicking. And me? I'm pretending my noise-canceling headphones are a magic cloak of invisibility.

I gaze at my monitor as it glows with snippets of glitter-covered chaos from earlier today. My cold fingers hammer at the keys, combing through the footage on the hunt for something—anything—that hasn't already been plastered across the internet. Thanks to Astrid's livestream from the altar, the "marriage ceremony" instantly hit viral status. Every news outlet, influencer, and digital loudmouth with an opinion is piling on. And the star of the spectacle? Reece Dare, YouTube's favorite daredevil turned punchline.

The headlines are brutal:

Prankster Gets Pranked!

Reece Dare's Wedding Day Meltdown!

Astrid Montclair's Savage Goodbye!

Reece Dare is Cancelled.

"Find Astrid!" Gordon had barked at Blaze earlier before we hopped into this moving prison. "Talk some sense into her. And for the love of God, don't livestream it!"

Talking sense into either one of them? Good luck. Astrid is the equivalent of a human jellyfish *(literally no brain and no heart, just vibes)*. And Blaze? Hand him a set of instructions, and you might as well be reading them to a beach ball with sunglasses.

I turned my phone off an hour ago because, apparently, I'm now LA's most wanted source of gossip. My sister Aria. Best friends Katie and Petra. Random college classmates I haven't spoken to in years. Hell, even my landlord texted me for some "tea." Well, that and to remind me that rent was due last Tuesday.

Reece is hunched in his seat, scrolling through his phone. His jaw is tight, his eyes dark, and if he grinds his teeth any harder, he's going to need veneers by morning. The guy is one notification away from jumping out of this moving car.

Through my computer screen, I cut together the footage where Reece's face crumpled when Astrid announced she couldn't marry him because *Mercury is in Gatorade.* That moment—that split second—is now immortalized as a meme. His pained face already has its own Instagram account and its own filter #SadGroomChallenge.

The internet is eating this up. And as much as I want to hate him for being a broody, insufferable boss, I can't help but feel bad. Nobody should be dragged through the mud like this, not even Reece Dare.

"Why is she still here?"

Reece's voice is a knife cutting through my thoughts. *She?* Well, I *was* feeling sympathetic, but maybe not so much now, *pendejo.*

"Ignore her," Gordon hisses. "She's getting your video up. We need to control the narrative before—"

"Guys, holy shit!" some beauty guru squeals from Reece's phone. "Reece Dare just lost another 500K followers! This is insane!"

I bite back a groan. Of course Astrid chose to livestream her breakup to get it out ASAP. You can't edit and upload that quickly unless you shoot it in advance. Trust me, I know. I'm the one who usually has to perform those overnight miracles.

My eyes dart between clips, searching for video proof that he's not the villain in this wedding debacle. This is normally my favorite part of the job. Hand me hours of raw footage, and I'll find you a hero's story that will draw you in. It's similar to a documentary, if that doc had more product placement and fewer moral takeaways.

I need that clip. That redemptive moment. Something to give Reece's video that clickbait thumbnail... I've got nothing. But what catches my attention isn't the circus or the crying or even Astrid's bedazzled coochie crystals.

It's Reece.

For a mere second, before shock painted his features, his face was filled with... relief. Unmistakable relief.

Interesting.

But that's not the kind of clickbait that'll save this sinking ship.

"Fuck! Fuck! *Fuck!*" Gordon's voice ricochets around the limo like a pinball of panic. He thrusts his phone at Reece. "She posted again."

Reece grabs the phone, scowling as he hits *Play.* Astrid's face fills the screen, framed by her signature soft-focus lighting. Tears slide down her cheeks in dramatic slow motion. "The truth is, Reece neglected me over and over. Like, he bought me a knockoff Gucci handbag and a freakin' gold wedding ring. He knows white gold goes better with my skin color. And queens? Don't we *deserve* to be loved like the royalty we are?!"

I resist the urge to snort. This from the woman who once made me reshoot her "natural" wake-up routine because her morning breath wasn't "authentic enough." Yes, that's a direct quote. No, I have no clue what it means either.

"I just couldn't do it anymore." Astrid's voice trembles perfectly. "That's why I'm having a freedom sale!" Her emotional U-turn gives me whiplash. "Fifteen percent off my entire Bad Ass Bitches collection because no queen should have to pay full price for—"

Reece's thumb stabs at the screen, cutting off Astrid mid-pitch. "How bad is it?" he growls, his voice low and dangerous.

Gordon tugs at his tie so hard, I'm worried he'll actually strangle himself. "Well, you're hemorrhaging followers. We've lost two major sponsors, and Astrid's fans are organizing an online takedown. I won't read you the comments, but her army of queens wants your head on a rhinestone-encrusted platter."

I peek over my laptop as Reece leans back, resting against the headrest and closing his eyes. For a moment, he doesn't say anything, and I swear the pressure in the limo could pop a tire. Then he exhales sharply, his hands balling into fists. "She's controlling the narrative."

"Exactly," Gordon says, snapping his fingers. "Which is why you need to get ahead of this. Hawaii is perfect for damage control."

Reece's eyes snap open. "I'm not going to Hawaii."

"The fuck you aren't. You've got a contract, Reece. They're paying big bucks for you to promote the resort."

"Another goddamn contract." Reece's laugh sounds like shattered glass. "I'm so fucking sick of contracts controlling my life."

Gordon slips into his smooth-talking persona faster than I can say "sponsored content." "It'll be good for you! We'll film some healing-your-broken-heart videos. The fans will eat that shit up." He waves his hands as if he's conducting an orchestra of bullshit. "Get a massage. Fuck a few locals. Really lean into that wounded-but-still-fuckable energy."

I feel Reece's eyes burning a hole in the side of my head, but I maintain my best statue impression. *I am one with the editing software. I am invisible. I am definitely not thinking about him getting massages or fucking locals or—*

"I should stay and handle this mess," Reece argues.

"That's what I'm for," Gordon counters. "I'll manage the companies. You're the face of the brand, and that *face* needs to be in Hawaii making our sponsors happy."

Reece leans forward, his elbows on his knees, dragging his hands through his hair with a heavy exhale. "Goddammit."

"And we're here!" Gordon announces.

I follow his gaze. A private airfield looms ahead, complete with sleek jets parked like overgrown toys for billionaires.

Reece lets out a sharp laugh, a cackle with zero humor behind it. "I never had a choice, did I?"

"Come on, superstar!" Gordon claps like a seal demanding fish. "Shake it off!" Then his attention is a precision drone, locking onto me. "Camera girl! Is that video ready or what?"

I keep my headphones firmly in place, focused on my screen. Two years of dealing with influencer drama has taught me when to play deaf.

"CAMERA GIRL!"

"Sorry, I was editing." I slide my headphones down around my neck.

"The video done?"

"Ready to upload. Only thing left is a title."

"Wedding Shocker: Groom Gets Ditched—See His Epic Meltdown!"

"Yeah," Reece says, shoving open the limo door. "Make sure the video's monetized. We wouldn't want my public humiliation to go to waste."

"Great, there's Wi-Fi on the jet. Time to go, you two!" Gordon says.

"Wait." I jolt up. "You're not dropping me off at LAX for my flight?"

"You're skipping TSA today," Gordon snaps. "G-Thorne needs you on that plane. Keep editing promo pieces. We need Reece to be seen as either a victim or a hero... or both. *Comprende*?"

I step out and the blast of LA heat hits me like a hair dryer. My camera bag weighs heavily on my shoulder as I grab my suitcase—the one packed with dreams of beach sunsets and tropical cocktails just this morning.

Gordon pulls Reece's suitcase as they walk toward the jet. "Plenty of places to pull stunts in paradise! We'll make it a whole heartbreak series!" His eyes spark with inspiration. "How about: Eating My Feelings Challenge!"

Reece makes a sound like a dying whale.

"Paddleboarding Away the Pain in Maui!" Gordon's on a roll. "I Biked Down a Volcano to Outrun Heartache!"

Reece groans again as he climbs the plane steps before yelling, "How about, Masturbating On My Honeymoon for 24 Hours."

Ignoring him, Gordon whirls toward me, his lavender tux now a wrinkled mess. "I want video ideas in my inbox before you land in Maui."

With a solemn nod, it dawns on me that for the next two weeks, I'll be filming the world's most expensive pity party.

But hey, I'm not going to let Reece's mood get me down—I'm still going to Maui!

***

I STEP ONTO THE private jet and immediately freeze in the doorway. My first thought: I should turn around, climb right back down those steps, and call an Uber. My second thought: I need my camera, because this? This deserves to be immortalized.

This isn't a plane—it's a honeymoon suite with wings. Every surface sparkles with fairy lights and heart-shaped decorations, including a cheesy MR. & MRS. DARE banner strung across the back wall in glittering gold letters. And there's a bed for fucking, but...

No.

Fucking.

SEATS.

Not even a sad little fold-down jump seat for the bodyguard or chaperone. Instead, dominating the cabin is a single, giant bed—king-size, no less—draped in white silk sheets, drowning in rose petals.

There's a champagne bucket on a side table, condensation dripping down its sides. In the middle of the mattress is a gold-rimmed tray, with an enormous bowl of chocolate-covered strawberries and... My eyes lock on to what I'd call a "romance survival kit." Massage oil. Feathers. And condoms. So many flavored condoms. My God, these flavors are a crime against orgasms: banana split, ranch dressing, fried pickle... bacon?!

My overaccommodating brain supplies images I didn't ask for—all too vivid images of Reece and Astrid christening this cupid's orgy fest at 30,000 feet. *Yuck!*

The pilot pokes his head out, his handlebar mustache twitching. "Mr. Dare, I'm Captain Mitchell, but you can call me 'Captain Love.' We'll be taking off momentarily. Wanted to let you both know that I'll be wearing noise-canceling headphones for your... privacy." He winks.

Ew. Gross. I know for a fact you can still hear everything. Pervy pilot's probably got a whole spank bank of mile-high club greatest hits stored in his brain.

"And if you'd like to fly with 'Cupid's Cockpit' back to LA when your trip is over," he continues, his voice oozing customer service smarm, "we'd be happy to accommodate. Just scan the QR code on the tray next to the—"

He gestures vaguely toward the pile of sex supplies.

"—the, uh, lube bottle for all the details."

The pilot glances at Reece's pocket like he's willing him to pull out his phone.

Reece exhales sharply, angling his device at the tray.

DING!

The man's mustache does a little victory twitch. "Excellent. I've been added to your contacts."

I stare at Reece, wondering how often he has to put up with this kind of crap. How many people shove business deals, opportunities, favor requests at him in the most insane ways?

The cockpit door clicks shut, and Reece flops back onto the bed. Rose petals explode around him in a red cloud. He's like a fallen angel—all broad shoulders and devastation wrapped in a wrinkled white button down.

My fingers twitch toward my camera. This shot would be perfect—the defeated groom surrounded by remnants of romance. The lighting is dramatic, casting deep shadows that emphasize his jawline and highlight the tension on his face.

"Do you want me to—" I gesture weakly with my Sony "—you know, film this?"

"No."

Cool. Cool cool cool. Just gonna stand here, then. In a sex plane. With my grumpy boss.

I perch carefully on the opposite edge of the bed—because again, *WHERE ARE THE CHAIRS?*—and pull out my laptop like it's a shield against all this awkward. My head is throbbing from hair being in an all-day ponytail.

I yank out my scrunchie, unable to hold back the moan of relief as my natural waves tumble free. My scalp is tingling. I massage it gently, trying to coax away my stress headache.

Then I feel it—the weight of his gaze—a slow burn that sends a prickle across my skin. Reece is watching me, his steel-blue stare locked in, intense and unreadable. Our eyes meet, and he flicks his gaze back to his phone. Heat crawls up my neck.

"Sorry," I mutter, trying to tame my wild mane. "I look like I stuck my finger in an electrical socket. My hair gets crazy when it's been up too long."

"Yeah, you really need a mirror." His voice is clipped. "Bathroom's in the back."

Oh, so that's how we're playing it? Game on, grumpy pants.

"Right, because my thick porn star hair isn't as flawless as Astrid's fake waves. Your hair isn't so great either, buddy. Maybe stop raking your hands through it every five seconds."

His eyes narrow dangerously. "Is this your thirst trap hairstyle? For seducing all those island boys?"

"I hadn't considered it, but you're right—the bed head look sends a clear message: 'I'm ready for some serious pillow talk.'"

"Lady and gentleman," the captain says, oozing with honey-flavored innuendo, "I hope you're ready for a smooth, satisfied ride."

I stuff my computer away as the engines roar to life. I press my face against the window like an excited kid. The runway lights streak past faster and faster until we're airborne, Los Angeles shrinking beneath us.

The jet lurches, and the champagne glasses rattle ominously in their holders. I clutch the bedframe, my heart going double-time as turbulence shakes the plane. A mess of strawberries, dripping in chocolate, goes airborne, and time slows down in the worst way.

I watch in helpless horror as fruit tumbles across the sheets in slow motion, rolling like edible wrecking balls. Several bounce off the mattress before splattering onto me, leaving streaks across my shirt and smearing a major glob of melted chocolate on my pants.

"¡Mierda! No, no, no—"

On impulse, I lick my finger and rub my pants.

"What are you—" Reece's voice sounds strangled. "You're smearing it. Oh my God!"

My brain screeches to a halt as he rips off his white shirt, buttons flying, revealing his tan muscular chest and six-pack abs. His pecs flex slightly with the motion, the light catching his tattoos. Reece snags a bottle of water from the table, splashes some onto the fabric, and crouches in front of me. "Hold still."

My mouth goes dry.

"Wait, what are you—" My words cut off as his hand grips my hip to steady me, firm and warm through the fabric of my pants. My heart skips, and I forget how to breathe.

"This is stain removal 101," he mutters, dabbing at the chocolate smears on my thighs with the damp shirt. Electricity zings through my body as if I've licked a live wire. Has it really been that long since I've been touched?

"You've gotta blot it. Rubbing makes it worse." He's concentrating way too hard for someone cleaning up melted chocolate. His movements are precise, focused—and when he applies a little too much pressure, it sets off a ripple of heat that tightens in my core. The cabin feels smaller suddenly, the air too warm, too close.

I swallow hard, trying not to notice how his thumb lingers near my hip bone or how his other hand presses into my thigh, dangerously high.

Way too high.

Did I mention high?

We both freeze, realizing his hand is one accidental inch away from having a meet and greet with my hoo-ha. I suck in a breath.

He jerks back as if I'm on fire, his fingers accidentally grazing my breast in his retreat.

"Jesus fuck—sorry! I didn't—shit, sorry."

"It's fine." I sound helium drunk, my voice way too thin. "Didn't know you were a stain expert."

"Uh, yeah." He sits on the other side of the bed, putting distance between us. "Mom made me learn after I destroyed half my wardrobe as a kid. I played hard."

The word *hard* makes my eyes automatically drop to his crotch and—*Why? Why did I look?* He's packing what appears to be the Everest of erections in his Armani pants.

Is it possible to climax simply by tracing the outline of his dick with my eyes? I think I'm about to find out.

He snatches a pillow, dropping it onto his lap. He's totally frazzled and frantic, and I know I am not imagining the flush creeping up his neck.

I grab my laptop. "Well! Time to brainstorm video ideas! For Gordon! Who wants them when we land! In Hawaii! Where we're going! To work! As professionals!"

"Yup." His response is brisk, almost dismissive. "I better take a sleep... go to nap. Don't disturb me."

He flops onto his side while I stare at my blank screen. *How am I going to survive two weeks without kissing him?*

Killing. I mean *killing him*. Not *kissing*.

Although, a little kissing wouldn't hurt anybody.

NO! KILLING ONLY.

...probably.

***

THE WIND DOES ITS best to ruin me, whipping my hair into my mouth, up my nose, and slapping it against my cheeks. With a huff, I wrestle it back into a ponytail, twisting my scrunchie around it. The breeze still sneaks in, tugging at loose strands, but I'm not even mad. Not when we're cruising down the Hana Highway in a black convertible, the ocean shimmering beside us and the sunset painting the sky like a screensaver.

This moment? It's straight out of a movie. All I need is a pair of oversized sunglasses, a chiffon scarf tied dramatically around my head, and maybe a hunky co-star... *Oh wait. Scratch that last part.* I scope out Reece, who's casually steering with one hand as if auditioning for a luxury car commercial. He's annoyingly good-looking, and he knows it.

"Hey, Reece. Why'd you pick this grandpa car instead of some crypto-bro Lamborghini? Isn't that more your speed?"

"Grandpa car? This is a 1958 Porsche 356 Speedster Convertible."

"Are those words supposed to make me fall to my knees in automotive worship?"

I watch his right eye do a cute little twitching thing. *Wait—not cute. Annoying. Definitely annoying.*

"This is the same car from *Top Gun*. The original? Tom Cruise?"

"Never seen it."

"You've never—" His jaw drops. "But you know who Tom Cruise is, right?"

"Duh." I roll my eyes. "What's with all the man-thusiasm?"

He straightens in his seat, clearly unbothered by the implied jab. "The guy does all his own stunts. No green screen, no CGI—just pure guts. You gotta respect that."

"Sounds like my daredevil boss."

That earns me my first ever genuine Reece Dare smile. And Dios mío, the man's even more sexy when he smiles.

"Is that a compliment, Morales?"

"Maybe."

"He's got this run," Reece continues. "It's a whole thing. The Tom Cruise run—perfect form, high knees, arms pumping, no hesitation. There are YouTube videos that break it down like it's a sport. You should check it out. He takes running more seriously than most people take their careers."

"Okay, I will."

"Good. You should."

I've never heard him talk like this, at least not to me. Usually, our conversations are *him* critiquing my every breath and *me* doing my best to ignore how his T-shirts stretch across his chest. *Who is this person?*

"Maybe you should try acting someday?"

His smile falters, and he shakes his head. "Nah. Memorizing lines isn't my thing. I prefer being authentic—in the moment."

There's a heaviness to his voice now, a distance creeping into his expression that I wasn't expecting. I've accidentally touched on a deeper issue, but before I can figure out what it is, he reaches for the radio and flicks it on.

We don't speak again until Reece offers to bring my suitcase inside the hotel.

Though I don't know if *hotel* is the right word for this place.

The Aloha Amour Resort...

Oh. My. God.

My senses are assaulted. The lobby is pure seduction, designed to strip couples of their self-control before they even reach their room. The air is thick with hibiscus and vanilla, rich and warm, and a mystery ingredient that's too spicy to be innocent. I'd swear the air itself was flirting with me.

The dim lighting, tinted in shades of red and gold, drenches everything in a permanent sunset glow—skin looks softer, lips more kissable, restraint a distant memory. The entire place pulses with suggestion, with romance, with unspoken promises of sexual conquest. It's a full seduction playground up in here.

And the décor? Oh, the décor. Dead center is a massive fountain featuring two lava-rock lovers entwined in a carnal pose so athletic I'm getting secondhand muscle cramps. The water cascades down their bodies in a deeply sensual way, and upon further study, it's hard to explain its strong visual effect.

The sculpture is more than suggestive. It's visceral. Evocative. A hedonistic piece of artwork that conjures arousal. The thing's dripping with sexual idolatry, somehow summoning increasing amounts of primal desire the longer you look. I quickly break its spell, glancing down at the fountain's base, where heart-shaped lights pulse rhythmically to an elevator music version of Marvin Gaye's "Let's Get It On."

I search the walls, which are covered in photos of animals... getting busy. Two flamingos nuzzling their necks together, two rhinos with horns interlocked in what must be rhino foreplay. And three starfish... I don't exactly know what they're doing, but it's dirty.

The reception desk is framed by heart-shaped arches lit with pulsing LED lights. Overhead, neon pink letters spell out: THE ISLAND WHERE PASSION FLOWS LIKE LAVA.

The staff uniforms are a mix of tropical chic and "we moonlight at a dance club." The man at the counter wears a Hawaiian shirt unbuttoned to reveal more chest than necessary, and his name tag reads, *Aloha. I'm Kai's Best Friend.*

I'm a little worried to ask, who's Kai?

"Wow," I whisper, spinning slowly to take it all in. "This place really commits to the theme."

Reece stops beside me at the check-in desk, suitcase in hand, his jaw tight. "It's... something."

"Welcome to the Aloha Amour Resort!" the man says brightly. "Mr. Dare." He frowns at his computer screen. "Oh... uh... seems we have a little hiccup with your reservation."

Reece exhales sharply through his nose. "Of course there is."

"Let me dial up Kai. He'll have this all taken care of in a flash."

"Fantastic," Reece mutters, his grumpy tone back in full force.

I nudge him. "Hey, bright side. Now we've got more time to enjoy the... ambiance."

Reece cuts me a side-eye, but I notice the faint quirk at the corner of his mouth. I'm about to mentally high-five myself for softening the Grump King, when a voice booms across the lobby.

"Yo, finally! You're here, bro!"

We turn, and there is... Blaze? Reece's bleach blonde best friend is strutting toward us in a tank top that reads Blaze of Glory in a glittery font and board shorts that look like an exploding tie-dye factory.

"Rough day, huh?" Blaze says, pulling Reece into a bone-crushing hug. "Don't worry, broski. Blaze has got your back, for realz."

Reece extracts himself from the hug, his expression a blend of confusion and irritation. "What are you doing here?"

"Huh? It's all part of the master plan." He double winks so hard, I think he may be trying to communicate in Morse code.

"Plan?"

"Yeah, the plan, bro! So epic."

Before my brain can process whatever dimension Blaze is currently inhabiting—

"Blazey-Boo! Your queen needs you!"

Enter Astrid, stage left, filming herself as she makes her grand entrance. Her neon pink dress appears painted on, platinum extensions flowing as if she's got industrial fans following her around. *How does she do that?*

"Yeah, babe, coming!"

Wait. BABE?!

Blaze jogs to Astrid, and she grabs him by the collar. "Action!" Astrid commands.

And then they *kiss*.

It's not just a kiss. It's a spectacle. A sloppy, over-the-top mess of lips and tongue that goes on far too long and should come with a splash zone warning. My stomach churns in secondhand embarrassment. Reece stiffens beside me, his breathing shallow, his jaw locked tighter than a bank vault.

When they break apart, Blaze grins and wipes his mouth. "Wicked, babe. Your vape breath tastes like cotton candy and chemicals."

"Cut! Blaze, what the hell was that? You are being a freaking Labrador. We're doing it again."

Blaze blinks at her, his confusion so pure it's almost endearing. "I thought it was good. Like, romantic."

"Ew no! That was so NOT it," Astrid snaps, already adjusting her phone for another take. "Can you please *not* drool on me? This isn't a dog park, and I am *NOT* your chew toy."

Blaze shrugs, unbothered. "Whatever you say, babe. Let's roll."

They dive in for round two, and I can feel Reece vibrating with barely restrained fury. Blaze pulls back after a shorter kiss, and Astrid inspects the footage.

"Better," she mutters. Then she swivels to face Reece, still recording.

"What! The! Fuck!" Reece looks ready to commit murder.

"Sorry not sorry, but like, the universe literally told me to live my truth!" Astrid's voice is sheer TikTok drama. "We're not hiding our love anymore. Blaze actually appreciates my crystal-infused lifestyle! And you're not going to ruin this for us, Reece."

"Yeah, she told me we're vibe soulmates." Blaze is a brainless bobblehead, nodding. "But pro tip, when you're going down on someone—those vagina gem things get stuck in your hair, and it hurts like a bitch to rip 'em off."

"Blazey!" Astrid screeches, smacking his arm. "What did we just discuss?"

"Right, right. Never talk," Blaze says sheepishly. "Got it, babe."

"Now, kiss me again. And... action! Don't forget to smash that *Like* button, bitches, if you want more sizzling love content!"

I glance at Reece, whose face is currently buffering between *WTF*, *I need a drink*, and *Jesus take the wheel*. This trip went from bad to *welcome to hell, enjoy your stay*.

Then, they're going at it again. *Oh, shit.* Blaze is Astrid's new boyfriend.

CHAPTER FOUR

REECE

MY VISION GOES RED, then white—am I blacking out? Because I *can't* be watching my most trusted friend swap spit with the woman who left me at the altar approximately eight hours ago.

Blaze. My fucking childhood best friend. My *brother*. The guy who once superglued his own ass cheeks together on a dare—standing there, next to Astrid, looking like I'm supposed to fist-bump him and say, "Congrats, bro, you tapped that ex-fiancée booty."

Why is he smiling? His arm is slung over her as if they're a goddamn couple. This can't be real. And why does he keep acting like everything's chill? Like I knew this was coming. Like he's not twisting the knife with each stupid grin and exaggerated wink.

How long? I want to ask. *How long have you been playing me, Blaze?*

But all I manage is "You know what, Astrid—"

Before I can get another word out, Cam steps in front of me, alarm in her hazel eyes.

"Don't," Cam whispers. "She's filming. This is exactly what she wants."

Of course it is. Because God forbid anyone experience genuine human emotion without monetizing it first.

I grab my suitcase, ready to flee this paradise-themed torture chamber, when—a wall of bronzed muscle blocks my path.

"Wonderful! Everyone has arrived!"

The voice is too big, too enthusiastic, and just way too much for my current mental state. My eyes snap to the source, and...

Jesus. Fucking. Christ.

This man—no, this *Hawaiian deity*—is towering in the entryway like he was hand-carved from Maui's cliffs. He's six-foot-five of pure warrior, with tribal tattoos that dance across his glistening chest. The guy makes Jason Momoa look like he needs to hit the gym. His dark hair is swept up in a man bun that would be idiotic on anyone else. On him it screams "Alpha." And the guy's wearing two things: confidence, and a paper-thin floral sarong barely containing his massive python.

I'm not staring at his giant dick. I'm *NOT*. But it's like a solar eclipse. You know you shouldn't stare directly at it, but your eyes are drawn to the spectacle anyway.

"I... am Kai."

His voice is distant thunder, reverberating in my chest. He spreads his arms wide, as if expecting applause. Hell, he might get it. The two women checking in at the desk are drooling into their cocktails.

"I am the owner here, and I welcome you to the Aloha Amour Resort, where desire flows like lava and love blooms eternal."

Oh, come on.

Kai strides across the opulent lobby, and as if the bulge isn't horrifying enough, it announces itself with every step. Definitely going commando under that sarong.

"Mr. Dare!" His smile could power the entire luxury hotel. "We weren't sure if you would make it. Miss Astrid said you had... opted out."

I glare at my ex. "Oh, she's been saying all kinds of things today."

Astrid gasps. "Reece, that's so unfair! I was only trying to help—"

"By lying? Classic Astrid move."

Kai clears his throat dramatically, stepping between us, and I swear I hear wind chimes somewhere. "I sense the energy in this room needs cleansing. I am here to promote love in all manifestations, both tried and not yet experienced."

"Don't," I say, cutting him off. "Just don't."

His smile doesn't falter. "Here at Aloha Amour, we believe in passion, connection, and renewal. I know your union did not unfold as planned, but each ending is an opportunity for a new beginning."

Beside me, Cam snorts, earning a raised eyebrow from Kai. "Ah, and you, wahine, my feminine creature," he says, his tone softening. "Your energy... It's untapped. Wild. Waiting to be harnessed."

He takes her hand and kisses her knuckles. Cam sucks in a sharp breath, and I catch her biting her lip. *I am not loving that reaction one bit.*

"My philosophy," the resort owner continues, his pecs somehow independently undulating, "is that intimacy should never be confined by monogamy."

No shit, Captain Obvious. That thing tenting your sarong is basically a dowsing rod seeking its next spring. *Stop pointing it at Camila!*

"Here, we honor affection in all its radiant and beautiful expressions." He glides toward Blaze and Astrid, wrapping his colossal arms around them both. "Which is why for your new love match

I've arranged a special couples' massage in your suite. With"—he winks—"happy endings for you both."

"Duuuude! You are the *best!* This is gonna be sick!"

The blonde queen bee throws me a smug glance as she hits *Record.* "Later, loser. Besties, don't forget to like and subscribe to see me slaying it after escaping that hot mess express!" She flips her hair and shouts over her shoulder, "Blazey-poo! Your queen needs her rubdown, stat!"

"Coming!" Blaze parkours over a decorative pineapple. "Later, bro!"

He's got the IQ of a corndog, but c'mon. He can't really think we're still best friends. Can he?

"Now then, Mr. Dare." Kai's voice drops an octave, making the nearby orchids tremble. "While there is an abundance in love, we find ourselves... limited in accommodations. Your nuptial... situation has created quite the booking tsunami. The only remaining room is reserved for your videographer, the enchanting Miss Morales."

His gaze lingers on her breasts, smoldering with a heat that could melt candle wax. "I was prepared to offer you this body on your first night to properly welcome you."

A dark and angry snake of possessiveness uncurls in my ribcage.

"Or perhaps," he purrs, "you'd prefer to share my private sanctuary? Let Mr. Dare have the suite to himself?"

Cam's cheeks flush, and that angry snake becomes a full-blown dragon. The thought of her spending one second in this Coconut Casanova's love lair makes me want to commit crimes.

"Not happening," I growl. "We'll take the room. Together."

He claps, and the sound is a gong striking the air, deep and commanding. "Excellent! Allow me to escort you to your sex den."

Den of what now?

***

I JUST NEED SLEEP. That's all. Just sweet, dark oblivion where I can pretend this whole day never happened. But as Kai throws open the door, the strong scents of pineapple, vanilla, and what I'm pretty sure is aerosolized Viagra engulf me like a wave of horny air freshener.

"Welcome," he purrs, his oiled chest glistening in the mood lighting, "to your Temple of Tropical Temptation!"

The hotel room pulses with a soft pink glow, as if the walls themselves are blushing. Genuine rainforest sounds fill the air—birds calling, water trickling, and... is that Barry White remixed with a ukulele?

"Oh my God, this is amazing." Cam's already filming, despite her shoulders shaking as she tries *(and fails)* to keep a straight face. "It's like a porn set had a baby with a Rainforest Cafe. I've got the video title: I Survived 24 Hours in the Love Den."

"No walls," I blurt, my voice louder than I intended. "There are no walls."

Kai claps a massive hand on my shoulder. "Precisely the point, Mr. Dare. Freedom! Connection! Vulnerability! Why hide from each other when you can share every moment, every sensation, with your partner?"

"It's... unique," she says diplomatically.

"Observe!" Kai glides to the centerpiece of this jungle-themed fever dream—a round bed that starts rotating at his approach. "She awakens! Your passion playground responds to movement, to desire, to—"

"Did you just call the bed 'she'?" I ask.

"All beautiful things are feminine—take your lovely camera-woman here." He winks at Cam.

The bed dominates the space, a circular monstrosity draped in red satin sheets that all but scream "sex tape waiting to happen." And if that's not enough, there's a mirror the size of a satellite mounted on the ceiling, ensuring no angle is left unexplored. Because nothing says "romance" like watching yourself fall off this spinning teacup of a bed.

To top it all off, the pillows are embroidered with spicy suggestions. One reads PLUNGE INTO PARADISE, and another says SWEAT NOW, CUDDLE LATER, but the one I'm throwing off the balcony reads, *PUSSY PARTNER.*

Kai pats the mattress like a monk blessing a temple. "This," he says, voice hushed with reverence, "is a masterpiece of structural integrity. Designed to support every kind of union—soft, frantic, experimental—this bed welcomes all. Whether that's two bodies moving as one, three finding harmony, or four testing the boundaries of spatial physics. No judgment, only support—emotionally and structurally."

"Reece, get in the frame," Cam says. "Your expression is hilarious."

"Morales, I swear to God—"

"What? I'm just getting establishing shots. You're always telling me to be thorough."

She turns the camera back to the walking manbun. "Please, please tell me there are more motion sensors."

"Yes, wahine. I'd be happy to show you how it's done!" Kai prances—legitimately prances—through the space. With each movement, new features reveal themselves: hidden panels sliding open to showcase champagne, rose petals dropping from concealed ceiling compartments, massage oils that emerge from the floor like some sort of aroused dumbwaiter system.

"And over here!" Kai bounds across the room with the enthusiasm of a man who's never felt shame. "The Swing of Sublime Surrender!"

He pauses theatrically, gesturing toward what I can only describe as Satan's playground equipment: a sex swing hanging from the ceiling, complete with leather straps, stirrups, and more attachment points than a NASA docking station.

Camila pans the camera to me with flair. "Reece, thoughts? Care to take it for a spin?"

"You're here to film, not offer commentary."

"Guess I'm really overachieving today."

"I will gladly demonstrate," Kai says. "The secret, my friends, is in the mounting."

He grabs the leather loops hanging at waist level and launches himself into the contraption like Simone Biles going for gold at the Sex Olympics. His massive body somehow gracefully settles into the seat portion, legs dangling through two stirrup-like loops, while his hands grip the upper straps.

"Balance is everything," he says, adjusting himself comfortably in the suspended chair.

The hanging chair begins to rock, and his sarong starts fluttering like a curtain in the breeze, about to reveal...

"Code Red!"

I lunge forward, positioning myself between Cam and the impending wardrobe malfunction. In my panicked rush, my right arm swings up, directly through one of the hanging loops. The leather strap immediately tightens around my forearm as I try to pull back. *Shit.*

"Ohhhh, excellent!" Kai beams. "Partner play! Beautiful! You're embracing vulnerability!"

"I'm not—this isn't—" I tug at my trapped arm, which only seems to tighten the strap's grip. Meanwhile, Kai's sarong has fully surrendered its duty, and there he is, in all his glory, casually spreading his legs as he swings backward.

"This is the Passionate Pendulum position," he announces proudly.

WHOOSH!

The momentum carries him back toward me, and suddenly I'm doing an awkward limbo to avoid a face-to-face meeting with his exposed equipment. I bend backward so far my spine cracks.

"Cam!" I shout, twisting to see her behind the camera. "Stop filming and help me!"

She's trembling with suppressed laughter, camera steady as a rock.

So help me God! I will chew my arm off to escape this.

WHOOSH!

Kai swings away again, eyeing Cam like a thirsty sniper. "Would you like to join us, wahine? The Passionate Pendulum becomes the Triangle of Bliss with three!"

"Pass," she giggles.

I yank my arm hard, but instead of freeing myself, my elbow catches in another strap. Now I've got two limbs ensnared, and my balance shifts precariously. My feet slip on the smooth floor, and suddenly—

"WAIT!" I yelp, but it's too late.

My feet leave the ground completely. One moment I'm standing, trying to free my arm; the next I'm hanging awkwardly beside Kai, my ass in his face, tilted at a forty-five-degree angle with no way to move.

"Excellent initiative!" Kai beams while his bamboo warrior swings freely between us. "Real intimacy requires submission—I see you surrendering to my dominance. That shows trust. Tell me, Reece, what is your safe word?"

"Nope. Get me down. Cam, tell him!"

She's absolutely no help, her face now purple with suppressed laughter, hiding her grin behind the camera.

WHOOSH.

And now I'm swaying.

My position adjusts again as Kai reaches over—thankfully using his hand, not another appendage—and pulls a strap near my hip. Instantly, my lower body lifts higher, my legs splaying awkwardly as I forcibly try to keep them closed.

"Feel nature's rhythm!" Kai says, giving me a powerful push that sends me spinning like a drunk compass needle. My arm is twisted at an angle that human limbs were not designed for, while my legs dangle helplessly.

"This is the Suspended Butterfly!" Kai announces, pulling another strap that shoots my right leg up ninety degrees.

WHOOSH!

The momentum carries me directly toward Kai's exposed anatomy. "SWEET MOTHER OF—" I jerk my head sideways, his island flagpole missing my face by millimeters.

"*¡Mierda santa!* Careful there, boss. You might poke your eye out," Cam calls out, laughing hysterically.

"Stop filming!" I snarl, spread-eagled in midair.

"Next, we have Unlocking the Secret Chamber!" Kai pulls yet another strap—*where are all these coming from?*—and now both my legs are higher than my head. The blood rushes to my brain, making the room spin even faster.

WHOOSH!

"JESUS CHRIST!" I crane my neck awkwardly, narrowly avoiding another face-to-face encounter with Not-So-Little Kai. The evasive movement sends me spinning wildly in the opposite direction, my body rotating like a rotisserie chicken.

"That's it!" Cam cackles, capturing every embarrassing frame. "Eyes wide shut, boss!"

"Next, the Five-Limbed Surrender!" Kai announces, pulling what must be the master strap of humiliation.

One moment I'm horizontal, facing up, and then... I'm not. My world inverts. I'm fully upside down, my shirt falling over my face and blinding me just as Kai gives another push. I'm disoriented. Up is down, left is right, and there's a very naked Hawaiian man in my orbit.

"I can't see! I can't—" My sentence cuts off as I swing back, and something warm and distinctly not-a-hand brushes against my ear. "OH MY GOD!"

I finally free one arm, but the sudden weight shift sends me into a death spiral. The swing gains momentum, rotating and swinging simultaneously. Kai has started speaking in Hawaiian, probably blessing me with ancient love prayers. And I'm ninety percent sure I just high-fived his dick.

"And now for the Inverted Lotus—" he begins, reaching for yet another strap.

"No more positions!"

"Reece! Wait!" Cam shouts, her voice cutting through my panic. "You're about to—"

THUD.

The strap releases without warning, and I face-plant into the tiger-print rug below, my legs still tangled overhead in the swing, my dignity now completely extinguished.

"Having fun down there?" Cam kneels beside me. She turns to Kai with a straight face. "It's bologna, Kai. His safe word is bologna."

I hate everything.

I want to die here.

Face-down in a sex-dungeon, a Hawaiian love guru's dong my last earthly vision, and Cam's laughter as my funeral song.

"And now!" Kai says as he gracefully dismounts. "The crown jewel of your jungle paradise!"

He strides to the other side of the suite, and I follow reluctantly, already bracing for whatever fresh hell awaits.

"This," Kai announces, flipping a switch to activate the jets, "is the rainforest shower. The water cascades down like a natural waterfall, cleansing both body ánd soul. It's the ultimate paradise experience."

What I *thought* was a decorative rock feature is a freakin' shower?! It's fully open-concept, no walls, no doors—just smooth stones, cascading sprays, and an obscene number of tropical plants.

Cam leans forward, letting the mist flow through her fingers. Her expression softens. "It's really beautiful."

"*Beautiful?*" I echo, staring at her like she's lost her mind. "It's a garden hose with no privacy."

"It's freeing," she counters, stepping onto the stones. The mist clings to her hair and cheeks, making her glow under the soft light.

Instantly, my brain betrays me.

I picture her naked under the jets, water sliding over her sudsy skin, tracing every curve. Her lips moaning—her head tilting back, hair dripping, cheeks flushed from the heat.

Kai pulls out a chrome spray wand hidden in the rocks. "And this toy is extremely popular, for those who desire more... *focused connection,*" he says with a wink, spraying an arc of mist into the air.

Cam spins to face me, focusing her lens. "Wanna test it out?"

"Tour's over!" I slam my hand on the control panel, nearly slipping on the now-wet floor.

"But I haven't shown you the fog machine! Or the special wand buttons! Or the vibrating—"

"Goodbye, Kai!"

I shove him out the door, his last words floating back: "Remember, Miss Morales, my door is always open!"

I lean against the closed door, exhausted. Behind me, the bed's still rotating, Barry White's still serenading, and for the love of God, the swing is somehow still swaying.

"So... which half of the sex bed do you want?" She deactivates the spinning motion sensor with a swift, decisive wave.

Sex. Bed. Cam.

A three-car pileup of bad ideas. *How can I not picture her sprawled across those red satin sheets?*

"I'll take the couch."

"What couch?" She does this exaggerated sweep of our surroundings with her camera, playing tour guide. "Welcome to the No Walls Resort, where privacy comes to die! We have exactly one door, and..." She bounces over to it—*seriously, who has this much energy after the day we've had?*—and flings it open as if she's revealing a game show prize. "Behind door number one... Ta-da! The toilet. So, unless you want to sleep in here, the 'sex bed' is your only option, boss."

This is hell. Actual hell.

No walls. No escape. My dick's already sending up emergency flares, and there are exactly zero private places to handle that situation.

"There is no fucking way I'm spending two weeks trapped in this *sex den* with you."

"You think I'm thrilled? I was supposed to have this whole suite to myself."

I choke out a humorless laugh. "Right. Sorry to cockblock your plans to bang your way through the hotel staff."

Her eyes narrow, and she gives me a sweet, sarcastic smile. "I'd accept your apology if I thought it was genuine."

Her lack of denial shoots a nuclear blast to my brain.

Cam. In this room. Having sex. Everywhere. Images of Hawaiian men flash like a parade of shirtless assholes, each one laying claim to her in my imagination. I want to punch something. Preferably something that wears a sarong and makes bedroom eyes at my videographer.

"Reece?" she says, cutting through my mental rampage. "We should probably establish some ground rules. Figure out the shower problem."

Shit. The shower.

I take a deep breath, giving myself a mental slap. *I can do this.* Fourteen days in the world's most X-rated hotel suite with the woman who's given me inappropriate dreams since the day she walked into Gordon's office. No problem.

Simply set boundaries and follow them. No touching her. No thinking about her in the bed or the shower. No imagining her naked—dripping wet with steam swirling around succulent tits—*I wasn't; you were.*

Who said that? Anyway... I nod sharply. "I agree. First rule, no—"

My phone buzzes, and it's Gordon—I shouldn't answer. I don't want to answer. I answer.

Gordon's face is so close to the camera, I can see the dots where his hair plugs are anchored, resembling something I can only describe as forehead astroturf.

"Dare!" he barks, leaning back enough to reveal he's using a ring light. "What the hell is going on? Astrid and Blaze? Why are you in her video entitled Falling in Love Again? Why am I finding out about this at the same time as the rest of the damn internet?"

"Because I was busy wrestling an anaconda on a sex swing."

Gordon blinks. Once. Twice. Then he tilts his head, and his Botoxed forehead doesn't so much as ripple. "What the hell does that mean?"

"You'll see it in tomorrow's video," I snap, already over this conversation.

"Kid, this is bad. Really bad. Astrid is destroying you in the click-bait game. You've lost over two million followers. At this rate, we'll have to shut down the shoe line before it launches."

My stomach drops. "We can't lay off people."

"I've got a solution. And before you say anything, you're not gonna like it."

I groan. "Just tell me."

"Is camera girl there?"

I hit him with a glare that could melt his ring light.

"Sorry, sorry—is *Cam* there?"

"Yeah." I glance over—she's perched on the edge of a decorative boulder by the shower, eyes locked on her camera screen. Her thick chestnut waves, loose and unruly, cling to her damp skin—it's a gorgeous, tangled mess that I suddenly want to run my fingers through.

"Cam!" he yells. "Come have a seat. Let's talk strategy."

I look at our options: spinning sex mattress or the Pleasure Perch that almost murdered me. "We'll stand."

"First, Cam, legally I need to tell you that you are in no way obligated to do what I'm about to propose, and I want to remind you of your signed NDA. But... if you agree, it could literally save hundreds of jobs."

"For fuck's sake, Gordon, skip the guilt trip and get to the point."

"You have to beat Astrid at her own game." He hesitates for effect. "To do that, the two of you need to pretend to be a couple."

"No."

Beside me, her mouth falls open. She glances at me then back at Gordon, as if she's waiting for the punchline to land.

"Hear me out! Instead of the heartbreak angle, we flip the script. Surprise romance! True love was right under my nose this whole time, blah, blah, blah. Paradise brought you two together or some shit. You've got the perfect backdrop, the perfect chemistry—"

"What chemistry?" I cut in, glowering at him.

Cam's face is still locked in pure disbelief. "That's... insane."

He smirks. "Insane? Sure. Profitable? Absolutely. And Camila, I can sweeten the deal. A $25,000 bonus for your two weeks of... let's call it romantic improv."

The mood shifts.

Her breath hitches, those gorgeous eyes lighting up like someone offered her the keys to her dreams. As a boss, it's an expression I've witnessed on countless faces.

She is definitely weighing her options.

"Why is your solution *another* fake-dating scheme? Look where the last one got us."

The words are a live grenade hanging in the air, and I realize too late what I've admitted. Cam's sharp inhale tells me she caught it—the truth about Astrid that only a handful of people knew. That the entire epic influencer love story was another algorithm-driven business decision.

Shit.

"Besides," I barrel on, trying to recover, "it would never work with Cam. She's not Astrid."

"Wow." She crosses her arms. "Sorry we can't all be AI-generated fantasy women. Some of us real, breathing humans prefer looking natural. You know, for the decent guys who don't need their women plastic-wrapped and filtered."

Ah, fuck.

"No! That's not—" I drag my hands down my face. "I meant because earlier, when I was filming you, I could tell you're shy in front of the camera." The words tumble out before my brain can stop them. "It's fine! Not everyone is meant to be on camera. Some people belong behind the scenes."

Her expression morphs from annoyed to lethal in zero point five seconds.

She doesn't say anything, just stares at me, her face unreadable. I start sweating.

And then—

"I'll do it, Gordon."

Wait, what?

"Excellent! G-Thorne wants ALL the clickbait! We need thumbnail gold... something that'll grab attention... Like: Hawaii Love Affair with My Boss. Who Seduced Who?!"

"I Fell for My Grumpy Boss in Paradise!" Cam adds.

I glare at her. "Don't encourage him."

"The Moment We Knew We Were Soulmates (SHOCKING CONFESSION)? Accidentally in Love: The Truth About Us! OR—ooh, okay—10 Signs I'm in Love with My Best Friend—"

"We're not best friends," I cut in.

"Okay, okay, scratch that one," Gordon says. "But Falling for My Boss? That one has legs. Let's one-up Astrid using her own tricks. I want hand-holding, sunset walks, some waterfall action—"

"I haven't agreed to any of this," I say quickly.

"Oh, and one more thing..." Gordon's tone shifts to dead serious. "No sleeping around, either of you. I can't have some random person posting a TikTok of you getting down with resort staff. I'm already juggling more bad press than a Kardashian crisis manager."

Cam's mouth drops open. "Hold up. You're saying I have to go *two weeks* without... you know."

"Correct," Gordon replies cheerfully. "Small price to pay for $25,000."

I snort. "This is what gives you pause? *This* is your dealbreaker?"

"Your concern is truly heartwarming." She rolls her eyes, muttering in Spanish.

"So that's it, Gordon?" I throw up my hands. "No plan B? This is your only idea?"

She spins on me, eyes blazing. "Seriously? I'm trying to help you out here, ya know. But please, continue acting like fake dating me is a fate worse than death."

"Please. You're not helping me. You're doing this for a payday like everybody else."

Her expression crumples, and I instantly regret my words, wishing I could shove them back into my big, fat mouth.

KNOCK! KNOCK!

"Let me grab that door for you, boss. Or should I say *boyfriend*." Cam's extra emphasis on the last word is as sharp as her glare.

My brain is spiraling. This is all wrong. I was making rules to keep us apart, not signing up for a two-week couple's cosplay. Why does this day keep finding new ways to torture me?

Cam opens the door, and naturally, it's fucking Kai.

"Aloha, beautiful soul! I almost forgot to give you this welcome swag bag." He hands the gift to her, his massive fingers lingering. "It's brimming with sensual treats to awaken your spirit... and to inspire heated passionate moments."

"Okay, well, gee thanks."

Gordon's still talking, something about engagement metrics and damage control, but I don't hear a word of it. Because all my attention is locked on the scene unfolding in plain sight.

The Curator of Pleasure is very obviously flirting with Cam.

And of course he is.

She's the hottest fucking girl at this entire resort.

That's not even an opinion, it's a fact. Like, scientifically proven. I know. I've spent the last two years trying to ignore it.

I watch the way Kai's eyes trace her lips, how he leans into her space enough to make his attraction clear. And Cam?

All smiles.

At him.

My fingers bite into my palm and I feel a slow, creeping sensation climb up my spine.

Through the static in my brain, I hear Gordon talking. "Reece, buddy, this is the right move. The fans are gonna—"

But his words fade out because she laughs at something Kai says. Then—

Cam wets her lips.

Oh, fuck no.

A territorial feeling slams through me, and then Gordon's earlier words boomerang back into my head. "No sleeping around, either of you."

If I agree to this scheme, then Cam can't get rammed by Kai's sarong python.

"Fine," I say into the phone. "Fake dating. Clickbait. Whatever I need to do."

"Great! I knew you'd—"

I hang up before Gordon can finish his victory speech.

I cross the room in three strides. "Thanks for the present." The door closes on the resort owner's shocked face with a satisfying click, barely missing his intrusive schlong.

"That was rude!"

"Sorry, you've got work to do. Contract's in your inbox."

She blinks, those long lashes fluttering. "You agreed?"

I move closer, close enough to catch the hitch in her breath. "That's right. You're my girlfriend now, Morales."

As soon as the words leave my mouth, I know *I am completely fucked.*

CHAPTER FIVE

CAM

You're my girlfriend now, *Morales.*

Reece hasn't moved, hasn't blinked since he shoved Kai and his magic rod out the door. He's just... standing there, staring at me.

"Are you having a medical emergency?" I ask, waving a hand in his face. "Should I be checking for signs of stroke? Arm weakness? Slurred speech?"

"This isn't going to work."

I tap my chin. "Gruffness intact. Full sentences. Still a pendejo. Whew! You had me worried. Thought I was about to lose out on my twenty-five grand."

He storms toward our red satin love nest. The moment his perfect ass hits the mattress, the bed springs into action, spinning him like a carnival ride.

"What the—" Reece plants his feet, trying to slow the spin, but that only makes it worse. He resembles an overgrown kid on a playground merry-go-round gone rogue. The more he tries to stop it, the faster it spins. "How do I—fuck—make it—goddammit—"

I giggle as he struggles. "Having trouble there, boss?"

"Fix it!"

I wave my hand near the sensor, and the bed jolts to a stop. "Motion sensors, remember? Kai showed us when he was demonstrating his... equipment."

"Ugh. Fucking Kai." Reece flops onto his back, one arm thrown over his eyes. The movement makes his shirt ride up, revealing a forbidden set of scrumptious abs.

Nothing wrong with looking, right?

I perch carefully on the edge, setting the gift bag on the floor. "Aww, is someone feeling a little inadequate? Because I gotta say, they grow 'em real big here in Hawaii." I fan myself dramatically. "Like, anaconda big. Skyscraper proportions. The sort of package that causes a girl to question whether it would—"

His head snaps up. "Do you always talk this much about sex?"

"Only when I'm fake dating my grumpy boss in a honeymoon suite designed exclusively for *maximum* penetration."

He groans, running both hands down his cheeks as if he's praying for strength. "Just so we're clear, being my fake girlfriend doesn't come with... any *physical respon*sibilities."

"You wish," I say, barely containing my laugh. "I'm a pretend girlfriend, not a sex worker. If that was the case, I would've negotiated a much higher rate."

Reece's features cycle through about twelve different expressions, landing somewhere between horrified and constipated.

"Lighten up," I continue. "Getting frisky may have been in your contract with Astrid, but as you so rudely put it... I'm nothing like her."

"Oh God, no, that's not—we didn't—I mean, we did, but it wasn't like—"

"That's your private business." I hold up my hands.

"I am not that guy. The kind that—"

"Has a harem of pretend girlfriends to fuck around with?" I finish for him and immediately wish I hadn't. Because a shadow crosses his face.

"Look." His tone softens. "I get that I don't owe you an explanation, but I need you to know—I'm not a bad guy. And it's been several months since anything happened between Astrid and me."

I blink at him, surprised. "I never said you were a bad guy. A cranky pain in the ass? *Absolutely.* But I respect the lengths you'll go to protect your employees. Including me."

His trademark smirk softens into a small, sheepish smile that's so genuine it makes my stomach flip. This new expression, soft and subtle, has transformed his mouth into something, dare I say... dangerously appealing.

I force my eyes away from his lips. "You don't have to tell me, but how many is *several*?"

"What?"

"You said it's been *several* months. Just curious about the exact number. Might explain why you're so moody. That much pent-up frustration can't be healthy."

The smile vanishes. "How about we discuss your dry spell? Since you were broadcasting it so enthusiastically to your friends earlier. Not gonna lie, volume control is *not* your strong suit."

"Pretty sure sharing my sexual history isn't in the girlfriend contract." Heat floods my cheeks. "Though if you're that curious, maybe we can add it as an amendment. Right after a new clause about you taking hourly scowl breaks."

"What type of men do you even date, anyway?" The question bursts out, and then he quickly adds, "As your boyfriend, I should know. For authenticity."

"Working for you hasn't left much time for dating," I say, sitting down on the bed. "Lucky me, you've been the main man in my life for years, and now I get to be your fake girlfriend. Not that different from being your camera girl. I'm already a professional handler of the Reece Dare Mood Swing Experience."

He doesn't respond right away, his gaze lingering on me, brows furrowed as if he's working hard to read between the lines. The room feels smaller, the air charged with something unspoken. I shift against the mattress, suddenly all too aware of his warm body.

"You're right though—this won't work." I wave between us, accidentally triggering the bed's motion sensor. We both grab the sheets as it starts to turn. "Your nonstop glares and nitpicking? No one will believe I'm your girlfriend when your face shows that you'd rather be scrubbing toilets."

"Fooled everyone with Astrid," he mutters, waving his hand to stop the rotation. His arm brushes mine, and my skin tingles like I licked a battery.

"Honestly, I always thought you were too good for her." My blunt admission surprises us both. "You're an asshole, yeah, but not a complete dick. And in this day and age, that makes you a catch."

For once, neither of us seems to know what to say next.

I snatch up the gift bag, desperate to break this weird tension. "Let's see what goodies Kai left us. Hopefully some snacks, because I'm starving."

The tissue paper crinkles as I dig in, pushing past a layer of rose-scented candles, a bottle of edible massage oil that I immediately shove aside, and then—Oh. *Oh, hello.*

I grab hold of what can only be described as the Godzilla of vibrators, its purple silicone surface catching the light like a beacon of bad decisions. This thing has *girth* and more buttons than my camera.

"I know you don't want me to talk about sex or Kai's impressive love stick, but..." I snort, pulling it out. *"¡Por Dios!* It's kind of hard not to when I'm holding what appears to be the eighth wonder of the world."

Reece releases the longest drawn-out groan, as if his final thread of patience just flatlined.

I rotate the vibrator in my palms. "Holy mother of orgasms, look at the size of this bad boy. Ten bucks says Kai used his own dick as the prototype. No wonder he walks that way—he's got a franchise opportunity in his pants."

"Give me that." Reece snatches it from my grasp. He moves to shove it back into the bag, but—

BZZZZZZZZZZZZZZZZZZ!

The thing roars, and I mean ROARS to life, vibrating so violently it's breakdancing in his hands.

"Shit!" He fumbles with it, his hands a blur of jerky movement, like it's a ticking time bomb. His breath hitches as he frantically presses buttons, flipping it over, shaking it, pressing everywhere *but* the shutoff. "What the—how do I—goddammit!"

I collapse onto the mattress, wheezing. "¡Ay, Dios! This is the best thing that has ever happened to me. Where's my camera?!"

"Where's the damn—why won't this thing—" Reece glares at me, growing more flustered by the second. "You think this is funny?"

I gasp, clutching my stomach as I do my best to breathe through my laughter.

"Here!" He thrusts it at me. "Since you're such an expert, you turn it off!"

I catch it. Barely. The vibrations travel straight up my arms, down my spine, and into places that should absolutely not be reacting to this situation.

And then the laughter dies in my throat.

Because Reece is staring at me.

Not scowling. Not fuming.

Staring.

His chest rises and falls, slow and measured, his lips parted just enough that my brain takes a sharp left turn into *unacceptable territory*. His pupils? Blown wide. His blue eyes? Nearly black.

No. No way. This has to be rage. It must be his *I'm-about-to-feed-you-to-the-sharks* face.

I find the power button immediately and chuck the beast back into the bag. Though my body clearly didn't get the memo, because everything low and deep inside me clenches at his intensity.

"So," I say, my voice embarrassingly breathy, "I really need to shower and get this glitter out of my bra. I'm itchy as hell."

"Fine," Reece says, rolling onto his side and burrowing into the pillows. "If anyone needs me, I'll be unconscious and pretending today never happened."

"Oh hell no. You are *not* camping out here while I'm showering." I gesture at our wall-less paradise. "I might not be your type, but you're a man, and all men have a built-in perv setting. I'm not about to beta-test your self-control."

His lips quirk. "So, are you planning to peek at me in the shower? See how I measure up to Aquaman?"

"Don't start acting like a jealous boyfriend, Reece. I might find it attractive."

"Jealousy does it for you, huh?"

I shrug, feigning nonchalance. "A little possessiveness never hurt anyone."

His brows lift slightly in intrigue. But before he has the chance to speak, I say, "But don't worry—you're not my type either. I don't care for brooding control freaks who critique my every breath."

At least that's what my brain says. My hoo ha, however, has other ideas.

Excuse me, what's happening down there? Since when are we into irritable prickwads?

"Great," Reece says, pushing to his feet. "We'll take turns on the balcony. Close the curtain for privacy."

"Perfect. I'm going first." I point to the sliding glass door. "Out. Shoo."

He prowls to the balcony with the casual grace of a guy who knows exactly how good he looks in motion. And I'm only human—my eyes definitely track the way those tailored pants cup his ass. He drops into the hammock, and even the ocean breeze seems thirsty, immediately messing up his hair.

I follow him out. "Seriously, no peeking."

"Don't flatter yourself, Morales."

Then, in one swift movement, he rips his shirt off and wears it over his face like the world's sexiest blindfold.

My mouth goes dry. Bone dry. Sahara-level dry.

I don't know what sort of cosmic miracle crafted this man, but I owe him *(or her)* a serious thank-you note for those abs.

"I mean it. Do not come in here. I am not your fake girlfriend with benefits."

He peels the shirt slightly off one eye, catching me *very clearly* checking him out. A self-satisfied smirk dances on his lips. "Sounds as if you're trying to convince yourself."

"Ha! Not interested. Unless you're packing a Kai-sized weapon in those designer pants."

His scowl returns with a vengeance. "Since poetry-spouting douchewads are your type, I have nothing to worry about."

"And since you like your women pumped full of plastic, I guess I'm safe. Too bad for you, cause my tits?" I make a grand gesture toward my girls. "They're real, and they're spectacular."

His nostrils flare. His throat bobs. And for a brief second—so fast I almost miss it—his gaze definitely flickers downward.

I smirk, victorious, then spin on my heel and *slam* the sliding door shut before he can retaliate. I yank the curtain closed with a flourish.

¡Mierda! I need to get this tingle factory under control before I do something epically stupid. Like jump my boss.

Listen up, vajayjay. This is NOT the tropical vacation hookup we discussed.

***

"**THE NERVE OF THAT** cocky dickwad!"

With a dramatic huff, I yank open my overpacked suitcase and—

Oh, shit.

My entire packing strategy slaps me across the face.

No. No, no, no, no, no.

I dig frantically, tossing delicate bralettes, microscopic satin shorts, and lacy thongs. Everything I packed screams "I'm here to get laid," not "no-privacy cohabitation with my buzzkill of a boss."

"¡Mierda! This was supposed to be my Hawaiian sexcation, not a two-week celibacy retreat."

My fingers brush against something strappy. I pull it out and—yep, there it is. The crown jewel of my "get some" collection. A red open cup bra that's basically a series of strings playing connect-the-dots with my nipples. The matching underwear? A single strip of fabric up my ass, which—let's be honest—exists solely to give a man an excuse to groan into my skin while yanking it off with his teeth.

And now? What a waste.

I know damn well what I'm working with. These curves? They've made better men than Reece lose their minds. My perky tits are the reason I've never had to change a tire in my life. And my ass? More bounce than a trampoline park. So yeah, I splurge on lingerie that flaunts the goods.

I groan, tossing the red set back like it's radioactive. RIP, orgasms.

After sifting through an avalanche of lace and satin, my fingers land on something marginally less scandalous. *Marginally.* A hot pink satin crop top with a deep V that plunges shamelessly between my breasts. And shorts that are more boy-cut underwear. If I sneeze, I'll be indecent.

I hold it up, squinting.

This? This is my most modest choice.

Fan-fucking-tastic.

"You know what?" I mutter, clutching the pajamas. "If Reece has a problem with my natural Latina curves, he can take it up with God."

SNAP. Suitcase zipped.

My blood boils as his words loop in my head: "Some people belong behind the scenes."

I'm sorry—did I ask for your unsolicited asshole opinion?

But dammit if he didn't nail my insecurity with terrifying accuracy. And then with typical smugness, he drop-kicked my self-esteem to the curb.

Because the truth?

Yeah. I *am* better behind the camera.

The thought sits heavy in my chest, right next to my dreams of launching my own channel. It's the dirty little secret I've been hiding behind my cargo pants and professional smile.

In this world of ring lights and "don't forget to subscribe," people aren't just here for your content—they're here for you. They want morning routines, coffee chats, and that bestie-next-door vibe that makes them feel connected. They expect to see your face, know your story, and be a part of your journey.

And me?

I've spent my entire career making sure I was the one capturing those moments.

Not living them. Not being seen. Not being judged.

It's safer that way, where no one can count your flaws in the comments section or turn your worst moments into viral memes.

After watching Reece's life implode over the last twenty-four hours? Not exactly making me want to step into the spotlight. No matter how much it pays.

I sigh, closing my eyes. "Cut the shit, Camila. Admit there's another reason you said yes to this ridiculous scheme. One that has nothing to do with your channel or your bank account."

The look on Reece's face when he saw Blaze with Astrid—God, I've never seen someone fight so hard to stay composed. He's completely alone in this. Gordon sees him as a brand in need of a refresh, not a person unraveling right in front of him.

Yeah, he's grumpy.

Yeah, he says rude shit and has poor taste.

And yeah, he doesn't find me attractive.

But deep, deep, deep down? Reece Dare has a good heart.

The guy will do literally anything to protect his employees. He carries the weight of everyone's livelihood on those stupidly broad shoulders. And he deserves someone in his corner.

"Even if that someone is fake girlfriend number two," I mutter then immediately cringe. "Yeah, not loving that nickname."

And there's the huge dent to my self-esteem at how fast he shot down the idea of fake dating me. I strip off my glitter-bombed cargos and chocolate-smeared shirt, only to be greeted by my butt-naked, bare ass reflection grinning back from the eight thousand mirrors in this gettin' freaky fun house.

I channel my inner Instagram baddie and strike a pose.

"Clearly I'm not hideous," I tell myself. "I mean, Kai for sure wanted me to jump on his pogo stick."

But I'm not... blonde enough. Not contoured enough. Not *Astrid* enough.

"¡Ay, Dios mío! Get it together, Camila," I scold my reflection. "You're a badass! You've filmed parkour stunts! You've scaled buildings for the perfect angle! You've eaten gas station sushi! And most impressively, you've survived two years with Reece."

I don't give a damn if some cranky-ass piece of man candy doesn't think I'm sexy.

"You're going to be the best ever fake girlfriend. Get that channel promotion from Reece. And try not to kill him in his sleep." I give myself a confident nod.

The second I hit the control panel for the open shower, I am in awe.

Hot water sluices over black volcanic rock, creating a waterfall effect, wrapping me in a warm, misty embrace. The air is thick with steam, the scent of jasmine and plumeria curling around me like an aphrodisiac. The stone floor beneath my feet is heated, because of course it is.

I tip my head back, letting the water rush through my hair, sliding over my shoulders, down my back.

"Damn, Kai," I moan, tilting my face into the spray. "You're right. This isn't a shower. This is an experience."

Logically speaking, he should be the star of my tropical hookup fantasy. The man is gorgeous. A Hawaiian god. Built like he wrestles sharks for sport. He's a walking, talking romance novel cover come to life.

But the idea of him thrusting into me while whispering deep, soulful things about love flowing like lava? Hard pass. That doesn't make me swoon; it makes me feel like I'm stuck in a cheesy porno movie.

Still, seeing Reece get all flustered around him?

That's fun.

It's like watching a grumpy cat try to out-alpha a Great Dane who's too busy wagging his tail and winning hearts to notice.

Every time Kai so much as breathes near me, Reece gets so irrationally irritated. I find it hilarious.

But also?

Confusing.

Because why does Reece care? Why does he get so pissed off when Kai flirts with me? It sure as hell isn't jealousy.

"Although…" I work coconut-scented shampoo into my hair, trying desperately not to replay the way Reece's hands felt on my body. The firm grip on my hip when he caught me. The heat of his palm sliding up my thigh on the plane. The way his pupils dilated, turning those steel-blue eyes almost black…

"¡Mierda!" My thighs clench involuntarily.

"'She's not Astrid,'" I mimic his deep voice, adding extra grump. "Yeah? Well, your attitude's not my type either, pendejo!"

Still this throb between my legs isn't taking no for an answer. Am I really so desperate I'm actively lusting after my grouchy, uninterested boss?

This is a new low.

For a wild moment, I consider retrieving the Godzilla vibrator from Kai's gift bag. But that thing's got more horsepower than a Harley—Reece will absolutely hear it buzzing through the door.

Then I remember…

I reach behind the slick stone wall, fingers skimming over the hidden panel, finding the shower wand Kai demonstrated. A sleek, curved attachment, perfectly positioned for, well… this.

I flip it over, inspecting the settings. Sultry. Pulse. Volcanic.

"Hello there." I eye the balcony curtain—still firmly closed—then turn the wand, positioning it where I need it most, and press the sultry button.

The first burst of warm, streaming water hits, and my breath catches.

"Oh... *Yes...*" A slow shiver rolls through me. I press my back into the rock, letting the rhythmic pressure do its work.

And since I'm here... There's no harm in fantasizing.

Unfortunately, my brain is dead set on one person.

Reece.

I shut my eyes, imagining him on his knees, that perpetual scowl replaced with hunger. Those capable hands spreading my thighs. His smart mouth finally doing something besides criticizing me.

My free hand finds my breast, rolling my nipple as I imagine Reece's hands caressing me, teasing until they form stiff, aching peaks, begging for more of his touch.

I switch to pulse, and the rhythmic sensation builds, escalating as I envision his tongue plunging and caressing my intimate core. Sparks shoot off like fireworks, his hunger insatiable, as if he hasn't eaten in years. He feasts on me with a ferocity that sends shockwaves up my spine.

"Almost... fuck..."

I grip the stone ledge, rocking my hips slightly, chasing the sensation. I'm climbing faster than I ever have alone at home. Must be that island magic.

My body starts to coil.

The pressure builds.

I am so close.

I twist the dial to Volcanic.

And SCREAM.

"¡HIJO DE LA CHINGADA!"

The wand launches out of my grip, thrashing like a live wire, the harsh spray slamming into me with the force of a pressure washer.

I stumble, flailing, attempting to clutch on to the hose as it whips around.

BANG.

It smacks into my arm.

BANG.

It whacks my ass.

I scramble to turn it off, but the dial is slippery as hell, and the sprayer is still attacking me.

"OH MY GOD, OW! STOP! STOP!"

I shriek again, arms flailing, slipping against the wet rock.

I try to seize it, but it might as well be a lubed-up eel. The burst blinds me, then shoots between my thighs like it's trying to power wash my hoo ha.

"¡DIOS MÍO! ¡NO! ¡PARA!"

I finally get my hands on the demonic shower wand, my fingers gripping the slippery handle like a warrior wielding a sword.

And then I notice...

A man. Standing. In. My. Shower.

I SCREAM.

Like, full-bodied, horror movie scream. And in my blind panic, I twist the nozzle, spraying him.

A direct shot... to the eye.

"Holy fuck!" He staggers back.

"¡Mierda! Reece, I'm sorry—"

BOOM!

Thunder crashes as lightning flashes, turning the entire room into a strobe-lit nightmare. I shriek, dropping the wand of doom.

Worst. Decision. Ever.

The thing goes absolutely feral, whipping around with the force of a fire hose. Red lights pulse through the spray from LED strips embedded in the stone walls, transforming ordinary water into streams of fake lava.

"¡Ay, Dios mío!" I scream as scalding water blasts my hip.

Choreographed lighting rigs fire up like we're in a Polynesian rave, complete with artificial monkey screams and... *is that a panther's roar?*

I feel Reece's biceps flex around me, his bare chest pressing against my soaked back as he holds me close, shielding me as he reaches for the thrashing nozzle.

And for a split second, I think, *Wow, this is kind of hot.*

An elephant trumpets through surround-sound along with more thunder as programmed lightning zigzags between perfectly placed fixtures. Kai's "Ultimate Paradise Experience" is a Rainforest Cafe on steroids.

Like a shirtless superhero who's been called in for emergency duty, he pushes me behind his ridiculous torso. "Stay back—"

"Reece!" I grab his wrist. "That's my boob!"

"Fuck! Sorry!"

"Watch out!"

Too late. *THWACK!* The metal nozzle whips around, fast as a cobra, and smacks Reece in the forehead.

"MOTHERF—OW!" he snarls, staggering back, hands flying to his head. He glares at me through one squinted eye.

Another crack of lightning erupts over our heads. A clap of thunder shakes every inch of the space. The room pulses between blinding white flashes and total darkness.

And suddenly, the walls come alive.

Animatronic birds descend from the ceiling, mechanical beaks opening and closing as they burst into a soulful gospel rendition of "Let's Get It On."

A robotic toucan swings out of nowhere, flapping fake wings as an animatronic conga line of parrots start bobbing along the rock wall.

What. The actual. Fuck.

I whip around, and the handheld sprayer attacks me again, this time blasting me in the stomach so hard I double over.

"IT'S POSSESSED!" I scream, flailing.

Reece lunges for the hose, gripping it like he's wrestling a 200-pound python.

The water thrashes, the wand jerking violently in his grip, red mist still spraying everywhere like an angry, fire-breathing dragon.

"SHUT IT OFF!" he bellows.

I scramble toward the control panel, my feet slipping on the slick tile. And instead of a graceful sprint—

I SLIDE.

I slam into the panel, hitting the off switch, and the chaos stops instantly.

No water.

No thunder.

No demonic light show.

The birds slowly retreat into the ceiling, wings flapping in one final mechanical farewell.

And for three long seconds, the only sound is our ragged, heavy breathing.

I push my drenched hair out of my eyes, relieved this nightmare is over. Then I spot Reece on the ground, hand pressed to his eye. "Oh my God, are you okay?"

I drop to my knees beside him, cradling his head between my palms. His uncovered eye goes wide, darting back and forth.

And that's when I remember. I am very, very naked.

My boobs are introducing themselves to his face.

"*¡Ay, carajo!*" I screech, jumping up. But because karma's not done making me its bitch and the floor is still wet, my feet slide out from under me.

WHAM!

I fall backwards and Reece catches me, yanking me against his chest with enough force to knock the wind out of both of us. His hands instinctively latch on to my—

Yep.

He's got two handfuls of premium-grade boob.

We freeze. My heart hammers against his palms. His chest heaves against my back. Water drips.

Finally, Reece breaks the silence, his voice rough against my ear. "You're right, Morales. Your tits are spectacular."

And just like that, my traitorous lady bits fire up again.

CHAPTER SIX

REECE

Those are her fucking pajamas?

My toothbrush scrapes against my molars with enough force to make my gums bleed. I want to cleanse this whole night from my brain. But no amount of minty-fresh toothpaste can scrub away the spectacle of her in that shower.

Cam. Wet. Naked.

As we speak, she's lounging on the bed in a sizzling pink lingerie set that hardly classifies as sleepwear—looking hot as fuck—while I struggle to keep my cock from breaking free from its four-layer security system.

Yeah. Four.

Briefs. Then boxers. Gray sweats. And now? A fucking robe. Because I'm at DEFCON 1 levels of throbbing, and if she so much as breathes the wrong way, I'm going to nut so hard, they'll be putting caution tape around my pants.

I stare in the mirror, hoping to intimidate myself into behaving.

Don't look at her.

DON'T LOOK AT HER!

My traitorous eyes flick back to her.

She's cross-legged, laptop open, completely oblivious that she's ruining me. Her headphones are on, and her long, wild waves spill over one shoulder as her mouth purses slightly. She's editing footage in her barely there shorts, which are riding up her thighs. The teeniest little straps of that silk top are fighting for strength against the weight of her perfect tits.

Jesus Christ, those tits.

They're real.

My hands are still tingling with the memory of her curves overflowing in my palms, soft and lush. Her nipples, peaked and pressing against my skin, were a sensation I'll never forget. I have fantasized about her naked more times than I can count, but the reality? Better than I could've imagined. Those incredible breasts will star in my spank bank dreams until the day I die.

I spit into the sink so hard, it splashes.

Stop. This is Cam. My employee. The woman I pay to mock my life choices and film my misery. I will not think about her gorgeous nakedness. Or acknowledge my current feelings that fully clothed (*sorta*), she is even more alluring.

I throw my toothbrush and toiletry kit into my suitcase with more force than necessary. My eyes scan the room—a futile search for privacy in this mirror-covered sex dungeon. There's literally nowhere to handle my... situation.

Breathe, Dare. Breathe.

I stomp over to the bed—to the edge farthest from her—and drop onto the mattress before yanking out my phone. Maybe I can distract myself—scroll my way out of this crisis.

Except...

The goddamn mirrors.

This hellscape of a honeymoon suite is nothing but reflective surfaces. And every single one is showing me Cam from a new, devastating angle.

The full-length mirror on the wall? Her legs.

The vanity mirror? Her breasts.

The ceiling mirror? *Oh, come the fuck on.*

I will not tilt my head back.

I will not—

I tilt my head back. *Shit.*

Instant VIP pass to Nipple Town.

I shoot upright like I've been electrocuted.

Cam chooses this exact moment to lift her headphones and rest them on her neck.

Her tits bounce. Like a personal attack on my willpower. *Like they know what they're doing.*

Desperate, I grab a pillow—ready to scream into it—until I see the stupid familiar words:

Pussy Partner.

"Are you fucking kidding me?" I mutter, chucking the damn thing across the room.

Cam snorts, "Not a fan of Kai's interior design?"

I glare at her with every ounce of my miserable, suffering soul. "Are you really going to wear that to sleep?"

She blinks innocently. "This?"

"That." I wave a hand at her. "It's not pajamas. It's lingerie."

She gasps dramatically. "Look at you. Are you scandalized? Should I cover my ankles too?"

"Maybe put on a damn hoodie."

"A hoodie? In Hawaii?" She gestures to the literal tropical paradise outside the balcony. "Oh, I'm sorry. Let me just slip into my thermal onesie so you can sleep better."

"Fine. Don't wear a hoodie. Just don't"—I wave my hand at her—"do that."

"Do what?"

I scowl. "Bounce."

Her mouth drops open. And then… she bursts out laughing.

I hate her. I hate what she does to me.

"Oh my God," she wheezes, clutching her stomach. "Did you just tell my boobs to stop bouncing?"

"I told *you* to stop bouncing."

"I'm sorry," she says, catching her breath. "Is that why you're wearing a bathrobe over sweats? Afraid you'll tempt me with your dick flopping around?"

"I'm cold."

"It's eighty-five degrees. The humidity alone is a weighted blanket."

"I run cold."

"Ha! You're powered by a nuclear reactor of pent-up rage."

"How are those pajamas *work-appropriate*?" I snap.

"Well, one: I wasn't supposed to be sharing a room with you. And two: you've already seen me naked, so what's the big deal?"

My dick perks up at the word *naked* like it's been given the *all clear* to rejoin the conversation.

"I'm your boss."

"Okay, Mr. Dare. Got it. Loud and clear. My skin offends you. So, what do you want me to do about it?"

I want to be honest and tell you how goddamn hot you are. I want you to ask me to fuck you so hard they'll hear you screaming my name on the next island.

"I just want to be clear that I wasn't *trying* to see you naked."

She smirks.

"I'm your boss," I repeat. "This fake relationship is for the cameras. That's it. You don't need to worry about me touching you."

"Says the guy who grabbed two handfuls of—"

My eyes betray me, darting to her breasts. I jerk my gaze back up, but I know I look guilty as hell.

"That was an accident," I bite out.

"Twice?" She taps her chin with her finger. "You know, most guys butter me up with carbs before rounding second. You owe me some breadsticks."

"I'm serious. I'm not trying to take advantage. I'm here for business and nothing else. Wear whatever you want."

Her smirk fades.

Wait. Why does she seem… disappointed?

"Are we done with the *you-find-everything-about-me-offensive* conversation?" she asks, clicking at her laptop again. "Because Gordon needs me to upload tomorrow's video."

She tosses a folded slip of paper at my face.

"Oh, and this itinerary for tomorrow was in the gift bag. Along with some pineapple-flavored popcorn. I hope you're hungry," she continues, smug as hell, "because I ate it all."

I unfold the itinerary. It's a Hallmark movie checklist for couples, only cursed. I shudder. "A romantic hot tub dinner? So like dinner, but wet? That sounds disgusting."

"I figured you'd react that way. Because it could be fun, *but* you're a joy vampire. You feed off the good feelings of others until you've sucked them dry."

"Only you would be excited about stewing in your own broth while eating spaghetti."

"Got it. Don't expect any fake romance from my fake boyfriend. If you don't mind, I have work to get done, boss. Someone has to blur Kai's giant dick out, frame by frame, on the sex swing. Don't want to get demonetized."

The headphones slam over her ears, and she's back to editing... but something's off. The usual sparkle in her eyes is dimmed, and her shoulders are tense beneath that damned pink satin.

Fuck me... Why do I notice?

I'm her boss.

Not the guy who should be reading into her expressions.

Not the guy wondering if I should've said something different.

Not the guy who currently feels like garbage, for reasons I do not have the emotional bandwidth to unpack.

Deciding I need a fifth layer of protection, I grab a fluffy blanket from the cabinet and mummify my body.

I am now Burrito Reece. I flop onto the bed, facing away from her. I need to protect myself.

Not from her.

But from me.

Because if I spend one more second seeing Camila Morales in that tiny pink excuse for an outfit, I am one hundred percent going to plunge headfirst into a whirlwind of trouble.

***

THE PASSIVE-AGGRESSIVE HAWAIIAN SUN is bathing me in its warm embrace, and I find it to be a full-body assault. I should be in heaven, sprawled out on a poolside lounger, gazing at the infinity pool, which is pure, liquid sapphire minus the few smiling couples getting handsy in the water. Palm trees sway like lazy metronomes, their fronds whispering in a breeze laced with plumeria, salt air, and what I'm pretty sure is the resort's signature *Essence of Sexual Healing* fragrance.

Paradise, right? Except my brain won't shut off last night's eight-hour torture session.

I've survived parkour fails, wrestled an inflatable T-Rex in a hurricane, eaten the world's hottest wings while dressed as a diapered cupid in Times Square. But sharing a bed with Cam? Pure, unadulterated hell. That woman sleeps like she's choreographing an elaborate Broadway production.

Her legs kept finding mine and sticking to me like some sort of needy octopus. Her arms would wrap around my neck, choking me out while she muttered something in Spanish that sounded suspiciously like death threats. And her hand—fuck my life—her hand kept landing on my dick. Repeatedly. As if my cock was a magnet.

Shoutout to my five layers of protection!

Every time I closed my eyes, there she was. Camila, in that steamy shower scene—hair slicked back, lips parted, water cascading over soft curves, steam clinging to bare skin—alluring and unforgettable. I tried everything. Counting backwards from a thousand, thinking about my car's maintenance schedule, even pictured Gordon eating soup. Didn't matter.

By five a.m., delirious from lack of sleep and an erection that wouldn't quit, I grabbed the camera and fled like a coward, leaving her a note that I hoped made me sound douchey: *"Thanks for zero sleep with your non-stop thrashing. Meet me at the pool for couples' activities. Filming the resort until then."*

My phone buzzes a text alert.

Gordon: *Dropped hints to the press about a big surprise in tomorrow's video. Followers are still dropping but slower. I'm handling it.*

Me: *Do I have to do these stupid couples' challenges?*

Gordon: *Yes. Part of your contract. We need this new girlfriend content to be a hit. Show sponsors you've still got it. Have fun, superstar.*

I groan so loudly that a nearby couple stops making out. *Fun?* The only fun I want involves becoming a permanent blanket burrito and sleeping this trip off.

But I've got a plan. A solid one. A strategy so foolproof, even Blaze couldn't mess it up. Use the camera as a chastity shield between Cam and me. If my hands are occupied filming, they can't grab anything they shouldn't.

No touching.

No inappropriate boners.

No career-destroying mistakes that end with us fucking like bunnies.

The last thing I need on my mountain of problems is a scandal where I get caught taking advantage of my employee. That would blow up the whole damn operation.

A shadow falls over my lounge chair, and before I even look up, I feel him—the overwhelming, oppressive *alpha male energy* radiating like a heat source. Kai looms over me, his oiled chest gleaming in the sun. *Is that a loincloth made out of fresh orchids?*

Seriously, why is this dude so shiny? What does he do, bathe in the tears of men after he seduces their girlfriends?

"Brother. I trust you and the enchanting Miss Morales enjoyed my welcome package?"

It's hard to hear the word *package* when *his* package is dangling so close to my face.

I stand abruptly. "What exactly are these couples' games?"

"Ahh, excellent question. At Aloha Amour, we believe love should be both playful and passionate. As I'm sure you know, even the most devoted lovers cannot pound each other twenty-four-seven."

He takes a cleansing breath. "The body needs to recharge. Therefore, in between moments of deep sensual exploration, we offer activities that nurture the bond between couples. Strengthen their connection. Prepare them for greater pleasures."

I regret asking.

"Kai, my man!" Blaze bounds over like a bouncy ball, hand raised for a high-five, which Kai returns with the seriousness of a sacred ritual.

Then Blaze turns to me, hand still raised. "Brooooo! Don't leave me hangin'."

"You cannot be serious right now."

"Tired? I get it." He winks so hard his whole face contorts. "None of us got any sleep last night." When I don't respond, he high-fives himself.

My best friend has always been a few fries short of a Happy Meal. He once got lost in his own backyard. Honestly, his childlike innocence is... *was* one of my favorite things about him. That and he's always down to try anything, no matter how stupid. But can he really be *this* clueless?

"Blazey-poo!" Astrid's voice cuts through the air. "I told you not to wander! We have to record our intro video!"

"Coming, babykins!" He parkours over a chaise lounge, nearly taking out an elderly couple.

There's movement by the pool entrance, and my throat goes dry. Cam's walking toward us in cutoff shorts and a fitted floral tank top. I've never seen her dressed so casually, so... free. A royal blue string teases around her neck, disappearing under fabric and—

No. No, no, no.

Please, if there is a God, do not let there be a bikini under there.

And then, being an actual masochist, I immediately hope there is.

Get it together. She's your employee.

I force my face into the scowl to end all scowls and bark, "You're late."

Cam saunters up, looking unbothered by my presence, which I do not appreciate. If I'm suffering, she should at least pretend to be flustered.

"Good morning to you too, Reecey-Poo. Got your love note. Nice to know you can criticize me even when I'm unconscious."

"If you need a third member to add harmony to your relationship," Kai says, "I have extensive experience—"

"Thanks, but no thanks," I cut him off sharply. "We need to film. You know, to promote your resort."

"Ah yes, of course." Kai nods sagely. "You are the expert. And the weeks ahead will present plenty of time for us to intertwine our bodies."

Kai finally—finally—saunters off, leaving behind a cloud of pheromones and uninvited sexual wisdom. I let out a breath, ready to regroup, when Cam grabs my camera from the recliner. I snatch it back before she can power it up.

"Oh no. I'll be filming today."

"Why?"

"Because you're *on* camera now, remember? Since you don't have experience, you need to focus."

"Right. Because I suck at everything. Filming. Sleeping. Being on camera. Tell me, boss, since I'm the worst employee in the history of employees, why haven't you fired me yet?"

"That's not—"

"Don't spare my feelings. You'll strain yourself." She lifts her chin, daring me to say more—a total turn-on. "You're paying me good money to play make-believe. So, call the shots, boss."

How about you peel off that tank top and let me see your glorious breasts in your swimsuit. Please, oh please let your nipples be hard.

I clear my throat. "We don't have time for wardrobe malfunctions, so you better not have worn a bikini."

"One-piece." She grabs the hem of her tank top. "Want a preview?"

"Jesus—NO! Can we just film the damn intro?"

I hit *Record*. "Hey, DareSquad! Coming at you with some insane content. Yeah, trapped on an island with my ex—" I turn the lens to show Astrid in the background. "Yikes! But don't worry about your boy. I'm moving on and moving up. Meet my new girlfriend, Camila!"

I pan to her and—*great, just great*. She's frozen like a statue. I hit *Stop*.

"What the hell was that?" The words come out harsher than intended. "You've literally filmed thousands of these."

"Newsflash, pendejo." She pokes my chest. "You didn't tell me what to say. I'm not Blaze. I can't read your mind."

Right on cue: "Yooooo!" Blaze says from the pool stairs. "Me and my girl are gonna slay these games today! That's how we do it!"

Both our heads snap toward the far end of the shimmering blue water, where beach chairs and neon inflatables clutter the deck. Blaze throws his overly muscular arm around Astrid, flashing a megawatt grin into the lens.

She tilts the camera so it highlights her cleavage. "That's right, Blazey. Smash that *Like* button if you're down to see us destroy my ex, Reece Dare."

I lift my hands. "Morales, how is this supposed to work when you have no clue how to be on camera?"

The moment the words leave my mouth, her expression crumbles, and I am officially the biggest asshole in Hawaii. I'm taking out my frustration—sexual and otherwise—on her. None of this cluster-fuck is her fault.

"Cam, I'm—"

PWOOOOOOOO!

The loudest goddamn sound in the world explodes from across the pool.

I whip my head around and see Kai standing dramatically at the water's edge, a massive conch shell pressed to his lips like a horn.

"Let the Passion Games begin!"

And I already know this day is about to get way worse.

***

A BIKINI WOULD HAVE been better. A fucking bikini would have been merciful compared to this stripper lingerie posing as a swimsuit.

It's a masterpiece in royal blue, the color so deep and rich that her olive skin is glowing in the golden sun. A thin strap circles her neck, drawing attention to the giant, scandalous, absolutely soul-destroying cutout between her breasts. The way this thing celebrates her mouthwatering cleavage should be illegal.

But oh, buckle up, it gets worse.

More cutouts on her hips, little delicate straps with white beads holding the bottoms in place. And a single strip of fabric connecting the top to the bottom, trailing over her stomach in a way that is so damn sensual, so effortlessly erotic, that I can't stop picturing her arching under me.

Fuck. Every guy here is staring at her like she's the best thing on the menu.

"Damn, Cam!" Blaze shouts from across the pool. "You've been holding out on us! All that fire hiding under them cargo pants? You're fine as hell!"

I'm going to kill him.

I move with clenched fists of rage. Cam steps in, blocking my path, and *Christ—the back view is even more sinful.*

"Blaze," she sighs, "if you want to keep your teeth, stop talking."

He grins. "What? I'm only spitting facts! Everyone's thinking it!"

"Hello?" Astrid pushes out her artificially round boobs, held in by her neon orange bikini. "These are literally right here!"

"What's wrong, Astrid? Jealous of my new girlfriend?"

Shit. Did I actually say that?

"What? Camera girl?" Her tone drips pure venom. "How about never?"

"Yo, you guys are dating?" Blaze claps. "That's sick. Congrats, bro! This is like when my pet hamster met my other pet hamster and they had baby hamsters!"

Astrid whips out her phone, locked, loaded, and recording, before I can blink.

"Besties! Stop everything! The tea is SCALDING! Reece is so desperate right now. He's like, copying me? With…" she zooms in on Cam, "…that? If you think you can win this competition with those thunder thighs, you're more delusional than when you thought I actually orgasmed."

Cam reaches up, twisting her hair into a ponytail with her scrunchie, and everything… bounces. "Why don't you come closer and say that to my face?"

"Oh honey." Astrid's tone could freeze hell. "You're not even in my tax bracket. Go hide behind your little camera where you belong."

Something in me snaps. I charge forward, my camera rolling hot. "See, that's your problem, Astrid. You work so hard chasing perfection, you've forgotten what real beauty is." I grab Cam's hand, spinning her slowly, showcasing every gorgeous curve. "This? This is what perfection looks like. You can snap a pic and take it to your next doctor's appointment. C'mon, Cam. Let's go win these games."

I wrap my arm around Cam's waist, and holy hell—her skin is soft.

"Don't let her get to you." I murmur, trying to ignore how right she feels.

"Thanks for defending me."

Reality backhands me—I'm touching her. Actually touching her. I quickly pull away.

Hands off, Dare! Pull yourself together!

***

RESORT COUPLES OF ALL types, from honeymooners to anniversary lovebirds, gather around the pool. They have no idea they're about to witness my descent into madness.

"First challenge!" Kai announces. "The couples' relay race! The stronger partner must carry the other through the pool as if rushing toward mutual pleasure."

Shit. Cam has to hold the camera while I hold... her.

The horn sounds, and we jump into the water. Blaze and Astrid are synchronized dolphins. They're on the move, and she's clinging to him like a horny mermaid, somehow managing to film and narrate the whole thing.

Me? I'm having a crisis.

I think of every position possible to not touch too much of Cam.

Piggyback? Her thighs would be wrapped around my waist. Hard pass.

Side carry? Her breasts would be pressed firmly into my chest. Hell no.

Front carry? I would die on the spot.

I opt for holding her like she's a ladder and take off running through the water.

"You do realize I'm not a surfboard, right?" she sputters as water splashes into her face.

"Reece!" Kai shouts. "Your erect body must support hers! Embrace those curves as the ocean embraces the shore!"

Cam squirms, turning into me, and suddenly her breasts are pushed up against my bare stomach, soft and full and—

SPLASH.

I drop her as Astrid and Blaze cross the finish line.

Astrid winks at the lens. "That's right, we won, bitches! Reece and his new 'girlfriend' didn't even finish. Guess Reece still can't get a girl across the finish line. Get used to it, honey!"

I don't care that she's filming me—I hit her with a death glare hot enough to fry her battery.

"Next challenge! The Balancing Act of Desire." Kai shouts.

Giant heart-shaped rafts bob in the water that resemble a fleet of mini Valentine's Day parade floats.

"Couples must become one with each other," Kai proclaims. "First you climb aboard the float, then you both must find balance while standing. Finally, you unite your bodies in a sensual embrace. This requires strength and stamina—much like what is needed for marathon love-making sessions!"

"There is no way in hell I'm doing that," I mutter to myself.

Cam's already moving, pulling herself onto the inflatable. Then—as if my suffering wasn't enough—she rolls onto her hands and knees in a *fuck-me-on-all-fours* position that has me reeling.

"Earth to Reece!" She snaps her fingers. "Camera! Now! Unless you want footage of the pool drain?"

I hand her the GoPro and grip the edge of the heart-shaped floatie. "I'm strategizing."

"What's there to strategize? Get your ass up here!"

I attempt to climb aboard the small raft without touching her—a maneuver that would challenge Tom Cruise's entire stunt team. My hands slip on the wet plastic as if I'm grabbing a greased pig, and—

The raft launches us into the pool.

SPLASH.

When I surface, Cam is sputtering, coughing, and glaring. "Are you actively trying to drown me?"

"Feel the rhythm! Let your bodies sync, your energies entwine—trust your connection together" Kai shouts.

"Oh, we're feeling the vibes," Astrid purrs from their float, where she's face-first wrapped around Blaze like a pole dancer, camera in hand. "Look at us being, like, so mentally connected or whatever."

"My Dude!" Blaze hollers. "You got this man. Just ease up into her."

"He's not even trying." Cam coughs up more water.

As resort staff clear the giant inflatables, I weigh my options while watching water trail down Cam's curves. They all lead to one conclusion: get out of this fucking pool. Because if I stay here one more minute, my dick is going to override my brain and convince Cam to go play its own games back in our room.

"We forfeit," I say.

"You already quitting?" Astrid grins for her audience. "Reece is finally admitting I'm superior. Because some of us"—she gestures down her figure—"were built for these challenges. While others... with that bargain basement booty? Are way too thick to handle, let alone balance."

"Did you seriously just come for my ass?" Cam's eyes narrow dangerously.

"Sweetie, I'm saving you from embarrassing yourself. Reece can barely look at you without cringing. You gotta admit, it's kinda desperate to date the help…"

"Time to go," I say, but Cam doesn't budge.

"Trust me." Astrid tosses her extensions. "Reece might look pretty, but his performance? There's a reason I upgraded to Blazey. Some boys can't rise to the occasion."

"Listen up, you walking mannequin." Cam's voice could freeze lava. "The only genuine thing about you is your audacity. And guess what? Reece is a nonstop pleasure machine. He's all man, all night, and he's only having trouble today because I didn't let him get any sleep."

There is no hiding the shock on my face or the erection tenting in my board shorts.

"We're doing this next challenge," she declares, pointing at me, "so get your shit together. Let's destroy them."

"Behold! The Totem of Passion!" Kai proclaims. "The totem represents man's most primal state! The women shall mount their men's shoulders, standing tall and proud, representing nature's most powerful sword!"

Nope, I am getting out of this pool.

"Yo!" Blaze bounces in the water. "Just like morning wood! Am I right, bro?"

"Quit talking to me!" I snap back.

"The men become the base, strong and firm, while their goddesses rise above, creating the ultimate tower of passion." He sounds the horn. "Begin!"

Cam is a spider monkey scrambling up my body, and I almost drop the camera.

"Don't move," Cam mutters, gripping my shoulders. Her hands squeeze my skin, warming every inch they touch. "Stay still—"

Blaze already has Astrid perched on his shoulders like a Vegas showgirl.

Then—

Cam's silky thighs lock around my neck.

My brain shuts down.

"Grab my hand!" she orders as she steps onto my shoulders. "Help me stand!"

I reach up blindly and brush against—sweet mother of fuck—the softest, most forbidden territory imaginable between her legs.

I yank back. Cam wobbles.

"Reece!"

Pure panic. I fumble to steady her, and—*SMACK*—my palm connects with her delicious round ass.

She pitches forward with a shriek, hitting the water face-first.

SPLASH!

Astrid, standing on Blaze's shoulders, cackles while filming. "He literally can't get it up."

"Dude! You gotta worship that booty. Respect the cake!"

"Blazey-poo!" Astrid yanks his hair. "Stop coaching him!"

Cam surfaces, looking homicidal. "Did you spank me?"

"I was trying to save you!"

"By slapping my ass?"

"It was an accident!"

"Right." She spits out water. "Just like 'accidentally' grabbing my pu—"

"We're quitting."

"We can't," Cam says. "This video is total garbage. We need at least one challenge where you don't drop me like a hot potato."

I'm done. So fucking done. Done with this day, this trip. And completely over these nonstop, bullshit, sellout videos.

PWOOOOOOOO!

Kai's obnoxious horn signals the final round.

"This last challenge," Kai announces, "represents the ultimate connection!" He gestures to what is unmistakably a floating labia-shaped inner tube. "The Ring of Pleasure!"

I'm going to drown myself in this pool.

"The man will be blindfolded," Kai continues, "symbolizing how true ecstasy requires faith. He must guide his woman using"—he lifts an enormous inflatable penis pool noodle as if it's Excalibur—"his mighty sword! Welcome to The Journey to Climax!"

Workers distribute blindfolds and giant dick noodles, passing them out as if they're party favors.

WHACK!

Pain explodes across my face.

"Bro!" Blaze splashes in the water. "Did you see that? I hit you with my giant dick!"

WHACK!

"Fuck! Blaze, what the hell—"

THWACK!

That's it. I swing my dick noodle, catching him square in the shoulder.

Blaze laughs, viewing the whole situation as another prank video.

"How could you do this to me?!" I unleash, whacking him again. Harder. Faster.

"How could I not smack you with my fake dick? It's hilarious," he says, genuinely confused.

"Not that. Her. YOU VIOLATED THE BRO CODE!"

"Huh?"

WHACK!

"Do you even realize what you've done?! We're not friends anymore!"

Blaze freezes mid-swing. Blinks. "Wait... what?"

I watch his face as the single brain cell does its best.

"Ohhhhh!" His eyes light up. "This is for the video. I get it!" He clears his throat. "Listen, Reece! People do crazy things when they're in love!"

I see red.

"Love?! You've been together for less than twenty-four hours!"

"Blazey!" Astrid stage-whispers, focusing the camera. "Remember what I said—be mad, baby!"

"Oh yeah!" Blaze straightens. "BRO... What we have is real. We're in love!"

"This is insane." I throw down my pool noodle. "You two deserve each other."

Blaze beams. "Thanks, man!"

"Oh my God, Blazey!" Astrid groans. "You're ruining my video!"

"And we're gonna get married too!" Blaze says as I exit the pool.

"Wrong!" Astrid's head snaps around. "Nuh-uh. Not that. Too soon."

"Oh, right, sorry. My bad, babe. Should we do another take?"

I storm away from this circus. I ignore Cam calling after me. *Astrid's no doubt already uploading the footage to humiliate me.*

"Great content as always, man!" Blaze yells after me.

I don't look back. Midafternoon or not, I'm officially Burrito Blanket Reece. Fuck this day.

CHAPTER SEVEN

CAM

GROUP CHAT : CPK FOREVER

Petra: *Quick Poll: How many island boys have you corrupted?*

Me: *Current count: negative zero. My vajayjay is in mourning.*

Katie: *Let me guess, Grumpy McCrankyPants is cockblocking paradise?*

Me: *¡Dios mío! You have no idea. Kai the resort owner keeps flirting with me...*

Petra: *Just googled Kai. You NEED to let that tattooed island God wreck you.*

Me: *Except my boss is everywhere. Get this, Kai gifted me a vibrator the size of Maui.*

Katie: *Take what you can get, but after feeling what Matteo can do with his tongue, batteries don't compare.*

Me: *Excuse me while I die of sexual frustration and live vicariously through your Italian adventures.*

I'm dreaming of... Marshmallows?

Warm. Soft. Deliciously dense but still plush enough to sink into, like some kind of fancy artisanal marshmallow at a boujee farmers' market. My fingers flex, testing the firm-yet-fluffy consistency beneath me. It smells good too—like sea salt, and something spicy, maybe... ginger?

Wait.

Marshmallows don't snore.

Every muscle locks up as I register the deep, rhythmic vibrations rumbling through my torso. I pry open one sleep-heavy eye, and... I'm spooning Reece Dare.

And not like, barely brushing against him in a *whoops, must've rolled too close* kind of way.

No. I am a needy koala—full-body latched on to him, my thigh draped over his hip, my face smushed into his shoulder blade, and—¡Ay, Dios!—my hand!?

Firmly gripping the unmistakable bulge poking up under the blanket.

I release him as if he's radioactive. My limbs go full *Mission Impossible* mode, slowly peeling away so I don't wake up the human furnace I've been unconsciously cuddling the hell out of.

The burrito blanket situation is not helping. Reece has wrapped himself up so tight that only one bare arm, the sharp edge of his jawline, and a sliver of messy dark hair are visible. The rest is a mummified cocoon of heat and muscle. No wonder I'm snuggling on top of him.

Because God help me, he's adorable.

Dammit. He should not be adorable.

He stirs right as I make it to my side, and I freeze faster than Gordon's Botoxed forehead.

He shifts slightly then—the snoring resumes.

SNNNRRRKKKKK! RAAAARRRKKKKK!

This is no ordinary snore—it's an auditory contradiction: part congested rhinoceros, part malfunctioning Roomba.

"Seriously," I mutter under my breath, "you might want to get that checked out."

I pull the covers over myself and stare at the ceiling, replaying yesterday's shitshow like an embarrassing highlight reel.

Astrid calling me "thunder thighs." Reece retaliating and publicly declaring my curves "perfection." The poolside penis floatie battle. Reece retreating to his blanket cocoon like a man on the brink.

Yeah. Yesterday sucked.

And no, I'm not still thinking about the way he pointed to me and said, "This is what perfection looks like." It was a ploy—had to be—a way to get back at Astrid and score some fake-dating credibility.

I know this because he has reminded me, approximately 3,542 times, that I am not his type and he is my boss.

"Cam, you're my employee.

"Cam, this is just for PR.

"Cam, you are my boss. Wait, no—I'm your boss. I am the boss."

I get it, Reece. You're not interested.

And yet... why was he being so freaking weird about touching me yesterday?

Like, he had zero issues accidentally groping me in the shower, but when it came time for structured, totally-allowed-in-the-rule-book pool games, suddenly he was handling me *(or rather NOT handling me)* as if I was made of live explosives.

Ugh. Men.

I glance over at his blanket-wrapped form as another seismic snore shakes the mattress. He's dealing with so much—a failed wedding, viral humiliation, his entire brand imploding because his ex replaced him with his bestie. I think he's finally cracked.

His words from yesterday slice through my confidence like a machete. "You don't have experience," he'd said, unknowingly sneering at my dreams. The guy who inspired me to buy my first camera thinks I belong permanently behind it.

No preparation. No guidance. Just *BAM!* "Hey, DareSquad, meet my new girlfriend!" And out of nowhere, I'm supposed to sparkle as if I've got glitter in my veins instead of anxiety. Two years of making him look good through the camera, and he couldn't give me five minutes to find my footing.

And boy did I bomb... *hard.*

I was stiff, awkward, and painfully aware of the way my face moved. Was I blinking too much? Was my smile weird? What about my hands? Should they be limp? Activated? By my sides? Moving so they accentuate what I'm saying?

And then there was Astrid, with her "everything's artificial" superiority complex: "Go hide behind your little camera." I played it off like her words were as fake as her eyelashes, but they hit me hard. Every second thought I've had about being good enough—about deserving to tell my own stories—came rushing back in a tsunami of self-doubt.

So, while Sir Blanket-a-lot was having his existential crisis yesterday, I practiced. Hours of talking to the camera, watching the playback, and confronting the horrors of my own awkwardness. My fake-happy voice sounded like an overly chipper Starbucks barista. But I kept going, because they're right—both of them. If I want this dream, I need to level up.

Plus, there's no place to take care of my *other* frustrations in this mirror-covered fun house. I might as well redirect all that sexual energy into something productive.

A growl erupts from my stomach loud enough to rival Reece's snoring. My eyes dart to him. He doesn't move. *Good. I'm not ready to deal with that hot mess yet.*

Next to the nightstand, I see the new gift bag that was left in our room last night. *I would kill for more of that delicious pineapple popcorn.*

I stretch my arm out from under the sheets, but it's just a little too out of reach. So I slide my foot out instead, curling my toes in a desperate attempt to hook the strap. *Victory!* My toes snag the bag's handle, and I drag it closer like the snack burglar I am—

BEEP. WHIRRR.

Oh, fuck.

The bed starts rotating.

I frantically swipe at the sensor, cutting off the motion right as Reece grunts in his sleep.

My whole body goes rigid.

He lets out a snort that resembles a warthog discovering masturbation and settles back into his sinus symphony. With such unholy sleeping sounds, it's a good thing this man is pretty.

Phew! Crisis averted.

I reach inside with the stealth of a ninja, trying to avoid the crinkling tissue paper.

My fingers brush against something... rubbery? *Definitely not popcorn.* I extract what appears to be a palm-sized penguin, complete with bowtie and a come-hither expression.

The tag reads: "The Pleasure Penguin—Slide, Glide, and Enjoy the Ride!

I turn it over in my hands, searching for clues about its purpose, when my thumb hits something and—

BZZZZZZZZZZ!

I start pushing everywhere on the poor bird, molesting it beyond comprehension. It just keeps buzzing.

My roommate stirs beside me, his snoring pattern changing.

With pure panic, I shove the vibrating penguin under the covers, squeezing it with my thighs to muffle the sound, and—

¡Jesucristo!

The spasming hellbird dances against my clit, and suddenly I'm having a very different kind of morning wake-up call. My legs clamp together on reflex, which increases the intense sensation.

This is inappropriate.

This is unprofessional.

This is... happening people. Holy fuck, that feels good.

I press the device more firmly against my clit. I should stop. *No, seriously.* But I've been on edge sexually since before we landed in Paradise Gone Wrong, and the anticipation of climax has been building, and the pressure... *God, the pressure!*

My traitorous brain floods with images of Reece. His strong, possessive hands on my breasts in the shower. Then when he first saw me in my swimsuit, his pupils dilated—fucking dilated! Those steel-blue eyes went black as they were dragging over my curves like he was mapping territory. The throbbing intensifies, and ¡Dios mío!, how am I climbing this fast just thinking about—

My bedmate snorts like a sleeping dragon getting ready to wake.

I'm seconds away from discovering enlightenment via my new tuxedoed friend with benefits.

Waddle faster, you sinful little bird!

Suddenly, the man rolls. All two hundred pounds of muscled male landing directly on top of me.

I'm somewhere between frozen and stuck—his arm wraps around me, his chin nuzzles into my shoulder, his morning stubble scraping deliciously against my cheek, and then—

"Mmm... Camila."

Did he say my name?

Red alert!

I cannot—CANNOT—orgasm while Reece "I'm Your Boss" Dare is moaning my name like I'm his favorite cheat meal.

He's as heavy as I am determined. I try to shimmy away under the covers, accidentally conjuring up more friction—

BZZZZZZZZZ!

I reach to retrieve the demon toy, gripping it like I'm rescuing my phone at 1% behind the couch, and—

BZZZZZZZZZZZZ!!!

Somehow I've cranked up the setting to MAXIMUM.

With a surge of desperation, I grip the vibrator and wrench my arm free. It pops loose like a champagne cork, sending Reece rolling onto his back and out of his blankets.

The flightless bird launches from my hand like a lust-fueled comet.

And lands.

Directly.

On.

Reece.

His body jolts like someone hooked him up to a car battery. Those devastating blue eyes fly open, still cloudy with sleep.

And then—

He looks down.

Right at the vibrating menace having a rave against his eight-pack.

He blinks once. Twice. Three times.

I stop beating... I mean breathing. That is, my heart stops breathing. I mean... *Whatever.* All I know is time stops.

He picks up the bird, examining it as if it's evidence in a crime. Which, let's be honest, it kind of is.

And then—

The slowest, most devastating, and most devious, panty-melting grin spreads across his face.

Fuck fuck fuckity fuck.

"Must have fallen from the ceiling!" I squeak. "You know, from Kai's jungle show. Probably got confused and thought it could fly. But penguins can't fly. That'd be crazy."

Oh my God, shut UP, Camila!

I snatch the beaked bandit from his hand, my fingers frantically violating its every crevice and no-no zone to find the off button. Its bill? Nothing. Webbed feet? Nada. Tail? Just more buzzing. I'm performing emergency surgery on a sex toy while he watches with that insufferable smirk.

Finally—*thank you, sex gods*—I pull on a wing, and the perverted penguin goes silent.

Reece gives me a look that's half amusement, half arousal, his hair sticking out in every direction like he's been thoroughly debauched. His eyes drop to my chest and—

My nipples are standing at attention in my dark-purple satin camisole set. This naughty number has a flyaway center that parts like curtains at a peep show, framing my belly button and giving a glimpse of underboob.

His eyes snap back to mine, and the heat in them could melt polar ice caps. I suck in a gasp, and my veins fill with lava as my core clenches. I can feel each pulse between my legs growing stronger, hotter, remembering a mere thirty seconds ago I was about to orgasm thinking about the man who's currently eye-fucking me.

"I just—"

"Need air!" he shouts.

"Oxygen. Right? We need oxygen?"

"Super important. Great idea. Me, air, and no... this."

We both bolt out of bed. He hits the floor, still tangled in his duvet, while I dash for the bathroom. He stumbles toward the balcony, and we both slam our doors shut.

I am so monumentally screwed.

Or rather—tragically *un-screwed.*

God, I hate this resort.

***

"HEY, DARESQUAD, IT'S YA girl Cam!"

No. Too influencer-y. I sound like I'm selling DareFuel.

"Hey! Camila coming at you from Maui—"

Ugh. Why am I giving off Disney Channel vibes?

I exhale slowly and evaluate my reflection. My hair is curled in soft waves that are actually behaving tonight. My makeup is freshly applied, and—surprise—my winged liner isn't even lopsided. My green leaf-print halter dress, however, is... on my last nerve.

I adjust my cleavage for the millionth time, wrangling my breasts into submission. They're staging a jailbreak, threatening to spill out of this dangerously low neckline. Three years ago in Cabo, Katie and Petra convinced me to buy this thing, insisting I looked like Jennifer Lopez in her iconic green dress.

I had agreed because, well—JLo. My sister Aria and I grew up idolizing her—the curvy Latina fashion icon who taught us to be proud of our figures and that our bodies were meant to be envied.

Normally, this dress makes me feel powerful, confident, perhaps even a little lethal. Normally...

But right now, I'm two deep breaths away from a full-scale wardrobe malfunction, and what's really not helping? My stupid brain flashing back to this morning.

To waking up tangled around Reece.

To the way he murmured my name as if he was dreaming about me.

Shutting that thought down right now.

"Just... stay put," I mutter to my cleavage while swiping on mascara. My eyes drift to the balcony, where he now sits like a haunted statue, staring at the ocean. He's barely moved all day except for a few bathroom breaks, each time avoiding eye contact as if I'm Medusa and one look will turn him to stone.

I shake out my hands and swipe on a second coat of mascara. I have to go to this stupid couples' luau alone. Fine. It's probably for the best. Except... I kind of want him to come, if I'm being honest. The thought of filming by myself makes my stomach twist into a pretzel. Or maybe it's because every time we're near each other lately, this electric current crackles between us, making my skin buzz and my thoughts scatter like startled birds.

Gah! I miss the old Reece. Mr. Critical. Mr. Pre-dictable-Pain-in-My-Ass. *That* version I knew how to handle. But this new one? This quiet, wounded man who I've caught staring like he wants to peel my clothes off with his teeth? He's making me feel... things.

"Hey squad, it's Camila! Reece Dare's girlfriend!"

For a split second, it sounds real.

And for another split second *(and I mean only like, half a millisecond)*, I don't hate how it sounds.

What if this wasn't pretend? What if I was actually getting ready for a date with him? A real date. I definitely wouldn't be trying to hide these curves. I'd be choosing this exact dress, putting my boobs on full display, knowing damn well he'd be looking and loving him for it.

I reach into my makeup bag for my favorite shade of deep-rose lipstick that begs, *Kiss me.*

I apply it with careful precision, letting myself indulge in the fantasy for a moment longer, picturing Reece's hungry eyes on me. I pluck a plumeria flower from the nearby vase and tuck it behind my ear.

"Damn," I whisper. "I could definitely pass for his girlfriend."

My phone vibrates on the vanity, flashing a name I wish I could ignore.

Gordon *(Actual Devil, Do Not Answer).*

I stare and wait. *Maybe he'll move on to bullying someone else... a poor intern, an ex-wife, an unsuspecting UberEats driver who brought him the wrong-sized latte.*

The phone keeps buzzing. Persistent. Loud. As if Gordon's already yelling at me.

I sigh, accept my fate, and swipe to answer. *Here it comes.*

Gordon's face explodes on the screen, his forehead smoother than a dolphin's backside, his pulled-too-tight eyebrows permanently raised in a way that suggests either imminent rage or a fresh round of Botox. Honestly, with Gordon, it's a toss-up.

"Where. The. Hell. Is. He?" Each word is a tiny angry fist punching through my speaker.

"Oh, you know..." I glance at the blanket burrito formerly known as Reece. "He's... meditating?"

Technically not a lie.

"Cut the crap, camera girl. Your resignation letter sounded like a YouTube mission statement. 'Following my dreams' and 'making content that matters'—very touching. Really pulled at my heart-strings. Well, it would if I had any."

Note to self: Maybe don't treat your two weeks' notice like a Live-Journal entry detailing your future plans.

"I offered you this girlfriend gig because I knew you wanted to start your own channel and would jump at the chance to bankroll it."

My stomach drops.

"Have you told him? About me quitting?"

"Fuck no. You think he needs more stress right now? Listen up, Spielberg. You need this opportunity more than it needs you, so stop. Fucking. Up."

"I'm doing this for more than the money." My grip tightens on the phone. "He needs someone in his corner right now, someone who—"

"Save the speech for the Oscars," Gordon says. "You can't bullshit a professional bullshitter. I put you on that island for one reason—to keep my golden goose laying eggs."

I don't need this shit. I open my mouth, ready to cuss him out in two languages, but he yammers on.

"Your job is to keep him in line. You're the man on the ground. He can't afford to spiral, and you sure as hell can't afford to let him."

"Maybe..." I try again, softer. "Maybe he needs a break? Ya know, a few days to—"

"Oh, that's cute. And maybe you should knit him a sweater while you're at it. Let me spell it out—no channel means no moolah. Either he performs, or the whole thing crumbles."

I shake my head. But my skin itches at the way he talks about Reece like he's a product. A machine to be reset and put back to work.

"Are you listening? No sponsors means no company means no paycheck for his three hundred employees, which includes you. Now, go give him the damn phone!"

My chest aches. Yes, I wanted the extra cash when I took the job. Yes, I'm trying to launch my own channel. But watching Reece break down, seeing him carrying the weight of everyone's expectations—I want to build a fortress around him and tell the whole world to fuck off.

I step onto the balcony, the evening air warm against my skin. Gently, I place my hand on his blanketed shoulder.

"Reece?" I keep my voice tender, as if I'm approaching a wounded animal. "Sorry to bother you, but Gordon is on the—"

"DARE! PHONE! NOW!" Gordon's voice makes several nearby birds take flight.

When he looks up at me, something in my chest splinters. Those blue eyes that usually spark with criticism or heat are dull, heavy. His jaw is buried under dark scruff, and his hair is a wreck—as if he's been clawing anxious fingers through it all day.

He sighs—a bone-deep sound of defeat—and takes the phone.

I'd love to snatch it back and throw it into the ocean. But I can't. I'm just his fake girlfriend with an exit strategy and a guilty conscience that's getting heavier by the second.

Gordon launches into his tirade before Reece can say hello. "You need to get your head out of your ass!"

I turn to leave, to give them privacy, but his hand shoots out and grabs mine. The contact sends electricity zipping up my arm, but this isn't some romantic gesture. His eyes stay fixed on the screen, jaw clenched, but his grip says *please stay* louder than words.

So, I stay.

His thumb strokes over my knuckles, tentative, as if he's unaware he's doing it. I squeeze back, hoping he gets the message. *I'm here. You're not alone.*

"That pool video was total shit! Astrid has better footage of you on *her* channel! And where's the chemistry between you and camera girl? It's like watching two male seahorses not sure where to stick it! The potted plant on my desk has more sex appeal!"

Reece doesn't react, simply stares straight ahead, but his grip on my hand tightens.

"Either sell this fake relationship, or we're going in a different direction. You hear me? DIFFERENT. DIRECTION."

I stiffen. I don't know exactly what *different direction* means, but considering Gordon operates with the moral compass of a... *Hell, who am I kidding? He has no moral compass.* This is bad.

Reece must know too. His hand slips from mine, and I immediately miss the warmth.

"It's not Cam," he says, voice rough. "It's me. I'll fix it."

Gordon doesn't miss a beat. "Damn right you will. Because this content is going to sink this ship faster than—"

"I will." He hangs up mid-rant. The silence that follows feels thick enough to chew. He releases a heavy breath and says, "Don't listen to that blowhard."

"It's fine." I aim for casual. "I'm used to it. Though I resent the potted plant comparison. I'm at least as charming as a succulent."

"You shouldn't be used to it." Something dangerous flashes in his eyes. "It's not okay from him or... me." He runs a hand through his hair, leaving it even more devastatingly disheveled. "I placed you in an impossible position yesterday. I'm sorry."

I blink. *Is this a real apology? From my fake boyfriend?*

Honestly, I don't know what to do with that.

"Ya know, Reece... you don't *have* to film. You could take a break. Actually breathe for once? Figure out what *you* want instead of what everyone expects?"

His head tilts slightly, as if he's considering it. Then his gaze drifts over me, and his face softens.

"You look really nice, Camila," he says quietly. "Beautiful."

Heat floods my cheeks. "Thanks. Just... you know. Getting my luau on. Living that tropical life. Attempting to not flash anyone when I hula."

His lips twitch, he smiles, and my heart liquefies into a warm, gooey puddle.

He gestures to the balcony. "If you don't mind waiting, I'll join you. I'll shower quickly."

"Sure! I mean, yes. That's... yes."

Someone please remove my speaking privileges.

He unwraps himself from his comforter cocoon, and even emotionally wrecked, he moves like a tragically majestic Greek god—chiseled, brooding, and devilishly dramatic. The curtain swishes shut behind him, leaving me alone with the sunset and approximately eight thousand racing thoughts.

I grip the terrace railing, watching waves crash below. Why did he hold my hand? Was I merely the closest warm body? Was I just temporary emotional support while Gordon yelled at him? Or does he actually feel comfortable with me?

My documentary filmmaker side can't help but analyze this, breaking him down like he's my next big project. Every good documentary needs three things: a compelling subject, a journey of transformation, and a truth waiting to be uncovered.

And Reece? He's a sexy, complicated mess of all three.

The compelling subject: YouTube's favorite daredevil turned burned-out showman.

The transformation: Going from grumpy boss to... what? To the man who stood up for me and held my hand when he was hurting. That's the story I want to tell.

Not that I'd actually make a documentary about him. *Although...* The thought takes root. The pressure of influencer culture, the toll it takes on mental health, the way social media turns people into products.

Hold on. You're supposed to be helping him, not turning his pain into content.

"Ready?"

I turn and—hot damn—the blanket burrito has morphed into a tropical dreamboat. I have *no* complaints. My boss-slash-fake-bae sports a pair of light linen shorts that hang low on his hips, giving me a sneak peek at those sculpted legs. His short-sleeved button-down is a vibrant explosion of blues and greens, the top buttons undone, offering a tantalizing glimpse of the tattoos on his chest.

His dark hair, still damp from the shower, curls at his neck in a handsomely boyish way, and I have a sudden craving to tangle my fingers in it. The camera strap crosses his body like some kind of unfairly hot accessory.

"You clean up hot," I blurt out, immediately wanting to jump off the ledge. "I mean, *fast*. You clean up fast."

"You already said hot, Morales. No take-backs." His blue eyes roam down the shape of my figure like an invisible caress. "You're pretty hot yourself. That dress is fire."

"Smooth talker," I say casually, pretending his words don't set off a chain reaction inside me.

"Seriously. You look incredible," he says before adding a smirk. "Almost as good as me."

My heart skips because right there—camera in hand, smile lighting up his whole face—I see him. The teenage boy who used to film backflips off his garage into pools of Jell-O. The Reece before the algorithms. Before the brand deals. Before the world's relentless demands turned him into a monetization puppet.

The camera settles naturally in his hands, like it belongs there. And in that instant, I know—*really* know—that I can help him. Not with fake dating, or saving his empire, or whatever project-of-the-week Gordon's throwing at him. I am going to make Reece fall in love with filming again.

Make him feel... that pure joy of creating something real, something that matters.

Give him... the rush of capturing a perfect moment, not because it'll get views, but because it'll make his soul sing again.

Help him find... the *real* Reece, the one who loves making content as much as I do.

"You're staring, Morales. See something you like?"

"Just wondering if you remember how to use that thing."

"You're the one who has a problem finding buttons on little toys." He offers his arm with a wink. "Ready to convince the internet we're madly in love?"

I slip my arm through his, startled by the pull—the quiet, electrical charge between us—and how undeniably right it feels.

CHAPTER EIGHT

REECE

I SHOULD GO BACK to the room. Every logical bone in my body says so. Because after two days at the Aloha Amour Resort, one thing is clear—this won't be a *normal* luau. This is gonna be Kai's version *(or rather perversion)*, which probably means fire dancers with dildos or strippers dry humping totem poles or us slow-twerking in hula skirts.

Tiki torches dot the edge of the winding path toward the beach, casting flickering shadows across the manicured lawn. The tropical night air is a light blend of plumeria and the salty sea, until it's overpowered by the deliciously charred scent of grilled meat. The smell is intoxicating—dangerous, even. This whole romance-on-steroids atmosphere is pushing me to do something primal, like kiss Cam senseless.

I clench my jaw, scanning the scene. Facing the rolling ocean is an elaborate stage, draped in crimson silk, billowing in the breeze as if it's about to host a burlesque performance instead of hula dancers. And with the tables, there's no "group seating" option, no buffer of extra chairs. Just tiny, candlelit tables for two, each designed for either making out or marriage proposals.

My gut tightens.

Cam starts filming a panoramic of the area. "A path of rose petals," she narrates, voice thick with amusement. "Wow, you do not see that every day. And next to that is a... pulsating volcano statue?" She zooms in on the obscenely phallic sculpture with water exploding from the top. "It's throbbing, right? Not just me. That's definitely a penis."

Jesus fucking Christ.

She had to say it.

The word shoots straight to my dick, which is already on thin ice after this morning. That toy penguin and how she blushed when I caught her. *It was hot—hot as hell.* The sight of her biting her lip, flushed and trembling. Soft curves spilling out of that purple satin top and her hard-as-diamonds nipples threatening to tear through the material.

How's a man supposed to focus?

I stare resolutely at a nearby palm tree, willing my cock to behave, when two massive arms wrap around me from behind.

"Aloha, love seekers!" a deep voice booms. I don't need to look. It's Kai.

Cam swings the camera toward us. "So what's the deal with this sculpture?"

"That, my curious wahine, is transgressive. The piece becomes whatever your subconscious believes it to be!" Kai spreads his arms wide, his hair flowing loose around his bare chest, his sarong fluttering erratically in the wind. "Perhaps you yearn for volcanic passion, or perhaps..."

"Yeah, I don't have a volcano fetish," Cam says with perfect deadpan delivery.

Despite my irritation, I snort.

"Then clearly your spirit recognizes the masculine energy." Kai's grin turns predatory. "Now come, let me get you properly lei'd."

I swear to all things holy, I am one inappropriate innuendo away from tackling this guy into the ocean.

Cam doesn't miss a beat, stepping forward with confidence as Kai's gaze zeroes in on her cleavage. That green fabric is holding on by a stitch and a prayer, one deep breath from giving up and letting Cam's stunning curves bust loose.

"The Getting Lei'd Ceremony is sacred!" he proclaims, leading us to a flower-covered station. "Each color tells a story of love! *Red* signals passionate commitment, *pink* suggests playful availability, and *gold*—"

"Gold. We'll take gold," I interrupt, attempting a quick escape with the flower necklaces.

Kai claps. "Ah! Gold! The color of scandal and secret passions! Perfect for forbidden trysts and midnight—"

"Red," I growl. "I meant *red*." I snatch two crimson leis and grab Cam's hand, her skin warm against my palm. I distance her from Mr. Sex Resort's knowing smirk.

"Enjoy the festivities!" he calls out. "The performance will begin once the moon goddess is upon us!"

It's only when we arrive at the buffet that I realize I'm still holding Cam's hand. I drop it like it's scalding. Then I cross my arms and scowl at the large spread of finger foods. Everything looks... *suggestive.*

"Oh my God, Reece, you have to try this." She locks on to some artfully arranged fruit. "This one's called the Coconut Kama Sutra Salad."

"No."

"Come on! How about the Forbidden Fruit Fondue?" She angles the lens toward a massive fountain, where dark chocolate and caramel flow in and out of each other like... like I don't know what, but it seems dirty. "I bet Kai infused it with love pheromones."

"You're enjoying this, aren't you?" I say, sounding sulky even for me.

"Grocery shopping will never *not* be hilarious now."

I scan the food spread, searching for something—anything—that won't try to seduce me. "Crispy Climax" Tempura. "Swallow Me Whole" Oysters. "Sizzling Man Stick" Meat Skewers. Of course, the mousse couldn't be just mousse—it had to be called "Midnight Moan."

I reach for what appears to be a harmless sushi roll, but before I can grab it, a server materializes. "Sir! We encourage guests to feed their partners. It enhances the sensual dining experience—"

"Not happening, friend of Kai." I pop the bite into my mouth, chewing with more aggression than necessary.

"You know..." Cam lowers the camera. "Being this grumpy at a luau is a felony in Hawaii. Pretty sure the punishment is aggressive hipshaking... in a coconut bra... at spear-point."

"I'm going to our table."

"Fine, run away from the sexy spread. I'll catch up after I capture some top-tier food porn—this papaya wants a mouth on it, and this mango is serving *take-me-now* energy."

I make my way through the sea of tangled limbs and love-sick couples, finding a table as far from the feasting as possible. Every pair here looks ready to conceive triplets.

I drop into my chair as if my strings have been cut. Heart-shaped fire pits dot the beach, while palm trees drip gold like they're part of Kai's personal fantasy. Even the damn cutlery wants to get laid—engraved with sayings that read "Taste the Desire" and "Let Passion Melt on Your Tongue."

I need a beer. Or a bottle of tequila. Or a meteor to hit this exact spot.

My eyes track Cam subconsciously at first. As she films, she moves with purpose and natural grace—first getting wide shots of the ambience then shooting close-ups of the ridiculous decorations. The silk canopy is an ivory wave rippling overhead, casting a soft glow that makes her appear... heavenly.

Not that she's ever anything less than gorgeous—whether she's rocking a ponytail and cargo pants, weighed down by filming gear, or strutting her stuff like in that killer swimsuit from yesterday. But tonight, she's next level. That dress is making her look so desirable, I want to sweep her off her feet.

I couldn't handle Gordon berating me again today—not in front of her. And he would've unleashed on her next.

It's *my* fault we are bombing these videos. And I will never, ever allow someone else to accept the blame for my mistakes.

I exhale sharply, dragging fingers through my hair. So fucking tired. Not just physically. I'm exhausted from all of it. From performing every second of my goddamn life.

Just... done.

"Yo! What up, my guy! This party is straight fire!"

For fuck's sake.

Blaze bounces into the chair across from me like an ADHD kangaroo who discovered Red Bull, grinning as if the two of us are still best friends... like he didn't help torpedo my life forty-eight hours ago.

"What the hell do you want?"

"Yo, checking in, bro. You seem stressed out lately."

"Ya think?" I lean forward. "Blaze, what the fuck is going on?"

"We're on vacation at a sex resort. It's awesome!"

I grip my side of the table as an alternative to strangling him. "I'm really trying to understand here. What the actual fuck is happening with you and Astrid?"

"Bro, I was confused too! But after the wedding, I found her like Gordon said to, and she laid it out. Told me about your guys' plan to break the internet. Damn, man, you did it!"

"Blaze, there was no plan."

"Yeah huh! Astrid said it was top secret. Not even Gordon knew. Only you guys." He leans in, whisper-shouting, "And that I was supposed to pretend to be her new boyfriend."

I stare at my idiot best friend, wondering if all those years of stunts have scrambled his last remaining brain cell.

I take a breath, my eye twitching. "What else did she say?"

His face scrunches up as if he's trying to divide by zero. Then, after a solid ten seconds of deep contemplation, he shrugs.

"I can't remember because then she got naked and ordered me to eat her out, which I did. She kept talking while I was doing it. Some of the stuff she said was like... orders of how I was doing it wrong. Man, apparently I do a lot of stuff wrong. Who knew?"

I grip my temples, massaging slowly. "Alrighty then. I think we're done here."

"Wait, let me try to remember better..." He grabs two dinner rolls and starts motorboating them while making slurping sounds.

"First she said to go 'up and down', but then she was all 'Circles, Blazey, circles!'" He starts rotating the bread in a *trying-to-buff-a-car* motion. "Then she got real specific about tongue pressure." He drops the yeast rolls and spreads his fingers in a V-shape, his tongue darting between them like a demented windshield wiper.

I slam my forehead onto the table.

Hard.

C'mon, Reece. Knock yourself unconscious, and this will all be over.

Blaze pauses mid-lick, staring at me as if I'm the one with problems. "Oh! And then we got on a plane! And I asked if you were gonna be there..."

He stops, thinking again.

Blaze snaps. "Yeah! Then she told me that I had to act really mad when I saw you."

Excuse me?

Blaze leans forward, hopeful. "How am I doing at that, by the way? It's tough to act like I'm mad at you, bro. Oh, and she gave me a blowjob."

I gape at him.

There are so many things wrong with what he's saying. Where to start?

I do the only thing I can.

I put a hand on his shoulder, look him dead in the eye, and accept the fact that my best friend is a complete moron. I'm about to... *I don't know, comfort him,* when Ástrid's shrill voice hits my ears.

"BLAZEY-KINS! Where are you? You need to feed me the orgasm oysters!"

Blaze bolts upright.

"Gotta go to work, bro." He winks, salutes, and books it. "Love you!"

Astrid is a bigger bitch than I thought. Manipulating my closest pal? Turning my personal life into a content farm? Diabolical. She needs to pay for this, but I don't have the energy to keep making more viral bait nonsense videos. *Why do millions of people watch this fake crap anyways, knowing it's all staged?* It's worse than reality TV, but... it's also the only thing that gets views nowadays.

I'm tired of it.

The channel.

The brand.

The bullshit.

I want to fucking quit.

I wish I had a choice.

***

THERE ARE A LOT of things I hate in this world. Paper straws. Astrid's existence. Filming shameless hot garbage for views.

But seriously, nothing—I repeat, NOTHING—could have prepared me for the deep, visceral, soul-sucking hatred I feel the moment Kai struts on stage. He's clad in nothing but a minuscule brown leather thong, his erection blatantly displayed in its snug leather sheath.

"Welcome to a tale as old as passion itself!" His voice booms across the beach. "Tonight, we witness the eternal battle between the gods of love and lust!"

One by one, muscular Hawaiian behemoths join him on-stage—each looking fresh off the set of a movie with gladiators, where the director answered "more penis" to every actor's question on their motivation. Tribal tattoos ripple across oiled biceps, their matching leather thongs leaving so little to the imagination that several elderly women in the front row have already fainted.

"We are the warriors!" Kai proclaims. "Sworn to protect lovers and defend every person's sacred right to orgasm!"

The muscled men let out a warped battle cry that sounds exactly like a mating call.

And then—because this night clearly needed to get weirder—Kai attaches a rope to the front of his thong. At the end dangles what appears to be a drum mallet.

A massive drum wheels out center stage.

The fighters begin to chant. "Grun. Grun. Grun."

Kai's hips start to gyrate, the rope circling as he hypnotizes the audience with his pelvis. The lasso mallet spins faster and faster until—

BAM!

It strikes the drum, and the stage explodes in synchronized lightning effects.

BAM! BAM! BAM!

The effect makes it seem like Kai is using his massive dick to beat that drum into submission. As I'm searching for an exit strategy, Cam is entranced—like she can't get enough—probably holding a tight close-up as she captures the erotic circus.

My brain flatlines.

"God of lust!" the emcee of my nightmares roars. "My gargantuan war tool is at your disposal!"

Suddenly, Cam bursts out laughing—actual snorting laughter—and clamps her hand over her mouth. She stops filming, her shoulders shaking. "Oh my God, I can't—I just can't anymore with this guy."

I blink. "Wait. You're not into his monstrous weapon?"

She snickers. "Oh, it's massive, but what it's attached to should not be taken seriously."

"Really?" Something in my chest loosens. "I thought you were wanting to, what was it? Climb him like a coconut tree?"

"Don't be jealous. This morning I got a pretty clear idea that you could be up there swinging your own mallet."

I choke on my own tongue. "Excuse me?"

Her eyes go wide. "¡Mierda! I didn't mean to say that."

I lean closer, suddenly very interested. "So tell me, Morales, did something else happen while I was sleeping? Besides the waddling penguin, of course."

Her face goes nuclear red.

"Please. Let's talk about literally anything else."

"For now." I grin. "But we *will* be circling back. Especially the part about my impressive equipment."

She groans, burying her head in her hands.

On stage, Kai's "war tool" continues its percussion performance, but I barely notice. I'm too busy watching Cam blush and wondering what other secrets might slip out.

"You wanna get out of here and go for a walk?"

She peeks at me through her fingers. "No talk of penguins."

I grin. "No webbed creatures of any kind."

When she smiles at me, a weight lifts off my shoulders. For the first time in days, I can breathe.

＊＊＊

"So how did you end up promoting the world's horniest resort?" Cam's bare feet leave perfect imprints in the wet sand as we walk. Her dress flows around her curves as if it's personally trying to drive me insane. "Did you pitch it yourself, or did Kai strap a dildo to a dolphin with his request and let it swim to LA like a raunchy carrier pigeon?"

The mental image blindsides me, and I laugh—an actual, genuine laugh that feels weird coming out of my mouth. *When did I last do that?*

The ocean stretches black and endless ahead of us, waves curling white at our feet. The distant *thump-thump-thump* of Kai's dick-drum performance carries through the air, but thankfully it's muted enough that I can stop picturing it... almost.

I grab a piece of driftwood, throwing it into the surf. "I don't handle sponsor deals. That's Gordon's territory. Usually brands reach out, and then we negotiate based on whether they're a good fit."

"And was this a good fit?"

I let warm water lap at my feet, considering. "I'm still deciding."

Moonlight catches in her hair, silvering her skin, and fuck me if she doesn't resemble some kind of dangerous siren sent to dash my heart against the shore. A gust of wind sweeps hair across her features, and my fingers itch to brush it away. To trace the curve of her cheek. To—

She catches me staring.

"Though clearly," I say quickly, "I didn't expect this place to be so off the deep end."

"Wait, so you didn't demand to have Kai's penis featured in every video?"

I roll my eyes. "Believe it or not, I did not agree to becoming a human prop in Kai's sex swing battle of the dicks."

Cam howls with laughter. She bends forward at the waist, shoulders shaking, full-body laughing as if I told the funniest joke ever. *And shit—I like it.*

I'd let Kai beat me with his drumstick dick a hundred more times to keep hearing that laugh.

What the hell is wrong with me? Two days ago I was wallowing in my failed wedding disaster, and now I'm thinking about ways to make Cam laugh? I might need a head scan. Maybe Blaze isn't the only one with brain damage from all our crazy stunts.

"Wow." She tilts her head toward the stars, a scatter of diamonds on black velvet. "They're beautiful. You never see actual constellations in LA."

I follow her gaze, and—holy hell—the celestial lights are insane, burning like a million tiny supernovas against the night sky. The black tapestry is vast and open, bigger than anything should be.

Her camera comes up instinctively, but when she reviews the footage, her nose scrunches. "Nope, you can't capture that kind of beauty."

"Let me try." I drop to one knee in the sand, taking the camera. "It's all about perspective."

I press *Record*, and in place of the sky, I frame her. The stars are a mere background to the real phenomenon. She's the centerpiece of it all, lips parted slightly as she studies the stars, her hair flowing in the breeze, and her eyes reflecting a million lights.

I hold up the screen so she can see.

She edges forward, her fingers grazing mine, and damn—my body aches to pull her close. To feel her warmth seep in and wrap around me like a slow-burning flame.

"You gotta know what to focus on," I say quietly. "And you... *you* enhance the sky's natural beauty."

She snorts. "Yeah, right. This place is getting to you. If you're handing out compliments, I think we need to check the sea air for hallucinogens."

"Huh? I'm not following."

"You told me I belong behind the camera, remember? So I already know you don't actually think I'm camera-worthy."

The reminder of my earlier asshole comment feels like stepping on broken glass. "That came out wrong. I didn't mean it as an insult. You're a talented videographer."

"Ha! Two compliments?" She scoffs. "Did you eat something weird at the luau? Was it the pineapple? Quick—how many fingers am I holding up?"

"I'm being serious, Morales." I step closer, sand shifting under my feet. "You're really gifted."

"Reece, I have worked for you for two years, and in that time, you have never—not once—given me a compliment."

"That can't be true."

"Oh, you want receipts? Remember the Can I Land a Jet Ski on a Moving Boat video?"

"Blaze convinced me that, yeah, obviously I could flip off a jet ski and land neatly onto the deck of a moving speedboat."

"I set up all three camera angles for that shoot. Had to anticipate your trajectory—which, let's be honest, even you didn't know—so I could capture the stunt, the splash zone, and the inevitable rescue. Do you remember what you said to me after?"

I exhale, bracing for impact.

"You described my footage as 'shaky garbage.'"

The waves crash behind us, but they're nothing compared to the storm of guilt building in my chest.

"Or that Sandboarding Down a Mountain Handcuffed to Blaze video. The one where I risked my life, strapped a camera to my own damn helmet, and chased you down the sand dune at thirty-five mph."

I grimace.

"You said"—she drops her voice low—"'The footage is decent, I guess. But maybe next time, try not to breathe so loud in the mic. It's called cardio, Morales.'"

Oof.

"Oh! And my personal favorite—the underwater shark cage stunt. I got scuba certified in two days, learned how to handle an underwater camera rig while actively *not* becoming shark bait... and you told me my cinematography 'sucked.'"

Fuuuuuuck.

I deserve to be punched in the dick... repeatedly. By her.

"The closest thing to a compliment from you was before your wedding, when you mentioned my camera angle was 'alright.' Which, I'm pathetic enough to admit, felt good. I almost called my mom."

"Cam, I am so—"

"It's fine." She cuts me off with a defeated wave. "And I think maybe you're right. I'm not meant to be on camera. And maybe my work is just... I don't know, average."

The shame hits like a tsunami. All this time, I've been using criticism as a shield, trying to maintain professional distance because I couldn't handle being attracted to her. And what did I accomplish? I made this talented, vibrant woman—this woman who took every insane risk to make me look good—doubt herself.

When it comes to Camila Morales, I can't stop fucking up.

"I'm sorry." The words feel pathetically inadequate. "I am a prickwad douchecanoe."

"Groundbreaking realization... Wait, where did you hear that phrase?"

"I've seen it pop up on your phone a couple times. I assumed it was about me."

"My friends and I also call you assbag prettyboy fuckhole."

"Also deserved."

That earns me a slight smile. The air feels a little lighter after a few moments of silence.

"I have no right to ask, but I'm curious—why are you so confident holding the camera, but not when it's pointed at you?"

She shrugs, digging her toes into the wet sand. "Not sure."

"Okay, then what makes you worried when the camera *is* on you?"

Cam goes quiet for so long, I almost think she's not going to answer. But then...

"People will judge me. Decide that I don't really have anything interesting to say." She inhales, as if forcing herself to continue talking. "That I'm basic. Or maybe talentless and stupid. And... being on your channel, millions of people will catch on."

The way she says it—so raw, so certain—knocks the breath right out of my lungs.

I turn to her, but she won't meet my eyes. Instead, she keeps her gaze fixed on the stars.

"Nothing about you is basic. Not one fucking thing."

Cam is the most talented person I've ever met, and the fact that she doesn't see that? That she thinks people will look at her and find her lacking?

It makes me want to wreck shit.

I want to tear apart every insecurity that's ever been planted in her mind by me and burn them to the ground.

I move into her eyeline so she's forced to see me. "And who cares what people think? Blaze is dumb as a rock, and he doesn't give two shits. He's the happiest person I know."

A reluctant smile tugs at her lips. "I... can't actually argue with that."

"The way you capture the world through your lens—it's not only skill, it's art. Passion you can see in every frame. I should have told you this sooner, but you're the heart of the channel. Without you, it wouldn't exist. Honestly, I would've quit."

"Really, Reece. I don't need you to be nice for my feelings. I'm used to it."

Man, I royally fucked up. Like monumentally.

I've spent the last two years picking apart her work, acting like nothing she does is good enough. And now?

Now she thinks she's not enough.

That's on me.

The thing I know for damn sure is that I need to fix it. Starting now.

CHAPTER NINE

CAM

Group Chat : CPK Forever
Me: *If you don't hear from me, it's because Reece finally snapped and buried my body.*
Katie: *What happened?*
Me: *He said I'm the "heart" of his channel.*
Katie: *Why does that feel like the beginning of a horror movie?*
Petra: *Run :-0 Get on a plane. Get off the island!*
Me: *If this is goodbye, you're the best ride-or-die besties ever.*
Petra: *We'll eat CPK in your memory.*

"**Good morning, DareSquad!** It's a beautiful day here in paradise with my favorite girl!"

I burrow deeper into the silk sheets, convinced I'm trapped in a fever dream. Because that voice? That cheerful, borderline chipper tone? That can't be...

My eyes crack open, confirming that yes, I am, in fact, awake. The Maui morning fills our wall-less love nest with golden light, the gauzy curtains dancing in the salt-kissed breeze. Outside, waves crash against the shore in a steady rhythm that would be soothing if I wasn't currently questioning my grip on reality.

Standing on the balcony, filming, is Reece.

A grinning Reece.

A happy, fun, almost bouncy Reece.

This can't be real.

He turns to me with tousled dark hair, sunlit blue eyes, and an expression way too cheerful for a guy who just yesterday was all grumbles and gargoyle.

"And good morning to you, my beautiful girlfriend."

What fresh hell is this?

The mattress dips as he plops onto the edge of our bed, camera phone pointed directly at my face. "How did you sleep? Did you dream of me? Of penguins?"

I'm about to tell him where he can shove his device, when I see a chat exploding across his screen in real-time. Hearts and emojis flood upward like a technical tidal wave.

"*¡Hijo de puta!*" I dive under the covers, yanking the blankets over my head. "You're doing a LIVE?!"

My heart pounds against my ribs. Betrayal. He's beaming me to the internet—*me*, pre-makeup, in full bedhead mode. No warning. No prep time. *Total surprise: here's your favorite YouTuber's sleep-deprived, unwashed, possibly feral girlfriend.*

"Sorry, DareSquad." Reece chuckles—actually chuckles. "Cam's *not* an early bird."

Buried in blankets, I am dying.

He's live. He's live. He's live.

"I can't—you can't—" I mumble through the blanket. "I'm not camera ready!"

My tongue feels like it's wearing a sweater, and I'm pretty sure there's dried drool on my chin. Not to mention my breath could wilt flowers. This is not the kind of content that Gordon wants to save the channel.

I'm sure the comments section is already sharpening their pitchforks.

The mattress shifts again, and suddenly Reece's head appears next to mine beneath the sheets. "Cam, you're always gorgeous." He pulls back the blanket, exposing my face to his millions of viewers. "Look at her. No makeup. No filters. Just real beauty. Tell her you agree."

The replies whir in faster than a high-speed elevator:

Cam is STUNNING!
Those EYES, holy shit!
Excuse me? She wakes up looking like that?
HER SKIN IS GLOWING WTF!
Wifey her up, Reece!

Okay, what? My brain slams into a brick wall.

Reece nods happily. "See? Told you. You're beautiful."

He pulls me up to sit beside him, and the comments take a turn:

Damn, her curves though.
Bro, I would sell my soul to lay on those thighs.
Them titties looking juicy even in—

His grin vanishes and his expression sharpens, eyes darkening.

"Hold on, guys," he says smoothly, his voice dipped in warning. "Let's keep it PG. I'm sharing my girlfriend with you, but not all of her." His free hand settles on my hip, warm and possessive, and my skin blazes.

The chat explodes again:

OPE, he said my girlfriend.
Oh he's claiming her, claiming her!
Reece being a protective king rn.
Daddy Dare just put us in our place.
Okay but how do I apply to be Cam?

I fixate on Reece, suspicious as hell, hugging the sheets to my chest, my mind firing off ten million questions. Who is this person? And what has he done with my grumpy boss?

"Thanks, everyone," I manage, my voice hesitant, my face heating under the unexpected wave of compliments. "You guys are... really sweet."

I start to gather up my hair, but—no scrunchie on my wrist. My lifeline to appearing semi-human has abandoned me. My eyes frantically dart around our sex circus of a bed.

"You looking for this?" My roommate dangles my hair tie like he's teasing a cat with a pom pom on a stick.

I snatch it and quickly twist my chaos waves into something that—hopefully—redeems me from my current *attacked-by-a-leaf-blower* aesthetic.

"Cam always has a scrunchie," he says into the lens. "Like, always. She takes filming very seriously."

He noticed that?

"I keep it close in case I need something to strangle you with."

He laughs. "There's the feisty girl the squad needs to see. And that's the perfect transition to tell everyone what we're doing today."

Oh geez. More public humiliation, and I haven't even had my first cup of coffee. What's next? A live broadcast of me crawling under the bed, half-naked, trying to escape?

"I need to admit something to Cam, and I want you all to be a part of it."

Don't panic. Act natural. I stare at my uncomfortable reflection on the screen.

No, not that natural—you're giving off serial killer vibes.

Smile! Not that kind of smile, you lunatic. You look like you're gonna bite someone.

Just cross your arms—wait, no, now your boobs are the main event. *STOP GIVING THE INTERNET A SHOW, CAMILA!*

"A lot of you know Cam is my new girlfriend," Reece continues, "but you may not know that she's also my right-hand woman behind the scenes." He turns those intense blue eyes on me. "How long have you been my videographer, Morales?"

"Uh, two years?" I manage, wondering if this is an elaborate setup to fire me on a livestream for views.

"And have I been an asshole to you that entire time?"

My eyes fly wide open because *WHAT IS HAPPENING?*

"I'll answer for her. Yes. I have been," he says, his tone serious now. "Making content for you can get super stressful. And I am not always the most pleasant off camera. So I am publicly apologizing to Cam for being a total douchebag. For not acknowledging how important she is. Guys, without her, this channel would be shaky selfies and stock footage with voiceovers. This filming powerhouse is literally in the trenches with me. She's a warrior, and it's time I told her."

Um, excuse me? Did I die? Am I in a coma? Because Reece Dare—the man who once said my drone footage looked like it was shot by a drunk, one-winged pigeon—is actually saying...

"You see, Cam's the one who has filmed all your favorite videos for the last two years. She's scaled buildings, jumped out of planes, and done it all like a pro. But not once did I thank her. I have *never* told her how freakishly talented she is." His jaw tightens, a muscle ticking beneath the stubble. "Which is a total dick move."

My newly enlightened boss looks at me, his eyes brimming with sincerity. He squeezes my thigh softly, like he's got something to say but wants to keep it between us.

"Quick, drop in the chat your favorite video Cam has filmed."

The responses fly in faster than Blaze's attention span:

Skateboard Rooftop Escape—Girls got SKILLZ.

The Haunted Asylum One—that angle when the door slammed? CHILLS.

OMG THE PLANE JUMP. HOW DID SHE FILM AND NOT DIE?

That underwater shark cage stunt had me SHOOK. Cam's got bigger balls than my boyfriend.

She's a total badass.

I'm speechless. Comment after comment, all praising... *me*. I'm just the behind-the-scenes girl, framing shots and editing this prankster's crazy stunts into something watchable. The internet saw his face, his daring antics, his irresistible charm.

Not me.

But here they are, calling *me* a badass.

I swallow, pressing my lips together as if that will somehow contain the weirdly emotional reaction brewing in my ribcage. "I mean, you were the one performing the stunt in midair. I was—"

"Filming while skydiving," Reece cuts in, deadpan. "That's like saying, 'I was only casually texting while riding a unicycle through a minefield.'"

I open my mouth to argue, but he barrels forward, eyes glinting like he's only getting started.

"Actually, let's put this into perspective. Cam, how many videos do you think we've filmed together in the last few years?"

"I don't know. A hundred?"

Reece lets out a low whistle. "Yikes. That's more than I thought." A grin spreads across his face—the kind that usually means someone's getting pushed into a pool dressed as a giant taco. "Then that's what I have to make up for. One hundred sorries for being a prickwad douchecanoe."

He winks at me, and my thighs press together like they're muffling a secret.

"No editing. No take-backs. We're continuing this live so you can see every second of my pain."

"That's... really not necessary."

"Yes it is!" He bounds onto our circular bed, waving his hand by the sensor and making it spin. "So stay with me and smash that *Like* button, because I'm spending the next twenty-four hours humiliating myself in today's video, Camila Morales, Please Forgive Me for Being a Total Dick Challenge!"

"Oh no no no, you're forgiven!" I flail my hands, stopping the bed from spinning. "Really. We're good. Clean slate. Look, I'll even pinky swear!"

"Nice try. I'm not getting off that easy. I must pay for my insults. Now, you better move. We have to be at the beach in twenty minutes."

I stare at him, my stomach doing more flips than an Olympic gymnast. *What on Earth is going on? Why is he apologizing to me?*

Wait.

No.

He's not apologizing. He is *performing* an apology.

The realization is a rogue surfboard to the face. It's not real. This is content. Prime clickbait material: *Grumpy YouTuber's Redemption Arc* or *Watch Me Grovel For Views!*

I'm another prop in his latest viral video.

But then he smiles at me again, that genuine, unguarded smile where his eyes crinkle at the corners, and my heart straight-up ignores my brain's *THIS IS FAKE* warning sirens.

Stupid heart.

It needs to re-read the fine print in our fake relationship contract.

***

SOMETHING IS SERIOUSLY WRONG with Reece.

We're walking to the beach—or rather, I'm walking while he pirouettes down the path. He's a one-man musical number, twirling and leaping as if the guy's on the lead float in a parade called Everything Is Awesome.

His phone is held high, livestreaming every over-the-top, horrifyingly wholesome second of what I've officially deemed his complete mental breakdown.

"Oh my gosh, is that a butterfly?" He gasps, stopping mid-spin and clutching his chest. "Everyone, check out its wings! Nature is... so incredible."

His voice actually cracks with emotion.

I am terrified.

"Cam! Tell the chat what you love most about Hawaii!"

"Uh... that on most days, my boss isn't having a full-blown personality transplant?"

He throws his head back and laughs. "She's hilarious! Isn't she hilarious? And beautiful. And—hey there! Kai's best friend!"

Before I can process the whiplash, Reece takes off like a golden retriever who just spotted its favorite UPS driver. The poor resort worker, wearing an ALOHA, I'M KAI'S BEST FRIEND name tag, looks fully unprepared to be body-slammed by joy incarnate.

"Kai has tons of best friends, but I'm guessing you are the best best *best* of best friends." Reece announces to his live audience of millions, "This guy makes the most incredible towel swans I've ever seen. Dude, you are an artist. A visionary. A towel-folding genius!"

I latch on to the filming lunatic's arm and drag him away, thoroughly apologizing to the employee.

"Reece," I hiss, "did Kai's war hammer hit you in the head? Because you're acting like Blaze after ten DareFuel drinks."

"I'm spreading joy, Sunshine!" He throws an arm around my shoulders, flashing his unhinged smile. It's disturbing.

His followers in the thread explode:

HE CALLED HER SUNSHINE OMG!
He's so in love with her it's painful.
SOMEONE BOTTLE THIS ENERGY IMMEDIATELY!
New DareFuel flavor, Reece's Crush Rush!

"Would you look at this magical paradise!" He spins around, arms spread wide as if he's starring in *The Sound of Music*. "The weather is perfect!"

"It's literally the same weather as yesterday. And the day before. Because we're in Maui."

"Exactly! Another perfect day. Thanks, Mother Nature. I love and appreciate you!" He blows a kiss to the sun.

I size him up. Now might be a good time to spring the news about my new channel launch. I bet Pixie Dream Reece will say yes to anything. Then again, exploiting someone mid-mental breakdown feels wrong. *Stupid conscience.*

"And do you know who else I love and appreciate?" he asks.

I try to flee, but he grabs my shoulders, yanking me into frame. "This goddess right here."

The chat has feelings on that statement:

Goddess Cam confirmed, bow down peasants.
BRO DIDN'T EVEN BLINK. HE MEANT THAT.
KING AND HIS GODDESS, THIS SHIP SAILS ITSELF.
How he hypes his girl. #RelationshipGoals.

"Are you... okay?"

"Never better!" He beams. "Let's do a Q&A!"

"No. No, let's not."

Too late. A question appears:

Describe Cam in three words.

Reece gasps dramatically. "Only three??" He angles toward me, dead serious. "That's impossible."

Oh God.

"Radiant. Spectacular. Visionary."

"Please stop—"

"No, wait! Magnificent. Extraordinary. Phenomenal."

I yank the phone down, genuine concern flooding my system. "Blink twice if you need help."

Instead, he skips away, high-fives a resort worker, and—*oh God*—hugs a palm tree.

A PALM TREE.

I catch up to him as he's thanking the tree for providing shade and asking permission to climb it.

"Um, Reece, how about we go back to the room?"

His grin widens. "Can't a guy appreciate life? And you? And—OH MY GOD, IS THAT A SEASHELL?"

He sprints toward the beach, leaving me standing there. *So this is how it feels when your boss has a psychotic break live on camera.*

I chase after him, and maybe, just maybe, his giddiness isn't completely unwarranted. This beach is absurdly gorgeous, like it's showing off. *Okay, nature, we see you—you're breathtaking.*

The waves are rolling in like they rehearsed all night, the golden sand is soft and warm like a freshly baked croissant, and the sun is casting everything in that obnoxiously romantic glow that makes people book vacations they can't afford.

And right in the middle of it all... an art class?

Rows of wooden easels stand proudly on the shore. Each holds a pristine, blank canvas waiting to be blessed—or brutally assaulted—by creativity. Low stools dot the setup, tiny wooden palettes stacked neatly on tables covered in old paint splatters.

"I hope you're good at painting, Morales."

"I'm okay." I shrug, watching other resort guests settle onto their stools.

"That's Cam code for 'I'm amazing,'" he tells his viewers.

"I promise you, it's not," I say, throwing my hands up in surrender. "I swear. Stop hyping me up. I'll be lucky to create an inkblot test for serial killers. People are going to be disappointed."

"Impossible." He grins. "Everything you do is spectacular."

Our gazes lock, and for a second, my heart forgets its rhythm. This sinfully attractive menace is staring at me with an intensity that makes my toes curl. I grab his face, squishing his cheeks together until he resembles a very handsome fish.

"Reece. Listen carefully. Did Kai give you something? Something in a drink? Maybe a mysterious powder? A tea infused with illegal substances?"

"Cam, Cam, Cam." He leans in, forehead nearly touching mine.

My breath catches.

His voice drops, serious for the first time all morning.

"I'm just... really, really happy to be here with you."

And then, like a true psychopath, he boops my nose.

"See, guys? This woman is literally the most honest, nicest, most gifted person I know. And I've been a complete, unforgivable asshole. So here is my first sorry of the day."

"I accept your apology. Now let's go get some breakfast."

"Oh, it's not that easy. I have to *earn* your forgiveness."

I don't like the way he says *earn*. There's too much mischief in him. Like a kid who recently found the *Don't Push Me* button that blows up the world but can't resist.

Before I can question him, he takes me by the shoulders and physically moves me into position at an art station. My seat wobbles in the sand, and I grab on to the tiny folding table to steady myself. There's already a small group of artists assembled around me, most of them older women in breezy resort wear, clutching glasses of wine.

"This is your spot, front row billing," Reece announces, making a grand gesture toward the easel like he's presenting me to an audience. "All set?"

I narrow my eyes at him, but he turns and skips away.

A woman in her seventies leans over and winks. "Oh, honey, you're in for a treat."

That sounds ominous.

Reece climbs onto the stage under the thatched-roof canopy, where a giant banner reads PAINT & SIP : FIND YOUR MUSE, FIND YOUR PASSION.

Uncomfortable energy hums through the crowd. *Or is that just me?* A quiet anticipation. Like something unholy is about to happen, only we can't comprehend how unholy it will be.

He adjusts the tripod and fine-tunes his shot, ensuring he's front and center before facing the artists. *Even crazy, he looks stupidly hot.*

"Welcome, everyone! For those of you who don't know me, I'm Reece Dare. And today, in the spirit of humiliation and forgiveness, I'm doing something a little different."

He subtly angles the camera. *What's he trying to show the livestream viewers that we can't see from our beachfront seats?* I quickly pull out my phone and jump onto his live. To my relief, the shot seems normal. It's a close-up of Reece, highlighting his DareSquad tee.

Phew, crisis averted.

"Camila Morales, this is for never appreciating you enough. My humiliation is nothing compared to the regret that haunts me. I made you feel unseen and unappreciated." Then, with a smirk that sends a shiver down my spine, he adds, "So consider this payback for the unforgettable view of your killer naked body in the shower."

And without warning, he strips.

Totally.

Naked.

Pause everything, because my life is rushing past me like a highlight reel. Every decision, every path that led me here—each one more questionable than the last.

And holy mother of abs.

The man is art.

It's not fair.

Shoulders? Massive. Arms? Tattooed perfection. Chest? Absurd. Stomach? *What even is that V-cut?*

And then there's his—

NOPE. NOPE NOPE NOPE.

Abort mission! Avert Eyes!

My lungs collapse. My vision goes blurry. My internal scream factory malfunctions.

The crowd loses their collective minds, especially the elderly woman wearing bifocals holding down the last row.

Catcalls. Cheers. Paintbrushes are being thrown.

Reece poses like a chiseled naked bachelor at an auction, one arm flexed, the other casually resting on his hip, chest gleaming, legs spread.

I CANNOT.

I snap my gaze to my phone screen, desperately making sure the entire internet is not getting any full-frontal.

Okay. Crisis somewhat averted. The live-stream is only framed on his bare chest—which is still an act of violence because those pecs were hand-carved by Zeus himself.

The chat is out of control:

BRO WHAT IN THE FANFICTION IS THIS?
SOMEONE SCREEN RECORD.
DADDY DARE IS OUT HERE BREAKING THE INTERNET.
GOD IS REAL AND HE WANTS US TO BE HAPPY.

Oh, fuck. It's official.
The man has indeed lost his goddamn mind.

"Please be kind with your brush strokes. It's a tad chilly up here." he says, winking at me.

"Sweetie, you've got zero reasons to be shy!" the bifocaled woman next to me hollers.

This is an all-out emergency situation. Like, code red, pull the fire alarm, hide all the sharp objects before this man shaves his head.

My phone buzzes.

Gordon: *What the fuck am I watching?*

Oh God. This is bad. This is career-ending bad. This is *Gordon Will Turn Me Into Protein Powder* bad. I can already picture the LinkedIn headline: FORMER VIDEOGRAPHER SEEKING WORK – PREVIOUS EXPERIENCE INCLUDES BREAKING YOUTUBE'S BIGGEST STAR.

Career? Over.

Dreams? Dead.

Sanity? Hanging on by a thread.

But I have bigger problems than Gordon's impending wrath. Because right now the throb between my legs has officially escalated into a magnitude 7.9 sexual earthquake. According to my contract, there is only one man I'm allowed to let fix it. And from where I'm sitting, he looks extremely overqualified for the job.

A dangerous thought slithers into my mind. *Maybe we should practice... ya know... to appear convincing on camera? For the brand. For content.*

My inner voice—which sounds suspiciously like Kai—whispers: *It would be more believable if you knew how his body felt against yours. You need to map every inch of those muscles with your fingers... and your lips...*

I clutch my paintbrush tighter, wishing I could concentrate on anything but the way his muscles ripple when he moves. It's no use. My logical left brain has been sidelined, replaced by pure, throbbing all-kinds-of-right brain desire.

¡Ay, Dios mío! I can't give in to these thoughts.

Sure, he's been blessed by the dick fairy.

And yes, I might actually combust from sexual frustration.

But no, I'm not letting him know that.

You hear that, Mr. Boss Man? A few sweet words and a striptease don't erase two years of criticism. The grump is still in there, lurking beneath the surface, ready to pounce and knock me back down.

What's with all these compliments anyway? "Cam's so talented" this and "She's incredible" that. It's for the audience, another performance for his precious DareSquad, right? It's seriously messing with my head.

Those yearning, stupidly blue eyes, every time he says something nice, each accidental touch that has my skin begging for more; I will not let him see how much he affects me.

I suck in a long, deep breath of salty ocean air, hoping it'll cool the raging inferno that is my damn libido. Nope. Still hot. Still wildly unhinged.

Like hell will I reveal what he's doing to me. No way can he know that I lie awake most nights, imagining his big hands and hungry mouth claiming me. *No!* Not happening. Not today, Satan.

Because he's my boss. And the jerk's made it abundantly clear that he's not into me—repeatedly, consistently, and with an impressive variety of criticism. Especially when the camera's *not* on.

But still, a tiny, relentless voice in the back of my mind won't shut up. What if he's as consumed by this as me? What if this daring man is feeling the same electric charge? What if we gave in?

I shake my head, pushing the thoughts away. No, I cannot go there. Can't let myself hope. Reece is acting insane today; tomorrow he'll be back to normal. I gotta stay strong and maintain focus. *He's off-limits and a jerk. Ignore him calling you "gorgeous." Push down how intensely your body is responding.*

I tighten my grip on the paintbrush, forcing my eyes to return to the canvas. I'm going to finish this painting and prove to myself that I can resist him. I *will* control these crazy, reckless desires.

I've spent years being told that I am not good enough. He doesn't get to flip the script in one afternoon. No way in hell does he get the satisfaction of knowing how badly I crave him.

CHAPTER TEN

REECE

SMACK. RIGHT ACROSS MY goddamn face.

Ouch! I jolt awake, eyes snapping open, and immediately get hit with round two—a solid palm to the jaw, followed by a knee to the thigh.

Jesus Christ. I'm under attack.

No. Correction.

Cam is in full cling-wrap mode, and once again, I'm the unwilling victim of her nighttime assault antics.

Violence shouldn't be this adorable, but here I am getting bitch-slapped at four a.m. by my videographer in her skimpy yellow pajamas. And holy hell—her toes are doing this lazy little dance against my dick through the blanket. Her skin is fever-hot even through five layers of protective fabric, and my traitorous body is memorizing every point of contact.

Carefully, I pry her off. It's a painfully delicate process. One arm, then the other. I slowly slide her leg from mine, peeling her away like removing a stubborn twenty percent off sticker from a book cover.

Cam makes a soft *hmm* noise as I roll her onto her side. My fingers graze warm, bare skin, and the edge of her pink lacy underwear peek out from her tiny-ass yellow shorts.

Fuuuuuccck.

She nuzzles into her pillow, lashes resting against her cheeks. Her lips are plush and relaxed, as if waiting for a kiss. So beautiful. And so completely unaware of the absolute chaos she's wreaking on my self-control.

I pull the blanket up and cover her then roll onto my back, staring at my reflection in the mirrored ceiling. Won't forget those peekaboo panties anytime soon. The ocean murmurs against the shore, each wave rising and falling in perfect harmony with Cam's gentle breath.

It's still dark and our alarm is set to buzz any second—ready to wake us for our early trek to watch the sunrise at Mount Haleakalā. But my mind is elsewhere, lingering on last night and the heat I swore I saw in Cam's gaze as we prepared for bed. *Did I imagine it?* Maybe I wanted to see desire in her after my little strip show for the art class.

There I was, standing naked in front of a bunch of cheering geriatric women, when I caught sight of Cam—her jaw dropped, her eyes locked on my dick. She stared for a full ten seconds, completely entranced.

And I thought—naively thought—she was impressed.

Until she didn't say a word. Not one appreciative comment about my body. She'd just... painted. And what did she paint? A fucking *pencil* where my penis should be. A yellow number two pencil, complete with a tiny eraser for the head of my cock.

"I present to you: 'The Littlest Pencil: A Portrait of An Erasable Ego,'" she'd announced with a smirk, her expression nothing but trouble. "We can hang it in your office. It'll keep you humble."

Disappointed yes, but unimpressed? Never. I actually love that about her. How she doesn't worship at the altar of Reece Dare like I'm YouTube royalty. She's not afraid to give me shit, to challenge me, to make me grin even when I'm grouchy.

Because everyone else? They idolize the brand. They kiss my ass, say whatever they think I want to hear, and treat me as if I'm the center of the universe.

Not Cam. She has never once put me on the celebrity pedestal. She knows I'm exactly the kind of man who deserves to be dragged.

And it makes me want her so damn much, it's ridiculous.

My cock perks up as if it's been summoned, and I grip the sheets. Because for the thousandth time, my mind's back to that fucking shower incident—how her full breasts felt in my palms, like slippery velvet pillows. *How natural it would be to step into her next shower, let the steam swallow us both, and pick up right where we left off.*

There'd be no hesitation. With adrenaline pumping, I'd press her against those rocks while water rushed over our bodies, fully immersed in the heat of her skin, dropping to my knees so I can worship her with my mouth and—

Dude, get your shit together. You have to stop this obsession. She's your employee.

We have a working relationship to maintain. And in less than two weeks, we go back to the real world. Where there's no way Camila Morales wants anything to do with me romantically after the way I've—

MWAAARP! MWAAARP! MWAAARP!

Holy shit! The earth-shattering blare of sirens is terrifying. *WTF?* I bolt upright, heart hammering, expecting a SWAT team to burst through the balcony windows.

I whip my head toward Cam's side of the bed, ready for a full-blown emergency, but—

She's asleep.

Completely unfazed, soft breaths escaping her lips, curled up like a content kitten.

MWAAARP! MWAAARP! MWAAARP!

"Cam," I whisper. "Hey. Your alarm. It's time to get up."

Nothing.

"We have to be in the lobby in forty-five minutes."

She doesn't so much as twitch.

Touching her seems like a death wish, given her history of sleep violence. Instead, I carefully stretch over her to silence the phone, trying to ignore her coconut scent that's a direct hit to my morning wood.

The second my finger hits snooze and the noise stops—

"¡MIERDA! I'M GONNA BE LATE!"

Cam explodes awake as if she's been launched out of a cannon, shooting upright.

CRACK!

Our skulls collide at full force.

A shockwave of pain detonates in my forehead.

I yelp, instinctively jerking backward, still wrapped in my protective blanket burrito. I'm a human log rolling off the mattress then hitting the floor face first. *THUD.* What's worse, my dick breaks my fall.

"Fuck!"

"Oh shit, Reece!"

I roll over on the ground, staring up. Her face appears over the side of the bed, hair wild and eyes wide with concern. She'd be adorable if my skull wasn't busy exploring new dimensions of pain *(along with my hopefully not broken dick)*.

"So we're clear," I groan, "if we ever film a Morning Routine with Cam video, I'm getting hazard pay. You're a one-woman workplace safety violation."

"Do you need help?" she asks, rubbing her head and biting back a grin.

"No. My balls think you've done enough." I shift, wincing as my two favorite body parts check in with complaints. "I need to lie here and try to understand how my life choices got me to this moment."

"Don't be a baby," she says with sympathetic eyes, and I've already forgiven her. "Besides, according to my artistic interpretation yesterday, there's not much down there to damage. More *golf pencil* than a 1-wood driver, if you ask me."

I shoot her my best death glare. "You're way too chipper for someone who just committed assault and battery."

She grins and for a second, my eyes soak up those fantastic gravity-defying breasts spilling out of her top, and all is right with the world.

I look back up and her gaze has changed—the teasing amusement replaced with something smoky and electric. The air goes taut *(same, buddy)*, my body tensing with the urge to move—to brush my mouth over hers, to swallow whatever breathy moans she'd make when I press her back into the mattress and devour her whole.

To tease her with the heavy, aching length of my cock, feel her squirm against me, gasping, needy, desperate for—

She licks her lips then quickly sits up, breaking the charged moment.

I gulp, forcing down a groan. "Go get dressed, you menace. Before I fire you for attempted murder."

"You can't fire me," she sings, bouncing on her feet. "I'm your girlfriend now, remember?"

"Fake girlfriend!"

"Still counts!" She disappears into the bathroom.

I exhale, rubbing the back of my neck and willing my body to cool the fuck down.

I'm officially losing my goddamn mind.

If this is how the day starts, I'm genuinely afraid of what else might happen.

***

IF THIS SHUTTLE TAKES one more hairpin turn, I'm going to hurl all over Kai's first-ever fully clothed appearance. The mountain road is a maze of curves and cliffs, barely lit by the headlights, and if the motion sickness doesn't get us, the plummeting to our deaths will.

"My sensual seekers, you are about to have a truly religious experience."

Please don't let this be another penis drum situation.

I shift in my seat, adjusting my gray DareWear hoodie, as Cam's head bobs beside me, her body swaying with every curve in the road. She's sporting my merch as well—matching olive green sweatpants and sweatshirt, with *DARE2BU* emblazoned on the front. Gordon sent us a mandatory merch kit to help sell our relationship and the product all in one fell swoop.

"This is no mere mountain," Kai says, now in storyteller mode. "This is Haleakalā. A volcano. A place of gods. Of fire and light. Legend says that the great demigod Maui lassoed the sun from the summit of Haleakalā, slowing its journey across the sky."

It's too early for one of Kai's innuendo-filled speeches. I check my phone, hoping for a successful repeat of yesterday's livestream. *Battery life, seventy percent. Should be okay.*

"Many visitors describe feeling an energy unlike anything they've ever known. Some may sense a deep, internal shift—a shedding of fears, a pull toward their most primal desires."

"It's a sunrise, not an orgy," I mutter.

Cam snorts, her shoulder bumping mine in the darkness. "Shh! Don't manifest that shit."

"As the sun ascends, so will your senses. It's natural to feel physical sensations—goosebumps, warmth radiating from within, and unexpected tingling in hidden places. Let it flow. Let it ignite your sexual spirit."

"Twenty bucks says someone tries to make a sunrise baby," Cam mutters.

"Fifty says it's the couple that turned the hot tub into an R-rated movie yesterday."

"—but first, please bundle up. It's quite cold at this elevation, about forty degrees. We have blankets for couples wishing to experience the mountaintop directly, or you may view in the warmth of the visitor center."

The shuttle lurches to a stop, and a whisper of dawn bleeds across the horizon.

"It begins," Kai whispers dramatically. "Soon your souls will—"

"Dude!" Blaze rockets out of his seat so fast you'd think his ass is on fire. "I got a stiffy just thinking about that kick-ass sun!"

"Blazey, sit your pervy ass down!" Astrid yanks him back by his shirt. "There's no way I'm risking my thousand-dollar extensions in that wind. We're watching from the visitor center."

Camila's already got her camera out like it's a fifth limb.

"What's your vote, Morales? Heated viewing lounge or mountain goat experience?"

"Life's not meant to be lived through windows," she says, grinning. "Neither are epic shots."

I love her adventurous spirit.

I grab a blanket from Kai, and we step off the shuttle. The cold hits us like a Will Smith slap to the face.

"¡Mierda!" Cam yelps. "My nipples disagree. They're telling me it's negative 13,000 degrees out here."

"We can head inside—"

"Hell no. Let's find the money shot."

We pick our way through the crowd, vying for the best viewing area. By the time we find an ideal spot away from the masses, Cam is shivering so hard her teeth are chattering. I hold out the blanket. "Here. You're gonna vibrate off the mountain."

She wraps it around herself, shoulders still shaking. I do my best to ignore the human earthquake, but less than a minute later, I cave.

"C'mere," I say before my overthinking kicks in. "Body heat is more efficient if we share."

Standing side by side, we try sharing a blanket that was apparently made for hobbits. Every time we get one side covered, the opposite side flaps open like a cape in the wind.

"This isn't working," she laughs.

"For fuck's sake…" I step behind her, wrapping the blanket around us and pulling her against my chest. "Only until our fingers thaw enough to hold the camera."

She doesn't argue, just melts into me—like she was made to fit under my chin. And then—

Sweet mother of fuck.

The sky cracks open like God himself is putting on a show.

The initial brilliant streaks burst over the horizon, setting the clouds on fire.

Colors I've never seen in my life, colors that probably don't even have names, explode across the heavens in a symphony of light. Orange bleeds into rose gold, violet weaves through amber, and the clouds below us—*holy shit, we're above the clouds*—morph into a sea of liquid sunshine. We're literally standing at the edge of heaven, watching the sun ascend into existence like we're witnessing the first dawn of time.

Goddammit. Kai was right.

The crowd around us falls into reverent silence, and for once, I have nothing negative to say. Because I'm standing here, Cam pressed against me, watching something bigger than all of us.

And then—

A realization cracks me on the head—blunt, hard, and impossible to ignore.

Yesterday, stripped down and on full display for that art class, I was…

Reckless. Dangerous. Irresponsible. And I fucking loved it!

Yesterday wasn't just another stunt for the fans—it was for her. But I didn't realize it would stir something up, something I can't shake. Being uncomfortable and pushing boundaries—it reignited a fire in my soul.

For the first time in years, I felt free. I felt like me again.

The *me* who used to come up with the most batshit stunts imaginable and then spend hours pulling them off.

The *me* who lived for the adrenaline of the unknown—the thrill of testing limits, of knowing something could go horribly wrong but doing it anyway.

I didn't give a shit what people thought because I was too busy having fun.

The fact that it turned into a career, that it paid for Mama's treatments? That was a miracle.

When did I lose that love for filming?

Gordon. All talk, no talent. The king of smoke and mirrors. More sizzle than steak.

He strutted into my life with promises of global domination—so much bullshit, it had its own gravitational pull. "You could be bigger than PewDiePie," he said, and like an idiot, I'd bought it. Hook, line, and designer sneaker.

And to his credit, he wasn't wrong. For a while there, I was untouchable.

But here's the thing they don't tell you about fame—you never know when you've peaked until your ass is sliding down the other side.

Fame fades.

Trends change.

New creators pop up, doing faster, crazier, dumber shit and grabbing the spotlight you thought was yours. You spend all your time trying to stay relevant, hustling and advancing but then forgetting what made you want to climb.

My original fans? They're all moving on with life. Getting married. Making babies. Building careers. They get to grow, to change, to evolve. Meanwhile, I'm frozen in time like some kind of perpetual frat boy Peter Pan, doing the same shit I did at twenty-one because I'm too terrified to lose what I have.

Losing myself in the billowing sky and seeing the vastness of this beautiful world, I'm floating. My heart can feel what my mind already realizes. *My life needs to change.*

I just don't know what *change* looks like.

Hell, I almost married *Astrid*. Things had gotten so fucked up with the business that I actually convinced myself marrying her was the solution to my declining views. Her ditching me at the altar might be the most humiliating thing that's ever happened to me, but honestly? She did me a favor. *How many more years would I have wasted on staged couple smiles and stupid pranks?*

Yesterday's livestream, that rush of not knowing how it would play out? That's what's been missing from my life. That spark. That authenticity. Not to mention finally being able to tell Cam how incredible she is. It felt great taking off my asshole armor, being real with her, and telling her how much this channel owes to her talent.

Yesterday, I got to say things I've wanted to for years.

But I'm nowhere near done apologizing. The shit I said to her because I couldn't handle myself wanting her? Grade A dickhead behavior. Premium douchebaggery. The way I made her doubt herself, made her feel as if she wasn't good enough?

It's unforgivable.

I was so fucking wrong.

And her self-esteem paid the price.

I was pushing her away, keeping her at a distance, making sure she never got too close. I was too scared to admit she matters to me. *How do I make up for years of being King Asshat?*

The reality is, I could spend the rest of my life apologizing, and it still won't be enough.

But I'm going to try.

"Oh crap." Cam shifts against me. "We're not filming."

"Let's enjoy this one," I murmur, pulling her closer, needing her warmth like my next breath. She snuggles back against me, and my heart expands, pressing against my ribs as if it's trying to make room for new emotions I'm not supposed to have.

Because this woman in my arms?

The universe is making it clear—she's my first step toward whatever's next.

***

THE SHUTTLE DOOR HISSES open, pouring us onto a roadside oasis, emerald cliffs and lush greenery towering on all sides. The humid air gives me chills. It's awe-inspiring. Kai walks by, and instead of some godawful body spray, he smells *exquisite*—like pheromones, a double rainbow, karma, and everything good in this world.

Okay, maybe I'm still riding high off that mountaintop.

"If you seek a gentle communion with nature, go this way." Kai gestures to a path that looks as easy as a shopping mall walkway. "And for those prepared to embrace their wilder side..." He points to a trail marked with a sign featuring a waterfall and skulls and crossbones.

I glance at Cam. "Tourist trap or death wish?"

"You know me—I like it rough."

The second those words leave her mouth, her cheeks flame.

She partially turns, eyeing the difficult trail, and her eyes light up with the notion of adventure. It's one of my favorite things about her—how she's always ready to chase the next thrill, camera in hand.

We quickly peel off our sunrise layers and zip them securely into our backpacks. *Time to take on this trail!* I'm in my standard Dare4Adventure merch—a blue logo tee with khaki shorts—and Cam... *Christ.* Those cutoff shorts and a white tank with the words DareGirl stretched across her boobs.

Death by hotness is looking real likely. She's got that red string tied around her neck, drawing my eye like a goddamn beacon. I'm glad my fans can't see the filthy ways I'm fantasizing about her.

Focus, you thirsty idiot.

"Uh, hellooo?" Astrid says, her voice so shrill it could neuter a dog on a neighboring island. "Isn't there, like, a shopping option? Or maybe"—she slides closer to Kai, batting her lashes— "a little one-on-one coaching? Y'know, something more... horizontal?"

"Ah, passionate one." Kai's voice drops an octave. "Sadly, Hawaii state law requires that the most vigorous activities happen behind closed doors."

"Mmm, yeah, that's what I was hoping for," Astrid purrs. "Maybe you could stretch me out? I hear you're very... hands-on with your instruction."

"DUDE!" Blaze bounces between them. "Are you guys talking about CrossFit? That shit's intense!"

I grab Cam's arm before I'm forced to watch any more. "Kai says this trail leads to a cliff jumping spot."

"Perfect for content."

"Speaking of…" I wave my phone. "Let's go live. You do the intro."

"That's gonna be a hard pass, boss."

"Counter offer: I'll do the intro, you work the camera for the hike?"

"Deal."

I study her face, catching anxiety in her features. "Why does going live make you nervous?"

"It doesn't—"

"Morales."

She sighs, twisting the scrunchie on her wrist. "No editing. No do-overs. Just me, live, probably saying something stupid while a million people wait to attack me in the chat."

"Okay, first of all—you're so wrong that it's physically painful," I tell her, resisting the urge to cup her face in my hands. "You're fucking incredible at this. The chat was geared up to start a Cam fan club yesterday."

She rolls her eyes, but I catch the ghost of a smile.

I'm going to fix this. Step one was apologizing for being Supreme Overlord of Dickheads. Step two is rebuilding what I helped break. *If I can only figure out how to boost her confidence without pushing too hard.*

Because watching her doubt herself?

That shit ends today.

I hit *Go Live,* and my screen explodes with notifications. The viewer count rockets past fifty thousand.

"Hey, DareSquad! It's your boy, Reece, coming at you live from the most insane mountain in Maui." I pause, grinning into the camera, and then bring Cam to my side. Her warmth instantly bleeds through my shirt.

"And, of course, I'm here with my stunning girlfriend, Camila."

Her body stiffens for a split second before she gives the lens a quick, awkward wave.

"Guys, let's take a moment here for some girlfriend appreciation." I turn the camera, starting at her face and then tilting downward in a slow, deliberate sweep. "I mean, look at this masterpiece. Those eyes, those lips, those—"

"Reece!" Cam's jaw drops, and she elbows me hard in the ribs.

"What?! I'm just admiring my lady."

"And we're done. That's enough of that."

"Well then, Morales, what's your favorite part of your man?" I gesture to myself as if I'm on a gameshow.

"Your unwavering confidence in the face of reality?" She smirks then adds, "Okay, fine. Your ocean blue eyes are sexy as hell."

Did she just say—

"What?" She catches my surprise. "You know you're hot. Am I right, chat?"

The comments catch fire with all the flame emojis:

DADDY DARE IS FINE AF.

THOSE EYES ARE A CRIME.

RAIL ME REECE.

HOTTEST COUPLE ON YOUTUBE.

"Although, I'm shocked he's still got a shirt on," Cam snarks. "I swear, he thinks covering those abs is a violation of his civil rights."

Well, damn. Girl came to play!

She's a goddamn Christmas tree that lights up when she roasts me, when she's meeting my challenge. The sass, the confidence, that playful edge that makes my blood hot—it all comes out when Cam is focused on destroying my ego.

Very interesting.

The chat suffers a complete psychological break:

I'M CRYING THEY'RE SO CUTE.
THE WAY HE LOOKS AT HER THO.
THEIR CHEMISTRY IS EVERYTHING.

"Today"—I pan the camera to showcase the steep incline—"we're taking on the craziest hike in Maui. At the top of this trail is...?" I swing to Cam.

"Oh! Um, a waterfall."

"That's right, babe. A secret waterfall."

Her eyes go wide at the pet name. I'd love to enjoy her reaction, but—

"OH. MY. ACTUAL. GOD!" Astrid screeches. "Do you see this? These are five-thousand-dollar Louboutins! And they're getting raw-dogged by mud!"

"It's cool, baby!" Blaze calls. "Mud's just like... wet dirt!"

"That's *NOT* the POINT, Blazey! They color-matched my fit for the gram! It's called aesthetic cohesion."

I catch Cam's eye, and she's fighting back laughter.

"So, Morales..." I nod at her feet. "You worried about your footwear?"

"No. Unlike some people"—she models her boots with exaggerated flair—"I chose *hiking* boots to go hiking. Crazy concept, I know."

"That's my girl." The words escape before my brain catches up. I recover quickly, fingers finding the red string at her neck. "More importantly, what does this connect to? Please say it's a bikini."

She smirks, and my whole body ignites. "You'll have to wait and find out like everyone else."

"My Louboutins did not sign up for this death march through nature!" Astrid wails behind us. "Like, why are we not taking a helicopter?"

"Babe, I got you!" Blaze flexes. "I'll carry you! I'm fast. How much do you weigh?"

"Are you calling me fat?"

Thanks to that ridiculous conversation, inspiration strikes.

"Hey, DareSquad, new challenge! First one to the top keeps their shirt on!"

I shove the selfie stick at Cam and bolt, the ground uneven under my feet. "Try to keep up, babe!"

"Oh HELL no!" Her voice rings out behind me. "If this clown thinks he's faster than me, he's got another thing coming!"

I already hear her footsteps closing in.

I risk a glance over my shoulder.

And there she is, neck and neck with me, breath coming fast, brutal determination on her face.

I push harder. "You're slowing down, babe! Getting tired?"

"Wow, is this your top speed? Kinda embarrassing for a guy who does stunts for a living."

The trail gets steeper, both of us gasping like asthmatic fish out of water but neither willing to back down.

"Didn't know—" *gasp* "—you were so—" *wheeze* "—thirsty to see me shirtless!"

I let out a choked laugh, my lungs burning.

"Big talk—" *gasp* "—from someone getting lapped!"

Cam lets out a growl of sheer determination, pushing forward and matching my pace stride for stride.

The peak of the hill is within reach, the incline a final cruel test of willpower.

And then—

Like two exhausted lunatics, we both reach the top. Bent over, hands on knees, sucking in air as if we barely escaped a bear attack.

Cam, still clutching the long selfie rod, wipes the sweat from her brow, panting. She shrugs off her backpack, letting it fall to the ground.

"Winner?" I gasp.

"Don't know."

"Ask the fans."

She glares but turns to the chat. "Alright, who won?" She pauses, reading. Then—her lips curl in wicked delight.

"Welp, it's a tie. Guess we both win."

My stomach drops.

"Rules are rules—shirts off, buddy." She hands me the selfie stick then lifts her tank top over her head.

I have made a tactical error of epic proportions.

Because that red string? It's connected to three meager inches of fabric masquerading as a bikini top. Two tiny triangles that dramatically respond to every breath she takes, threatening *(no, promising)* to reveal more with each movement. Her seriously hot underboob has my eyes quaking. That swimsuit is working harder than my self-control.

On autopilot, I lose my shirt, barely registering the movement because my eyes are fixated on her.

Cam, seemingly unaffected by my mental collapse, lifts her arms to gather her hair into that always-there scrunchie. The gesture reveals miles of olive skin, toned arms, and delicate collarbones that practically plead for my tongue's attention. She returns her backpack to her shoulder.

"You coming, Dare? Or did I break you?"

I will not stare at her ass. I will not stare at her ass. I absolutely will not—

God fucking dammit.

I'm pretty sure the chat is having a collective aneurysm over Cam's curves. I can't actually tell because I'm too busy trying to remember how legs work.

She sets my whole body on fire! *How the hell am I supposed to keep my professional distance? Just breathing the same air makes me forget why I should stay away. There's no way I can keep going on like this.*

I know I don't deserve her. Not after the way I treated her. But still, I'm running out of strength to deny it—she's becoming my obsession.

I want her.

CHAPTER ELEVEN

REECE

"Check it out, DareSquad. Maui is next level!" I say, grinning to my audience. "One of my favorite things about Hawaii is the insane variety of ecosystems on the island. Like right now"—I pan the camera slowly, showcasing the trail—"we're in a straight-up jungle. I mean c'mon. Tell me this *isn't* giving major *Jurassic Park* vibes."

I keep the selfie stick steady as the two of us move side by side, boots crunching softly under the packed dirt of the walkway. The hiking path snakes through towering trees, their thick branches swallowing up most of the sunlight, casting dappled shadows against the ground. The air is crisp. Wild. Alive.

I deserve a goddamn prize for keeping my eyes forward. That sprint up here nearly ended me—not from the workout, but from watching my favorite parts of Cam's anatomy defy gravity. My breathing's finally regulated, which I'm counting as a win, even if the rest of me is buzzing like a stadium under Friday night lights.

"Trust me, it smells amazing, too. Like—really, *really* good. If someone bottled this air and sold it as a cologne, I'd do brand deals for them for free. And listen..." I stop walking, and Cam halts beside me. Her breasts bounce slightly, and my brain records it in slow-motion.

We both hold still. Complete silence. Except the viewers can probably hear my heart hammering because she and her intoxicating coconut shampoo scent have overtaken the forest air *(and my senses)*.

"Cam, how would you describe it?"

She breathes in deep, tilting her face to the sky. "So calming... really peaceful."

I shift the GoPro toward her without thinking, capturing the way the filtered light catches the curve of her cheek and how her forehead does this cute crinkle as she listens.

And then, I do something stupid.

I *look* at her. *Really* look at her.

Not like a boss. Not like a guy faking a relationship for clicks. Just... as a man standing beside a beautiful, forbidden woman. One he shouldn't want but definitely does.

"We hope you guys feel like you're here with us," I tell the audience, forcing my voice to sound normal.

Cam glances at me out of the corner of her eye, sensing the slight tension in my words. *Of course she does. She notices everything.*

The trail tightens ahead, with centuries-old trees creating a natural tunnel. Their roots burst through the earth as if they're trying to escape, while overgrown foliage blocks the path, making nature's version of a ninja warrior set.

This is my element. No brand deals, no Gordon breathing down my neck.

"Be careful. There's a—"

Too late. Cam catches her boot on a gnarled root and stumbles forward with a sharp gasp.

"¡Mierda!"

It happens in bullet time. I dive and spin, dropping the phone and throwing myself in front of her. My arms instinctively wrap around her waist as she crashes into me.

WHUMP.

I land on my ass, the impact knocks the wind out of me, but I barely notice because Cam is sprawled across my lap, her hands braced on my shoulders, her mouth inches from mine.

I don't move. I *can't* move.

Her hazel eyes are wide—lips slightly open—like she's caught between an apology and something more dangerous. Her breath, quick and shallow, fans against my lips. My grip on her hips tightens, not because I mean to but because my fingers are staging a fucking mutiny and have decided *we're staying right where we are, thanks.*

God, she's warm.

For a second—one long, excruciating second—I swear she's looking at my mouth. And if she is... if there's even a *chance* she's thinking about it—

Don't do it. Don't do it. Don't do it.

I want to.

So bad.

One moment. One real taste of her. To *really* know how she feels pressed against my lips—not the fantasy that haunts my thoughts at two a.m.

"You okay?" I manage, my voice sounding as if I gargled gravel.

"Yeah," she whispers. "My hero."

"I always knew you'd *fall* for me eventually."

"A pun? Really?" She groans as she stands and brushes dirt off her legs. "That was terrible."

"You're smiling though."

"I'm grimacing in pain."

"Got any other graceful moves you're itching to try?" I ask as I stand.

"Depends. How many times can you play human mattress?"

"For you? I'll clear my schedule."

Her eyes search mine, as if she's trying to figure out if I mean it. Then— "Reece! You dropped the phone!"

"Oh shit..." I scramble for the selfie stick. "Sorry, squad. Cam tried to high-five a tree root with her face. Don't worry, though. Your boy's got reflexes."

"I would've been fine."

I shake my head no to the fans.

"I saw that!" She smacks my arm. "And let's be real—you weren't the hero here. It was your ass. That thing's got perfect bounce and excellent shock absorption."

"Are you objectifying my ass on livestream?"

The chat lights up:

OBJECTIFIED IN 4K: Booty had it coming.
REECE KISS HER ALREADY.
Just make out OMG.

"Okay fam—" I clear my throat, scrambling for a subject change before I make a catastrophically dumb move... like actually listen to the chat. "Q&A time! Let's get to know the woman behind the camera, the star of my dreams, the sass master herself—Camila Morales."

That earns me an eye roll. But she needs to get comfortable talking to the viewers, and she needs *me* to push her.

I scan the questions. "Ooh, here we go. "What's your favorite thing about Reece?"

"His unpredictable mood swings. It's like dating a rollercoaster, without a harness."

"Wrong. It's my eyes. Sorry, but there are wrong answers. Or you could have said my abs, since you can't stop staring at them."

"I'm staring because there's a spider on you."

"WHAT?!" I do a full body shimmy, and she doubles over laughing.

"Made you dance!"

"You're evil. Sexy, but evil. Next question..." I scroll through the comments. "Where did you grow up, and did you like it?"

"New York City! And yes, I loved it. I haven't been back in a while though. I really miss my family."

"Maybe I'll surprise you with a visit home so I can meet them."

Her eyes snap to mine, searching for the joke.

Am I messing with her?

Huh... I don't know.

"You'd like to meet my family? You do realize a visit with my *abuela* includes force-feeding and overshares. You think you can handle that?"

"Sounds like a good time."

"She'll try to marry us for real when she sees those abs and that Amex."

"Smart woman. I like her already. And guys, Cam has a sister named Aria who's a chef in New York," I add, watching her reaction.

"You... remember that?" She recovers quickly. "Well, when we're in New York, Aria's opening up her own food truck. All our favorite Puerto Rican recipes. If you fly me home, we'll go eat there. Keep your notifications on, squad!"

She flashes a smile—one that says she's nailing our fake relationship performance.

I tilt her chin to meet my gaze. "Wherever you feel like going, I'll take you."

She sucks in a breath. And for a solid five seconds, we drink each other in.

"Careful with those promises, Dare. A girl might start believing them."

"Maybe she should."

"Says the man who ate the world's hottest curries then cried for three hours."

"First off, it was a heroic display of emotion. Secondly, those curries were clearly marinated in dragon's breath."

"Sure, blame the curry. Not your inability to handle spicy foods."

"My abs and my spice tolerance are the stuff of legends!"

"The same six pack that got scared by an imaginary spider?"

The chat crumbles into chaos:

I'VE NEVER SHIPPED anything harder.
The WAY he looks at her... HOLY SHIT.
NO BUT FR, how do I insert myself in this Love Story?
DARE: I'm a legend. ALSO DARE: Cries over spicy food.

"Oh, here's a good one—somebody asked when you decided to become a YouTuber."

The transformation is instant and jarring. Color drains from Cam's face, and she's suddenly as pale as bleached bedsheets. I don't get why the question hits her so hard, but my protective instincts surge.

"Actually," I jump in, hand finding the small of her back, "Cam is an award-winning documentary filmmaker, and we're super lucky she joined DareProductions. Someday Cam will leave us to go make important stories about people and causes that need her. But I hope that's a long, long time from now."

Cam's eyes lock on to mine, and something vulnerable flickers.

The group loudly protests:

NEVER LEAVE, CAM!!!
NOOO, Reece NEEDS you!
DARESQUAD won't be the same.

"Don't worry," she says, forcing a small smile. "I'm not going anywhere... *not yet.*"

That last part? Yeah. Not a fan of that.

I want to dig deeper, but something catches her eye.

"Oh my God, wait until you see this!" She grabs the selfie stick and takes off toward a break in the trees.

I run after her, but she's fast! All legs and restless energy, she kicks up dirt while her ponytail snaps like a flag in the breeze. Her laughter is a challenge, daring me to keep up. I whip into action, ready for the chase. We crash through the dense foliage, and—

Damn.

Standing at the cliff's brink, the valley unfolds beneath us like a living painting—countless shades of green below mountains that pierce the clouds. The ocean stretches to infinity, a sheet of sapphire that bleeds into the horizon. There's an absence of human interference—no buildings, no cars, not a hint of civilization. Pure, untamed paradise. It's as if we've stepped into a hidden corner of the world.

She pans the camera with reverent slowness. "This is why they call Maui 'The Valley Isle.'"

"It's humbling, isn't it?" I say, my voice rough with emotion. "Makes you feel small."

"But in a good way, right?" she continues, her gaze drifting back to the horizon, "it's like we're all just tiny pixels in this massive, beautiful picture. When you zoom in, each pixel has its own story, its own purpose. And when we connect with others, our stories intertwine, creating something more beautiful and meaningful."

I nod, taking in her words.

"It's why I love making documentaries. Our lives are these intricate patterns, and every person we meet, every connection we make, adds a new thread to the tapestry. And even though we're small, our impact is immense."

Her philosophy hits me hard, stirring a sense of purpose and connection. In this vast, untouched oasis, yes the stunning view steals my breath, but even more, it's her. The way she sees the world, the depth of her heart, and the quiet strength of her spirit. She's a force of nature—as captivating as this vibrant, untamed landscape.

"I need you to know," I say quietly, "there's no way I could've managed these last few years without you. Even now, I... I'm glad you're here."

Cam's eyes study my face, and I hold my breath, terrified of what I might be revealing. But I can't look away. She stands framed by the sweeping vista behind her—a living metaphor of all the untapped possibilities she makes me believe in.

I'm flooded with emotion. It hits me. *Could we make something work between us? Does she feel this too?* This woman stayed by my side, offering support despite me being a complete jerk. Another truth slams into me: She's more than someone I care about—she's someone I trust.

And in my world of fake relationships, greedy users, and staged content, trust is rarer than authentic comments on YouTube.

"Actually, Reece," she starts, her voice wavering slightly, "I've been meaning to ask you. I was um, hoping..."

No. She's doing that thing... withdrawing... bottling herself up. I reach for her hand, wanting—needing—to help her through whatever this is. My fingers barely graze hers when—

"Blazey, slow down, you animal! You're gonna drop me again!" Astrid's voice shatters our bubble like a hammer through glass.

"Yo, we gotta see that waterfall—it's gonna be so sick!" Blaze calls back.

Cam and I jump apart, eyes wide.

"Shit, we gotta get there first!" She takes off running. "Come on!"

I follow, but not before stealing one last glance at the stunning view. An idea stirs. My life might be in a tailspin, but maybe—just maybe—I can help Cam make her dream happen.

***

OH, FOR FUCK'S SAKE, *look at her ass.*

Cam hooks her thumbs into her belt loops, shimmies out of her sinfully short denim shorts, and I'm salivating. My eyes are bulging out like a cartoon dog, all because of one perfectly executed strip-tease that I know—I fucking know—wasn't even for me.

And yet, my dick is standing at full attention as if she just gave me a lap dance.

Because Camila Morales is wearing a red thong bikini bottom.

Thong.

Why is she doing this to me?

This is it. This is how I die. Not from a stunt gone wrong. Not from one of Blaze's "genius" ideas. Nope. Death by Cam's ass. Melting my brain down.

That baby deserves a spot in a virtual museum; her derriere is next-gen art. The kind of masterpiece that would make AI artists retire all other models because they've found the ultimate muse.

She does this little bounce-and-wiggle to adjust her ponytail with her sexy scrunchie, and I swear my soul leaves my body. Then when she bends to stuff her shorts into her backpack... my brain sends emergency signals to my cock. *Houston, we have liftoff!*

I wonder which of these trees would best support her weight while I...

What the actual fuck, Dare? This day is supposed to be about empowering her. Building her confidence. Not mentally calculating load-bearing capacities of tropical foliage because you can't keep your dick in your pants.

"Earth to Reece?" She waves a hand in front of my face. "Want me to hold the camera while you strip down to your board shorts?"

Little Reece to Big Reece. Incoming message! She asked you a question, dipshit.

"Yes, uh, yeah, cheers, great, thanks."

Stellar response. Just hand her your ever-present filming rod, you moron.

Cam bites her lip, a way-too-amused glint in her eye.

She knows.

She fucking knows.

"DareSquad, feast your eyes on this!" She stretches the selfie stick out over the edge, giving viewers a vertigo-inducing shot of the falls.

The water thunders down like God himself turned on the world's biggest shower, crashing over rocks carved by mythical giants. White spray explodes everywhere, creating a constant rainbow mist. Vines cling to the cliffside, their emerald-green tendrils swaying in the humid breeze. This place is otherworldly, a miracle.

The pool below? Straight-up turquoise magic. So clear you could probably read a book through it. The whole thing is ringed by rocks wearing fluffy moss coats and decorated with wild orchids that you would think were placed there by a Hollywood movie set designer.

"Can you hear this monster?" She holds the phone closer. "It's like standing next to a jet engine. My whole body is vibrating!"

I watch her work the camera, talking directly to the audience without me, and something warm spreads through my chest. I was right. She was made for this.

"Hey, Dare!" she shouts over the roar. "Temperature prediction—refreshing splash or a cold kick to the balls?"

"No idea." *I hope it's freezing. So my cock forgets how much it wants her.*

"Well gang, we're about to find out together! Although..." She peeks beyond the cliff again. "That's definitely higher than what it looked like on Google Maps."

I join her at the edge, and suddenly every survival instinct I possess starts signaling internal alarm bells as if it's a freaking fire drill. My brain flashes back to that ominous sign at the trailhead—the one with the waterfall image with the skull and crossbones.

"Uh, Cam? I don't know if this is such a great idea. That's... that's a lot of down between here and there."

She snorts. "Okay, yeah, right. Wait. Are you serious right now?"

"I just... Who's to say if it's safe for you to jump. I think you should—"

"Oh *hell* to the no. The guy who literally tied me to a bungee cord and launched me off a bridge for the Will This Kill Us? video. You think *this* is too dangerous?"

I open my mouth. Nothing comes out.

Cam takes a step closer. "Do not start with that overprotective machismo crap, Dare. Or did you forget about Jamaica? You know, when your genius self belly-flopped from fifty feet up and I had to fish your unconscious ass out of the water while still holding the camera steady?"

"Yeah, well, that was different." *That was before the thought of you getting hurt made me want to build a fortress of bubble wrap around you and hire a squad of superheroes as your personal security detail.*

I've spent my entire career laughing in the face of danger. Heights? Just another Tuesday. Wild animals? Bring it on. But this is different. This fear is foreign. Overwhelming. Bone-deep terror.

Picturing something bad happening to Cam feels like someone reaching into my chest and trying to rip out my fucking heart.

I swallow the lump in my throat. "Let's hike down to the bottom. Could be fun? Lots of... walking... and... safety?"

"Oh, that's cute." She pats my chest. "You want to take the scenic route? Maybe stop for a snack? Sing to all the woodland creatures on the way down?"

I scowl. "I'm serious."

"So am I. How about you take your little leisure stroll and enjoy the show from down there?"

Shit. The livestream. Our audience:

MOMMY AND DADDY ARE FIGHTING.
Protective Reece is making me feel things.
JUMP CAM, JUMP!
She's not your property!
If this is about her thong, blink twice.

Oh, good. The internet thinks I'm a joy-blocking control freak.

The determination blazing in her eyes tells me I'm fighting a losing battle. I could throw down the authority card—play the boss angle—but that would only make her more likely to do something reckless the instant I turn my back.

"Fine." I snatch the selfie stick. "But I'm jumping first. When I decide it's safe, then you can jump."

"Whatever you say, boss." She crosses her arms under her chest, giving her cleavage an extra boost that's impossible to ignore. *Talk about a power move.*

Focus, dammit. Someone's gotta protect those magnificent boobs, and apparently, today that someone is me.

I edge closer to the drop, mentally calculating trajectories. The water below is crystal clear—thank fuck—making it easy to spot the deepest section. My eyes scan for any hidden rocks, debris, or other threats. The darker blue patches signal deeper waters, so I map out the safest entry point with military precision.

"Listen…" I turn back to her. "You don't jump unless I give the all-clear. Got it?"

She rolls her eyes but doesn't argue.

"Squad, I do tons of stupid shit on this channel, but quick PSA—I'm a professional stunt person, and I take safety very seriously. Please, for the love of God, don't try this at home. Unless you want your mom to hunt me down and shave off my eyebrows."

I take off running.

The ground flies beneath my feet.

My blood pounds in my ears.

The edge is there—one final step—then nothing.

For a split second, I am weightless.

The wind tears at my skin, ripping through my hair, rushing past my ears with a deafening roar. My stomach lurches as my body surrenders to the fall, gravity yanking me toward the water below.

"WOOOOOOOOO!!!"

SPLASH.

The impact is a freight train slamming against my feet, water engulfing me, swallowing me whole. Cold. Sharp. Invigorating. My body surges to life, muscles tightening, lungs burning for air.

I kick up hard, breaking the surface with a gasping inhale, my body shaking from the rush.

Still got the camera. *Hell yeah!*

Above me, I see Cam's face peering over the edge, ponytail blowing in the breeze—she's a goddess surveying her kingdom.

"How was it?" she yells.

"Well, I don't usually say this, but keep your legs closed upon entry."

She laughs, asking, "Is it cold?"

"You might want to give your nipples a pep talk first!"

"What is it with you and my breasts?"

Yeah, let's not unpack that particular obsession right now.

"Jump EXACTLY where I did!" I swim to the side. "I mean it, Cam—RIGHT here!"

"I heard you the first time, pendejo!"

Before I can protest further, she's already running. I hold my breath. She launches herself off the cliff, arms stretched, body sleek and powerful, her hair whipping behind her. Her battle cry echoes off the rocks as she arcs through the air. She's a damn action movie heroine.

SPLASH!

She surfaces with a gasp. "Holy shitballs, that's cold!"

"Warned you." My eyes automatically drop to her chest and—yep, those nipples are standing at attention. I jerk my gaze away before she catches me being a perv. *Real classy, dude.*

"What do you think, fam?" She grins at the fans. "Should we go again?"

I search for an ally in the chat like a fool:

YESSS DO IT AGAIN!

Cam you're a badass!

Marry me Cam! I'll treat you better than Reece!

Shoot your shot bros, she's too good for him!

"Guess you've got some competition, Dare." She smirks then starts swimming toward the rocks, her powerful strokes cutting through the water with practiced ease.

I don't just follow. I'm a goddamn hawk watching every movement.

She hauls herself up, water cascading off her skin like something out of a *Sports Illustrated* photoshoot. The rocks are slick with algae, treacherous under her feet. Once again, every cell in my body screams to protect her.

"Maybe I should go first—"

She whirls on me. "If you don't knock off this suddenly overprotective caveman routine, I will personally introduce your balls to these very pointy rocks. If you're so worried about my safety, stay below to catch me if I fall. Now come on!"

A shriek splits the air like a banshee with a megaphone.

"BLAZE! STOP! PUT ME DOWN! NOOOOOOOO!"

I swing the camera to catch my former best friend holding my ex-fiancé, who thrashes in his arms, as they leap from the cliff in one chaotic lurch.

"Woo-hoo!" and "Whhyyyyyy!" fill the air.

SPLASH.

When they surface, Astrid's makeup resembles a raccoon who climbed out of a washing machine.

"MY LASHES! My extensions! Do you know how many vape pens I had to sell to pay for these?!" She thrashes in the water like a mermaid with aquaphobia. "How am I supposed to film now? I look disgusting! This water is gross! Everything is RUINED!"

"Bro!" Blaze's face lights up when he spots me. "Did you see that epic entrance?"

"Yeah man, but…" I nod toward the cliffs. "You've got a problem. There's only one way outta here… UP."

Astrid's shriek can be heard on the next island over. "Are you freaking kidding me? I have to climb those rocks?"

"Good luck with that crisis." I smirk. "It's pretty obvious who got the better gal."

It's nice to see the fans agree with me:

Is that Astrid or a WET DOG?
Reece, buddy, you really dodged a bullet.
Karma's a b*tch and so is she!
Bro definitely upgraded with Cam.

I gaze up, and Cam's already halfway up the rock wall.
Does she ever wait?

Shoving the filming stick into the holster I'm carrying, I grab the first rock and start climbing.

Every muscle in my body reminds me to lock in on the rocks *(and only the rocks)* above me. The grip. The next handhold. The safe foothold—

But my stupid eyes betray me instantly. When I glance up, her booty moves in hypnotic motion. I'm blinded by that ass-terpiece. With each step, her butt cheeks clench that wet string that connects to a whisper of fabric covering her pussy.

Fuuucccckkkk me.

Her thighs flex, calves tightening as she hoists herself onto the next ledge. Her hips curve, twisting with each step, and I'm entranced by her ponytail that's sticking to her sweaty, damp neck.

Focus on the rocks. The rocks are your friends. The rocks don't make you want to hump them silly.

I climb faster, gritting my teeth.

We make it to the top just in time to witness Blaze pushing Astrid onto the ridge like he's trying to load an angry cat into a carrier.

"MY NAIL! This is YOUR fault!"

"We gotta hurry, babe!" Blaze bounces on his toes. "So we can jump again!"

"We are NOT jumping again, you walnut! And when we get back to the resort, you are in SO much trouble!"

Blaze grins widely. "You mean like hate sex? That sounds hot!"

Astrid lets out a deep groan as if she's summoning the underworld.

Cam adjusts her skimpy bikini top—*don't look, don't look, absolutely DO NOT look*—and reaches for the phone.

"My turn to film."

"I'll make you a deal. You can have the camera if I can hold your hand and we jump together."

She eyes me suspiciously, but I catch a hidden smile. "Fine."

Her hand slides into mine, warm and small but strong. We back up together. "Ready?"

She squeezes my hand. We run. We leap. We fly.

SPLASH!

The cold is a shockwave ripping through me, but when I break the surface, I'm grinning. Hard.

Cam swipes the dripping strands from her face, laughing, breathless, holding the streaming device up triumphantly.

She's so goddamn beautiful. Flushed. Excited. Totally unguarded.

"That was amazing!" she gasps.

Then... I panic. Because something is missing.

Something important.

Something red.

"Shit. Cam? Where's your top?"

I pull her against my chest, shielding her from millions of prying eyes. The feeling of her bare breasts pressed against me is torture. Her hardened nipples graze my skin like tiny sparks of electricity, her mouth almost touching mine as we tread water. Even with the waterfall roaring behind us, I swear I can hear her quick, shallow breaths. Despite the cold water, the heat of her body bleeds into mine, and something inside me just... snaps.

I kiss her.

Two fucking years of longing and holding back, of telling myself no—I finally taste her. We bob in the water, and I kick harder to keep us steady as her lips crash into mine. It's like discovering fire. This is why lips were invented.

She makes this tiny gasp of surprise against my mouth, but then her lips part for my tongue, and her free arm clutches the back of my neck, pulling me closer.

My fingers tangle in her wet hair, tilting her head to deepen the kiss, to taste more, to devour. I pour every ounce of pent-up desperation into her. Water splashes wildly as we kiss and kick, frantic and breathless. I should slow down. I should be gentle. But then she wraps a leg around my waist, using the water's buoyancy to press herself flush against me, grinding directly onto my now painfully hard cock.

The moan she releases is filthy perfection—half surprise, half need—and it shoots through me like my blood is now lava. My hand finds her ass under the water, gripping, guiding her movements as she rocks against my shaft. Our legs tangle as we try to stay afloat, but I don't care if we sink to the bottom of this pool.

I kiss her how I want to fuck her—hard, fast, devastating—

"Bro, get it!" Blaze's voice shatters the moment.

Reality crashes in. We're not alone.

I'm still treading water and supporting her with one arm when I pull back, and my heart plummets at her expression. Her eyes are wide, shocked, but there's something else in her gaze—confusion, vulnerability, the slightest bit of panic.

Like I just crossed a line. One we can't uncross.

She's in complete and utter disbelief. And I hate that I did this to her.

I grab the selfie stick, my hand shaking as I check the screen. Fuck me sideways. The chat is moving so fast, it's just a rainbow blur. The viewer count sends ice through my veins: fifty million. I kill the stream without even saying goodbye.

The whole damn internet just watched me maul my employee like a pent-up teenager. The one woman who was supposed to stay firmly in the "do not touch" category. *She's your fake girlfriend. FAKE!*

Way to go, dickhead.

You were supposed to make things up to her, not make out with her.

But Jesus Christ, those lips. Those little whimpers she makes. The way she tastes...

No. Mistake made. Lesson learned.

Pull your shit together. Keep your fucking distance. This can't happen again.

CHAPTER TWELVE

CAM

Group Chat : CPK Forever

Me: *911 HELP: How do u cope when ur boss melts ur brain with a kiss... then ghosts you?*

Petra: *THAT LIPLOCK TOOK DOWN THE OF-FICE WIFI. My bro legit paused a meeting to replay it.*

Katie: *Aunt Deb's exact words: "When a man kisses like that, darling, you better start stretching, because that's just the appetizer"*

Petra: *What happened to fake dating for views?*

Me: *WE ARE! Someone needs to tell my vajayjay.*

Katie: *There was nothing fake about the way he devoured you.*

Petra: *Or the way you wrapped those legs around him.*

Katie: *Your whole body must still be buzzing.*

Me: *Worst. Lady. Boner. Ever.*

Reece might be dead.

Or maybe he simply forgot how to function as a human being.

I should probably check for a pulse, but that would require touching him, and he's currently doing his best statue impression. Like, hasn't moved, spoken, or possibly even breathed since we climbed into this shuttle of sexual tension. He's angled toward the aisle as if I've got a contagious disease he'll contract through prolonged eye contact.

My hands grip the seat tightly as we navigate this bumpy, nausea-inducing ride down the Maui mountains. Fat raindrops begin to sprinkle against the window glass, trailing down in slow, lazy patterns. The gorgeous coastline stretches before us, and I try to focus on the water instead of acknowledging the wall of frustration radiating from the man beside me. But my brain keeps spinning, kinda like our rotating sex bed—replaying everything that's happened since sunrise.

Will the real Reece Dare please stand up?

Reece—the one from this morning—was different. He was... attentive. Present. His laugh was genuine, his smile captivating. The way he wrapped that blanket around us at Mount Haleakalā, his chest pressed against my back, his breath warming my neck as we watched the sun ignite the sky. For a moment, I let myself believe he actually wanted to be there. *With me.*

And don't even get me started on the chat comments. How the fans went absolutely crazy over us, over *me*... It made me feel seen. Important. Like it's possible I wasn't just the lackluster videographer he's been criticizing for two years. Maybe I *do* belong in front of the camera and people *would* care about the stories I want to tell.

But I totally blew my opportunity to ask Reece to promote my channel. After he confessed, *there's no way I could've managed these last few years without you. Even now, I... I'm glad you're here.*

Don't ask me to string two words together after that truth bomb.

Did he really mean that?

Does he need... me?

A bump in the road shifts me closer to him, and memories of that kiss flood back. Steam was definitely visible on the livestream from the heat we generated in that waterfall pool. How his hands gripped my ass, guiding my movements as I rocked against his—

¡Mierda! I squirm in my seat, trying to dispel the ache pulsing in my core.

And now? He's over there pretending it never happened, as if fifty million viewers (*and counting*) didn't just witness our full-body, hot as fuck, dangerously erotic moment.

I squeeze my thighs together, willing my traitorous lady bits to *calm the fuck down*, but that only makes things worse because my entire body craves the feel of him. My shoulders wiggle as the delicious sensation zings through me.

Reece's head snaps toward me, his eyes dark with what seems like irritation—or desire. Then, his gaze goes directly down to my tits.

And *ohhhhh shit.*

Because let's not forget that little detail where I lost my bikini top. Which means I am sitting here wearing nothing but a wet, white DareGirl tank, with my very enthusiastic nipples making a guest appearance.

He stiffens from head to toe. His throat bobs. His fingers flex. And then—he averts his eyes, jaw clenching so hard I swear I hear his teeth cracking.

So, that's how we're playing this?

Kiss me like your life depends on it, grope me so passionately my mind explodes, but then ignore me?

If he wants to be distant and broody, FINE. Two can play that game.

He can sulk in silence while I daydream about all the things his lips could be doing—besides staying shut. *Wait, no. That's not what I meant.*

Kai's voice takes on a rare serious tone as he stands near the driver, facing us. "My friends, if you look to your left, you'll see Lahaina town. The fire was one of Maui's darkest days. A lot of you may have seen it on the news, the former capital of the Kingdom of Hawaii—our crown jewel—lost many of its iconic structures. Countless homes reduced to ashes."

The rain streaks down my window like silent tears as the devastation comes into view. Where vibrant storefronts and houses once stood, there's only... emptiness. Charred remnants and hollow foundations stretch toward a gray sky, as if the town itself is reaching out, begging to be remembered. The humidity fogs up the glass, but nevertheless, I can make out the brutal evidence of nature's fury—blackened walls, twisted metal, spaces where entire buildings simply ceased to exist.

A heavy silence fills the shuttle. Even the newlyweds in the back stop their canoodling to listen.

"The loss runs deep," Kai says, the usual swagger in his voice completely absent. "Heritage runs deep. But the people here? They are resilient." He draws a breath before adding, "If anyone is interested, Aloha Amour Resort partners with local volunteers to help rebuild.

We also hold a weekly spiritual ceremony to honor those lost. You are welcome to participate."

I fumble for my phone, trying to capture something—anything—through the foggy, rain-streaked window.

"You're not gonna get a good shot."

Oh, look who decided to speak. Mr. Critical is back, right on schedule.

"Really? Thanks for the hot tip, Captain Obvious." I zoom in anyway, refusing to give up. "I had no idea windows could be difficult to shoot through. Is that the kind of premium insight that comes with your millions of subscribers?"

"Why are you wasting your time?"

"Right, because if it won't go viral, why bother? I know it's not another shirtless Will It Explode? video, but God forbid we document something that actually matters."

He opens his mouth to respond, but I'm livid. "This was somewhere I wanted to visit, but between your aggressive content schedule and Gordon's demands, I didn't have time." My voice catches embarrassingly. "Do you realize how many people are still displaced? How many reconstruction efforts have stalled because of funding? Some residents can't even get basic services restored because of bureaucratic bullsh—"

I exhale, trying to steady myself. "I... I wanted to take some photos. Remind others on social media that this cause still needs attention. These people *still* need help. Just because it's not trending anymore doesn't mean it's fixed."

"And the pictures would... help?"

"Yeah. Probably… I think so. I hope so. You definitely can't know if you don't try. Not everything needs a million likes to make a difference."

For a heartbeat, his expression changes—like I've caught him off guard—and the way he looks at me makes my breath catch. Then, his eyes fall to my mouth, and everything shifts. A fiery anticipation ignites within me, coursing through my veins like liquid sunshine. Every inch of me is alive, yearning for the electric touch of his lips, the rough caress of his hands. His gaze lingers, and I want to reach out, to bridge the gap between us…

But I'm frozen in place, held captive by his swirling storm of emotions.

Then, as if a switch is flipped, his features harden into that familiar scowl. "Well, I don't think blurry rainy photos are going to cut it."

He turns away, ending the conversation, and I do the same. Through the window, Lahaina disappears from view, along with my chance to capture even a glimpse of its story. But it's not the missed opportunity that has my blood boiling—it's him.

How is it that, despite his whole Jekyll-and-Hyde routine, I crave his touch? *Seriously, get it together, girl!* Yet the torturous push and pull of him is addictive—as if I enjoy being breathless and internally screaming. What kind of dark magic is this?

Somebody call a priest—my vagina needs an exorcism.

***

THE RAGING STORM IS biblical—a darkened sky unleashes its fury with thick sheets of rain, while trees are furiously being battered by the winds. It's nothing compared to the seething storm inside of me. I burst out of the shuttle like a sprinter at the starting gun, desperate to escape the suffocating weight of Reece's silence.

Rain hammers the pavement as guests scramble toward the hotel lobby, where the standing, smiling workers resemble a welcoming committee. They're armed with fluffy white towels, ponchos, and those stupid gift bags that probably contain more of Kai's sex toys. Wind whips through the open-air space, knocking over flower displays and sending brochures flying in every direction.

I don't stop.

I walk straight through the crowd and right out the nearest door.

I step outside, and the rain swallows me whole.

It's so cold, it steals the breath from my lungs, instantly soaking my tank top and shorts, plastering them to me like a second skin. Water slides down my neck, trailing over my collarbones, pooling in the hollow between my breasts. I sprint through the downpour, my feet splashing through puddles reflecting the violent sky.

I don't care. I need space. I need distance from him.

"Cam!" Reece's voice cuts through the thunder.

I keep walking.

"What the hell are you doing?" he demands, his voice closer now.

I whirl around, barely able to see him through the thick curtain of rain. "Getting away from you!"

"It's not safe out here." Lightning flashes, highlighting every ridge of muscle beneath his soaked shirt. "You need to come back inside."

Fury explodes inside me. "I think you're confused about your role in my life. You are not my real boyfriend. You're my *fake* boyfriend. Which means you don't get an opinion about what I do and whether or not it's safe."

"I may not be your boyfriend, but I am your boss."

"¡Ay, Dios mío! Has it been ten whole minutes already?" I throw my arms wide as thunder shakes the ground. "Hey, Hawaii! Did you hear that? *Reece Dare* is my *BOSS*! Quick, someone carve that into a totem pole for everybody to read! Oh wait. The world already knows because you never shut up about it!"

Reece drags a rough hand down his face, cursing under his breath.

The rain pounds against my skin as I march up to him, jabbing my finger to his chest. "Being my boss does not mean you get a say in my personal life."

We're toe to toe, so close I feel the heat radiating off his body. Water drips from his dark hair, trailing down his neck, and my traitorous gaze follows its path. His breathing is sharp and uneven, matching the frantic rhythm of my own.

God, I want him to kiss me. To finish what he started in that waterfall.

My skin burns where raindrops hit, every nerve ending alive with anticipation. What would happen if I just... leaned in? Would he push me away? Or would he grab me, crush me against him, remind me exactly why I can't think straight when he's near?

The thought of him taking me right here on the rain-soaked grass makes my core clench so fucking hard with need, my knees buckle. I want his hands on my skin, his mouth claiming mine, his body pressing me into the earth while the storm rages around us. I swear I can hear my own heartbeat over the thunder, can feel the charge in the air, buzzing, building, pressing against my ribs as if it's yearning to get out.

And Reece? He's standing there, rain running off his dark, soaked hair. His breathing is measured, as if he's trying to hold something in. His storm-blue eyes flick over my face—burning, calculating—before he takes a giant step back, putting physical space between us.

"I hear you." His voice is rough. "Will you *please* come to the room and get out of the rain?"

"Fine. Since you said please... but mainly because I'm freezing."

When I say "freezing," his gaze drops to my chest. The rain has turned my shirt completely see-through, and he doesn't even try to hide his stare at my stiff nipples.

"Are you fucking kidding me?!"

I let out an exasperated groan and stomp back to the hotel. I'm done. Done with this storm. Done with his unreadable grumpy face. Done with his mood swings.

I hear his footsteps behind me as I march down the hallway. "Cam, wait—"

Nope. Not happening. I pick up the pace, a woman marching on a warpath.

"Will you stop—"

Absolutely not. I reach our room first and slam the door in his face.

Two seconds later, the door unlocks.

"Real mature." He barges in looking like a wet dream in a bad mood then strides over to stand in the shower area. He snags a towel and starts roughly drying his hair.

I cross my arms, still dripping wet, shivering, and seething with anger.

Finally, he yanks the towel down and glares at me. "You're getting water all over the floor."

"Oh, I'm sorry. Is my inconvenient wetness bothering you? I guess you better report me to the Housekeeping Police."

He gestures—wildly—at the carpet. "You're standing there leaking, while I'm over here being a responsible adult and drying myself off."

"You want me to dry off? Sure thing, boss." I march over, grab the hem of my tank top, and start pulling it off.

"Whoa! What are you doing?"

"Getting out of these wet clothes that you can see through anyway." I arch an eyebrow. "What's the big deal? You've been staring at my boobs all day. You're practically best friends now."

He clears his throat. "We both need to change. Let's just... not face each other."

"Whatever."

We turn our backs to each other, as if preparing for a duel, and I begin to peel off my wet, sticky clothes from my chilled skin. Every reflective surface reveals a different angle of him doing the same. I notice him stealing glances at me too, our eyes meeting briefly in the mirror before shifting away.

In record time, we put on the fluffy white hotel robes, both tying the belts with more force than necessary. I'm ready to give him another piece of my mind—maybe mention how that kiss didn't mean shit.

KNOCK! KNOCK!

Reece exhales sharply, rubbing his temples. "What now?"

I yank open the door and immediately regret it. One of "Kai's Best Friends" beams at me and holds a sleek white bag with a gold ribbon wrapped around it.

"Aloha, lovers!" he beams, handing me the gift pack. "We noticed you didn't take your Rainy Day Pleasure Bag when you arrived, so we wanted to make sure you got it! Also, room service is available whenever you need. And if there's anything else we can do to help you have an orgasmic evening, please don't hesitate to ask!"

"Thanks," I grit out before closing the door.

I peek inside and—¡Mierda!—there's another obnoxiously large vibrator. I yank it out of the bag and hold it up like a weapon, gripping it tight and pointing it as I lay down the law.

"That's fucking it! I cannot keep pretending this tension between us isn't making me absolutely feral."

Reece's eyes go huge, his gaze ping-ponging between my face and the vibrator I'm waving.

"I know this relationship is fake—but the throb between my legs? That shit is very fucking real."

"You think you're the only one who's sexually frustrated? I fucking kissed you, Cam."

And that's when it hits me.

The kiss. It wasn't about me. It wasn't some earth-shattering moment of passion where he couldn't resist me anymore.

It was pent-up, sex-starved frustration. Exactly like mine.

I narrow my eyes. "Then I propose we do something about it."

Reece goes completely still.

The only sound is the fierce storm outside, wind battering the windows, rain pounding against the glass as if Mother Nature herself is a co-conspirator screaming, *Just fuck already!*

His voice is tight, careful. "Together?"

"Well, Gordon made it pretty damn clear we can't do it with anyone else."

For the first time, I see his internal battle—logic battling animalistic need.

"I don't think it's a good idea," he finally mutters, voice gruff, but there's a crack in his restraint now. I can feel it.

"Why not? How long has it been since you've had sex, Dare?"

He says nothing. That hesitation? Dead giveaway.

"You already know my sad story," I say. "Six months. You said 'a while.' Fess up. How long?"

"... A year."

"¡Mierda! No wonder you kissed me."

He starts to apologize, but I cut him off. "You can't take it back. That kiss happened. And now my poor, deprived, pathetically touch-starved body has officially reached its tipping point." I step forward, tilting my chin up, locking eyes with him. "So either you have sex with me, or I'm going to fuck myself."

And then something happens I've never seen in my entire life.

Reece's dick jumps.

Not a twitch.

Not a flinch.

A full-on, fucking leap—right under his robe.

I deliberately drag my gaze down. "Huh. That's interesting."

"I should go."

"Go. Stay. I don't care."

I fiddle with the buttons on the device, finally managing to turn it on. The V-shaped gadget buzzes to life, one end spinning while the other vibrates intensely.

"God, what the hell does that do?"

"Simultaneous clit and G-spot stimulation." I grin, turning it over in my hand, admiring it like a fine wine. "It'll get the job done. And then some."

His eyes turn molten.

I step closer. "We've established we don't like each other, yeah?"

He hesitates. "Uh huh."

"So I'll give you the option. Stay, and if you decide to join me, great. I get some extra orgasms."

The vibrator purrs between us, and I switch it off.

"But regardless, I'm experiencing some pleasure right fucking now."

I strut toward the bed, my pulse pounding, my skin burning with a need so intense it's insane. I drop my robe, letting it slip off my shoulders and pool onto the floor like a discarded afterthought. The room chills my bare skin, but I'm already on fire, already too far gone. Slowly, I lie back on the massive, luxurious bed, stretching lazily and savoring the cool silk sheets against my flushed skin.

And then I do the most reckless thing I've ever done in my life.

I spread my legs wide open.

And Reece falls to his knees like I've punched the air out of his lungs.

"Oh my God."

His voice is broken, reverent, as if he's at the pearly gates but knows he doesn't deserve to be there. His fingers tremble at his sides, every inch of him tense and frozen, staring as if he can't decide whether to flee or bury his face between my thighs and beg for redemption.

I grab the vibrator, click it on, and slide it inside myself—never breaking eye contact.

"I... c-can w-w-watch?"

I smirk, shifting my hips as I press the toy deeper, dragging it slowly, teasing, until a shuddery moan escapes me.

"If that's all you want." My voice is breathless, knowing, challenging. "I'm happy to get off to your gorgeous, tortured face. Seems to be all I think about anyhow."

The second it slips out, my stomach flips. Because—*shit. Where the hell did that come from?*

Reece's breathing stutters; his brows pull together as if he's processing the confession, dissecting it, maybe even tucking it away for later use.

And then the vibrator switches speeds on its own, the sensation turning sharp, insistent. "Oh fuck, yes." The words slide out on a ragged moan, my back lifting off the sheets.

Reece growls, slamming his palms onto the mattress, his chest heaving, his fingers digging in. He looks ready to launch himself onto the bed and wreck me.

"Goddammit, Cam. I can't. We shouldn't—"

I press the buzzing device farther in, roll my hips rhythmically to meet the sensation, and moan shamelessly. "Finally. This feels so fucking good."

A strangled curse tears from Reece's throat, and before I even register the movement, he rips open his robe, shoves it off his shoulders, and grips his cock in one big, desperate fist.

Jesus.

I knew he was packing, but *fuck.*

Watching him pleasure himself, muscles tensing along his jaw, abs flexing with each deliberate stroke, his free hand gripping the bed like he's fighting the urge to pounce on me.

It's too much. It's not enough.

It's everything.

"Tell me," he grits out, his palm gliding over his thick, hard length. "Does it feel warm and deep, like it's my cock inside you. Stretching you, filling you?"

I shudder, his words sparking an inferno within me—heat licking through my core. "Yes."

"Fuck, you'd feel so good," His mouth is close to my inner thigh, hot and teasing, but he doesn't touch me. "Would you squeeze me with those hot-as-fuck inner muscles?"

I pant through the building pleasure, my thighs trembling. "Hard."

His groan melts my inhibitions, urging me to go further than I should.

"So hard... you'd pass out... from forgetting to breathe."

His breath hitches, muscles going rigid as he teeters on the edge.

"Fuck, I'm close."

"Me too, Dare."

Reece stands over me, steadying himself with one arm beside my head, his face hovering near mine, so close we could kiss. His breath is harsh and ragged, his cock jolting in his grip, like he's about to detonate all over me.

And God help me, I want to be the one to push the button.

"Let's finish together," he growls. "Turn it on high."

"I don't recall asking you to be in charge."

"I think your pussy wants me to take control."

His eyes flash, his smirk wicked, and suddenly, his hand moves. Straight for the vibrator. He switches it to high.

"Reece—"

A sharp wave of pleasure rips through me, my hips jerking violently, my moan breaking into a whimper.

"Holy shit, that's intense!" I cry out.

"Don't turn it down." His voice is low, commanding. "You can take it because it's how I would fuck you. Now, thrust it harder. I want to come with you."

My hand moves faster, matching the frantic rhythm of Reece's strokes above me.

His hand skims the edge of my pubic bone, the faintest whisper of contact, but he doesn't pull away. His knuckles press against me as he pulls his shaft, hovering over me, his hips jerking forward with every slick stroke.

Reece makes a noise so low, so primal, it skates down my spine like fire.

I pant. "Imagine you're inside me. How does my pussy feel?"

"It's fucking heaven. Soft, wet, perfect. Your velvety walls are squeezing me, hugging every thrust. It's—" He cuts himself off as his head tilts back, the tendons in his neck pulling taut as he fists his cock harder.

I roll my hips, thrusting the vibrator deeper, chasing that white-hot burn beneath my skin. "I'm throbbing for you," I rasp.

"Jesus, yes." His chest rises and falls in sharp, heavy movements. "I bet I would feel you pulsing, baby. You want to come for me right now."

"Fuck yes." My voice breaks, my thighs tightening, my movements frantic. "I want you harder."

Reece growls, his hand pumping himself in time with my thrusts, his gaze glued to my body falling apart beneath him.

"You can have whatever the fuck you want, baby."

And God, the sight of him—his thick, strong frame shuddering, his stomach clenching with every stroke, his cock leaking, as if he can't hold on—

I want his come so bad it hurts.

Inside me. On me. All over me.

I want to reach up, grab him, push him in deep, feel the stretch, feel the weight, feel every thick inch of him filling me up until I can't take any more. I whimper, squeezing the toy harder, picturing it's his cock doubling down on me.

"Reece! Now."

The words barely make it past my lips before I explode, my orgasm ripping through me with violent force, my back arching, a high, broken moan spilling from my mouth as I shatter completely.

Reece lets out a powerful, wrecked groan, his body convulsing, his strokes stuttering.

"Camila—fuck, yes—Cam."

Thick, hot streams of his release coat my stomach, warmth spilling over my skin, his lower half shaking, his breath ragged, uneven, his forehead dropping to my shoulder as he's erupting.

My chest heaves, my skin damp and overheated, my limbs weak and boneless.

I reach down, click off the vibrator, my head still spinning, my pulse erratic, the room now thick with our scent of sex and sweat. I turn my head, ready to say something, to crack a joke, to anchor us back to reality before we fall too far off the deep end.

But before I even move.

Reece jerks up, pushing off the bed so fast he stumbles, his chest rising and falling as if he just ran a marathon. He grabs his robe, yanks it around himself, his fingers fumbling with the belt like he's afraid I'll rip it off.

His warm release cools on my skin as his face shuts down completely. I blink, trying to process why he's acting as if he's committed a goddamn felony. "Reece, that was—"

"So wrong."

What?

"Jesus, Cam." His hand shakes as his gaze darts everywhere but me. "I'm sorry. Are you—good? I mean, fuck. Are you okay?"

"I'm more than okay. I think that's obvious—"

"I'm sorry." He grabs his phone, fumbling with it in a mad dash to exit.

Like he regrets what happened.

So then why did he shout my name when he came?

Before I can say a single fucking word...

He's gone.

And the door slams shut on the hottest orgasm of my life.

CHAPTER THIRTEEN

REECE

"**Can you hear me?** Mr. Dare?"

A man's voice pierces my consciousness like an aggressive alarm clock. I grunt in protest. Something feels... off.

Shit. Where the hell am I?

Reality trickles in slowly—the hardwood floor beneath me, a crick in my neck, and the distinct sense that I made some monumentally stupid decisions last night.

I crack one eye open, and—motherfucker—there's Kai in all his glistening glory, towering over me like a tropical Hercules. His long dark hair is swept up in that signature man bun. And his sarong? Crafted from fabric so flimsy it's basically a paper towel trying to house his anaconda.

The thing moves, and I bolt upright so fast my spine cracks like a glowstick. "Fuck!"

"Ah, wonderful!" Kai's voice booms. "Let us welcome the divine light of a new day!"

Blinding sunlight floods in as resort staff fling open the massive sliding wall doors. The whole space transforms to an open-air oasis in one point five seconds. Sheer white curtains ripple in the morning breeze, smacking me upside the head with waves of floral and salty sea air. The ocean crashes in the distance, and birds chirp—a little too smugly for my liking—because I know what they're saying.

Bro, you done fucked up.

The floors are polished bamboo *(which my spine now despises),* and a thatched roof arches high above the white walls. The room seamlessly blends with the outside world, offering a straight shot of blue sky and ocean. It's the kind of place Cam would sigh over, framing it perfectly, while I stood next to her, secretly eyeing her instead of the horizon.

I glance down at my wrinkled robe, and everything comes rushing back. Cam. The vibrator. Her stretched out on our bed—my wildest fantasy come true. The way she moaned my name. Touching myself while watching her. Then... oh yeah, I ran away like a fucking coward.

I'd wandered around the resort in a daze last night. Pondering what it meant, what it could mean, if it meant anything at all? *Of course it did, didn't it?* I kept overthinking in circles until, eventually, I saw the YOGA & MEDITATION sign. It seemed as good a place as any to hide from my problems. Clearly, I passed out mid-crisis.

"Will your curvaceous goddess be joining us for morning mediation? Camila's energy would bring such... passion to our practice."

The use of her name makes me possessive, and frankly it pisses me off. But it's early, so I'm calm-ish. "No. Actually, I should—"

Go where, genius? Back to our room where I left her? Where I bolted after the most intimate moment of my life? Where she made me feel so out of control, so needy, so utterly unsure of what it means.

I want her so badly it scares me. WTF am I gonna do?

"Stay. Clearly, your mind is not at peace. My class will quiet the inner chatter, melt away your problems, and guide you to release whatever you're holding on to."

My hands clench at my sides. My whole body is tight. It's a fucking coil wound up and ready to snap. I should say no. I should definitely not take life advice from a man who conducts drum circles with his dick.

But.

Maybe Hawaiian Thor is right. I need to figure out why I keep sabotaging myself. Understand why every time she gets close, I panic and run.

"Fine." I sigh, already regretting this decision. "But if I see any warriors or drums, I'm out."

The meditation room becomes a spiritual sardine can as guest after guest files in. People take their places on colorful mats, settling onto oversized floor cushions, their stupidly relaxed faces starting to annoy me. I claim a cushion near the front, hoping to focus on the beach view instead of Kai's... fully awakened chi.

Kai settles beside me, a preening peacock finding his favorite perch. "Aloha, lovers. I am honored to be your guide on this relaxation journey—where we'll unlock your most sacred tool." He pauses for dramatic effect. "Radical self-love."

Oh for fuck's sake. Crossing my legs, I plant my hands palms-up on my knees. I roll my shoulders, trying to shift the uncomfortable tension knotted in every muscle.

"Today we step out of the endless river of doing and drop into the act of *being*."

When was the last time I focused on just being?

Before the brand deals. Before the sponsorships. Before the grind of keeping this whole damn empire from collapsing under the weight of expectations.

I close my eyes, but the second darkness hits, she's there.

Cam.

Spread out like an offering. Her skin flushed, her eyes hungry, her legs open wide. That pretty pink cunt glistening, calling me to it. And the way she moaned my name like a dirty secret, how she writhed on the bed, needy and shameless, taking her pleasure.

And here we go again. My stiff cock has me shifting on the cushion, trying to adjust without drawing attention. Because that's exactly what I need—a boner in meditation class.

But I can't stop the memories. Can't stop wondering—*did she want me? Really want me? Or am I another cabana boy on her fuck list?*

No. The way she looked at me... Nobody's ever looked at me like that. She knew the *me* I was hiding behind my walls, and the kicker... she wanted me anyway.

The image of her face, confused and hurt, when I bolted flashes in my mind. Was that *regret* I saw? Or, more likely, the *wow, what a dickhead* expression I deserved. Yet again.

DING!

A chime rings through the room.

"With each inhale, feel a sense of calm and peace washing over you. With each exhale, let go of worries and distractions."

Ha! I came to this island with enough problems to fill the Pacific.

Cam's thoughts on Lahaina and the struggles of those uprooted resurface in my thoughts. Hearing her be so passionate about using social media for good. I used to be excited like that. I'd wake up energized about creating, about pushing boundaries, about inspiring people.

Now it's all about metrics. The views. The never-ending hamster wheel of churning out mass quantities of stock content to keep the machine running. Three hundred employees and their families depend on me.

My entire life is tied to this persona I've built.

DING!

"Now, let's take this connection to the next level." Kai holds up a book with a shirtless photo of himself on the cover. "Each of you will receive an autographed edition of my new book, the 'Kama Kai Sutra.' Consider it your passport to heightened levels of pleasure and—"

The Kama what now?

I scan the room, and—oh, fuck me—everyone here is paired up. Couples. All of them locked on to each other with that glazed "morning sex" expression. Linked fingers. Gentle thigh touches. This isn't meditation—this "mindfulness" is thinly disguised foreplay.

I have to leave right n—

DING!

"I call this breathing exercise the *Panting Passion*. Place your palm on your partner's chest and channel the energy flowing between you. Connect your breath."

Kai grabs my hand and places it on his greasy pecs. Damn! This man is made of granite. Okay. Deep breaths. *This isn't awful. Just two dudes, being bros, platonically vibing on each other's life force or whatever the hell this is.*

I shut my eyes to focus, but Kai's infuriatingly powerful heartbeat reminds me of his giant dick drum luau routine.

Ugh! This whole connection exercise is bullshit.

Trusting someone is like holding nitroglycerin—handle with extreme caution because one wrong move and everything explodes. I've got the emotional scars to prove it. The walls I've built are high for a reason—they're necessary, the difference between surviving and being gutted by someone else's greed.

Let's say for a minute that Cam could forgive me—could I trust her?

How do I know she's not Astrid 2.0? Another pretty face using me as her personal ladder to fame? My platform, my influence, my hard-earned brand is all people ever want. Why would she be any different?

That's not who Camila is. You know it. And that's what's scaring you shitless.

DING!

"This next pose, known as *Clasped in Climax*, is powerfully intimate and the most sacred of them all. Wrap your legs around your partner, rest your forehead against theirs, and allow your breaths to synchronize. Feel the beat of their core merging with your own."

All around me, people are entwining themselves around each other as if they're auditioning for Cirque du So-Laid. It's a goddamn synchronized sex wave.

Kai scoots his pelvis closer, his tree trunk legs widening open. "Shall we merge our sacred energies, my virile friend?" Kai purrs.

"Jesus—NO." I launch up, my body moving instinctively. "Sorry! Great class! Really... enlightening! Keep up the... orgy breathing exercises!"

A worker shoves Kai's book at me as I sprint for the door, taking out a potted plant in my escape.

"Your complimentary signed copy of *The Kama Kai Sutra*," she beams.

I take it and run. *Where am I going? No idea.*

There's no way I can go back to face Cam. Avoidance is clearly the only adult response here. Totally fine. I'll just... never see her again. Live in this robe. Hide in the meditation room in-between sex classes until my flight home. Problem solved.

Now if I could only mute the relentless soundtrack of her moans in my head.

***

I'VE SUCCESSFULLY DODGED CAM all day.

It's been a delicate balance of strategic maneuvers and tactical avoidance. I know I'm a spineless, avoidant, emotionally stunted scaredy-cat. At this point I'd rather run into actual gunfire than face her, because she's gotta be pissed, and rightfully so.

The bonfire flames flicker and dance in front of me, each amber fleck matching the acid churning in my gut. I'm sweating balls, and not due to the fire. It's because I'm completely screwed and I know it.

My eyes sweep over the growing crowd, my heart hammering against my ribs. No sign of her. Both a blessing and a curse, all rolled into one.

Behind me, dozens of white tents line the beach in perfect Instagram-worthy rows, their canvas walls rippling in the breeze. Each one is equipped with—I shit you not—massage oils, LED mood lighting, and what the info pamphlet calls "a passion enhancement kit." It's like someone gave Kai an unlimited budget and said, *Make camping sensual.*

I glance down at my outfit—living proof that desperation makes you do stupid things. After fleeing the meditation class, I raided the resort gift shop rather than return to our room. My shirt reads, SAVE THE RHINOS... ONE RIDE AT A TIME, in eye-searing neon, featuring two extremely enthusiastic rhinos mid-coitus. And, as if my humiliation wasn't enough, the matching Hawaiian-print shorts boast another literary masterpiece: WELCOME TO THE LU-WOW!

With hibiscus flowers arranged in the shape of an arrow and pointing to my dick.

Three hundred dollars of panic-induced shame. But hey, that included a much-needed phone charger.

All day, I've been strategizing how to survive this night: shoot the livestream, then GTFO before my dignity waves the white flag. Because no way—NO. WAY.—am I making eye contact with Cam and admitting that I'm obsessed with watching her fuck that vibrator.

RING! RING!

My phone shakes against my thigh. Gordon. Again. There are only two reasons why my manager FaceTimes me.

1. He's about to deliver bad news disguised as "great news.

2. He got a new skincare procedure and wants validation.

I answer quickly before he can send a string of threatening emojis. His face pops on screen. Whatever emotion he's having is hidden by that disturbingly smooth, chemically frozen forehead, stretched so tight I could ice skate on it. Then he flashes his overly whitened, blinding veneer smile that's too big for his face.

It's as if every cosmetic procedure is fighting for dominance.

I brace myself. "Gordon."

"There's my comeback kid! Views are through the roof—they're insane! We're talking record-breaking engagement. The algorithm is sucking you off like a Dyson vacuum."

"That's... great."

"Great? Kid, it's astronomical! The sponsors are crawling back, begging to work with you. And guess what? G-Thorne is charging them triple what they were paying pre-Astrid. Who, by the way, is yesterday's news. Dead content walking. You and camera girl? Hottest thing since Bennifer 2.0!"

His manic energy ratchets up another notch. "DareGirl merch? Sold out. Backordered through next quarter. I've got designers creating new couples' lines as we speak. And don't even get me started on the DareFuel flavors we're rushing to production. Yeah, overtime's gonna cost us, but trust me—it'll be worth every penny."

"So the shoe line? Everyone's jobs? We're good?"

"Better than good, superstar! We're golden."

The stress ulcer that's been my constant companion since Astrid went full runaway bride finally unclenches—

"Which is why I'm working with your publicist on a launch tour. You and Cam, ten cities minimum. Every major outlet wants you two. People can't get enough of America's new favorite couple."

—and instantly reclenches. "Gordon, we only planned this fake relationship for Hawaii."

"That was before your waterfall makeout session became Gen Z's *The Notebook*! That smooch has over a billion replays. People are recreating your kiss everywhere—pools, fountains, kitchen sinks. I saw one couple try it in their fish tank! The DareDuo is dead. Long live DareLove!"

"Fake girlfriend reporting for duty, *boss*!"

Every cell in my body freezes, then ignites.

Cam stands there, the embodiment of all my wet dreams combined. Her white tennis skirt is so short it barely qualifies as a napkin, and I want to wipe my mouth with it. Paired with a hot-pink tube top that might as well be airbrushed onto her skin. *Goddamn!*

And right across her perfect, braless tits?

DareGirl.

My name.

Over her un-fucking-mistakable pebbled nipples.

I *should* be concerned about the wicked glint in her eyes. But my brain? PRE. OC. U. PIED.

Her hair falls in wild waves, one side pulled back with a pink hibiscus flower, and those lips—*fuck me*—glossed in pink like she's begging to be kissed. Or maybe they want to be wrapped around my—

It takes me a second to realize... I haven't blinked. Or breathed. Or remembered how to form words. My mouth feels as if I've been gargling sand.

That sly grin tugging at the corner of her lips tells me she's fully aware of her effect on me. Either that, or she's admiring my shirt design of rhinos getting frisky.

"What?" She blinks innocently. "You don't like it? I'm wearing your merch like the good fake girlfriend I am." She does a slow twirl, and—*fuck me*—hot-pink lace flashes under her tantalizing mini skirt.

"Exactly!" Gordon's eyes rake over her as if she's the merchandise. "Looking like a whole snack, gorgeous!"

I grip my phone so hard it cracks a little.

"So dish! What's the next viral moment from my favorite power couple? We need something bigger! Spicier! More—" he chef-kisses the air "—marketable!"

"That's up to Reece. He's the boss, after all. He decides what gets initiated." Her eyes lock with mine. "He doesn't like it when *I* initiate things."

First shot fired—she's coming in hot. Direct hit!

"We'll figure something out."

"That's my boy! Just remember—" Gordon wags his finger, "keep it advertiser-friendly! This isn't OnlyFans!" He swivels his attention to Cam—a shark smelling blood. "And, camera gir—I mean, Cam. We need to talk contracts. Legal's drafting something big. I've got your whole schedule mapped out when you get back."

Her expression flickers. Unease. *Does she seem panicked?*

"But Gordon, after this... Remember the email about my—"

"Exposure is everything! This is the big leagues, and when the algorithm gives you a gift, you jack that bull off until he's shooting blanks, comprende?"

The light dims in Cam's eyes. I watch her shoulders tense. She's being strong-armed into extending this lie, and I'm the useless asshole letting it happen.

"We gotta go. Livestream's starting."

"Remember to keep that money train—"

I end the call. Silence stretches between us.

The waves pound against the shore, the bonfire crackles, and the humid night air clings to my skin like a punishment.

"Cam—"

"Save it. Let's do our job and give Gordon his content."

She's furious. And fuck, she has every right to be.

"I won't touch you."

"Wise choice. You're not ready to see what happens if you try."

I pull out my phone, hit *Go Live*, and—*POOF*—transform into YouTuber Reece faster than Peter Parker slipping on his Spidey suit.

"What's up, DareSquad! Coming at you live from this insane beach bonfire with my beautiful—"

"Who wants to play a GAME?" Her smile is pure mischief.

Oh no. No no no.

Why does it feel like Cam's dropping the mic into the chat and then lighting it on fire?

YES! THE KISSING GAME.

KISS KISS KISS.

WATERFALL KISS 2.0!

CAM FOR PRESIDENT.

"I was thinking truth or dare with the one and only Reece Dare..."

Bad idea. Very bad idea. But... I'll take it over the kissing suggestions. "Alright fam, let's start with truth—"

"Why did you kiss me?"

"DARE! I meant dare."

She is a tiger stalking prey as she sashays to the food table, and I have to aim the camera up because that skirt is one breeze away from giving the internet an all-access pass.

"Oh, the choices!" She surveys the spread as if she's picking weapons. "We've got 'Passion's Peak Poi,' 'Seven Minutes in Heaven Sushi,' or"—she lifts a glass with all the dramatic flair of a movie villain—"Kai's Special Love Potion! Crafted with rare Hawaiian aphrodisiacs guaranteed to 'enhance pleasure and maintain peak performance for hours.'"

The chat detonates:

CHUG CHUG CHUG.

His dare is to drink it.

Reece do it for science!

MAGICAL BONER JUICE TIME!

"Yeah, not happening."

"Aw, is the big bad YouTuber scared of a little magic relationship juice?"

I have no idea what this performance of hers is, but it's sooo much worse than just being yelled at.

Something hot and reckless snaps. I grab two full glasses and down them both, maintaining eye contact like it's a high-stakes poker game.

The liquid burns like lava mixed with DareFuel Passionfruit Pizzazz. *What the fuck did I just drink?*

"Okay, my turn." I force my voice to stay steady despite the strange warmth creeping up my spine. "Truth or dare?"

"Dare, obviously. I am your DareGirl, after all."

That fucking nickname.

She gives a playful shimmy, her smile widening as my jaw drops open. I have to use my hand to physically close my mouth to stop gawking at her breasts. Whatever Kai put in that drink must be premium grade because suddenly I'm channeling my inner frat boy.

"I dare you to show the squad a tour of the passion tent."

"Then I better hold the phone because you'll run away as soon as we step inside."

Before I can overthink it, I grab her hand and lead her toward the nearest tent. This is an epically bad idea. The kind of bad idea that makes jumping off cliffs seem downright responsible.

The moment we step inside, Cam's confident smirk falters as she takes in the space. The tent is too intimate. Too seductive. *Kai, you've done it again. You pervy bastard!*

Golden lanterns glow low and warm, casting everything in soft, flickering light. There's a massive plush mattress draped in white fluffy blankets that looks more sex cloud than bed.

"That is a lot of... supplies. Are those edible body paints?"

Her eyes scan over a tray of glistening glass bottles filled with oils, neatly arranged water bottles, and—

A pile—no, a fucking *mountain* of condoms.

Her uncomfortable expression cuts through my competitive haze. *What the hell am I doing?* I should stop this. Call it off before—

"Okay guys, well, there's a lot of interesting, questionable things in here. Maybe I should dare Reece to—Whoa!"

I track her gaze upward. The tent's top is wide open, revealing a starry night sky. The Milky Way sprawls across the darkness like a trail of spilled diamonds. Each brilliant pinprick of light feels as though you could reach out and touch it.

Cam moves first, lying down on the fluffy mattress. I lie beside her, hyper-aware of every inch where our bodies connect. My fingers move on their own, drawn to her hand like a magnet. Just a brush. Testing. She doesn't instantly pull away, so I loop my pinky with hers. It's barely anything—the world's most G-rated hand-holding—but my heart's beating wildly.

I notice a few comments so I flip the phone camera to give the audience a better view of the sky:

SOMEBODY CALL NASA CUZ THIS IS OUT OF THIS WORLD.

THIS IS SO ROMANTIC I'M DYING.

THE WAY HE LOOKS AT HER THO!!!

WAIT, ARE THOSE RHINOS F@C#ING ON HIS SHIRT???

The waves crash outside in a steady rhythm. Our pinkies are locked like a grade school promise, and I'm frozen. Because moving might break whatever cosmic spell is happening here.

And then—

"YES! YES! RIDE ME, YOU STALLION!"

What can only be described as a whale having an orgasm erupts from next door.

"HARDER, DADDY! SPLIT ME LIKE A COCONUT!"

Cam loses it first, dissolving into giggles and breaking our contact. The sound is so genuine, so unguarded, that I can't help but join her.

I turn the camera, framing us lying side by side. Her flower has gone slightly crooked, one strand of hair falling across her cheek. The urge to brush it away is so strong my fingers actually twitch.

"Guess our tent neighbors are having a different reaction to the view," I say loudly over the enthusiastic moans.

She snorts then covers her mouth. It shouldn't be so cute, but it freaking is. "Let's go back to the game. Your turn. Truth or dare?"

"Truth."

The word is a lit fuse between us. I know what she's going to ask. About the kiss that broke the internet. About why I ran after the hottest, sexiest encounter of my life. The love potion burns in my veins, but something else burns hotter—the need to finally stop being a goddamn coward.

"¡Ay, Dios mío! Your shorts!" Cam bursts into hysterical laughter, pointing at my crotch.

I glance down and—fuck. My "Welcome to the Lu-WOW" shorts are now competing with the actual tent we're sitting in. The hibiscus arrow isn't just pointing anymore—it's saluting. Standing at full attention resembling a soldier who spotted his commanding officer.

"Son of a—" I snatch up the nearest pillow.

Cam wheezes, trying—and failing—to get a word out.

And the chat? Full-blown hysteria:

REECE DRANK THE BONER JUICE, I REPEAT, HE DRANK THE BONER JUICE.

RHINO STYLE? CONFIRMED.
My guy's about to burst out like the Kool-Aid Man.
NEW DAREFUEL FLAVOR: ERECTILE ERUPTION.

I fumble with my phone. "That's enough for today! Stream's over. Bye!" I punch the *End LiveStream* button.

Cam's still sprawled on the mattress, cackling.

"Enjoying the show?" The words come out sharper than intended.

Her laughter dies. "Right, because this is somehow my fault?"

"You're the one who dared me to drink Kai's love potion!"

"And you're the egomaniac who chugged two glasses!"

She sits up, all curves and fury, and fuck-me-if-that-isn't-the-hottest-combination-I've-ever-seen. That tiny excuse for a skirt rides up her thighs and I don't know how, but my cock gets even stiffer.

"What is your actual problem with me, Reece? Because I'm getting whiplash from your hot-and-cold routine."

"I don't have a problem with you."

"Oh, *please*. You've been a nonstop prickwad since I started working for you. And this week? It's new levels of crazy. You can't decide if you want to kiss me or fire me."

What can I say? Admit she's invaded every thought, dream, and fantasy I've had for two years?

"Use your words, Reece." She leans forward, unleashing a wave of coconut-scented passion fumes. "What did I do that was so terrible?"

"You made me fucking obsessed with you!"

My confession is an exploding bomb. Her lips open in surprise, and I'm dying to taste that shock right off her mouth.

"What? You can't stand me. All you do is criticize me. I swear your life's mission is to point out my every little flaw."

"There is nothing—not one fucking thing—I don't like about you. Your smart mouth. The way you shut down my bullshit. Your perfect ass. You're a goddamn fever I can't sweat out, Cam. I want you so bad I can't think straight. When someone else looks at you, touches you, even breathes near you—I lose my goddamn mind. The urges to commit violence this week are more than I've ever felt in my whole life."

She stares at me, her hazel eyes wide, and suddenly I'm dangling off the edge of a cliff with no safety gear. Whatever this confession means, I'm about to free-fall.

"I know I've been an unforgivable asshole. I'm... gonna go—"

"Don't move." Her voice trembles. "I don't know what this is between us, but it's consuming me too. Ever since that shower—when your hands were on my skin—I can't think straight." She inches closer, and the tent suddenly seems microscopic. "I want your hands on me again. I want you, Reece. All of you."

Fuck it. I can't fight this.

I surge forward, crushing my mouth to hers, dragging her into my lap, feeling her soft curves mold against my body as if she belongs there.

She gasps into my mouth, her hands fisting my shirt, yanking me into her like she's been aching for this as long as I have.

"Tell me you're sure."

"Yes."

"Be fucking sure," I growl against her lips, "because the second I'm inside you, that's it. Game over. I'm never going to want to leave."

A whimper escapes her. She grabs my hand and places it against her core, the heat of her burning through delicate lace. My head tips back, a groan ripping from my throat as my fingers press into the hot, wet mess she's made for me.

"Reece, do I feel like I want you anywhere else?"

I'm done for.

"Baby, I can't be soft with you." My hands shake as they slide up her thighs. "Later—I swear to God—I'll worship every inch. But right now, I'm three seconds away from combusting just looking at you."

"Shut your gorgeous face up and fuck me."

I'm smiling like an idiot as I scramble on top of her. I graze the skin of her throat with my lips, pressing a kiss to her jaw. "Nope, I've changed my mind..." Rolling onto my back, I pull her on top of me. "I want to watch your gorgeous tits bounce while you ride my dick."

I yank my shorts down just enough to free myself, then look up to see her top fly off. Her breasts spill free, those rosy nipples already stiff and begging for attention. I slide my hands up her body, finally—*finally*—FINALLY—getting to touch the most incredible tits in fucking existence.

Holy fuck!

I've never given much thought to how I hoped to die, but this is it: palming Camila Morales' perfect tits while she straddles me in a beach tent.

"I want to do everything. Touch you. Taste you. Kiss. Fuck. Cuddle the hell out of you."

"We'll do it all, I promise. Multiple times," she says, rocking against me and creating a friction that makes my eyes cross. "But I need you inside me... now."

"Jesus." I send up a prayer to whichever Hawaiian god blessed me with this gorgeous, impatient woman. I fumble for a condom with shaking hands, nearly ripping it in my rush.

Her jaw drops as I roll it on. "Holy shit, I thought you were huge before you got drugged."

"So you lied when you painted me as a flimsy little pencil?"

"You didn't need your ego inflating this beast you call a dick any bigger."

"Think you can take all of it?"

She rises to her knees, determination blazing across her face, and shoves her panties aside—too impatient for proper undressing. I expect her to ease down, squeeze me in gently, but instead—holy fucking hell—she grips me like it's a challenge, lines us up, and drops down so hard my vision whites out.

"Motherfu—baby—" My words strangle in my throat at the sight of her taking me completely. "Are you okay?"

"I'm not some delicate flower. Don't you go easy on me."

That does it. I slam up into her, and the sound she makes? Pure filth.

"Do you feel that?" My fingers dig into the flesh of her ass, guiding her up just to slam her back down. Again. Again. Each thrust more savage than the last. "Two years of wanting this. Wanting you. Taking my cock like you were created for it."

I lose myself completely, fucking her like a man possessed. Her incredible tits bounce with each thrust. Each delicious slam—flesh against flesh—builds my climax. The glorious stars, framing her overhead, have nothing on the view of Cam's breasts bouncing viciously to our brutal pace.

She keeps getting tighter, impossibly tighter, as if she's trying to trap me inside her forever. And damn if I don't want to let her.

Her nails dig into my chest as she rides me like she's trying to break us both. The marks she leaves? I'll wear them like trophies.

"Fuck, Cam, I'm gonna explode."

"I dare you not to come yet." Even breathless, she's still challenging me.

"Right back at you, Morales."

"Fuck me harder."

"You want harder?" I grip her hips tight enough to bruise. "I already told you—you can have whatever the fuck you want, baby."

My movements are unhinged, but she matches me thrust for thrust. I swear we're breaking the laws of physics. We're fighting gravity... We're flying. She anticipates every erratic snap of my hips, meeting my intensity, slamming hard, and I mean *hard*, against me.

Spanish tumbles from her lips between ragged breaths, her pleas and demands tangled together in a frenzy.

I release her ass with one hand to find her clit, circling her nerve center and making her entire body quiver. Then—SMACK—my palm lands on that perfect ass. "Now baby, now!" I pinch her clit and she screams my name like a battle cry, her orgasm a volcanic eruption.

Her inner muscles clamp down, rippling around me, and I'm gone. Absolutely fucking gone. My hips keep driving up, chasing every last spark of pleasure until she collapses on top of me, both of us sweat-slicked and shaking.

We lie there panting in our post-orgasmic haze. Truth hits me like a revelation: I've swum with hammerhead sharks in crystal-clear Bahamian waters, freefallen from a plane at 20,000 feet blindfolded, and navigated treacherous Class V rapids of the Colorado River in a unicorn pool floatie.

But nothing—not one single adrenaline rush—comes close to the pure euphoria of Camila Morales.

The woman who just ruined me for anyone else.

Forever.

CHAPTER FOURTEEN

CAM

Group Chat : CPK Forever

Me: *Quick Poll: Hypothetically, can you break your vagina from too much sex?*

Petra: *SPILL IT! Every filthy detail required IMMEDIATELY.*

Me: *Let's just say my drought is now a full-on monsoon.*

Katie: *Twinsies! My Italian Stallion has my vajay-jay begging for mercy. She's all, "Ciao bella, I need a personal day."*

Petra: *I hate you both. The only action I'm getting is from my email notifications.*

Katie: *Give us everything. No holding back.*

Me: *Best sex of my whole fucking life. My boss is an orgasm wizard.*

Petra: *Some of us are trying not to fantasize about our*
bosses, okay?
Katie: *Sorry... How IS it going with the Bryce situation*
anyway?
Petra: *No comment.*
Katie: *Cam? You still with us? CAMILA?*
Petra: *And she's gone. 100% getting railed again.*
Katie: *Can't blame her. Get it girl!*

WE HAVEN'T LEFT THE room in three days.

If someone had told me a week ago that I'd be tangled up in bed with Reece Dare, watching *Mission Impossible: Fallout* while he absentmindedly traced patterns over my underwear, I would have laughed so hard I'd need a rib replacement. And yet... here I am. In his arms. In our little happy bubble where time doesn't exist, reality is on pause, and apparently, my vagina needs a PTO day.

The man has barely let me out of his sight. Or off this mattress. Or let me pee in peace. And while I'll let him do pretty much anything else to me in this room *(and have, repeatedly)*, bathroom time is still a sacred, solo mission. A girl needs boundaries. ¡Por Dios!

His scent—ocean saltwater mixed with spicy ginger and sex—has become my new favorite fragrance. It clings to me—my skin, my hair, my lips—like he's marking me from the inside out. Nestled against his side, my leg draped over his and his arm wrapped securely around me, the heat from his exposed chest seeps into my shirt. The way he holds on to me is a total turn-on—not needy, not demanding, just... possessive. Like he's afraid if he doesn't keep a physical connection to me, I'll evaporate.

I'm still trying to wrap my head around how much has changed between us in a matter of days. From a reluctant fake girlfriend to whatever this is. This surprisingly tender thing. All I know is that my heart soars every time his eyes lock on to mine.

The sheets are a twisted disaster zone of our making. My laptop balances on his lap, flickering light across his absurdly handsome face, the one I have, regrettably, now grown violently attached to. On screen, Tom Cruise is in full action mode, driving a motorcycle into oncoming traffic.

"You ever think Ethan Hunt just wants to... take a break?"

Reece stops tracing the lazy circles on my thigh. "What did you say?"

"I mean, the guy is always saving the world. What if, deep down, he wants to, I don't know, learn to play the ukulele? Or maybe"—I smirk—"pick up knitting?"

"Ethan Hunt doesn't do downtime. He does impossible. His idea of a relaxing weekend is disarming a nuclear bomb while hanging upside down from a helicopter."

"Sounds like someone else I know," I say, poking him in the ribs.

He meets my eyes, the corners of his mouth lifting in that devastating half-smile. My toes curl. He leans down, pressing his lips against mine in a kiss that starts gentle but quickly veers into heated territory. His tongue slides against the seam of my lips, demanding entry I'm all too happy to grant. Right as I'm getting into it, the iconic action movie theme intensifies—and his attention snaps back to the screen.

"Seriously? Tom Cruise over me?"

"We agreed on rest time," he reminds me, his eyes glued to the screen even as his hand gives my thigh a squeeze. "This is me being the mature one and giving your perfect pussy a well-earned rest."

I settle back against his naked torso, feeling the steady rhythm of his heart beneath my cheek. *How is this fake relationship feeling more real than any real one I've ever had?*

"All right, keep watching. It's almost the chase scene."

Who knew that hidden beneath all that grump was this adorkable man-child who gets giddy over Tom Cruise action sequences?

Still, he's right—we *did* agree to some rest time, and holy hell, we needed it. Because the romp-fest we had? Relentless. Ferocious. Mind-altering.

Bed? Obviously.

Shower? Slippery yet successful.

Sex swing? Five stars.

I can't get enough of the new Reece. The one who's uninhibited and ridiculously playful—who performed Tom Cruise's *Risky Business* dance routine, going full "underwear slide," while being serenaded by those creepy mechanical birds and their pre-programmed mating calls.

Then the sock-sliding goofball transformed into a sex god in zero point five seconds, hoisting me into that hanging contraption with biceps and a ferocity I've never seen.

He went to town on me, and I'm still feeling... not sure what you call it. Residual bliss? Phantom sensations? Whatever it is, this tingling aftermath is all his doing.

I look up and—yep—he's still smiling. No trace of the signature scowl he's worn since the day we met. He hasn't stopped grinning, not even in his sleep. It's like he's been infected with some rare happiness virus, and apparently, I'm the carrier.

The wildness. The joy. The heat. The absolute filthy things he whispers in my ear as he's buried deep inside me.

This Reece Dare is totally free and un-fucking-believably happy.

He turns and catches me staring. "This scene is crucial to the plot," he says, tapping the screen. "You need to focus so you don't miss important details."

"But then I'd miss out on the real action—watching you watch the movie," I reply, tracing a finger along his jawline.

He passes me a stern look that would be more convincing if his lips weren't twitching at the corners, fighting a grin. I redirect my attention back to the laptop, but my mind wanders.

All this time, I thought Reece was a tightly wound control freak with impossibly high standards, someone with a permanent grudge against happiness. But it turns out he was controlling himself—around me. With that perspective, I rewatch every moment from the past two years like a brand-new director's cut. The fleeting smiles he tried to hide. The way his jaw clenched whenever I adjusted my shirt. Every frustrated sigh. Every unnecessary bark of criticism.

After the way he's completely ravaged me these past three days, it's no wonder he struggled to hold back.

I am well aware there are big things to be discussed that we are neglecting. Such as Gordon's contract extension and continuing to play Reece's fake girlfriend—which I can't do because I'm finally leaving to start my own channel. The resignation email I sent to Gordon hangs over me like a tropical storm. Reece has no idea I gave my two weeks' notice way back before we got on the plane to Hawaii.

He doesn't have a clue that while he's planning our fake relationship tour, I'm planning my exit strategy.

No more morning routines.

No more sponsorship stunts.

No more jumping off things for clicks.

It's time to move on and make videos about important things. About people who need help. About places like Lahaina, still struggling to rebuild while tourists take fun sunset selfies at resorts half a mile away.

It's my calling—the path I've always known I should take but kept putting off. No more. I will not let my insecurities convince me I'm not good enough, not experienced enough, not ready enough. Reece has shown me that I am ready. That people absolutely want to hear what I have to say.

Still, I want to stay in this bubble with him a little longer. In this dream world where the only thing that exists is us and this bed and the ridiculous amount of pleasure we can wring from each other's bodies. Where he makes me feel worshipped and cherished and so fucking sexy that I strut around in nothing but his rhino shirt as if I'm JLo herself.

Because once we step outside this room, once I tell him about my resignation... everything changes. And I'm not ready to lose this version of Reece—playful, tender, and openly affectionate—not when I've just discovered it exists.

And then—

DUH-DUH. DUH-DUH.

The movie's theme song blasts through the speakers—a sign if there ever was one—that Tom Cruise is about to do some dangerous shit.

"This is it, the running scene!"

I turn my attention to the screen where the action hero sprints so fast he's practically a blur.

"He looks like he's trying to break the sound barrier."

"Exactly! And you know he does all his own stunts, right? He doesn't use a stunt double. He's all, 'Nah, I got this. Just hand me some running shoes. I already have the death wish.'"

I can't help but snicker at this fanboy.

Reece turns, his expression intense. "I can tell you're not taking this seriously." Without warning, he pushes the laptop off his legs and springs from the bed as if he's been launched. "To run like that takes incredible endurance."

He starts running in place, the movie's action scene providing the perfect soundtrack to his impromptu demonstration. His form is actually perfect—arms bent at ninety-degree angles, knees lifting high, landing on the balls of his feet.

Suddenly, he takes off, running circles around our sex-disaster of a room. "It takes a consistent stride and strong core engagement to do that sprint for extended periods of time," he lectures, dodging room service trays and discarded clothing as if they're obstacles in a *Mission Impossible* training course.

"I wonder how that run looks naked?" I suggest, propping myself up on my elbows to better enjoy the show.

The fanboy doesn't miss a beat, continuing his sprint around the room. Then—because apparently running in circles isn't dramatic enough—he parkours over the bed in one smooth motion, barely disturbing the sheets.

My stunt boy runs in place, pointing at the screen. "This scene is cinematic history. Watch! Right there, he broke his ankle and kept running! That's so fucking badass."

"Would you run on a broken ankle to save me?" I ask, purposely making my voice breathy and flirtatious.

He stops running immediately, his chest heaving from exertion, sweat glistening on his temples. Those blue eyes lock on to mine with an intensity that steals my breath.

"Cam, I could have a bullet in my head and I would keep running and refuse to let my brain accept it until I made it to you. I'd climb mountains, swim oceans, do whatever it takes to keep you safe, to make you happy."

His voice is so sincere, I want to believe it. Heat grows in his eyes, turning them from ocean blue to midnight, and then—an explosion rocks the laptop screen, making us both jump.

"Oh no!" Reece yells dramatically. "I'll rescue you!"

I barely blink and he's scooped me into his arms like I weigh nothing, one arm under my knees and the other supporting my back. My arms curve over his shoulders, and he launches into a run with me clutched to his bare chest.

"Oh no, your clothes are on fire!" he announces with fake panic. "I need to get you out of them immediately—this is an emergency!"

He tosses me onto the mattress and peels my rhino shirt over my head, exposing my naked breasts to the Hawaiian sunshine pouring through our balcony doors.

"Oh thank God," he says reverently, cradling my breasts in his hands. "They weren't harmed." Then he fake cries, complete with exaggerated sobbing noises. "I don't know what I would do if anything ever happened to you," he wails, addressing my boobs directly. "Especially you, Ilsa."

"Seriously, you rescued my breasts? And you named them?"

"Yeah, after the two main heroines in the movie, Ilsa and Julia." Reece's eyes widen as he stares at my chest. "Wait Did you hear that voice?" He studies the room in mock confusion. "Where did that come from?"

I roll my eyes hard but I'm smiling.

"Oh no!" he gasps, eyes darting wildly. "Someone else needs to be rescued!"

"Shut up."

He ignores me, hoisting me higher in his arms and taking off again. This time he runs with exaggerated steps, raised knees, face scrunched in his best Ethan Hunt impression. "We've got a situation here! Priority rescue in progress!"

I squeal as he spins me around, my naked breasts bouncing with each dramatic step.

"It sounds like this gorgeous Latina."

"That's better."

He shoots me a devilish smirk. "A gorgeous Latina's hot little cunt."

"Reece!" Before I can process the shock of his words, he flips me back onto the mattress and rips off my panties.

He stands at the bed's edge, soaking in my naked body with a happy sigh. Then he leans in, slowly kissing up my legs, starting at my ankles. "I'm looking for injuries," he explains with faux seriousness between kisses. "This is a very thorough inspection."

I squeal in delight as his lips skim my lower thigh, then keep moving—slow and deliberate.

When his mouth finally reaches the apex of my thighs, he pauses, hovering mere inches from where I'm embarrassingly wet for him. His lips graze my pussy, and he blows a breath of hot air directly on my most sensitive spot.

"Is rest time over?"

My mind screams, *Hell no—give me a break, you insatiable maniac!* while my body has an entirely different opinion on the matter. Three days of near-constant sex should have me begging for mercy, but one wink from him and I'm ready to go another three rounds.

He blows on me again, this time following it with a gentle, teasing lick from side to side on my clit. The sensation sets me on fire.

My hips lift involuntarily, seeking more contact, more pressure, more of his sinfully talented mouth. Right as he's about to deliver, the *Mission Impossible* soundtrack blares from the forgotten laptop, the dramatic music an absurdly fitting theme to what's happening between my legs.

"Show me what you got," I challenge, threading my fingers through his hair. "Let's see if your tongue is as fast as Tom Cruise."

The wicked gleam behind those eyes tells me I'm about to regret challenging him. But as his mouth descends and my hands pull him where I need him, I think, *Some regrets are absolutely worth having.*

***

FOR THE SAKE OF my poor, exhausted vajayjay, we finally made our escape from the room.

I'd forgotten what the outside world was like—three days deep in our little sex paradise. The sun feels incredible against my skin, like it's getting reacquainted with an old friend. I stretch my legs out on the plush, oversized lounger and tip my face toward the warmth.

"Can I get you anything else?" The pool waiter with his KAI'S BEST FRIEND nametag hovers near our private cabana, his expression so eager to please that I half expect him to start tap dancing.

"I'm good," Reece says. "You want anything, baby?"

My heart skips three beats. *He called me baby again.* He says that one simple word and I turn into a swooning teenager. It shouldn't make me melt, especially after seventy-two hours of sin and succulence, but here we are.

"Maybe some more pineapple?" I ask, eyeing the substantial spread of food around us.

The waiter nods enthusiastically. "Of course! I'll return in a bit."

Reece shifts closer, his lips brushing my ear. "You know, if you want something sweet to suck on, I've got—"

"This is a sex-free zone," I interrupt, pointing a warning finger at him.

"We'll see." He smirks, and *God, I love that look.* It's my favorite out of all the new smiles he's given me over the last few days—slightly wicked, entirely confident, with a hint of boyish mischief that makes my insides flutter.

We're lounging poolside in our own private cabana that's so luxurious, it makes me wonder if actual royalty vacation here. The structure is massive—white billowing curtains flutter in the warm breeze, currently tied back to showcase the stunning infinity pool view.

The double chaise lounge chair we're sprawled on could easily fit four people, covered in the plushest cushions my tushy has ever felt. It's like we're relaxing on a cloud. White gossamer fabric hangs from the ceiling, along with tiny twinkling lights that must transform this space into a fairy tale at night.

The infinity pool stretches out before us, its crystal blue water blending with the ocean horizon. Palm trees sway gently against a sky so perfectly blue, I'd swear it was created by AI. It's the kind of day that makes you believe in paradise—warm but not sticky, with an ideal breeze that's just right.

Around us there's enough food to feed an entire film crew. Fresh fruit platters overflowing with pineapple, mango, and passion fruit. A tower of coconut shrimp. Some kind of poke bowl. Two different kinds of sliders. Truffle fries that smell so good I cried when they arrived. Half-empty glasses of tropical drinks with names such as Passion's Promise and Tropical Ecstasy are scattered across the teak side tables.

My stomach growls so loudly Reece can hear it, but I don't even have the decency to be embarrassed. Since emerging from our room, we've been ravenous—like our bodies remembered orgasms are not actual sustenance. Though the man did eat me out a few hours ago, so technically he's had a head start on breakfast.

"Someone's hungry," the troublemaker teases, popping a piece of pineapple into my mouth.

I chew happily, savoring the sweet explosion on my tongue. "It's your fault. You've been working me like a marathon coach who thinks the finish line is on Mars."

"I heard zero complaints." His finger traces the V of my yellow string bikini, and I'm still not complaining.

"It's good we left the room," I say, reluctantly pushing his wandering hand away. "This is a workcation, not a sexcation."

Reece groans. "Gordon threatened to fly to Maui if we don't start livestreaming again soon." He holds up his phone. "Should we get this over with?"

"Is it weird that I miss the fans? They're so funny."

"They definitely miss you, but I hate sharing you."

"Then we'll make it quick."

I lean in, giving him a light, teasing kiss that he immediately tries to deepen, his hand coming up to cup the back of my neck. I push him away, laughing. "Nuh-uh." I grab his phone from his grip and press *Go Live* before he can argue.

"Hello, DareSquad! We missed you!" I beam into the camera, angling it to catch both of us in the frame.

Chat comments blow up like a firecracker:

OMG THEY'RE ALIVE!
Mom and Dad are back from making us siblings!!!
The hickey on Reece's neck—I CANNOT.
Cam is a tasty SNACK in that bikini.
KISS NOW OR WE RIOT!

My fake boyfriend edges closer, his arm sliding around my waist, his picture-perfect influencer smile on full display. "I think today we do a challenge video"—he pauses, milking it—"in the pool!"

Before I get what he's really saying, he scoops me up

"REECE, NO—"

One moment we're dry and civilized on our lounger. The next we're airborne. My scream gurgles as we hit the water.

SPLASH!

The phone keeps streaming from its waterproof case.

We surface and I immediately splash him. "You are going to regret that."

He pushes his wet hair back. "I'm hoping to," he says with a wink that makes me want to drag him back to our room.

And then we turn the livestream into an all-out pool war.

Swimming relay? Reece wins.

Holding breath underwater? I win.

Marco Polo? If Reece finds me, he gets to kiss me.

And spoiler alert. He finds me instantly.

"Cheater," I accuse, my legs instinctively wrapping around his waist.

"I don't need to peek. Blindfolded in a crowd, I'd still find you. Your smell, your energy... you are a magnet to me."

The kiss he gives me isn't for show or for winning a pool game. It's gentle and tender and tells me I'm his. Strong palms cradle my face, thumbs stroke my cheekbones, and his warm mouth glides over mine.

When we break apart, I'm breathless. The chat is an absolute frenzy, wild comments that are almost as out of control as the roaring in my ears. Because as I look into Reece's gaze, I'm in serious trouble.

I'm falling for my boss. The man I'm supposed to be fake dating. And he's oblivious to the fact that I'm quitting this job as soon as our vacation's over.

An hour later, we've wrapped up the livestream and are now sprawled out on our oversized lounger, a pair of lizards basking in the sun. My fingers are intertwined with his. We're hypnotized by the beautiful late-afternoon colors in the Maui sky.

It's... peaceful. Exactly what we need.

"Fruit plate, rum punch, and poolside reading material, compliments of Kai," announces the returning waiter, setting down a borderline pornographic platter of fruit. The punch glasses are served in coconut shells with orchids floating on top and straws shaped as—*wait, are those...?* Yep. Plastic penises. Subtle as a sledgehammer.

But what really catches my attention? The thick book with a sizzling shirtless Kai that reads: THE KAMA KAI SUTRA: A TROPICAL JOURNEY TO PLEASURE PARADISE.

"What's this?" I snatch it up.

Reece groans like a man who's just realized he left his wallet in the Uber. "It's Kai's book. He wrote his own take on the Kama Sutra."

"Get out!" I squeal, flipping it open. Inside is a treasure trove of sexual positions all starring Kai himself, his gleaming, muscled body paired with various women looking blissfully exhausted.

"'The Reverse Dolphin Blowhole!'" I announce, my eyes bulging at a photo where Kai and a willowy blonde are entwined in a position that defies gravity, common sense, and one of the Lord's commandments. Below the photo, Kai's poetic wisdom reads: "Just as the majestic dolphin breaches the waves at sunset, allow your spirits to soar in unified ecstasy. For optimal alignment, the smaller partner should visualize their heart chakra opening like a lotus flower while maintaining a 45-degree pelvic tilt. WARNING: May cause spontaneous vocalizations reminiscent of whale song."

"Listen to this," I say, flipping to a page where Kai and a brunette are balanced as a human pretzel. "'The Volcano's Mighty Eruption'—Like the powerful forces of nature that shaped these islands, so must your passion build and explode in magnificent glory. *NOTE* Unexpected dismounts may occur. For your safety, ensure all nearby surfaces are padded and that pets are removed from the room."

"Dismounts? Please stop. I've seen Kai's dick so much I can sketch it from memory—I wish I was kidding."

"But this is educational!" I protest, flipping through more pages. "'The Surf's Up Spiral,' 'The Tsunami Twist,' 'The Lava Flow'—wait, why is every position named after something that could kill you?"

I'm about to snap the book shut when I flip to a page that makes me slam on the mental brakes so hard I'm surprised I don't get whiplash. "Oh my God. OH MY GOD!"

Reece sits bolt upright. "What? Did he Photoshop my face in there somewhere? I will burn this resort to the ground—"

"NO! LOOK!"

The page shows Kai with a vibrant strawberry-blonde woman demonstrating "The Tidal Wave Twist." Despite being in her seventies, she's absolutely stunning—toned, flexible, with an expression of pure, uninhibited joy as she's locked in an impressively athletic position with Kai.

I scramble for my phone. "I'd bet my entire collection of cargo pants that is Katie's aunt Deb!"

I snap a picture and send a quick text to Katie:

Me: *Are you with Deb? Can you ask if this is her?*

"Aunt who now?" my SFBWB *(snoopy fake boyfriend with bene-fits)* asks as he peers over my shoulder.

"My friend Katie's aunt, Deborah Fox. She's who I wanna be when I grow up. She's seventy-two but has the stamina of a twen-ty-year-old, and she's had more lovers than I've had cups of coffee. She's never been married—'why settle for one flavor when you can taste the whole buffet, darling?' is her motto. Been single her entire life and is 'always ready to mingle,' as she puts it."

"So she's in Kai's book because…"

"Young guys, old guys, rich guys, poor guys—if there's a spark, she's lighting the fire," I say, flipping through pages. "She once told us her vagina has had more visitors than Miami Beach on spring break."

Reece chokes on his rum punch and sprays it everywhere like a busted sprinkler.

"And right now," I continue, dabbing at his face with a napkin, "Katie's in Italy with her! Deb told her to pack condoms, sunscreen, and an open mind—in that order."

"So, no future suburban life for you? Just globetrotting, making documentaries, and a sad trail of heartbroken guys?"

"Says the guy who's equally as restless. Adventurers like us are not meant to settle down."

We share a charged look, and I can't quite read his expression. *DING!*

My phone lights up.

Katie: *Oh, it's her alright. Aunt Deb wants to know if you've ridden Kai's giant love stick yet. She says ask him to do "The Breadfruit Bounty" on you. It will, and I quote, "make your uterus sing La Traviata."*

A giggle escapes me. The image of my uterus belting opera notes is too much to handle.

"What's so funny?"

"Nothing," I say, tilting my phone away from his prying eyes. "Girl talk."

"Girl talk, huh?" He snatches my phone, blocking the screen with his body—thumbs flying as he types.

"Stop! What are you doing?"

"I'm helping," he says innocently. "There. Sent."

Me: *Tell her it's like a pencil compared to the dick I'm currently riding.*

"¡Dios mío! Give me that!"

DING!

Reece reads my text aloud.

Katie: *I'm supposed to tell you that Kai is a wonderful lover but be aware ... he can get a little clingy. Plan your exit strategy. Aunt Deb says she's had to fake her death in three countries to get rid of persistent lovers.*

He bursts out laughing. "Your friend's aunt is a fucking legend," he says, finally relinquishing my phone.

I snatch it back, my fingers firing off my reply. "Oh, I'm getting you back for this," I warn, narrating as I type. "Ask her for more strategies because the guy I'm screwing is also super clingy."

Faster than I can hit *Send*, he grabs my phone, tosses it onto a pillow, and rolls his body on top of mine. His weight presses me into the plush surface, arms caging me, face hovering inches from mine.

"Damn right I'm clingy," he growls, his lips finding the sensitive spot right below my ear. The scrape of his stubble against my neck sends shivers racing down my spine. He trails hot, open-mouthed kisses down my throat, each one stoking the fire building low in my belly. "I had no idea what I was missing. I'm not about to give it up now."

"Do you really mean that?"

Reece lifts up on one arm, his eyes serious as they search mine. "Cam, I would give anything to go back in time to get those two years back with you."

Something expands inside me, a balloon of emotion threatening to burst through my ribcage. I know, I know—I shouldn't let these feelings grow. Not when I'm keeping secrets. Not when I'm leaving. Not when this relationship has an expiration date.

"And now that I've had you, there's no way I can go back to jerking off just thinking about you." He grins, his tone shifting to playful. "So yeah, I'm gonna fucking be clingy."

"No you didn't."

"Damn right I did. Who do you think starred in every fantasy while I stroked myself stupid this past year? I've mind-fucked you in every position imaginable... Well, except..."

"Hold up. Are you saying there's a filthy daydream you haven't done with me? Because I think we've done it all after the last three days."

Reece slowly takes his fingers and traces the swell of my breast, his touch featherlight through the thin fabric of my bikini top. Goose-bumps race over my skin and my nipples stiffen, straining against the material like they're reaching for him, desperate for more.

"First off, everything we've done, I want to do a million more times because I fucking can't get enough of you."

The naked hunger in his eyes makes me squirm.

"But yeah, there is something I have fantasized about... a lot."

He bites down, gently, on my breast. And I lose my damn mind.

"What is it?" I whisper, barely recognizing my own voice. "Tell me."

"I've dreamed of fucking your perfect breasts." His hand slides up my ribs, thumb grazing the underside of my boob. "If you'd let me."

"Here?"

"Why not? I can pull the curtains closed."

He leans down and draws his tongue in between the valley of my breasts. The wet heat of his mouth against my sun-warmed skin sets off a rush of desire to my core.

My breath hitches audibly. I've never thought about anyone fucking my tits before. Suddenly it's all I can picture—Reece above me, his hard length sliding between my breasts, his face twisted in pleasure.

"Would you let me," he asks, his voice rough with need.

"Yes," I whimper.

He gives my breast a firm squeeze, his thumb finding my nipple through the thin fabric of my swimsuit. Even through the material, the sensation is so intense that my back arches involuntarily, pushing me farther into his touch.

"I can't wait to slide between those glorious tits and come all over them. You'll be dripping."

"God, yes. I want that."

Instinctively, I reach for my wrist, fingers searching for the familiar feel of my scrunchie to pull my hair back. But my wrist is bare.

"No. Oh, crap." I pat my wrist again as if it might magically materialize. "I don't have a scrunchie."

"That's fine. You don't need it."

I sit up suddenly, breaking the heated moment like a bucket of ice water. "Oh no. Sorry. No scrunchie, no *boob job*. I've learned that lesson the hard way."

He pulls back, disappointment etched into his features. "Do I want to know?"

"If you want to hear about how I jerked off this guy in college who shot his load in my hair and—"

"Stop!" Reece clamps his hand over my mouth. "Moment ruined. Not hearing about you with anyone else, ever."

He shifts our positions, tugging me so that I'm nestled into his side, my head on his chest, his arm a protective band around my shoulders. He presses his nose into my hair, inhaling deeply.

"Cock-blocked by a scrunchie. And I was so close." He laughs, his voice thick with contentment. "Let's stay like this for a while—take a nap in the sun."

I should resist. I should make a sarcastic remark, keep things light. But instead, I stay warm in his arms, my heart swelling. *I refuse to accept any reality that will intrude on our Hawaiian fantasy.*

Is this the real Reece?

I came here to quit. To tell him I was leaving, to push him to promote my channel, to put myself first... finally.

But now?

Now, I don't know if I can.

If I tell him I'm leaving, am I throwing this all away? Throwing *him* away?

But if I stay—keep letting myself fall deeper into him—will I ever be able to leave?

CHAPTER FIFTEEN

REECE

"Tell me the surprise. Pleeease," Cam pleads for the thirtieth time, bouncing in the passenger seat.

"Nope."

I smirk, adjusting my grip on the wheel as the Porsche hugs a curve along the shoreline highway. The early morning light glints off the ocean, casting sparkles across the water like it's trying to seduce the coastline.

The engine growls beneath us—a mechanical purr that vibrates through the seats and up my spine. Nothing compared to the way Cam's moans reverberate through my chest when she's under me, but it's a close fucking second.

"Just one hint? A single syllable? Morse code? I'll take anything."

"You know what I'm discovering, Morales? There are a lot of ways to make you squirm. I'm adding 'surprises' to my mental list, right after 'shower water pressure' and 'that thing with my tongue that had you screaming in Spanish.'"

"You're the worst."

"That's not what you said last night."

She smacks my arm, and her laugh is a shot of pure dopamine to my veins.

I'm thrilled to be behind the wheel of this car again—a replica '58 Porsche 356 Speedster model like Tom Cruise drove in *Top Gun*—but I'm even more excited about what I've planned for today. For her.

The sun beats down, turning everything golden and warm, but the breeze rushing through the open top of the convertible keeps us cool—or it would if my blood wasn't running hot whenever I look over at Cam.

I steal another glance at her. The wind whips through her hair, loose strands escape from the ponytail she tied up with a scrunchie. That damn scrunchie she didn't have yesterday to fulfill my dirty fantasy. My hands grip the wheel tighter, knuckles white with the effort it takes to *not* pull over and drag her into my lap right this second.

Christ, get it together. Your dick can wait. This is about her.

Never in my life have I felt anything like this before. Cam has suddenly become my whole world. This feeling clawing at my chest is... *an epiphany? An addiction? A braingasm?*

I want to be with her every second of every day. Not just inside her—*though fuck yes, that too*—but next to her. Watching her. Getting her to laugh. Making up for all the time I spent belittling her work instead of recognizing what was right in front of me.

But does she feel this too? Or am I only convenient? A vacation fling? I mean, she made that pretty clear yesterday by repeating that Aunt Deb lady's life philosophy, "Why settle for one flavor when you can taste the whole buffet." Maybe she's not interested in anything serious, but imagining her with somebody else makes it hard to breathe.

"Pleeeease tell me," she interrupts my spiral. "Is it a puppy? A new lens? A lifetime supply of patience for dealing with your grumpy ass?"

"It's something you deserve. The least I could do to make amends."

"That's a long list, Dare."

"I'm well aware."

As I take the final turn, Cam's rapid-fire chatter dies abruptly. I pull to a stop, the vintage engine purring a final time before I kill it. Before us...

Lahaina—charred remnants of a once-vibrant community. Burned-out storefronts. Blackened foundations. Condemned shells of homes. The air itself is different here—heavier, carrying the lingering scent of char despite the months that have passed since the fires.

The destruction is staggering, sobering, and suddenly my master plan feels woefully inadequate.

"Are we... livestreaming here?"

"No streaming today. We're taking the day off." I shift to face her. "Today you're teaching me how to be a documentary filmmaker."

"I'm sorry, what now?"

I take her hand in mine, craving that connection like a lifeline. "This isn't some stunt. It's not a PR move or content for the channel. This is for you, Cam. I'm trying to know everything about you—your dreams, your passions. I want to understand it. To understand you."

Her face flickers—like a secret she didn't mean to share—sharp and real enough to stop me cold. She blinks, and poof, it's gone. Her smile slides back into place, but it's shaky now, as if it has to work overtime to hide something.

"So... is that why we're wearing matching cargo pants and white T-shirts?"

"The outfits were a last-minute addition," I admit, kissing her knuckles. "Don't be jealous if I look sexier than you in your filming uniform."

The truth is more pathetic. I spent half the night texting Kai for help. I swallowed my pride and asked him to connect me with locals who could guide us. And I begged the resort concierge to find me cargo pants identical to hers by morning.

I gotta keep a few things to myself to maintain some dignity.

Climbing out of the car, I circle around and pop the trunk open. "Today, I'm *your* assistant."

Cam comes over and her eyes pop at all the equipment I've packed. Camera bags. Tripods. Extra batteries. Mics. I don't know what documentary filmmaking actually requires, so I rented one of everything.

"Wait, are you wearing women's pants?"

I start unloading gear from the trunk, passing her a lightweight camera bag. "If you're asking if these pants are tight in the crotch, the answer is yes." I adjust myself with zero subtlety. "So don't do anything to turn me on, because seriously, there is no room down there."

A mischievous gleam lights her eyes. Never breaking eye contact, she bends over to check one of the bags, her butt mere inches from my hands. And then she fucking winks at me.

My palm connects with her ass before I think twice. The sharp smack is satisfying in ways I cannot articulate. Sonnets should be written about that thing.

"Oh, you want to be a little troublemaker?" I give her another slap, slightly harder this time. "I'll remember that when we get back to the resort."

I start distributing equipment between us, stuffing memory cards, lens wipes, and a collapsible reflector into my many pockets. "I see why you like these pants. You can fit everything in here. Is this what women are always complaining about? The pocket inequality thing?"

"It's a genuine feminist issue. The patriarchy doesn't want us to have storage options because then we wouldn't need men to carry our stuff."

I grab her by the belt loops, pulling her against me. Her softness meets my hardness in all the right places. "Your ass in cargo pants when you work is art in motion." I press my lips to hers, drinking in her sweetness. "I will do my best not to stare at it all day." I kiss her again, deeper this time, my hands finding their way to the curves in question.

She makes a sound somewhere between a laugh and a moan that shoots straight to my groin. Shit. *These women's pants were not designed for arousal.*

Reluctantly, I release her, shouldering a camera bag and grabbing the tripod. "Okay, boss. Where to first?"

I watch her transform into work mode—shoulders straightening, eyes scanning the landscape with purpose. Goddamn, I'd follow this woman anywhere.

We walk in silence down Lahaina's once-bustling main street, the weight of destruction draping over us like a heavy blanket. The bones of the battered town remain—foundations stripped to concrete slabs, steel beams sticking out like fractured ribs. Blackened doorways leading to nowhere. Some buildings still stand, but they're beyond scorched, hollowed out by the fire that tried to erase them.

Lahaina is no longer the town from the postcards.

The streets are eerily quiet but not empty. The hum of machinery rumbles in the distance, workers clearing debris, rebuilding what they can. A woman sweeps ash from what used to be her front porch, despite there being no roof above her anymore. A group of men reassemble the wooden beams of a storefront, their movements slow and steady.

I've seen destruction before. Hell, I've caused it intentionally, for videos.

But this? This isn't content. This is real.

The folks here are trying to pick up the pieces of their life.

"This is why I wanted to come," she says finally. "The news cycle has moved on, but this place—these people—are still living in it."

She gestures toward the town, toward the workers, toward a man hammering boards into the remains of what might have been his storefront.

"People lost everything. Homes, businesses, family histories passed down through generations." She shakes her head. "Most are still displaced, stuck in temporary housing, not knowing when—if—they can ever come back. Sadly, with the town's infrastructure being such a mess, many wonder if it's even worth trying."

We round a corner and halt dead in our tracks.

Before us stands the famous banyan tree.

Sacred.

Majestic.

Haunting.

Grieving.

It looms proudly and defiantly behind the skeletal remains of the Old Lahaina Courthouse. The behemoth, with its massive trunk and sprawling limbs, once boasted a canopy spanning nearly an acre. Now diminished by the scars of fire, large sections of its once-lush foliage are gone, branches blackened and twisted. Yet somehow, against all odds, green shoots emerge from the less-damaged areas—life finding a way in the face of devastation.

"It's a symbol of hope and resilience," I murmur reverently.

"You're right. And you just discovered the start of our story." Her confident gaze locks on to mine, seeping into my soul. "Let's dive in. I want to get some sweeping wide shots and drone footage of the town."

For hours, we work together filming different areas, moving through the ruins of Lahaina as if we're documenting a war zone. Which, in a way, we are—Mother Nature's war against this historic town. With each new location, Cam becomes more and more of a different person, someone I've not fully seen before.

"See how this shot captures both the ruins and the ocean behind them?" She points to the viewfinder. "That contrast tells a story without saying a word. Paradise and destruction in the same frame."

I nod, absorbing her words like the student I am today.

We move to a different spot where an elderly man is sorting through what's left of his shop. Cam approaches him with gentleness, explaining what we're doing. To my surprise, he agrees to talk.

"For intimate moments like this," she whispers to me, "we need close-ups. They reveal emotion, vulnerability—the human element that connects viewers to the story." She demonstrates, focusing tightly on the man's weathered hands as he holds a charred photo frame, the one and only item he could recover from his business of thirty years.

Later, as we're filming B-roll along what once was a main thoroughfare, Cam sighs in frustration.

"I'd like to do a tracking shot that follows the length of the street, showing the progression of damage," she explains, "but I don't have a dolly or any of the proper equipment."

I scan our surroundings, eyes landing on an abandoned skateboard propped against a partially standing wall. I hold it up triumphantly.

"How about a DIY solution? You sit on this, I'll pull you, and you can get your shot."

Her eyebrows shoot up. "That could work."

I position the skateboard on the smoothest part of the road, and Cam sits down, camera balanced carefully in her hands. "Ready when you are, chauffeur."

"Hold on tight." I grab the front of the board and begin walking backward, pulling her along as smoothly as I can. She watches through the viewfinder, hands steadying it despite the bumpy ride.

"Great!" she calls out. "Just like that! Keep this pace!"

There's a stupidly satisfying rush in helping her nail the scene—backing her vision instead of forcing mine. When we finish the tracking shot, she turns to me, all lit up and grinning, and I'm wrecked. I feel pride, sure, but there's something deeper, something I'm not ready to name.

I thought I knew Camila Morales. I didn't. I only knew the version who pointed a camera at me. But this woman? She's a freaking revelation.

***

"PERFECT—NOW HOLD THAT ANGLE. I need to frame the shelter with the mountain in the background," Cam instructs, her body bent slightly forward in concentration.

I hold the reflector panel and do my best impression of a statue. "Almost done?"

"Don't move. At all. And no breathing!"

Sweat trickles down my spine, dampening my ridiculous women's cargo pants that have squeezed my junk into oblivion. "You realize I'm not a tripod, right? I have basic human needs like blinking and eventually rescuing my balls from the chokehold of these pants."

"Quit fidgeting," Cam whispers, not looking away from her viewfinder. "You're making the light bounce."

"I'm not fidgeting. I'm adjusting this fabric sauna. Totally different."

We're standing outside a metal box masquerading as a home—a FEMA-issued temporary housing unit. I don't know what I was expecting. It's a single-room structure, one of a dozen crammed into a repurposed elementary school parking lot. The walls are thin. The roof is corrugated metal, the kind that turns a storm into a percussive nightmare. A clothesline is strung between two trees, kids' T-shirts and towels swaying in the breeze.

This is home for the Akana family now.

Kai really came through with this connection. He didn't simply hand us some random contact—he sent us to his actual longtime friends. Pono and Hina Akana weren't just homeowners. They owned a gem among Lahaina's most beloved family businesses: Paradise Burger Hut, right on the waterfront. From what Kai told us, it was a local staple—a place where you could grab the best beach burger in town and people knew your name.

They lost everything.

Their restaurant and their home. Their kids have been uprooted, their employees—who were basically family—are struggling, and they're drowning in bureaucratic bullshit, working out whether they even *can* rebuild.

"You think we're intruding?" I whisper to Cam, suddenly unsure about this whole endeavor. "These people have been through hell. The last thing they need is cameras in their face."

"They want their story told, Reece. That's why they said yes." Cam's voice is steady, confident. "And we're not here to exploit them. We're here to listen."

Before I'm able to respond, the door swings open and a lanky teen boy freezes mid-step, his eyes going comically wide.

"Holy shit! You're Reece Dare!" he yelps, then immediately clamps his hand over his mouth. "Sorry about the language," he adds, glancing nervously behind him.

I fight back a grin. "No worries, man. I've said way worse on camera."

His face lights up as if I've handed him the keys to a Ferrari. "I've seen all your videos! The double-back flip into the foam pit while eating a burrito? Legendary! And the vid where you spent twenty-four hours in that shark cage? My friends and I tried to build one in my cousin's pool with PVC pipes!"

"Keoni, who are you talking—" A woman appears in the doorway, her eyes tired but kind. She gives us an apologetic smile. "I'm so sorry. He gets excited."

"Mom! It's Reece Dare!" Keoni bounces on his toes. "He's YouTube royalty!"

Cam shoots me a smirk. "Royalty, huh? Should I bow, Your Majesty?"

"Stop encouraging him, Morales."

Keoni's attention shifts to Cam. "Wait, you're his girlfriend! The girl from the waterfall video!" His cheeks flush slightly. "My friend Marco rewatched that video fifty times."

Great. The kid's seen me with my tongue down Cam's throat. Not the first impression I was going for.

"Come in, please." The woman—Hina, according to Kai—ushers us inside. "Don't mind the mess. We're still figuring out how to fit all of our belongings."

"Mess" is a generous description. The space is meticulously organized out of necessity—every inch serving multiple purposes. A couch that's clearly a pull-out bed. Plastic bins stacked as makeshift shelves. No photos, no knickknacks, nothing but a general vibe of a life put on hold.

The air inside is stuffy, tinged with the sharp scent of fresh carpet and the lingering ghost of a delicious meal that was cooked hours ago. An air conditioning unit rattles in the window, fighting a losing battle against the Hawaiian heat.

A curtain serves as a room divider, and through a gap I spot a little girl with two perfect braids, her dark eyes wide with curiosity as she peers at our equipment.

"Nalani, come meet our guests," Hina calls softly.

The girl—maybe six or seven—steps out cautiously, holding a stuffed turtle against her chest like a shield. She lingers slightly behind her mother, half-hidden, her small fingers curled into her mom's floral-print dress, ready to duck out of sight if needed.

A man emerges from the kitchen area, wiping his hands on a towel. "Pono Akana," he introduces himself, extending his hand. His grip is firm, his eyes scanning mine—he's sizing me up. "Kai says you're filming a documentary? About Lahaina?"

I gesture to Camila, who's already adjusting her camera settings. "Actually, she's the documentary filmmaker. I'm her assistant."

Pono's eyebrows lift slightly, a flash of respect crossing his features. "Good to hear Kai wasn't making things up. He said you wanted to tell real stories, not just get disaster footage for clicks."

"We want to understand what families such as yours are facing," Cam says, stepping forward with a voice so tender, my heart surges. "The struggles that don't make the headlines. The reality of rebuilding—or trying to."

"Well, we've got plenty of reality to share," Pono says with a hollow laugh and tired eyes. "Come sit. We don't have much space, but we've got stories."

We settle into the cramped living area—Cam and me on a worn loveseat that's seen better days, the Akanas clustered together on the pull-out couch. Keoni perches on the arm, while Nalani tucks herself against her mother's side, turtle still clutched protectively to her chest.

Cam sets up two cameras on tripods with smooth efficiency. The first positioned to capture the family, the other angled to include both us and them in the frame. *I'm impressed.*

"Reece, in that one video—" the boy starts eagerly.

"Keoni, no. Let them prepare before you bombard Mr. Dare," Hina says.

"No worries." I grin at the kid. "Shoot me a question."

"Did you actually jump your motorcycle over a swimming pool full of snakes? Or was that fake? My friends and I have a bet."

"Rubber snakes," I clarify. "My insurance wouldn't cover real ones. But don't tell anybody—ruins the magic."

His laugh hits me hard. It's the first genuinely joyful sound I've heard all day.

Cam gives me a subtle nod—we're ready.

"Thank you for welcoming us into your home," she says, her tone taking on a quality I've never heard—direct and intimate without being intrusive. "Can you tell us about Paradise Burger Hut? Kai said it was special to the community."

At the mention of their restaurant, Pono's expression transforms, as if someone switched on a light inside him. "It was our life's work. Started with my father's recipes fifteen years ago. Nothing fancy—just good food made with aloha."

"The best burgers on the island," Hina adds, pride momentarily eclipsing the exhaustion in her voice. "That's not only us saying it—we won 'Best of Maui' five years running."

"And the most insane milkshakes," Keoni interjects. "We'd make these monster creations with, like, whole slices of cake on top. People would take pictures before they even tasted them."

"Social media was good advertising," Pono nods. "Tourists would come in with photos on their phones, saying 'I want this exact shake.'"

"It was more than a restaurant," Hina says softly. "It was where the community gathered. First dates, marriage proposals, baby luaus..."

"Our employees were family," Pono adds. "Some had been with us since opening day."

Cam nods encouragingly. "And it was also your home?"

"We lived above the restaurant," Hina confirms. "Everything we owned was in that building."

"Now it's all gone," Pono says, the light in his eyes dimming. "Fifteen years of our lives. Up in smoke in less than an hour."

The air in the room thickens, heavy with loss and memory. Nalani hugs her turtle tighter. Cam lets the silence breathe—a technique I've never mastered. On my channel, silence is the enemy. Dead air means lost interest, viewers scrolling away. I fill every second with jokes, commentary, action. But Cam knows to pause, giving the moment the weight it deserves.

I find myself holding my breath, not wanting to disturb the magic.

"We had twenty minutes to evacuate," Hina continues finally. "The smoke was already so thick, we could barely see. What do you grab when your whole life is on fire?"

"I took the cash box and our wedding album," Pono says.

"I grabbed the kids' birth certificates and baby books," Hina adds.

"I got my PlayStation and external hard drive," Keoni admits, looking slightly embarrassed.

"I brought Wiggles," Nalani speaks for the first time, her voice small but clear as she holds up the turtle.

The simplicity of their answers hollows me out. Twenty minutes to decide what matters. Twenty minutes to grab the fragments of a life you're leaving behind.

What would I save if my life was on fire? My YouTube awards? My phone? My fucking DareWare merchandise?

"What's been the most challenging part of rebuilding?" Cam asks, her focus steady even as I'm having an existential crisis two feet away.

"The waiting," Pono says without hesitation. "Insurance claims in processing limbo. FEMA applications. Building permits. The whole system's backlogged; everyone's overwhelmed."

"And while we wait, life keeps happening," Hina adds. "The kids need school supplies. The car needs repairs. We must pay rent while we are trying to rebuild."

"Do you know when you'll be able to start reconstruction?" Cam asks.

Pono and Hina trade a silent exchange, thick with unspoken truths.

"We're still deciding if we should," Pono says carefully, his voice low. "The land's still there, but restoration costs are astronomical. Insurance covers only about forty percent. Taking out loans means debt we might never escape, especially if..."

"If what?" Cam prompts gently.

"If the tourists don't come back," Hina finishes. "If we're the only people who rebuild. A restaurant needs a community to survive."

"What about your employees?" I catch myself asking, unable to stay quiet. "Are they waiting for you to reopen?"

Pono's expression tightens. "Some found other jobs. Some left the island entirely—housing prices being what they are. You can't keep people waiting on a 'maybe someday' promise."

"We feel responsible for them," Hina adds. "These people trusted us with their livelihoods."

"But you aren't helping anyone if you drown while trying to save them," Pono says with the resignation of somebody who's had this argument with himself many times.

My throat constricts. I have three hundred employees who depend on my channel's success. It's why I keep churning out the same content, why I agreed to marry Astrid, why I'm going along with this fake girlfriend plan. At least I still have a platform.

What would I do if I lost everything overnight? Would I have this same dignity? This same concern for others?

Cam continues asking questions—perfect questions that unlock layers of the Akanas' story that I wouldn't have thought to explore. The endless insurance paperwork. The community support that materializes in surprising ways. The challenge of maintaining hope.

I watch, mesmerized, as she builds trust with this family. She understands when to push and when to pull back. When to let emotion fill the space and when to redirect to facts. She's not just collecting soundbites—she's weaving together the complex reality of what it means to be a family that loses it all and keeps going.

This is Cam in her element, and she's fucking magnificent.

How badass would my content be if I'd recognized her talent earlier? If I'd seen her as more than "camera girl?" *Jesus, am I as bad as Gordon?*

"Why do you do all those crazy stunts?" Keoni suddenly asks me, jolting me from my thoughts.

The question catches me off guard. "Uh... views, I guess. People like watching crazy stuff."

"No, but, um, why? Aren't you scared you'll die?" His eyes are wide, genuinely curious.

I laugh, running a hand through my hair. "Sometimes. That's part of the rush—doing things that scare you."

"Did you always want to be a YouTuber?"

I glance at Cam, who's studying me with undisguised interest. Great. An audience for my existential crisis.

"No. It started with my best friend, Blaze, and me goofing around. Then this one video went viral, and suddenly people wanted more. Bigger stunts. Wilder pranks." I shrug. "Before I knew it, I was selling shirts, releasing energy drinks, and all this crazy stuff. Now, it's this big company and I have all these people who work for me. Definitely not what I expected."

"Do you still like it?"

I hesitate, acutely aware of how absurd my career seems in this context—in this tiny prefab unit where a family is fighting to rebuild a life that actually matters.

"I mean, I used to be obsessed with it," I say finally, the unfiltered truth slipping out. "Now... I don't know. Half the time it feels as if I'm just filming stuff to remind people I exist."

Keoni considers this with surprising seriousness. "You know what would be really cool? If you used your channel to help people. Like, you have millions of followers, right? Imagine if they all did something small to help. That would be massive."

"Keoni," Hina warns gently, shooting me an apologetic look.

"It's okay," I assure her.

"Can you help us?" Keoni asks directly, his eyes full of unmistakable hope that makes my stomach drop, like I stepped off a ledge I didn't see coming.

The question paralyzes me.

Can I help? I have money, sure. I could write a check right now to cover their rebuilding costs. But that's a single family, and there are so many others. Plus, I can't fix all the bureaucracy and red tape that keeps them stuck in this position.

And my platform? Millions of followers who watch me do dumb shit for laughs. Would they care about the struggles of Lahaina? I can't see them donating to a GoFundMe. They'd just scroll past to the next viral challenge.

My entire brand is built on superficial entertainment. My audience comes for the adrenaline, the pranks, the stunts—not real issues requiring actual attention spans.

I'm drowning in my questions when Cam speaks up.

"We're going to do what we can to make sure people hear your story," she says with quiet conviction. "That's the first step—breaking through the noise, making sure you're not forgotten."

The certainty in her words both impresses and intimidates me. She knows exactly what to say, exactly what matters. Meanwhile, I'm still trying to figure out if anything I've ever made has mattered at all.

What have I been doing, really? Entertainment that evaporates from memory as quickly as the next video can load. Whereas Cam's capturing real stories about real people facing real challenges. Content that actually fucking matters.

Why would she tie herself to somebody like me? A jackwad who jumps off cliffs for views.

Oh my God, wait! This emptiness I've been feeling isn't burnout. It's not Gordon's relentless demands. Hell, it's not even the grind of day in and day out filming.

It's the cold, hard fact that I can't outrun. None of it has ever meant a damn thing.

And watching Cam today—seeing her connect with people, tell their stories with dignity and care... I want that. I want to make things that matter. I want to use my platform for a purpose bigger than myself.

Something in me has shifted, irreversibly. I can *not* go back to creating the same empty content.

But will people believe I genuinely want to help? Will she?

CHAPTER SIXTEEN

CAM

Me: *Hey sis. Serious question. Ever think about letting go of your dream?*
go of your dream?
Aria: *Hell no.*
Me: *Okay, okay. What about switching it up a bit?*
Aria: *Not a chance.*
Me: *But come on, your goal isn't to cook in a food truck. You want a restaurant, right?*
Aria: *Exactly. The food truck is a stepping-stone. It's my way of making the dream happen.*
Aria: *FYI Abuela won't stop showing everyone that video of you two sucking face at the waterfall. She's telling them you're engaged and has her wedding dress ready for you.*
Me: *¡Ay, Dios mío! We're having fun, that's all.*
Aria: *Fun, huh? I've seen the videos. That looks like more than just fun to me.*
Me: *I don't know what it is, alright? I'm just rolling with it.*

Me: *Sorry I haven't texted more.*

Aria: *No worries, mija. You're busy kicking ass. We both are. Love you.*

Me: *Love you more, chica.*

"THIS VIEW IS INCREDIBLE."

The blue sky overhead is so rich, I swear I can taste it—cool, crisp, like the first sip of cold water after a day in the sun. Sunlight seeps into my skin, warming me from the inside out, while the steady northeast wind teases me with breezy comfort. The humming catamaran cuts effortlessly through the water, leaving a foamy trail in its wake—an easy, rhythmic soundtrack to an afternoon that feels too perfect to be real.

"I agree," Reece murmurs.

But he's not focusing on the ocean. He's staring only at me, his deep-blue eyes giving me the full smolder, as if I'm the only woman on this boat. Hell, the only woman in Hawaii. A delicious thrill dances up my spine as he leans close and presses his lips against mine—gentle, sweet, yet still humming with the echoes of tangled sheets and whispered moans.

When did this shift happen? When did the obnoxious, grumpy, always-critical Reece Dare morph into this attentive guy who gazes at me like I'm the center of his universe?

And why does it make my grateful heart want to burst out of my chest?

"If you think that's distracting me from snorkeling today, you're tragically mistaken," I mumble against his lips.

"I'd never dream of stopping you from seeing fish, Morales. But I reserve the right to provide... incentives for after."

The heat in his gaze promises the kind of incentives that have left me boneless and breathless every night since we crossed that line.

We're sprawled across each other on the top deck of what can only be described as a floating Chuck E. Cheese for adults. This triple-decker catamaran is what would happen if a cruise ship and a water park had a baby after a tequila bender. The gleaming white monstrosity cuts through the waves with impressive speed.

Below us, the main deck shines with floor-to-ceiling windows. Most of the fifty tourists onboard are on that level enjoying the breakfast buffet—platters of fresh pineapple, mango, and papaya arranged in rainbow spirals, alongside grilling mahi-mahi that releases wafts of mouthwatering aroma even up here. The bottom deck features a glass floor panel where people can watch fish without risking their blowouts.

But the real party tricks of this floating amusement park are the twin water slides corkscrewing off either side and the "walk the plank" jumping platform extending from the stern.

"I hope I get to see a turtle today," I say, already mentally rehearsing what settings I'll use on my waterproof camera.

"I hope you're wearing a thong bikini under these very modest shorts," Reece counters, his long, strong fingers finding the hot-pink string peeking out above my waistband. He gives it a gentle tug that sends electric currents racing across my skin. "Preferably one that ties at the sides for easy access."

His fingers slip beneath my shirt, exploring with the confidence of a man who's spent the last several days mapping every inch of my body with obsessive attention to detail.

"There's no way my bikini is more stunning than swimming with exotic fish in a volcanic crater," I argue, trying to sound stern but failing spectacularly as his fingertip traces the underside of my breast.

"Agree to disagree. I've seen exotic fish from Fiji to Japan, *and* I've seen you in a bikini. No comparison."

Right before I properly roast him for his priorities, he dips his head and attaches his mouth to my neck like a sexy vampire. The heat of his tongue against my skin is a direct hit to my happy place, and I have to bite my lip to keep from making a sound that would scandalize the nice midwestern family two rows over.

"You sure you want to play this game?" I gasp as his teeth graze my pulse point, "because I can get aroused without visible proof, but you? Board shorts aren't gonna hide that thick cock of yours." I deliberately glance at his board shorts, which are already showing I'm the clear winner.

He growls against my skin—an honest-to-God animal sound that vibrates through me—before reluctantly pulling back. His pupils are so dilated his eyes are almost black, and I feel a surge of feminine power knowing I did that to him.

"Fine. Later," he promises, threading his fingers through mine and pulling me closer. He rests his head on my shoulder with a contented sigh, the kind that lingers, that sinks under my skin and burrows in dangerously deep.

We sit in comfortable silence as the Molokini crater grows from a smudge on the horizon to a distinctive crescent shape rising from the water. It looks like something from a sci-fi movie—the partially submerged remains of an ancient volcano, its curved spine creating a natural harbor of turquoise water. Half a dozen other boats converge on the spot like colorful beetles drawn to the same flower.

It's perfect. Beautiful. Everything I could want from a Hawaiian vacation.

Except for the storm brewing inside me.

What happens when this ends?

I still can't believe Reece set up yesterday for me at Lahaina. The memory floods back—him assisting me with the documentary, learning my process, supporting my vision with such genuine interest and enthusiasm. I wanted so badly to tell him that this is exactly the type of content I want to make for my channel. The channel I've yet to mention, never mind asking for his help to promote it.

But reality lingers beneath the surface, circling like a shark. I'm leaving. I have to tell him about my resignation—but when? Cause once I do, our fake relationship is over. And I'm terrified this version of Reece—the man who watches *Mission Impossible* in bed with me, who runs around our room making me laugh, who calls me "baby" like he means it—will disappear forever.

What if I stay? The thought is an ambush. *What if we could be a couple and make meaningful content together?*

The Lahaina footage proves that I'm not delusional. The way he showed up, helped me, actually gave a damn about telling those people's stories. That wasn't for clout. That was real—a glimpse of what we could do together. His platform could be more than thirst traps and viral stunts. He has the power to make real change, to spotlight causes that deserve more than fifteen seconds of attention. To be more than the sultan of Shallow Content.

The possibilities unfurl, tempting and dangerous. I won't sign Gordon's contract, but I'll continue working with Reece as his... what? His videographer with benefits? His actual girlfriend? The uncertainty makes my stomach clench.

He acts obsessed with me... but is he, really? Or is this just Island Reece—relaxed, playful, affectionate because we're trapped in paradise with nothing but time and each other? Once we head back to real-world pressures, demanding sponsors, and the relentless content machine, then what happens?

The sex is mind-blowing, earth-shattering, *thank-you-Lord-for-making-male-bodies-capable-of-THAT* incredible. But it's the other moments that have my insides all gooey—the way he looks at me when he thinks I don't notice, how he remembered my sister's name, how he cuddles me and never wants to let go.

I'm still waiting for the rug to be pulled out from under me. For Reece to go back to grumpy boss mode, Mr. Critical. Because this Reece Dare—the one who's thoughtful and protective, who listens when I talk about camera shots and lighting with genuine interest—I'm falling for him. Hard.

I know that regardless, I need to make a decision and fast, because in two days we return to LA, where I've already given my notice. Where Gordon is waiting with a contract that would extend our staged romance for months—a contract I have no intention of signing. Yesterday made it clear: it's time to pursue my plans to start helping others.

"OMG, besties! The view from up here is literally everything!"

Astrid explodes onto the top deck like a confetti cannon filled with narcissism and lip fillers. She prances around in her gold metallic bikini, shoving the camera into Blaze's hands. "Hold this. I need you to capture my full goddess energy."

"On it, babe." Blaze salutes her, nearly dropping the camera in the process.

Blaze's outfit today is an assault on fashion—extra in the worst way, like a fever dream curated by a colorblind clown in a hurry.

Tie-dye tank top? Check. Tacky board shorts that look designed by a glitter-obsessed kindergartner? Check. And a sparkly pink baseball cap that reads, BLAZED AND CONFUSED. Which, let's face it, sums him up perfectly.

"Bitches, this exact turquoise shade is in my new Ocean Vibes eyeshadow palette, dropping at midnight!" She twirls—part prima ballerina, all marketing genius. "Use code GLOWJOB for fifteen percent off and free shipping on orders over fifty dollars! Your eyes will pop out of your skull—ideal for that trendy zombie vibe this summer!"

Astrid strikes several poses, puckering her lips and sticking out her tits to the camera. "Blazey-Boo, tell everybody how amazing my contour looks."

Blaze's face goes through a wild mix of emotions: confusion, panic, scrambling for thought, and then total freak-out. "Uh, your face is, uh, totally fire, babe. Like a super hot... statue? Yeah! Like those old guys who made ass statues, but on your face!"

I bite the inside of my cheek to stop from snorting.

"A statue? What does that even mean?" She snatches the camera back. "This is why we rehearse these things! Whatever."

She continues her monologue, her voice an unsettling blend of baby talk and an overly enthusiastic cheerleader, as she documents every inch of the boat.

Meanwhile, Blaze's attention span struggles to stay focused and then forgets why it was here. His eyes dart everywhere: a passing cloud, a splash in the water, his own reflection in a nearby window. And then he spots us.

"Yo! My dudes!" He bounds over, arms wide, pulling us into a group hug. "Miss you, bro! This reminds me when we went snorkeling in Australia and we met those two local girls who—"

"Nope," Reece cuts him off.

"Yeah, remember!" Blaze persists. "Yours was really hot but made those donkey noises when you—"

"Look, a dolphin!" Reece interrupts, pointing wildly at absolutely nothing.

Blaze's head whips around so fast I worry for his neck. "Where?" He bounds to the railing, leaning dangerously far over the side. "I don't see it! Is it doing tricks?"

"So, animal noises? Is that another kink I should know about?" I lean closer, lowering my voice to a mock-seductive whisper. "Titty fucking while I—" I let out an exaggerated "HEE-HAW! HEE-HAW!"

"Hilarious, Morales," he deadpans. "New rule. Not talking about exes goes both ways."

"You sure have a lot of rules for this fake relationship."

In an instant—his entire mood shifts.

His expression locks down, his eyes go hard, and there it is.

The wall.

The one I knew would come back eventually.

The one I dreaded.

I watch the tension creep into his shoulders, the way his jaw clenches, the way his fingers twitch, as if they can't figure out if they want to hold me or shove me away. Instead, he drops my hand and pulls out his phone, scrolling aimlessly, leaving me in awkward silence.

My stomach churns, and it's not from the rocking boat.

This is exactly what I've been afraid of. The silent Reece. The brooding Reece. The man who can go from playful to impenetrable fortress faster than Astrid can say "Like and subscribe."

But then—his hand slides over mine.

He lifts our joined fingers and touches his lips to my knuckles. The gesture is so unexpectedly tender, so jarringly intimate after the frost only moments before.

"I hope you get to see your turtle today."

Emotional. Whiplash.

I should tell him about quitting. Should rip the Band-Aid off and end this fantasy before it hurts even more.

But for now, I can't. I won't. I refuse. The truth—and whatever heartbreak it brings—can wait.

At least until we're back on dry land.

***

"DAMN, YOU'RE SEXY. HOW can you make flippers and a snorkel look so fucking hot?" Reece's eyes rake over me from behind his dorky, oversized mask.

"I'm beginning to think you hit your head when we jumped off that cliff." I tease, repositioning the strap digging into my scalp. "Or maybe it's heatstroke. Should I check your pupils? Alert medical professionals?"

We're standing near the stern, where everyone's gearing up for snorkeling, aligning masks and squeezing into fins. The energy is chaotic—excited tourists fumbling with equipment while crew members offer assistance with the patience of preschool teachers on a field trip.

One woman is engaged in an impressive wrestling match with her snorkel mask, the strap tangled hopelessly in her hair. Her husband—judging by the matching Hawaiian print swimwear—is pretending not to know her.

Reece and I decided our first shot will be jumping off the plank together, holding hands—a callback to our viral waterfall kiss. My heart rate kicks up just thinking about it, but honestly I can't tell if it's from the memory of his lips or the thought of plunging into the open ocean.

"I'm kinda glad it's impossible to livestream underwater," I say, giving my snorkel a quick test blow. I can finally get some real cinematic shots without the constant narration for viewers."

"You're so seductive when you get all passionate about filming. There's something about the way you get all intense and focused…" He steps closer, lowering his voice so only I can hear. "Like how you look right before you co—"

"Okay! Camera check!" I interrupt before my warming face spontaneously combusts. "Let's make sure this thing is recording properly."

He grins, holding up the special underwater GoPro setup—a selfie stick with extra grip texture so it doesn't slip from wet hands, encased in waterproof housing thick enough to survive the Mariana Trench.

Reece takes my hand as we step onto the plank, our fins making that ridiculous squeaky rubber sound. It should be impossible to feel romantic while waddling like penguins, yet somehow his touch still makes my whole arm tingle.

The plank extends from the rear of the boat, resembling a diving board to nowhere, suspended over crystal-clear water that shimmers in a dozen shades of blue. I can already see colorful fish darting beneath the surface, teasing us with flashes of yellow and electric orange.

He presses *Record*, aiming the camera at our faces.

"DareSquad, you are NOT ready for how gorgeous this water is." His voice shifts into YouTuber mode, enthusiasm dialed up to eleven as he swings the camera toward the ocean. "Check it out. You can see all the way to the bottom!"

The visibility is unreal—like staring into the world's largest natural aquarium.

Reece turns the camera back to capture both of us, his hand in mine. "Baby, tell them where we're at."

"We are snorkeling at the Molokini Crater," I say, smoothly transitioning into presenter mode, a role that's become surprisingly comfortable over the last week. "Home to over 250 species of colorful fish and 38 types of coral—"

"But," Reece cuts in, "my girl wants to see a turtle, so let's go find her one."

Before I can react, he moves closer and kisses me—fast and fiery, his lips firm and demanding. My heart rate skyrockets, and as I'm about to melt into the kiss, he pulls back with that devilish glint in his eyes and gives my hand a squeeze.

"Come on!"

And then—

YANK.

I'm airborne. My startled scream is cut short as we plunge into the water. *SPLASH!* The ocean swallows my yelp whole as we break the surface, cool air rushing over my skin.

I push my mask up, spitting out salty water. "Oh, you are so dead when I edit this footage."

"Totally worth it."

"After that stunt, it's my turn to hold the camera."

Reece doesn't hesitate. He passes it over, but then—he grabs my other hand. Laces his fingers with mine.

"That's fine. As long as I can still hold you."

Once more, my stupid heart goes all squishy on me.

We adjust our masks, popping snorkels into our mouths like awkward plastic pacifiers. Reece gives me a thumbs-up. I return the gesture and take a deep breath.

We dive.

The world transforms.

The bright, chaotic boat noises vanish, replaced by a peaceful, liquid silence. The only sounds are the gentle hum of the ocean, the occasional whoosh of a fellow snorkeler kicking past, and the stream of tiny bubbles floating toward the surface.

It's fucking magic.

The water is warm, enveloping us in liquid silk, a welcome contrast to the cooler air we'll feel when we surface. I tilt my head, watching beams of sunlight pierce through the translucent blue and illuminate the coral reef below.

Reece's fingers stay tangled with mine, his grip firm, as if he doesn't want to lose me in the vastness of the ocean. I lift the camera, getting my first underwater shots.

My calf tickles—the gentle brush of a fish swimming past, too curious or too confident to be bothered by our intrusion into its world. I turn the camera in time to capture a yellow tail darting away, its body a perfect slice of sunshine against the blue backdrop.

Before I realize what's happening, we're in the middle of a school of fish.

Hundreds—maybe thousands—of gleaming silver bodies with electric-orange racing stripes pulse around us, parting ever so slightly before reuniting behind us.

My mind races with the thrill of documenting something so wild and unpredictable. When I glance at Reece, his eyes are filled with wonder behind his mask. In this moment, he's not YouTube royalty or my complicated boss-turned-lover—he's just a man, utterly captivated by the world's beauty. It stirs an emotion deep within me, an unfamiliar feeling that I'm not prepared to dissect.

We kick forward, gliding over a forest of vibrant coral—a neon city pulsing with life. Beneath us, schools of tiny, iridescent fish flicker in and out of sight, vanishing between the coral's jagged ridges.

Reece jerks his hand from mine, pointing frantically at a creature beneath a rock. He motions for the camera, his expression shifting to that boyish excitement that makes him look sixteen instead of twenty-eight. I pass him the GoPro, watching as he dives deeper with powerful kicks that showcase every muscle in his thighs and calves—anatomy I've become intimately familiar with these past few days but still haven't tired of admiring.

The eel gets a sense of this absolute menace invading its personal space and vanishes into the coral.

Then, Reece is a torpedo shooting to the surface. I follow, breaking into the cool breeze, dragging the snorkel from my mouth.

"I saw it! I fucking saw its teeth!" he says, gasping for air. "There was a massive moray eel back there! It was horror-movie huge! It opened its mouth right when I got close, and I swear to God, Cam, it had a second set of jaws inside. Like that movie *Alien*!"

"Did you get a close-up?"

"Hell yeah! Here, I'll do some underwater reactions for the video."

He takes a deep breath and dives back under, leaving me to follow with the camera, lining up the shot.

What unfolds is the most hilarious underwater performance I've ever seen. He strikes a bodybuilder pose, flexing his biceps while puffing his cheeks out like a pufferfish. He slow-motion runs as if he's auditioning for an underwater *Baywatch* reboot. But the grand finale is his attempt at an underwater somersault, which goes so hilariously wrong that bubbles explode from his snorkel.

This playful, goofy side of Reece—the side that'll do anything to make me smile—is my new addiction.

We surface together, gasping and laughing, the sun hot on our faces, and everything feels perfectly, ridiculously right.

I freeze.

"What? What? Do I have a jellyfish on my face?"

"TURTLE!"

He spins around, and there it is—a massive green sea turtle, gliding past us as if it owns the place.

"Quick, go! I'll film it."

Reece grabs the GoPro, flipping it on and following as I dive down. The turtle moves slowly, unbothered, its shell catching the sunlight filtering through the waves.

I swim closer, hovering just beside it, turning slightly, posing like a full-on tourist. I'm so close I could reach out and touch it *(I won't. I don't need Mother Nature smiting me today).* The turtle acknowledges my presence with a slight turn of its head, its eyes meeting mine for a brief moment that feels profoundly spiritual before it continues its unhurried exploration, gliding away into the blue distance.

I'm still staring, transfixed by the encounter, when Reece's hand finds mine. He pulls me closer, wrapping an arm around my waist as we drift in the underwater silence. Through our masks, our eyes meet in a moment of shared wonder.

We stay suspended like that, holding each other in the gentle current, until our lungs remind us we're not actually equipped with gills. With synchronized kicks, we rise to the surface.

I rip off my mask, grinning so hard my face hurts. "Tell me you got that on video! ¡Dios mío! That was the coolest thing I've ever seen in my life!"

"Baby, I think I did, but I can't be sure. Your ass was pretty distracting."

I splash him. "Seriously? That's what you were focusing on? My dream of seeing a sea turtle, and you were filming my rear end?"

"I got the turtle too," he laughs.

"Give me the camera so I can check the footage."

I reach for the handle—but instead, he pulls me in. His lips find mine in a kiss that tastes of salt water and adventure.

When we break apart, Reece's expression shifts, his gaze so intense that it makes the rest of the world fade to nothing. "My dream is floating right here in my arms. Everything else is just bonus footage."

My heart stops, skips, then races as I slam my lips onto his, hungry to communicate to his body what I'm not ready to acknowledge to myself.

***

I SHOULD NOT BE this comfortable.

Wrapped up in one oversized beach towel, legs tangled with Reece's, his chest firm and warm against my back, I'm completely cocooned in him—trapped in the best possible way. His arms are locked around me, not as a restraint, but as a claim, a silent promise that I'm not going anywhere.

Which works for me. I have no interest in wiggling free.

"These moments," he murmurs against my ear, his breath entirely too distracting, "are why I love filming."

I angle my head back, resting against his broad, stupidly comfortable chest. "Snuggling with me? That's your takeaway?"

"Obviously," he teases, placing a gentle kiss on my forehead. "I'm saying... most people will never get to experience swimming with sea turtles or being above the clouds watching the sunrise. So at least I can help them experience it, you know? With my videos."

His arms tighten around me, pulling me closer.

"Especially for my younger audience," he continues. "Kids like Keoni—it shows them how big the world is, sparks ideas about places to visit, careers to explore, and adventures they may want to try someday."

"I've never thought about it that way, but you're totally right." I turn my head slightly to meet his eyes. "You are the reason I picked up a camera in the first place."

"Wait. Seriously? You meant it when you told my moms that?"

"I used to rewatch your videos the way film students dissect their favorite directors. I'd take notes on your transitions, your tracking shots, how you built tension before a stunt. My friends were all thirst-following for your abs. I was fangirling over your dolly zooms and depth-of-field choices."

His chest vibrates against my back with silent laughter.

"You drew me in with your visual storytelling. Nobody else was making skateboarding down a hill resemble an epic Hollywood production."

"But what about my abs? You liked them too, right?"

I elbow him lightly in the ribs, earning another laugh. "Yeah, yeah, they were and are spectacular."

"I never imagined that filming my dumb videos would lead me to the most incredible girl I've ever met."

I twist in his arms, nearly dislodging our carefully arranged towel fortress, needing to see his face—to assess whether this is just another line, another performance, another practiced charm offensive.

But his eyes... God, his eyes. They're wide open, vulnerable in a way I've never seen before, holding none of the calculated charisma he deploys for his audience.

"I think you're incredible too, Reece," I manage.

"I know I don't deserve to be here with you, but there's nothing I wouldn't do to make this last."

Panic flares hot under my ribs. My chest is so tight, my stomach is in knots, and if I don't break eye contact, I'm going to do something profoundly stupid.

Like tell him that I'm in love with him.

Oh shit, I love him.

I do. I really fucking do love him.

The boat's speakers crackle to life, interrupting my internal crisis. "Attention, passengers! We'll be departing for shore in approximately thirty minutes. Please gather your belongings and prepare for our return journey."

Reece stands. "I want to jump off the plank a few more times. You in?"

I clasp his hand, allowing him to pull me to my feet with effortless strength. "Yeah, but first I need to use the restroom."

"Hurry back. You can rate my dives on a scale from 'embarrassing belly flop' to 'Olympic gold medal.'"

We separate with a kiss. I make my way down the stairs to the main level, walking through the hall to the restroom when a wall of peroxide blonde materializes.

Astrid.

Her attention appears fixed on her phone, thumbs tapping with robotic precision.

"I gotta ask," she says, her voice oozing with fake innocence. "Does Reece even realize you've been playing him from the start?"

Keep walking, Camila. Don't acknowledge her.

"All this time, I thought you were just the shy little nobody behind the camera, but you're playing a whole different game, aren't you?"

"I'm not playing anything, Astrid."

She tilts her head, giving me a calculated once-over. "So you're telling me this relationship isn't the perfect setup for your little documentary channel? That you haven't already calculated how many subscribers Reece's endorsement could bring you?"

My stomach drops to my ankles. "How do you know about my channel?"

"Gordon gets super chatty when he drinks. He went off about his best videographer quitting right before this trip to start some 'bleeding heart documentary nonsense that'll never hit six figures.' Her smile is toxic. "And then—surprise, surprise!—you magically turn from employee to girlfriend in forty-eight freakin' hours. Crazy, huh?"

I feel the color drain from my face but remain vigilant. "You have no idea what you're talking about."

"Trust me, I get it. You're hungry for those subscribers. You've been playing the long game. Of course you see the power of Reece's platform because you've helped build it for two years. It's genius. Ruthless, but genius. That's what makes us so alike."

"I'm not using him like you did," I say, hands curling into fists at my sides,

"I bet you've been practicing your pitch in the mirror." she continues, twisting the knife. "'Oh, Reece, I've been thinking about starting this little channel. Would you mind giving it a shoutout to your followers? It would mean so much to *lil*'ol' me.'" Her mimicry is nauseatingly accurate.

"That's not—"

"You know what's truly impressive?" Her eyes gleam with malicious delight. "That waterfall kiss. Brilliant strategy. You've got the whole internet shipping you. But some advice: it's not so easy to fake chemistry long term when there are millions of subscribers and sponsors on the line."

Something snaps inside me—the last thread of restraint giving way to unchecked fury.

"Unlike you," I snarl, stepping closer, "I'm not treating him like he's disposable. My intentions are genuine. Yes, I want Reece to promote my channel. I'm not going to lie, I've thought about his followers becoming my audience. Yes, I've calculated how his endorsement could help my career." The words tumble out and I can't stop them. "Because I'm not stupid, and only a complete idiot would ignore the professional opportunities that have fallen into my lap!"

Her evil smile widens.

"But none of that matters," I continue, barely pausing for breath, "because I actually care about him. I care about the person, not his brand."

"Oh, totally believable." Her tone drips with sarcasm. "So, spill it—what's the big exit strategy? Wait until he promotes your channel, build your starter audience, then release a tear-jerking breakup video? Or are you thinking of stretching it out for a few more months, really securing your follower base before you ditch him?"

"I don't have an exit strategy!"

"Girl, everyone does." Her laugh is soft, almost pitying. "That's how this industry rolls. We all use each other to get ahead. I used Reece to boost my cosmetics line. You're using him to launch your channel. He's using you to save his company. Different reasons, same outcome."

She reaches out, patting my arm with faux sympathy. "Don't feel bad about it. It's smart. Actually, we should collaborate once this is all over. My followers love a good redemption arc."

"Listen, you manipulative, two-faced snake," I snap. "Go ahead and think I used his platform for views, but I never faked my feelings for him! There will not be a messy public breakup to boost my career. Reece is not a steppingstone. And when my channel launches, it's gonna be huge and make a real difference. So if you think I'm another social climber chasing the money, you're dead wrong."

"Oh, sweetie, that's cute. And slightly pathetic. Hit me up when you're ready to collab."

Then she struts off, grinning, leaving me to wonder if she's right.

Am I truly no better than Astrid?

If I confess the truth to Reece, will he believe me? Or will he think I'm using him, shut me out, and close the door on us?

CHAPTER SEVENTEEN

REECE

CAMILA IS AVOIDING ME.

She's spoken maybe three words since we got off the boat, and she hasn't looked at me once.

I don't know what changed between snorkeling and now, but one minute we were wrapped around each other under the surface of the Pacific, and the next she's treating me as if I'm invisible.

And I fucking hate it.

She didn't join me in the shower, even though I left the water hot and my arms wide open. Instead, she retreated to the balcony, muttering something about needing to "get to work editing the video because Gordon will want it ASAP."

Which, sure. Gordon is indeed a relentless content vulture. But the obvious distance Cam's putting between us is making my skin crawl with uncertainty.

So here I am, alone on the beach while the sun bleeds into the horizon. The sand is cool beneath my ass, gritty against my palms as I lean back. The waves crash against the shore in a steady rhythm.

We're leaving in less than forty-eight hours. The countdown is on, and I need to sort out where we stand—before we get on that plane, before reality bursts whatever bubble we've been living in.

Or maybe it already has?

What exactly do I hope for with Camila Morales? For her to be my... girlfriend? For real?

The word "girlfriend" crashes into me like a freight train of desire so powerful, my dick actually twitches in agreement. Yeah, I really fucking want that. The thought of her by my side—not only in bed but at breakfast, at events, in my everyday life—hell, I'd love that. *But is it the right decision?* Not just for me but for every other part of my life.

What about my employees—three hundred people whose mortgages and health insurance and kids' braces depend on me keeping the Reece Dare brand relevant? What about the sponsors who pay obscene amounts of money for me to use their products while I jump off cliffs and eat ghost peppers and pretend my balls aren't on fire?

Can I manage a real girlfriend while maintaining an empire? The constant pressure to be "on." The unending content treadmill. The crushing awareness that my entire career is built on the modern equivalent of "watch this idiot hurt himself for your amusement."

Astrid never cared for my attention beyond the videos, but with Cam, it would be different. I'd love spending every minute with her. Minutes I don't know if I have to offer.

Before I can spiral further, I yank my phone from my pocket, ignoring the twelve text notifications from Gordon (all in caps, all with multiple exclamation points, all about metrics and merchandise numbers). Instead, I flick through my contacts until I land on the people I trust most in this world: my moms.

Mama picks up the video call on the first ring, her dark curls arranged in familiar artful chaos. Her Parkinson's disease may put a slight tremor in her hand, but it does nothing to dull the sparkle in her eyes. She makes me feel like I'm the center of her universe.

"Helen!" she yells immediately, not bothering with hello. "Our son has finally called! Get your ass over here! Bring the good wine!"

I can't help but grin. "Hi, Mama. I've missed you too."

Before she can answer, Mom appears on screen, a glass of red in hand. Her silver-streaked hair is pulled back in its usual no-nonsense bun, sharp blue eyes narrowing as she assesses me through the camera.

"Reece," Mom says, "your mama has been making me nuts with conspiracy theories about what's really going on with you."

"Camila, Camila, Camila!" Mama singsongs. "Is it real? Please tell me you guys are real. She's such a nice girl. I've watched that waterfall kiss a hundred times, and if that's acting, then you both deserve Oscars."

"Vera," Mom sighs, "we discussed letting him bring this up, remember?"

"Life's too short for beating around bushes, Helen! Our son is in a romantic crisis. I can feel it in my bones."

"Yeah, well, that's kind of why I'm calling. I don't know if it's real. I mean, I want it to be, I think. But... Hell, I'm not sure what I'm doing with my life anymore."

Mama's face crumples into immediate concern. "Sweetie, what's wrong? Are you having a quarter-life crisis? Is it early balding?"

"It's not balding, Mama." I check my hairline on the screen to be sure. *Thanks for the new insecurity.* "It's... Do you think what I do matters? Like, at all?"

"Matters to whom?" Mom asks, ever precise, sipping her wine.

"To anyone. To the world. Is filming myself doing riskier and riskier stunts while telling dumb jokes actually adding value to humanity? Or am I more like a fleeting internet freakshow?"

"One hundred and fifty million subscribers think you matter quite a lot," Mama says.

"I get that people watch my videos," I say, digging a small trench in the sand with my heel. "But watching something and it actually mattering are two different things. I met this family in Lahaina whose entire life burned down in the fires. Their kid asked if I could help them. And I didn't know what to say."

My moms exchange one of those looks that have an entire conversation embedded in it—thirty years of marriage giving them their own visual shorthand.

"And what would you have wanted to say?" Mom asks, her voice now gentle.

"I don't know. Yes? But also... would my audience even care? Would they donate to help rebuild? Or would they just scroll to the next video of me doing something stupid for views?"

"Well, first thing," Mama says, "don't imagine the worst. If you imagine the worst and it happens, you've lived it twice."

"But what if I change everything and it fails? What if I let everyone down? What if people lose their jobs because I choose to make documentaries with Cam instead of filming my millionth stunt video? What if I can't pay for Mama's treatments because my whole business tanks?"

"Reece Hudson Dare." Mom's voice turns stern. "Is that what you think? That we need you to keep making videos so we can afford to survive?"

"Well... yeah." The admission might as well be me ripping open my chest and exposing my still-beating heart. "I mean, Mama's treatments aren't cheap, and the specialists, and the—"

"Stop right there." Mom raises her hand. "We are your parents. It is not—nor has it ever been—your obligation to take care of us. I swear to God, sometimes I think we raised you too well."

"But—"

"No buts."

"Yes, your success helped with medical expenses when you first started. And yes, we appreciated it more than we could ever express. But we are not financially dependent on you."

Mama nods emphatically. "We have savings, investments, insurance. Helen has her pension from the architecture firm. I have my teacher's retirement. We're comfortable, sweetheart."

"But what about the extra specialists?" I press, a decade-old fear clawing at my insides. "The experimental treatments? The therapies insurance won't cover?"

"Which I chose to stop a year ago," Mama says as her hand trembles slightly against her cheek. "Remember? We had that whole discussion at Thanksgiving. You were rage-texting Astrid the whole time, but I told you this. They weren't getting results, and I decided quality of life was more important than chasing a miracle cure."

I blink, the memory flooding in. She had told me that, hadn't she? I'd been so caught up in my own problems: Astrid, the content treadmill, the relentless pressure from Gordon—I'd never fully processed what it meant.

"Your happiness," Mom says firmly, leaning toward the camera, "is our most important concern. Always has been. Always will be."

"But—"

"We've seen you've been unhappy for quite some time," she continues. "The spark went out of your eyes. Your laugh changed—it became performance instead of genuine joy. We noticed, Reece. But you're an adult, and it's not our place to tell you how to live your life."

"Sweetheart, happiness is so important. Watching your livestreams these last few weeks, I've seen joy in you that has been missing since you were a boy. So if making a change to your videos will bring you that joy, then you do it. Future be damned."

"The things that frighten us the most are often the ones most worth doing." Mom takes a long sip of her wine, her gaze never wavering from mine.

I let out a long breath, detecting a shift inside me like tectonic plates rearranging. Not a complete resolution—there are still a gazillion questions swirling—but a clarity I haven't felt in months. Maybe years.

What brings me joy?

The answer comes so fast it's almost embarrassing: *Cam.*

Every breath, every thought, every beat of my heart sings the same name. *Cam. Cam. Cam.*

This girl's become as essential as oxygen or water or those ridiculously perfect fish tacos from the food truck near my house. Cam pushes me—no, inspires me—to be a better person. She's dug up parts of me I feared were lost under years of branding and image control.

"Reece? Did you cut out?" Mom's voice breaks through my trance.

"Shhh," Mama hushes her, voice dropping to a theatrical whisper. "He's thinking about her. Look at his face. Let him work it out."

Mom's expression softens. "You're such a romantic, Vera. It's the thing I love most about you."

Mama grins. "I know."

And then—they kiss. Not in an obnoxious way, not in a get-a-room way, but in a this-is-what-love-looks-like way.

The kind of love that makes it through job stress, bad days, and medical diagnoses. That weathers chaos and bullshit and still chooses each other, over and over again.

That's what I want.

I want her. I want real. I want forever.

Someone in your corner who sees past your facade to the person hiding underneath and chooses you anyway. *Oh. Shit.*

"You're in love with her," Mom states.

"I... Fuck. I think I am."

Mama makes a sound resembling a teakettle reaching full boil, clapping her hands with enough enthusiasm to jostle Mom's wineglass. "I KNEW IT! Helen, what did I tell you? I said, 'That boy is head over heels.'"

"Moms, I gotta go," I say suddenly, surging to my feet so fast I send a spray of sand flying into the air. "I love you both."

"We love you too," they chorus before I end the call.

I open up my text messages and click on Gordon's name, my thumbs flying across the screen:

Me: *Gordon, I've made a decision. We're done chasing trending content. It's time to focus on videos that mean something. Content that* *gives back. Cam wants to start by helping the people of Lahaina, and I agree. We'll talk more when we return.*

G-Thorne is going to lose his shit. He's going to yell, talk about branding, talk about numbers, and say things like, "Reece, going viral is what matters!" and "This is a business, not a charity!"

But I don't care.

Because for the first time in years, I'm not thinking about the DareSquad.

I'm thinking about me.

I want to create something that matters. To help people. To live a life that belongs to me, not my followers.

And there's only one person I want to share this with. Camila.

Time to be honest—with her and with myself. This isn't mere physical attraction, or a vacation fling, or great sex *(though fuck me, the sex is incredible).*

This is love.

It's time to put my heart on the line to find out if she feels the same.

***

ONE GOAL. ONE MISSION. Find Cam.

I've faced a live bear while wearing a salmon suit, sprinted through flaming obstacle courses, and even endured the deeply regrettable stunt where I let Blaze shoot arrows at balloons taped to my chest. But nothing—and I mean nothing—has ever made my internal organs as twisted as stepping into this hotel room right now.

Operation Tell Cam I'm Stupidly In Love With Her is a go. Or it will be, as soon as my hand remembers how to turn this doorknob that I'm sweating all over.

Come on, you're Reece goddamn Dare. You routinely fling yourself off structures normal people wouldn't consider climbing. You can handle a simple conversation about feelings.

Even if the potential for rejection seems seventy billion times scarier than that time I rode a shopping cart strapped to a rocket.

The resort key card beeps green, and I push open the door to find Cam, cheeks flushed, fresh from the shower, wrapped in a fluffy white robe. She's toweling off her damp hair, and the whole room is filled with the scent of her coconut shampoo. My mouth goes dry, and every version of my carefully rehearsed speech disappears.

"Hey," she says, her voice carefully neutral.

"Hey," I respond as the brilliant wordsmith that I am.

Real smooth, jackass. Shakespeare would be jealous.

As I work to get my brain back online, she gestures toward the far corner of the room.

"Those arrived while you were out."

I follow her gaze and spot a mountain of boxes. I couldn't care less. Cam is the only thing on my radar. I open my mouth to speak, but she's locked and loaded. Too little, too late.

"Is it more merch for us to wear? I do need to plan my outfit for tomorrow. Ziplining and a private Jeep tour." She's all business.

Something is seriously wrong. Cam's walls are so high and thick, I'm wondering if I need a wrecking ball—or possibly a nuclear strike—to bust through them. This isn't her being busy or distracted—this is deliberate distance. Distance that could be a precursor to goodbye.

I walk over to the boxes, my mind racing through strategies as if I'm planning a complex stunt. How do I approach this version of Cam? I've seen her frustrated, annoyed, turned on, amused, horrified—the full emotional spectrum. But distant? Cool? Clinical? This is uncharted territory, and it's freaking me the fuck out.

I scan the shipping label on one of the boxes: TWIST & TIE.

Oh, hell yes. This might actually help.

"These aren't for me. They're for you. It's a surprise."

Cam lifts an eyebrow. "Another surprise?"

There's something there in her tone—a little bit of the old Cam creeping back in. I go with it.

"Yeah, I like to surprise my girl."

She winces when I say "my girl," a flash of almost physical pain crossing her face. *Fuck.*

But I'm not backing down. Not now. I know what I want. *Who* I want.

I stride toward her with false confidence, like I know what I'm doing—like I'm not mortified that every step closer could mean my happiness slipping away. She looks up and I take her hand—still slightly damp from the shower—and pull her toward the boxes.

"Come on, see what I got you."

"Reece, you really don't need to get me things," she says, her voice softer, almost apologetic. "I'm not expecting it."

"I didn't say you were," I say, squeezing her hand gently. "I enjoy spoiling you."

She gives me a smile that's so clearly forced, it might as well have "FAKE" stamped across it in big red letters. It triggers a knot of dread in my stomach, heavy as a nine-pound bowling ball.

"You have to guess what it is before you can open it." I say, grabbing a box and handing it to her.

Cam gives it a test shake, brows furrowed, lips pursed—as if she's a bomb technician listening for ticking. Inside, something rattles, a muffled cascade of objects tumbling against the cardboard walls.

Then her eyes drift to the shipping label, and I catch the tiniest twitch at the corner of her mouth.

"That's cheating."

"The rules were not established up front." She shakes again. "Is this some sort of new sex toy? Like fuzzy handcuffs?"

I grin. "Maybe."

Her mouth falls open. "Oh my God, is it butt stuff?"

"Jesus, Cam." I chuckle.

"Hey, I don't judge. I simply need to know how prepared to be."

I press my lips together, biting back a smirk. "Will you open it already?"

Cam tears into the box, the sound of cardboard ripping filling the room, and when she sees what's inside, her jaw drops.

Hundreds of scrunchies in every color imaginable spill out as she reaches in and pulls out a giant handful. Reds, blues, yellows, patterns, glitter—she tears into another box, and another—each packed to the brim with more scrunchies, an avalanche of hair ties tumbling onto the carpet.

"¡Dios mío! You can't be serious!"

Her laugh explodes out of her, head-tilting-back, full-body-shaking, stomach-clutching laughter. And my entire body unclenches in relief.

I grab a handful of scrunchies and start sliding them onto my wrists. "Call me selfish. But I made sure you'll never, ever, *ever* be without one again."

Her gaze locks on to mine, that spark flaring back to life—pure mischief and heat. Her robe slips slightly, revealing the smooth curve of her shoulder, and I'm yearning to press my mouth to that spot and work my way down.

"You must really, really, *really* want to fuck my tits," she says, her tone dropping to a husky register that makes my cock instantly hard.

I let my gaze drag over her with deliberate heat. "Is it that obvious?"

Cam leans forward, closing the distance between us, and presses her lips to mine. I pull her close, grateful for the embrace after the strange coldness mere minutes ago. My hands slide to her waist, sensing the soft terry cloth of her robe and the curves underneath.

She pulls back just enough to whisper against my lips, "Then what are you waiting for?"

My breath catches as she takes a deliberate step backward, maintaining eye contact as her fingers find the loose knot at her waist. She shrugs, and the robe obeys, sliding down her arms before slipping off completely, pooling at her feet. Her breasts break free—soft, full, utterly perfect.

I drink her in, lingering on her tight, erect nipples. My hands twitch with the urge to squeeze. With a flirty look, she takes the scrunchie in my hand, lifts her arms above her head, and gathers her damp hair in a messy bun.

The transformation is instantaneous—from freshly showered resort guest to absolute seductress. The moonlight streaming through the balcony doors caresses every inch of her naked skin, highlighting the curves and valleys I've come to know so intimately.

I'm suddenly faced with a dilemma—as if I'm being asked to choose between oxygen or water. I came here to talk, to get everything out in the open, and to find out what caused her sudden distance. But my body has other, very insistent ideas about what should happen next.

My dick, currently straining against my shorts with enough force to bend steel, reminds me that we can do both. Fuck now, talk later.

You're a genius, I silently tell him.

Cam's eyes darken. A devilish glint that spells the best kind of trouble—the kind with her flat on her back and praising whatever God sent this woman to ruin me. Cam drops to her knees in one smooth, sinfully confident motion, her hands gliding up my thighs like she owns me. They reach the waistband of my shorts, and with torturous, cruel patience, she pushes the fabric down, freeing my already rock-solid cock.

Seeing her like this—naked, kneeling before me, hair up in a scrunchie—threatens to shatter my last thread of control.

She edges closer, her tongue swirling around the tip of my cock with a teasing lick—sparks shoot up my spine. Wrapping her hand around my base, she pumps slowly while her mouth engulfs me, sucking harder and deeper with each bob of her head before pulling back with an obscene pop that echoes in the quiet room.

When she glances up, her expression shifts slightly, her head tilting as she studies my face. "You're trying to decide if you want a blow job or a titty fuck, aren't you?"

"What? No. I—" I pause. Then sigh. "Okay, yeah. How the hell do you always know what I'm thinking?"

It's unsettling how easily she reads me, how she can take one quick glance and know exactly what filthy scenarios are playing in my mind. Sure she's written her own playbook these past few days, but this girl has direct access to the darkest corners of my desires.

She doesn't answer because my dream girl's too busy completely derailing my ability to function. She strokes me once, twice, then lowers her mouth again. Slowly, torturing me, pumping me in time with every slick glide of her tongue, her pace unbearably perfect.

I groan, my head dropping back. "Jesus, Cam…"

She hums against me, and when she releases my cock, there's an infuriatingly smug look on her face. She's edging me and loving every fucking second of it *(same baby, same)*.

Rising slowly, her body presses against mine as she stands. With impatient hands, she yanks my shirt over my head, throwing it onto the growing pile of discarded clothes. Her nipples graze my chest, sparking trails of fire in their path.

Standing on her tiptoes, gripping my cock in her hand, she drags me against her crease—right where she's already wet for me. Her slick heat gliding over my shaft, making my pulse stutter.

"I'll help you decide," she whispers in my ear. "Fuck my tits first."

I release a low groan, barely holding it together. "And then?"

"Then," she murmurs, dragging her lips over my jaw, "I'll suck you until you're hard again."

A shocked gasp bursts from my chest when she pushes her tongue into my ear, chased by a wave of hot breath.

"And then you can finish in my mouth or my pussy. Your choice."

I can't take it anymore.

I drag my mouth over her neck, sucking hard enough to leave a mark, needing to brand her as mine even as the rational part of my brain knows she isn't—may never be.

"I would've burned my entire empire to the ground two years ago if I knew I could've had you," I confess against her skin. "How can you make me crave you more and more? I don't think I'm ever going to be satisfied."

Her hands clutch at my hair, and she breathes out, "I feel the same way."

Those five simple words make my fucking heart explode.

I capture her mouth in a kiss that's all-consuming hunger, devouring her confession like a man dying of thirst. She craves me too. Whatever's been bothering her, whatever caused that strange distance earlier—it can wait. Right now, all that matters is this woman who has completely upended my world.

I push down all the questions, all the what-ifs, all the fears about the future that have been circling my mind. I want to exist fully in this moment with her. Touching. Tasting. Cherishing.

Slowly, deliberately, I guide her backward, one hand at the small of her back, the other tangled in her hair, careful not to dislodge the scrunchie. She only realizes where we're headed when the backs of her legs hit the edge of the mattress. Her lips curl with anticipation.

I lift her effortlessly—her body molding to mine, thighs wrapping around my waist—and lay her down in the center of the pillows. She's spread out beneath me, watching me with hooded eyes, her lips swollen from my kisses. I climb on top of her, straddling her ribs, experiencing the heat radiating between us.

"Lick me like a lollipop until I'm dripping like your sweet, wet cunt."

"You're the boss," she murmurs, sitting up on her elbows.

I watch, mesmerized, as she drags her tongue repeatedly up and down my shaft until I'm nothing but exposed nerve endings, drenched and hungry for release. My hips buck involuntarily.

She pulls back, smirking up at me. "Patience, Dare."

"Let's see how you like it," I growl, pushing her back against the mattress, bending down, licking the valley of her breasts, and trailing moisture over her skin, layer after layer, lick after lick, until she's squirming beneath me.

Her head tips back, a moan spilling from her lips.

"I still can't believe I get to touch you. You're so fucking perfect," I rasp, dragging my palm over the curve of her waist, up to the full, perfect shape of her breasts. My thumb brushes over her nipple, and Cam shudders, her lips parting, a sound that goes straight to my soul.

"Reece," she whispers, pressing her soft curves together in a tantalizing invitation.

I don't make her wait.

I position myself beneath her breasts, pushing in with a slow, controlled thrust, my breath hitching at the sensation. My abs tighten as my cock glides between the slick warmth of her flawless tits.

"Now, that's a new smile."

"I don't think I've ever made it before."

She's watching my face, eyes locked on me, studying my reactions. If I could memorize this moment, I would—but fuck, I'm barely holding on.

"Do you want me to press harder?" she asks.

I don't get a chance to respond before she squeezes tighter, her hands framing her breasts, amping up the friction, the heat.

I curse, every muscle in my body flexing, straining, desperate to make this last. But Cam? Not done ruining me. She leans forward, her lips parting—

And when I thrust again, she tilts her head up and licks my tip.

My brain goes into a frenzy.

"Cam, no," I grit out, my fingers fisting the sheets.

"What?" she purrs, eyes locked on mine. "You don't want to fuck my breasts and my mouth at the same time?"

She licks me again.

"Jesus Christ," I mutter, my control unraveling at the seams.

Thrust.

Her tongue flicks.

Thrust.

Another long lick.

"Baby, fuck," I groan, moving faster, harder, trying to keep from absolutely losing my mind.

She's watching me intently, like she knows exactly what I desire but haven't said out loud.

That I need her.

That I want her.

That she's mine.

And that I love her.

Cam angles her head, allowing my tip to pulse into her mouth with each pump.

She moans, loud and unapologetically sinful, sending a rumble straight to my cock. The vibration courses down my length, making my balls tighten with anticipation.

"Camila, baby, I—fuck, I'm gonna—"

She moans louder. Her teeth graze me. The slightest scrape.

And I lose it.

I pull back just in time and roar her name—my release painting her skin, claiming her while my entire body pulsates.

Cam arches her back, eyes fluttering shut. "God, yes. Cover me."

My vision blurs at the sight of her, tits dripping in me, her lips glistening. I collapse forward, catching myself on my forearms, my face buried against her neck, panting.

"That was so fucking hot."

I let out a hoarse chuckle, kissing the soft spot behind her ear.

I wish I could just tell her that I love her.

That she's it.

The only person who's ever made me feel this way—alive, grounded, like my entire life before her was nothing but noise.

But then I remember—the distance, the hesitation. I won't allow this moment to end.

So instead, I press one last kiss to her temple and say, "I am yours."

Cam freezes beneath me. "Reece, I—"

I hear the shift in her tone. And it stings.

So before she can say anything else—before she can ruin this with something that might break me—I push up onto my elbows, giving her a wicked grin.

"Oh, no, you don't get to talk with that naughty mouth after what you just did," I tease, my voice husky, raw, but light enough that she relaxes.

Her lips twitch, but she's watching me carefully.

I reach for a scrunchie still on my wrist, twist it into my hair, and pull my bangs into a ridiculous unicorn horn.

She stares in disbelief. Then bursts out laughing so hard she nearly chokes.

"You won't think it's so funny, when you see how much trouble your pussy is in."

Her laughter turns to a gasp when I flip our bodies so she's on top of me. Her eyes go molten in an instant.

I wave my hand over the sensor, and the bed begins its slow, steady rotation. She clutches my shoulders, steadying herself as my palms slide down her smooth, exposed thighs. I grip her firmly, pulling her onto my chest, her clit pressing against me.

"Now, be a good girl and come sit on my face."

With a wicked smile, Cam obeys.

And as she lowers herself to my eager mouth, I think—no, I know—this woman is mine. Whether *she* knows it or not. I need to make her see it.

Because I love her.

And I'm not letting her go.

CHAPTER EIGHTEEN

CAM

Hnrfff-zzzthbt. Mmrrph. Hhnkshpoo... Snkxxkchh!

I turn my head on the pillow and bite my lip, shaking with silent laughter. Reece snores like a broken symphony—a chorus of clogged kazoos with chainsaw overtones, each breath ending in a high-pitched wheeze *(is that a whale mating call?)*. And yet, somehow, it's adorable. As in, I could happily listen to this wrecked accordion for the rest of my life.

Holy hell, I'm down *bad* for him.

Last night he wrecked me in the best, walking-today-will-be-a-problem way. The man has stamina. And an oral fixation. And a surprising ability to make me forget the limits of my flexibility.

Muscles I didn't know I had are screaming in sweet protest. My thighs burn. My lips feel puffy and tender. And the spot between my legs? Let's just say I'm going to request one of those inflatable donuts for our Jeep tour today.

Worth. Every. Ache.

I reposition myself on the rumpled sheets, inhaling the intoxicating cocktail of scents that surrounds us—his spicy ginger cologne mixed with my coconut shampoo, plus the faint musk of sex. My gaze falls to the floor, where the scrunchies lie scattered like leftover party favors.

My eyes land on Reece's wrist, where a hot-pink scrunchie clings—the same one that, a few hours ago, was keeping my hair in place while he fu—

¡Dios mío! Calm your tits, Camila! Focus up, or we will never leave this bed.

The fact that he's still wearing it as a bizarre trophy makes my heart sing. I should be panicking. Should be freaking out about how hard I've fallen. Leaving was always the plan. The whole point. But now? None of that matters. Not after last night.

I don't want to leave.

I want to stay. With him.

It's suddenly clear what I have to do—something I've avoided this entire trip.

Lay it all out. Confess the truth... Admit I love him.

No games, no half-truths. Just the messy reality.

If there's one thing I've learned about Reece, it's that he'll never make the first move. Not when it comes to feelings. He's too scared of being used, too burned by people turning him into a paycheck. Someone has to be brave. And it might as well be me.

All I need is to shake off the ugly voice in my head whispering Astrid's words.

"You're just using him to launch your channel."

"You and I are the same."

"We all use each other to get ahead."

My twisted stomach is a pretzel of guilt. Did I come here hoping he'd promote my channel? Absolutely. Was that a little opportunistic? One hundred percent. But that was before I knew the man behind the YouTuber persona was someone I could fall in love with.

Reece Dare, my scrunchie thief, tenderhearted grump, and secret Tom Cruise fanboy.

I'd rather throw my camera into the ocean than risk him thinking I'm mining his influence for personal gain. I won't ask for his endorsement. Not now. Not ever. If he offers, that's different. But I refuse to be another entry on the long list of takers in his life.

Because I love him, not his followers. *Him.*

I reach out, unable to resist tracing the sharp cut of his jaw with my fingertips. His stubble scratches my skin, the sensation shooting straight to my core. His snoring stutters then abruptly stops. His lips curve into a devastating smile that would break the internet if his fans saw it.

"Morning, gorgeous," he murmurs.

"You haven't even opened your eyes. How can you say I look pretty?" I say, trying to sound sassy instead of hopelessly smitten. "I could be hideous, or maybe I transformed into a monstrous eel after you dozed off."

One eye lifts, ocean blue peeking out. "Eels don't have these, Morales." His hand slides without warning, cupping my bare breast, his fingers giving a slow, teasing squeeze.

"¡Mierda!" I gasp, heat flooding through me. "Some people just say good morning, you know."

"They aren't waking up to a breathtaking sex goddess." Both eyes are open now, focused on me with an intensity that causes me to melt. "You're so damn beautiful it's painful, Camila. Even half-asleep, I'd recognize you. The air feels different when you're close."

How does he do that? Go from playful to soul-deep in two seconds?

"I'm either sex-drunk from last night, or that's the sweetest thing anyone's ever said to me," I joke, trying to mask how completely undone I am by his words.

His mouth quirks up on one side. "You're too far away from me." He hooks an arm around my waist and hauls me to him with embarrassing ease. I collide with the solid wall of his naked chest, his skin blazing hot against mine in the air-conditioned room.

His lips find my forehead, my cheeks, the tip of my nose—I shiver. Each press of his mouth is gentle, almost reverent, completely at odds with the filthy things he said last night.

"Can we just stay here? Forever?"

His arms tighten around me, one large hand splaying possessively across my lower back. "I've been thinking the same thing. We could become beach hermits. Live off room service and skinny dipping."

I pull back enough to take him in, studying the quiet storm in his eyes. *What is he holding in?*

Blood rushes to my ears, the sound drowning out the gentle crash of waves outside. *This is it. The moment.* I need to tell him now, or I'll lose my nerve.

Three little syllables dancing on my tongue, ready to shake up everything between us. I'm ready.

BANG! BANG!

The words die in my throat as someone pounds on our door like a jackhammer with a raging hard-on. *So much for romantic timing.*

"GO AWAY!" Reece bellows. "WE'RE BUSY!"

He rolls over to pin me beneath him. His nose nuzzles into the curve of my neck, legs tangling with mine. A giggle escapes as I wiggle under his weight, loving every second of it.

"Busy getting busy," he whispers before leaning in to kiss me.

BANG! BANG! BANG!

The pounding intensifies, somehow becoming even more aggressive. Whoever's out there is either running from a zombie horde or doesn't understand the concept of "do not disturb."

A man's voice penetrates the door, sharp and demanding. "REECE! OPEN THE FUCK UP!"

He freezes mid-nibble. His head jerks up, brow furrowed in confusion. "Is that... *Gordon*?"

Our eyes lock, mutual horror dawning between us. Gordon Thorne—Reece's manager and professional narcissist—is supposed to be in Los Angeles, not pounding on our Maui love nest door at the crack of dawn.

"Put something on. No one gets to see my baby naked but me."

The possessive growl in his voice sends a shudder up my spine that has nothing to do with the AC blasting against my suddenly exposed skin. I scramble for my hotel robe and cinch it at my waist while Reece yanks up his shorts, not bothering with underwear or a shirt.

He strides to the door resembling a panther whose territory has been invaded—all deadly swagger and coiled tension. I smooth down my sex-rumpled hair, aiming for *well-rested professional* instead of *someone who's been riding her boss like a mechanical bull.*

Reece barely cracks the door when Gordon forces his way in, his short stature vibrating with fury. Despite his agitated state, his hair—clearly fresh from a salon touch-up—doesn't move, a testament to whatever industrial-strength product he's shellacked it with. His skinny jeans look painted on, and his crimson blazer—*dear God, he's wearing velvet in Hawaii?*—strains against his narrow shoulders.

"I knew it," Gordon hisses, beady eyes darting between us and the rumpled sheets of destruction behind us. "I fucking knew it."

"Gordon." Reece crosses his arms over his bare chest, biceps flexing and nostrils flaring. "I'm sure you're pissed about my text, but flying to Hawaii is a bit much, even for you. Besides, my mind is made up."

Wait—what text? What decision?

Gordon waves his hand dismissively. "We'll talk about your little identity crisis later." His eyes swivel to me, narrowing into venomous slits as he shows me his phone. "What the fuck is this?"

His scathing tone, dripping with contempt, forces me to take a step back. I've been on the receiving end of Gordon's wrath before—like when I've suggested Reece take a day off or refused to film a particularly dangerous stunt—but this? This is seething rage.

Reece steps between us, an arm positioning me safely behind him. His fingers grip my hip protectively, and that dominant reassurance calms the storm in my chest.

"You better calm the fuck down," Reece threatens. "No one talks to her like that."

Gordon's too-tight face twists into something ugly. "Before you defend her, look at this."

I don't like how he says that.

He thrusts his phone at Reece, who receives it with obvious reluctance. I peer around Reece's shoulder and when I see the screen, my heart plummets like a malfunctioning elevator.

There's a YouTube thumbnail of Astrid—her expression a masterpiece of calculated devastation. Crocodile tears streak her perfectly contoured cheeks, her signature overdrawn lips trembling for maximum sympathy.

But it's the title that makes my blood turn to ice water in my veins:

Exposed: Camila Morales Confesses to Using Reece Dare!

Oh no. No no no no no.

"That's typical Astrid bullshit," Reece says.

"Play it. The whole damn internet already has. Eighty million views in twelve hours."

Reece taps *Play*, and it displays blurry, shaky footage—undoubtedly filmed with a hidden camera. The middeck of yesterday's catamaran comes into view, rocking slightly. Astrid appears on screen, her gold bikini glinting, and my throat tightens.

"I gotta ask," she says, voice honeyed with fake innocence, "does Reece even realize you've been playing him from the start?"

And then—

There I am.

"I'm not going to lie. I'm using him."

A dramatic *DUN DUN DUN* sound effect blasts from the tiny speaker, making Gordon flinch. Bold red text flashes on the display: SHE SAID IT HERSELF!

"I didn't say that!" I grab Reece's forearm. "She's taking it out of context! That's not what I—"

Reece shrugs off my grip without looking at me, his eyes locked on to the video with razor-sharp intensity. Panic turns my body into a trembling disaster zone, radiating out from my gut to my shaky fingertips.

This isn't happening. This can't be happening.

The video mercilessly continues.

On screen, Astrid's manicured hand tosses her blonde extensions over one shoulder. "So you're telling me this relationship is the perfect setup for your little documentary channel?"

"Yes, I've calculated how his endorsement could help my career. I've thought about his followers becoming my audience."

"You've been playing the long game. You're hungry for those subscribers."

"Only a complete idiot would ignore the professional opportunities that have fallen in my lap!"

I taste copper—I've bitten the inside of my cheek so hard it's bleeding. Each spoken word is another nail in my coffin. I recognize fragments of what I actually said, viciously dissected and reconstructed into something monstrous. A grotesque puppet show starring me.

"What's the exit strategy? Wait until he promotes your channel, build your starter audience, then release a tear-jerking breakup video?"

"There will be a messy public breakup to boost my career. Reece is a steppingstone. He's disposable. And when my channel launches, it's gonna be huge. I'm just a social climber chasing the money."

Those aren't my words—not in that order, not with that meaning, not with that intent.

The footage transitions with a star-wipe effect to Astrid sitting in her hotel room.

"Reece, baby," she says softly, voice thick with manufactured emotion, "I am so sorry you had to find out this way. I really, really hoped I was wrong, but the receipts don't lie. You are being played.

Camila Morales doesn't love you. She loves what you can do for her. We may not be lovers anymore, but we're friends, and I find this disgusting."

Bold white text fills the screen: #CancelCamila #SaveReece

Astrid leans in for effect with exaggerated sympathy. "DareSquad, hear me loud and clear. If you care about Reece like I do—and I mean, I *really* care—you won't let a fame-hungry nobody keep playing him. Y'all know what to do. Take. Her. Down."

The video cuts to black.

"That's not true!" I blurt, my voice cracking. "She edited that to make me sound awful. Those weren't my words, not like that!"

Reece is stone cold, his face unreadable. "So you're *not* leaving to start your own channel."

"I... I was planning on telling you," I whisper, each word scraping my throat like broken glass.

"She put in her two weeks' notice before you left for Hawaii," Gordon says, blunt and brutal. "Sorry, kid. I thought Cam was the best solution for you, but clearly I fucked up. And the fans? They're out for blood. Listen to these comments."

He scrolls reading them aloud:

Classic move: sleep with the boss, steal his audience.
Can't believe Reece fell for her act. So obvious.
Always knew she was using him for clout. #TeamAstrid.
Camera girl should stick to staying BEHIND the camera.
DareSquad, it's time to #CancelCamila once and for all.

When Reece's gaze meets mine, I'm staring into the soul of a man who's being gutted alive. Pure agony.

Gordon sighs. "Cam and I had discussed you promoting her new channel as part of the fake girlfriend contract. That's why she was so eager."

"No!" I surge forward, desperation clawing up my throat. "*You* said that. I hadn't decided if that's what I wanted or not!"

"What *do* you want, Cam? Because I sure as hell don't know." Reece says gruffly. "I was hoping it was me. But apparently I'm a schmuck, because I'm just the 'willing hottie at the resort for you to climb like a coconut tree.'"

My heart stops. Those words. My words. From my FaceTime call with Petra and Katie back in the church on his wedding day. The plan he overheard—coming to Hawaii to have sex with hot cabana boys.

"Reece, you have to believe me. Don't shut me out. Not again. Let's talk about this alone. I can explain."

I watch it happen in real time—the shuttering of his expression, the hardening of his features, the emotional retreat I've witnessed many times before when emotion run too high.

Gordon checks his diamond encrusted watch. "The PR firm is waiting on a video call to discuss damage control. I've got the conference room set up."

Blind panic courses through me. I grab his hand. "Reece, please. Don't go."

He stares at our joined hands for three excruciating heartbeats. Then he extracts himself from my grip, the neon pink scrunchie still on his wrist grazing my skin.

"I thought you were different." He moves to the door, pausing at the threshold. "I was going to ask you to be my girlfriend. For real."

The admission hangs in the air between us, a beautiful dream extinguished before it could live.

He completes his dark transformation, and it destroys me. The playful, passionate man who stole my heart is gone—lost behind walls built from years of betrayal and mistrust.

He walks out without another word.

"You're fired, effective immediately. If you come near Reece again, I'll bury you in legal paperwork so deep your descendants will be filing motions." Gordon slams the door, the bang echoing through our once-intimate space.

My heart doesn't just break—it disintegrates, pulverized beyond recognition. My legs give out, and I collapse onto the pile of colorful scrunchies that Reece ordered for me, each one a testament to possibilities now lost forever.

The memory of his eyes—gutted, betrayed, devastated—sears itself into my brain. My stomach revolts violently, bile scorching my throat. I don't know whether to sob or vomit, so my body chooses both. Hot tears stream down my face as I stumble for the trash can, retching painfully while clutching a purple scrunchie to my heart like it's the last piece of him I'll ever hold.

***

I STAB AT PETRA'S contact with a trembling finger, my vision so blurred from crying I can barely see the phone display. Each long ring is an eternity. *Pick up, Petra. I can't be alone in this nightmare.*

When her face appears, she's squinting, her black hair a wild nest around her head, dark smudges of yesterday's eyeliner giving her raccoon eyes.

"Cam, it's fucking six a.m.," she says with a raspy groan. "Someone better be dead or—"

A sob rips from my chest so violently it actually hurts.

Instantly, her eyes snap open. Gone is violent sleep-gremlin Petra, replaced by alert, protect-at-all-costs Petra.

"Whoa, whoa—what happened? What's wrong?"

"I—I—I—" My words disintegrate into hiccuping sobs. I try again. "Reece... video... Astrid... Gordon... fired..." Each word punctuated by a gasping breath followed by a pathetic blend of sobs and a wheezy, mucus-laden whimper that makes me hate myself.

"Okay, who's fucking fault is this? I want blood," she demands as she sits up abruptly, the covers sliding off her tattooed, bare chest—Petra Brinkman doesn't believe in pajamas, or modesty.

I catch a glimpse of my reflection in the tiny FaceTime box and—¡Ay, Dios mío!

I look rough—like if a hangover had a hangover.

My hair is doing so many things, none of them good. My face is red, blotchy, and beyond shiny with mascara smeared down my cheeks. There are actual snot bubbles forming. *Snot bubbles!*

I. Am. A. Hideous. Mess.

"S-Sorry," I stammer through a hiccup. "I w-would've called Katie, but sh-she's in Italy, and I don't know what time it is there, and—" Another sob erupts, snuffing out the rest of my sentence.

"Hold on," she says, snatching a crumpled tee from the floor and tugging it over her head. "I got you, Cam. Whatever it is, we'll handle it together."

Petra enters an insanely fancy sitting area, which can only be described as a 'casual billionaire's jungle sanctuary.' She plops down onto a pristine white leather couch that looks like it's never met a human butt.

The room behind her oozes wealth—the quiet, terrifying kind. Like, you won't find gold faucets here because that's too *new money*. Floor-to-ceiling windows frame a panoramic view of lush jungle meeting the vast ocean. There's a super yacht in the distance and I'm pretty sure that the abstract painting on the wall behind her is a real Picasso just casually hanging there like it's a $20 Target print.

"Start over," she says, running a hand through her chaotic bed-head. "Tell me exactly what happened."

A deep male voice interrupts from somewhere offscreen. "Is this a cappuccino situation or espresso?"

She turns slightly, tilting the phone. "Espresso. A double."

My sobs come to a screeching halt as I spot the man in fancy silk pajamas talking on his phone. Tall, gorgeous, with blonde hair more perfect than any Ken doll.

But he's not just any blue-eyed hottie—it's Bryce Freaking Sterling. Billionaire heir to the Sterling empire, with buildings named after his family in every major city. The same guy Petra's been hopelessly in love with since high school and who happens to be her brother's best friend.

"Okay, spill it," Petra says, unfazed. As if I'm not witnessing her most closely guarded fantasy come to life.

"Is that... Wait, are you...?"

"It's not what you think. It's... complicated. I'm in Mexico for my brother's wedding. We can talk about it later. Focus, Cam. What's wrong? How can I help?"

The memory of Gordon's face...of Reece's broken expression...of Astrid's manipulated video...comes crashing back. The tears return with reinforcements.

"I fucked up. It's all gone to shit." My voice cracks. "I want to come home."

"Should I send the jet?" Bryce asks offscreen. "Wait, sorry, my jet's in New York with my mother. I can charter one though, be there in four, maybe five hours."

"Slow down, Mr. Moneybags." Petra rolls her eyes. "Normal people just buy a plane ticket."

She turns back to me. "Cam, I'll book you on the next flight out. And when you get home, I'll arrange Reece's takedown," Petra says, voice cool, dangerous, like a woman who absolutely knows where to hide a body. "Something public and humiliating. Maybe involving a scandal."

Bryce appears in frame, offering Petra her espresso on a fancy room service tray. "I forget how legitimately terrifying you can be."

"Money can't buy your safety," Petra replies, accepting the tiny cup with a smile that's equal parts threat and promise.

They share a look that's so X-rated, I'm secondhand blushing—might be time to hang up.

She knocks back her espresso as if it's a shot of tequila. "I'm gonna hang up to get your ticket sorted. Text me when you're at the airport, okay? And Bryce will have a car pick you up when you land."

"I will?" Bryce asks.

"Oh, so now you're shy about flaunting your fortune?"

"Love you," I interject, hoping to dodge the crossfire of their bickering, which sounds suspiciously like foreplay.

"Love you too bestie."

And then she's gone.

I yank open my suitcase and start throwing things in like a lunatic.

Scrunchies.

More scrunchies.

Armfuls of scrunchies.

Because if I don't have at least a hundred mementos of him, I will die.

A soft knock at the door sends my heart soaring. Hope lights a fuse of fireworks in my chest.

Reece. He came back. He realized Gordon was lying. He—

Not Reece.

Kai stands in the hallway, shirtless. His sarong is tied with suspicious precision, his sun-kissed skin glowing like a damn sunset, his expression that usual Zen-master-meets-thirst-trap combo that makes women book extra nights at his resort.

His smile fades the instant he notices my tear-ravaged face. "Oh, wahine. What is wrong?"

"Um, I..." I struggle to form words, swiping at tears that won't stop. "Never mind. What do you need?"

"I came to ask if there was any way I could help with the video about my friends from Lahaina," Kai says, his eyes soft with genuine concern. "Our community is very grateful for Reece's interest. Not many celebrities bother to look past the resorts to see the real Maui."

He glances behind me at the explosion of clothes and toiletries. "This is a bad time. I will return later."

That does it. The dam breaks again.

"I had hoped the video would help too," I say between hiccupping breaths. "But I... I don't work for Reece anymore."

Kai blinks, processing what I'm saying. "May I hug you?" he asks, spreading his arms tentatively.

I nod mutely, and his arms wrap around me—not in the flirty, suggestive way he hugs female guests by the pool, but in a solid, comforting embrace.

It's nice, but definitely not a Reece hug.

"I feel your heart's pain," he says, voice quiet and thoughtful. "At times like these, I recall what my grandmother said to me about the ocean. No matter how stormy the surface, deeper waters always remain calm. And every tide, no matter how far out it goes, always returns."

My phone dings, the sound demanding my attention. I pull away to inspect the display—it's from Petra, confirming my flight details.

I check the departure time. My flight doesn't leave for several hours, but I can't stay here. Not one more second.

"I need to go to the airport."

"I will arrange a car," he says, immediately pulling out his phone and sending a quick text.

Where the hell does he keep that thing? Does that sarong have pockets?

"Before you embark on your journey homeward, would you allow me to share the words stirring inside me?"

"Sure?" *At this point, what's one more bizarre Hawaiian memory?*

Kai places his large hand on my shoulder, his touch surprisingly gentle for a man who can bench press a small car. His eyes latch on to mine with a gaze so powerful that I forget to keep crying.

"Beautiful soul-seeker, find the hearts that beat with yours, for they are your tribe. Then dance with those who match your rhythm without masks or expectations. The universe has scattered kindred spirits along your path, like stars that light the way home. You do not journey alone."

I exhale sharply, his words settling into me, cracking me open.

I realize...

I know exactly what I have to do.

It won't win Reece back, but it will allow me to turn my mess into something good.

"Thank you," I whisper. "For everything. This has been... an unforgettable experience."

"Aloha, Camila. May you find the fulfillment and happiness that your soul desires and deserves. The world is waiting for you to shine. Our paths will cross again."

I wipe away my tears.

Then, I grab my laptop.

I have work to do.

***

HAWAII CAN SUCK IT.

Like, genuinely, truly, all the way up its gorgeous volcanic ass with a pineapple.

I stare at my laptop, nursing a lukewarm lemonade at the airport California Pizza Kitchen. My BBQ chicken pizza festers beside me, barely touched. The cheese has congealed into a sad, plastic-looking mess—a perfect metaphor of my heart.

I barely notice the bustling restaurant crowd—tourists in flip-flops and souvenir shirts, buzzing with vacation energy. *Must be nice.* Meanwhile, my cargo pants hug my thighs like emotional

Bubble Wrap. I'm wearing the T-shirt Reece wore when we made love under the stars *(yes, the one with rhinos fucking)*. I'm clinging to anything familiar since my whole damn life has gone up in flames.

Tap. Tap. Tap.

I have never edited a video so fast in my life. My fingers fly across the keyboard, making brutal cuts to the footage with a speed and efficiency that would impress even Mr. Critical. It's not about perfection. It's about truth. About what I should've said all along, before Astrid's manipulated video went mega-viral and ruined everything.

I don't have much time. The second Gordon realizes I still have access, he'll change the passwords to all of Reece's accounts. He probably already has some poor intern in a corporate dungeon drafting up an ironclad NDA to make sure I never utter Reece's name again.

But I'm getting this out first.

Every frame I cut through shows Reece's face—his real face, not the crafted YouTube persona, but the man I fell in love with. The one whose heart I broke.

"Fuck." My eyes sting with fresh tears.

Of course he went to his default setting—shut down, locked me out, tossed me into the pile of people who've used and abused him. That's all he's ever known. And right when he took the risk—let himself trust again—I betrayed him.

I can't get his expression out of my head. The way his jaw clenched—he was barely holding himself together. Then his blue eyes turned hollow, as if I'd taken the first real thing he's felt in years and mocked him for being so gullible.

That look is tattooed on my eyelids, right along with my shattered heart.

The laptop fan whirs angrily as the upload bar creeps across the screen, the little blue line taking its sweet-ass time, as if it's aware that my entire soul is riding on this moment. The airport Wi-Fi is a miserable, crawling, wounded sloth, and I resist the urge to start pounding the table *(just barely)*.

"Come on, come on."

Reece might never see it. Hell, he might delete it the second he gets a notification. But if he does watch it, he'll learn the truth. The unedited, unfiltered, brutal truth.

I was never using him. I was simply too scared to admit I love him.

He was going to ask me to be his girlfriend.

For real.

My chest tightens and I feel like I might suffocate.

The upload bar finally hits 100%. I hover over the "Post" button before jamming my finger down as if I'm detonating explosives. Which, in a way, I am.

"Processing... Processing... Video posted successfully!" I say out loud.

The confirmation appears, and I power down my laptop before shoving it into my carry-on.

I glance at the departures board—one hour and twelve minutes until my flight whisks me away from this paradise-turned-hellscape.

I grab my phone, opening the YouTube app to check how many views the video has already gotten. Instead, I'm bombarded with alerts, thumbnails, and recommended videos—digital *wanted* posters with my face plastered across them.

Justice For Reece: Why #CancelCamila Is Trending Worldwide.

Reece's Face When He Found Out The Truth About Cam (Heartbreaking).

10 Times Camila Morales Was Shady—Red Flags We Missed!

YouTubers React: Camila's Shocking Betrayal of Reece Dare.

The Hawaii Con: Camila's Master Plan That Made Her the Internet's Most Hated.

Why We'll NEVER Forgive Camila Morales (And Neither Should Reece).

¡Ay, Dios! This is so much worse than I imagined. And it's blowing up so fast. I close the app, my stomach twisting painfully as if I swallowed barbed wire. The endless flood of notifications are a series of tiny, electrical shocks stinging my already bruised heart.

PING! PING! PING!

More notifications.

I don't want to stay in Los Angeles. I can't.

LA is Reece's kingdom. His adoring fans fill every coffee shop, every grocery store, every sidewalk—too many memories, too many places where we filmed together.

I can't live with reminders of him... of what I had... and of how I lost it.

I will not live under judgment from his fans, their sideways glances, their whispered hateful comments as I walk by. Reece has been in the public eye for years. He's strong enough to weather that kind of storm, but I'm not.

This is why I always chose to stay behind the camera. No one picks you apart if they don't know you exist. No one cares what you wear or who you sleep with.

But now? I'm the villain in a story being told by millions of people who have never even met me.

I need to disappear. I need a shoulder to lean on. I need my sister.

Aria, with her tiny New York apartment and her food truck and her complete detachment from YouTube drama. Aria, who once told a catcaller to "Go fuck a blender" without breaking stride. Aria, who—like Petra—would burn down the world for me no questions asked.

I send off a quick text.

Me: *Can I come stay with you for a while?*

Aria: *Of course. My couch is always yours. But what's wrong? You ok?*

Me: *No. I'll explain when I get there. I gotta pack up some stuff, but I'll be on the red eye to New York tonight.*

I turn off my phone, unable to handle another notification, another message, another fucking reminder of what a spectacularly shitty person I am.

I want to unplug. To forget the headlines, the hate, the people who think they know me. To sink into the only place I still feel whole—his memory.

CHAPTER NINETEEN

REECE

SHELL-SHOCKINGLY GOOD IN BED is splashed across my chest in blinding neon green, along with two turtles mid-hump like no one's watching. Their goofy little turtle mouths curved up in pure bliss. I stare at my reflection in the bathroom mirror and shake my head. *When did I become such a fucking masochist?*

Since her, that's when.

The second I saw it in the gift shop, I had to buy it—it reminded me of Cam spotting that sea turtle, her eyes huge behind her snorkel mask, flippers kicking with childlike excitement, her hand squeezing mine in the warm tropical water.

"Congratulations, Dare. You've officially hit rock bottom," I tell my reflection. "You're wearing turtle porn to a business meeting."

I splash cold water on my face, hoping it'll shock some sense into me. It doesn't. Cool liquid drips down my chin as I grip the edges of the marble sink. I glance at the scrunchie—neon pink and way too bright—still wrapped around my wrist like I'm a lovesick teenager.

It's the same one she used last night when I fucked her tits. *Jesus. Was that really just hours ago?* When I thought that maybe, just maybe, we had something real?

Christ, I'm pathetic.

With a growl of frustration, I yank it off, the elastic snapping against my skin. For a moment, I hold it between my fingers, remembering how she gathered her hair up right before...

"Fuck this and fuck her." I toss it into the trash can with enough force to rattle the metal bin.

It lands on a pile of crumpled resort stationery and tissues, a bright spot of color in the garbage. It's a magnet, pulling my gaze. Three seconds pass. Four. Five.

"Shit. I guess it's fuck me." I bend down, fishing it out. "What is wrong with me?"

I slide it back onto my wrist, hating myself a little more.

"Get your shit together. You're the boss. Act like it."

But the mirror reveals who I truly am: a man who, just this morning, had his heart yanked out through his asshole.

I should be plotting my comeback video, my "why Camila Morales is dead to me" speech. She lied. She played me. She did exactly what every other person in my life has done—used me.

Fame is a fancy word for "everyone wants a piece of you." My followers crave entertainment. My sponsors expect profit. My manager demands his cut. My ex-fiancée chased clout. And Cam? She wanted my platform. My influence. My ability to catapult her little documentary channel into the stratosphere.

I just wanted... *her.*

Straightening my shoulders, I push through the door into the adjoining conference room, instantly hit by the artificial chill of resort air conditioning. It's a corporate war zone now—an oversized black table dominating the center, leather chairs lined up like soldiers awaiting orders, tropical paintings on the walls trying hard to remind us we're in paradise.

Another scandal. Another viral disaster. Another day in the life of Reece Dare.

I'm so fucking exhausted.

I collapse into the chair at the head of the table, slumping so low my ass nearly slides off the edge. At the other end, a massive screen waits to be filled with the people who will determine how to salvage my career from the smoking crater Cam and Astrid left behind.

Gordon paces in tight circles, his designer shoes clicking a staccato rhythm on the gleaming floor. Those absurd Italian leather lifts add a good three inches to his height, giving him the perpetual look of a guy about to face-plant.

"Listen here," he snaps at the resort employee trying to set up our video call. Gordon's eyes narrow at the guy's name tag. "'Kai's Best Friend'—is that your *real* name? Never mind. I need this up and running in the next ten minutes. I don't know how they do things in whatever protein-shake-fueled fantasy you stepped out of, but at G-Thorne Enterprises, we execute. We succeed. We do not let the screen display a goddamn error message. Fix it."

"I'm very sorry, sir," he stammers. "Our tech team is—"

"Fix it. I don't care if you have to sacrifice a virgin to the Wi-Fi gods. Make. It. Work."

The guy scurries away as Gordon continues his phone tirade.

"This is code red. Everyone on that list needs to be in front of their computers in ten minutes, or I start collecting LinkedIn profiles. Clear?"

He glances over at me, covering the phone briefly. "Sorry about this clusterfuck, kid. When I flew in this morning, they promised state-of-the-art facilities."

I offer a halfhearted thumbs-up, but it's wasted effort. Gordon's already on to his next call.

Shouldn't I feel... something?

Adrenaline, anger, or at least a flicker of indignation that—once again—I'm about to be roasted like a marshmallow over the bonfire of internet outrage.

But there's nothing. I'm coming up empty.

Gordon catches his reflection in the glass wall, zeroes in on a poppy seed stuck in his veneers. "Reece, you good? I'm gonna get camera-ready. Back in five." He disappears into the adjoining bathroom, shouting, "No comment means no fucking comment, dipshit. Now put your boss on the phone before I take the next flight out and become your personal nightmare."

I can feel the stress ulcer building in my stomach again, a slow-growing, fury-fueled tumor. I try to remind myself of my survival mantra—the one that's kept me from losing my shit all these years:

Keep smiling. Stay relevant. Don't let them see you crack.

It's not working.

The meeting room door swings open, and Blaze shuffles in—less a human tornado, more a slow, dejected trudge. His bleach blonde hair is flat on one side like he slept on it wet, and his signature tank top has been replaced with a wrinkled Hawaiian shirt missing two buttons. Even his go-to grin is MIA.

Blaze flops into the chair next to mine, "Hey, bro," he sighs.

Oh shit. This is serious.

"Hey," I sigh back. Then my grief-clouded mind splits wide open. "Wait—what the hell are you doing here?"

"G-Thorne told me all hands. It's DareDuo 2.0." He attempts a fist pump that gives up halfway, his arm dropping limply back to the armrest.

"Of course he did."

That's how Gordon operates—telling literally everyone except me what's happening in my own fucking life. Want to know the plan for your career? Sorry, that's need-to-know, and the actual human whose face is on the merch doesn't need to know.

I'm so fucking sick of it.

"Uh... Reece. I'm really sorry, man."

"Did you accidentally torch something valuable again?"

He exhales hard. "Astrid and I filmed our breakup video last night. She said our relationship had run its 'promotional course.'

Classic Astrid—chew 'em up, spit 'em out, then monetize the tooth marks.

"I had to cry on command while she announced her new lip plumper line."

He attempts to demonstrate his cry face, scrunching up his features and resembling a constipated bulldog.

"She kept saying 'More tears, Blazey! My followers need authenticity!' And after we filmed it, I felt weird. So I was wandering around the resort, and my insides felt shitty—ya know, like someone had stolen my favorite surfboard. And I was thinking, um, maybe she just needed space? Maybe we could still work things out?"

Oh no. I am familiar with that particular tone. It's Blaze's *I-have-a-brilliant-idea-that's-actually-a-terrible-idea* voice—the same one that preceded the Great Wasabi Challenge of

2019, which ended with a trip to the ER, a very angry Japanese chef, and a lifetime ban from Benihana.

"I figured I could surprise her, right? Go all out! I got Kai to hook me up with the full romance package—flowers, penis-shaped candles, anal beads—"

"Please skip to the end."

"Right. So I'm filming the whole thing. Recording my heart-felt speech about how we're meant to be together and how her lip plumper makes me want to kiss her, even though it tastes like gasoline."

He's sitting up straighter now, his hands animating the story with characteristic windmill-like gestures.

"I decided to parkour up to our balcony to be romantic and shit. But there she was—getting smashed like a piñata by another dude. And that's when it hit me. What I did to you was fucked up."

Dude! That's when it hit you? I keep silent.

Blaze holds my gaze, genuine regret in his eyes. "I should've asked if you were cool with Astrid and me goin' to pound town. I totally thought it was all, like, staged for views or whatever. But watching her move on from me that fast—literally hours after our 'emotional' breakup video—I finally get it. I messed up. Big-time. Like, I dropped-my-phone-in-the-toilet kind of messed up. I'm really fucking sorry, man."

The apology catches me off guard, hitting me like an unexpected left hook.

In our decades-long friendship, Blaze has broken my possessions, several of my bones, and once, my grandma's antique vase that apparently contained her ashes. But this is the first time he's come close to breaking our friendship—and the only time I've seen him genuinely remorseful.

I reach over, clasping his shoulder firmly. "Thanks," I say, meaning it. "We're cool."

"So... the DareDuo is back?"

"DareDuo is best bros forever," I confirm, the words unlocking something tight in my chest. *At least I still have this—a friendship that predates the fame, the brand, the absolute circus my life has become.*

Blaze's face breaks into that familiar goofy grin as he launches himself at me, pulling me into a hug so tight it's painful. I endure it, giving him an awkward pat on the back before extracting myself from his bear hug.

"Where's Cam?" he asks, eyeing the corner of the room as if her five-foot-four-inch body is hiding behind a twelve-inch potted plant. "I thought you two were, like, sex friends." He waggles his eyebrows.

The brief moment of normalcy shatters. The hot-pink scrunchie on my wrist suddenly feels as if it's made of lead.

"You're not the only heartbroken idiot at this table."

Ten minutes later, the blue error message finally disappears, and there's a wall of faces that are making up the world's most depressing Zoom meeting. Twenty different people stare back at me, each tiny window a peek into a different flavor of the corporate world.

Some sit in sleek office settings with tasteful art, as if they're ready to go on CNN. Others are clearly on vacation, squinting against the tropical sun or sipping coffee on a European balcony. Then there are the true victims—rumpled, dead-eyed, looking like they were dragged from their beds with disheveled hair that screams, *What ungodly hour is it?*

I clear my throat, sitting up in my chair. "Thank you everyone for coming on such short noti—"

"Let's get down to business," Gordon cuts me off. "Tell Reece what has happened to sales overnight."

The first face to enlarge belongs to Marcus, the head of DareProductions. Behind him, an office wall covered in film equipment and framed YouTube Play Buttons serves as a reminder of better days.

"We've had three sponsors pull out of branded content," he says, his voice tight. "BeastMode Barbells, TripleX Protein, and FearLess Sunglasses all terminated their contracts this morning, not wanting to be attached to the scandal. Without that revenue..." He swallows hard. "We don't have enough projects to sustain our current staff. Layoffs are inevitable unless we can find replacement sponsors immediately."

My gut churns at the word "layoffs." DareProductions alone employs forty-seven people—editors, camera operators, production assistants, all with families and mortgages that depend on my videos getting views and my face selling products.

The screen shifts to Vanessa, the impeccably dressed head of DareWear, who appears to be sitting on a luxury yacht. Her designer sunglasses are perched on her head, and the sparkling Mediterranean Sea appears to be mocking our collective misery.

"I was on a call with the DareWear factory," she says with crimson lips pressed into a tight line. "Orders have dropped by fifty percent overnight. On top of that, we've already invested heavily in the new DareLove line following your waterfall kiss with Camila." She pauses, letting the words sink in. "It's most likely a loss in the millions unless we can turn public opinion around immediately."

The screen shifts again to Derek, head of DareFuel, who's in his kitchen. His usual polished appearance has been replaced by a rumpled T-shirt and a bad case of bedhead.

"DareFuel has the same problem with the new couples' flavors we were rushing to market," he explains, running a hand through his disheveled hair. "Production is already underway for 'Love Potion Peach' and 'Coconut Kiss.' We've invested—"

"Daddy! I have to go poo-poo!"

A tiny tornado in princess pajamas crashes into the frame, clutching a well-loved teddy bear. Her pigtails are askew, one significantly higher than the other, and her face bears the remnants of what might be chocolate milk.

"Can we PLEASE keep your offspring out of this CRISIS MEETING?!" Gordon explodes.

"Sorry, sorry!" Derek looks mortified as a lovely woman—presumably his wife—darts into the frame, scooping up the toddler.

The little girl's innocent face tugs at my chest—a memory of Nalani, the Akana family's daughter, clutching her stuffed turtle while standing in the doorway of their temporary housing unit. Cam captured their tragedy with grace and kindness. Her storytelling instincts turned what could have been exploitation into a powerful, deeply human moment.

That day in Lahaina had sparked a fire in me—a realization about what my platform could be. What it *should* be. For the first time in years, I'd felt a sense of purpose beyond chasing views and selling merch.

I'd thought maybe Cam could be part of that vision.

I trace my thumb over the scrunchie clinging to my wrist—the tiny pink elastic carrying the weight of an entire imagined future.

But that was before I knew the truth. That I was dreaming about our future together while she was calculating how to use me to launch her career.

Now I'm back where I started. My companies are imploding, hundreds of jobs are at risk, and millions of dollars are disappearing by the minute. And for what? Because I was stupid enough to trust her. To think she saw me for more than my subscriber count?

"—been up all night securing a solution." Gordon's voice snaps my focus to the nightmare at hand. "A plan that will definitely pull us out of the downward spiral."

With the dramatic flourish of a magician revealing his final trick, Gordon strides to the conference room door and flings it open.

And in struts Astrid Montclair.

Her outfit is a masterclass in showing skin—a yellow bandage dress vacuum-sealed to her body, highlighting every surgically perfected curve, with cutouts exposing way too much spray-tanned skin. Stilettos jack her up six inches, and her red soles hit the floor like warning flares with each calculated step.

"What the fuck?"

Gordon pulls out the chair beside me, and she takes his hand with a smirk, her viper-like confidence radiating as she sits. "G-Thorne always gives it to you straight. This isn't about Astrid, though yeah, her numbers are blowing up. It's not about camera girl's takedown video, which is viral as fuck."

A sharp pang hits me thinking about all the online hate Camila's getting. Yeah, she played me, but she was only chasing what she thought mattered. I'm pissed off, but... no one deserves cyber hate like this. I've been there—it's brutal, even when you kinda have it coming.

Gordon claps a hand on my shoulder. "This is about giving a hungry audience what they expect—you and Astrid back together. For real this time. Kid, everything we've done has led to this. They're shipping you two. Hashtag ASStreece has over seventy million impressions. She's your golden ticket."

"I break the internet for breakfast," she says, her baby-talk voice at odds with the calculating look in her eyes. "Come on, Reece. You and me? We're social media crack."

There's churning in my gut, and acid climbs up my throat—my body is physically rejecting the Astrid pitch. But what choice do I have? Hundreds of jobs on the line. Millions in investments. Real people with real bills.

But for some inexplicable reason, at this moment of peak desperation, I hear Cam's voice in my head.

From the shuttle, driving past Lahaina: *"You don't ever really know if your efforts will help. But that doesn't mean you don't try. Not everything needs a million likes to make a difference."*

"Not everything needs a million likes to make a difference," I declare to a room full of people but mostly to myself. The truth of the words burns my tongue.

I rise to my feet, my chair scraping against the floor with a dramatic screech that perfectly punctuates this moment of clarity.

"I was serious about the text I sent you last night, Gordon," I announce, my voice leveling out. "Effective immediately, we're changing content strategies. No more clickbait. We're focusing on giving back."

I turn to the screen, facing the grid of shocked executives directly. "I want us to be a company that produces something meaningful. It's scary to switch strategies, but I've spent the last two weeks really thinking about what matters—for me and for everyone who depends on the Dare brand."

My pulse pounds in my ears as the words tumble out. "No more fast fashion that trashes the planet. No more energy drinks loaded with chemicals no one can pronounce. No more trending bullshit. Everything we put the DARE brand on from this moment forward will be customer-focused, earth-conscious, and built with purpose."

I take a breath. Twenty stunned faces stare back at me from the monitor, in a *we've-seen-this-before, this-has-to-be-a-prank* expression. And then—

Clapping.

It's the dad from earlier, the one who got interrupted by his daughter needing to go poo-poo. He's sitting in his kitchen, smiling, hands coming together in steady applause.

Then someone else joins in. Then another. And suddenly, the whole screen is clapping.

"Gordon, you swore this was a lock if I posted that vid." Astrid's voice is a blade slicing through the applause. "Seriously, what the hell is happening?"

"Not now, Astrid," Gordon hisses, his usually smooth face flushing red. Wrinkles, suppressed by years of cosmetic intervention, break through.

My eyes narrow. "Tell me straight—did you make that deal with her? Because if that's the case... you're done."

"Don't threaten me, kid," he says, voice dangerous. "I didn't promise Astrid anything."

Blaze lets out a long, slow whistle. "Uh, that's a load of shit, G-Thorne. You're straight-up lying."

I swivel toward him. "Bro, what are you talking about?"

Blaze fiddles with his phone, thumbs flying across the screen. "Gordon was making all the promises when I caught him fucking Astrid last night. I got it on video, see?"

He holds out his phone, and I take it with a sense of morbid curiosity. The screen shows a hotel balcony view—presumably filmed during Blaze's ill-fated romantic mission. The footage is a bit shaky, but there's no mistaking what I'm seeing: a very sweaty, very hairy Gordon Thorne, his suit pants bunched around his ankles, enthusiastically banging a clearly bored Astrid.

"I'm gonna make you a superstar!" Gordon's voice echoes from the phone speaker. "You and this hot ass will be bigger than Reece!"

"I want my own clothing line and my makeup in Sephora." She pauses. "And an album."

"You wanna be a singer?" Gordon pants. "Prove it. Scream my name."

Astrid complies with the mechanical enthusiasm of someone ordering take-out. "Gordon, oh God, G-Thorne! Give it to me, Daddy Thorne!"

I pause the video, making a mental note to tell Blaze later that explosive details like this need to be shared immediately.

Then all hell breaks loose.

Astrid lunges across the table like a feral cat, her talons extended. "Give me that phone!" she screeches. "Blaze, you backstabber, delete that video!"

She grabs Blaze's phone, but it's *not* a video on his phone—it's a YouTube video. She lets out a bloodcurdling scream. "OHMY-GAAAAAAHHHHHD!"

Her entire face crumples in horror.

Blaze grins wide. "Yeah," he says, stretching his arms above his head. "I uploaded it to YouTube. #AstridScam is trending. Guess I do know how to fuck you."

She bolts like her ass is on fire, screaming loud enough to shatter glass.

I turn to Gordon, who stands frozen. "You're fired." Then I swivel back to the screen of executives, who've just witnessed what amounts to a live reality TV meltdown. "All passwords are to be changed now. Gordon's office is to be packed up and delivered to his home. Tell Legal to prepare for pushback if he threatens or violates his NDA." I pause, drawing a deep breath. "I'll be back in LA today for an emergency meeting. I expect ideas from everyone on a new plan moving forward."

I end the call. Twenty stunned faces vanish as the screen goes black.

Gordon stares at me, jaw tight, hands clenched. "I did you a favor by getting rid of camera girl and her bleeding-heart agenda. Giving back is not how successful companies are run."

"You don't know until you try."

"I'm your rock," he counters, desperation creeping into his voice. "I'm the only one on your side."

"Wrong," I say, feeling lighter with each passing second. "You're only on *your* side. Now you better go chase after Astrid, because she's your new big client... starmaker."

I turn and walk the fuck out of the conference room, with Blaze bounding close behind. The door slams shut on Gordon's sputtering protests.

***

THE LOBBY DOORS SLIDE open, and I barrel through like a man possessed. My heart thumps wildly, and I squeeze my phone as if I'm trying to wring the truth out of it. I hit Cam's number again.

Straight to voicemail.

"I'm probably hanging off a cliff somewhere with Reece Dare, so if I'm still alive after I'M DONE FILMING, I'll call you back!"

I hear her voice—that sarcastic, warm, *everything-I-fucking-need* tone.

"Camila? Where are you? Call me. Please."

The hotel lobby swirls with activity—happy tourists in flowery shirts clutching tropical drinks, bellhops pushing carts stacked with designer luggage, a newly arrived couple kissing passionately by the check-in desk.

"Bro, where we goin'?" Blaze skids to a stop beside me.

"Cam. I gotta find Cam. Let's check my room." I'm already moving, dodging guests and suitcases as if they're obstacles in one of my stunt videos.

"Dude, what if she's gone? Like, whoosh, vanished like that time we tried to tame those wild lizards and they—"

"Not helping, Blaze."

An alert pings on his phone. "I found her!" His face scrunches up in confusion. "What's La *Hane, La Hiney*?"

I snatch his phone, my eyes zeroing in on the YouTube notification.

"It's Lahaina," I correct, tapping on the new video I see posted on my channel: The Truth About Lahaina, Hawaii… and Me.

It starts playing and there she is—Cam, my Cam—and the sight of her hits like a harpoon to my heart. She's filming from an airport restaurant, the CPK sign visible in the background. Dark circles shadow her eyes, which are red and swollen from crying. Her hair is piled into a scrunchie bun, and she's wearing my Save the Rhinos… One Ride at a Time shirt of rhinos banging. The one I wore when we made love for the first time, under a sky full of stars.

She takes a deep breath, stares straight into the camera. "I suppose I should introduce myself, although if you watch this channel, you probably already know me. I'm Camila Morales. And before anyone comments—yeah, I'm aware my eyes are puffy. I'm not having the best day."

I want to reach through the screen and pull her into my arms. I wish I could apologize for not listening, for trusting my walls over her and not letting her explain. For being a fucking coward—again.

"You all know me as Reece Dare's new girlfriend. But that's not true. I was never his real girlfriend. Our relationship was *fake*, only for views."

"Ohhh shit," Blaze drawls.

I shush him, pressing the volume higher.

"Reece works his butt off for every fan," she continues. "You don't see the endless planning, the safety checks, the sleepless edits—all for those ten minutes that make you smile. He's got true integrity, pushing through exhaustion not only for you, but for his team. Three hundred people rely on him to show up, no matter what."

I can't tear my eyes away from her face—from the sincerity etched into every feature.

"I've been a DareSquad fan since high school," she says, a faint smile on her lips. "But I never knew the pressure and isolation Reece faces. The grind of being a full-time creator is brutal and leads to burnout. The internet is fickle.

It's true I wanted to start a documentary channel and hoped to get Reece's endorsement. But in Maui, I got to see a side of him fans never see—his big heart. That's why he arranged a visit to Lahaina Town, which was ravaged by fires a year ago."

Images of Lahaina before and after play on the screen. The contrast is gut-wrenching. Front Street as it used to be—vibrant storefronts, the historic, sprawling banyan tree, tourists and locals mingling together. Then comes blackened foundations, skeletal buildings, and the scorched tree somehow still standing.

"A fan asked Reece if there was a way he could help," she says, and the video cuts to Keoni's hopeful expression. "Now, I'm asking you, the DareSquad, to rise to the challenge. Let's show Reece that there's more to his impact than just stunts and pranks. Together, we can help him help others."

"Holy shit," I whisper, and I swear my heart is swelling to twice its normal size.

Out of nowhere, Kai places a steadying palm on my shoulder, his usual unsettling presence offering me a strange comfort.

"The warrior goddess fights for your honor as her heart bleeds," he intones softly. "Such is the rarest form of devotion—that which gives without expectation of return."

"I was going to post this video on *my* new channel, but it can do so much more good for the people of Lahaina if the DareSquad sees it and stands up for something meaningful—not another scandal."

Her words are a wrecking ball to my chest. She gave up her own opportunity—her chance to launch her dream—to help these peo- ple. To help me.

"I've added a donate button to help Lahaina families rebuild," she says, leaning in. "I dare you all to contribute, even a dollar. Every bit counts. Together, we can make a difference, just like hitting a million likes—one click at a time."

Pride surges through me. This woman—this incredibly brilliant, passionate, take-no-shit angel—is fighting for a cause that matters. She's turned a personal disaster into a chance to help others. She's showing me the way, embodying everything I was too scared to embrace.

"One more thing. I'm sorry, Reece, for not telling you how I felt. I never expected this trip to change me, no clue I'd feel..." She pauses, her hazel eyes drowning in emotion. A tear escapes, cutting a path down her cheek. "I would've said yes."

The world stops spinning.

She would've said yes. To being my girlfriend. To being mine, *for real.*

The video cuts away to footage of Lahaina: the Akana family standing outside their temporary shelter, and the interview where they shared their struggles with losing everything.

The views skyrocket before my eyes.

Ten million.

Fifteen million.

Twenty-three million.

The comments flood in:

Help Reece Help Lahaina! #DareToRebuild.
Just donated $50! Who can match me?
#Dare4Change.
This is why Reece is the GOAT! Always helping others!
I donated my coffee money for the month! Worth it!
THIS is the content we need—not drama, but ACTUAL HELP!

A donation counter ticks up in at the bottom of the screen.

One million.

No.

One point two million.

No.

One point five million.

And climbing.

I turn, scanning the resort lobby.

Every single person—hotel staff, guests, tourists fresh from the pool, everyone—is watching Cam's video on their phones.

A guy in a Tommy Bahama shirt is frantically tapping his screen. "Babe, I donated. I dare you to match me."

His girlfriend slaps his arm. "Double it."

"She's rallied your army," Kai says with admiration. "The DareSquad marches not for entertainment, but for purpose."

And now she's gone.

Jesus Christ, I'm a fucking idiot.

Cam is at the airport, probably booked a one-way ticket as far away from me as humanly possible.

My breath comes too fast, too shallow, like my body can't catch up to my stupidity. I rake my hand through my hair, replaying every single goddamn moment I was a total dick to her.

And wow, there are so many.

I should've trusted her. Trusted her heart.

But no. Instead, I had to spiral and assume the worst. Assume she was the same as everyone else—a user. Cam is different.

She always has been.

"Kai, do you know anything about her flight?" I ask.

He shakes his head. "No. I only arranged her ride to the airport."

I whirl on Blaze. "Go to valet. Get my car."

He dashes off without a word.

I turn back to Kai, a sudden certainty rising within me.

"I AM going to help the Akanas and the other families from Lahaina," I say, my voice steadier than it's been all day. "I promise you, I'm going to financially match every contribution my followers make. Dollar for dollar."

Kai beams. "May I hug you?" He opens his arms. I take in his sarong-wearing, oily, muscled torso. "A true warrior's bond is forged in embrace."

I sigh. "Fuck it. Why not."

Kai wraps me up in a full-body, rib-crushing hold.

And yep. That's Kai's dick.

I stiffen *(not like that)*.

"Mmmmm," Kai hums contentedly. "We have finally merged our sacred energies, my virile friend."

I immediately wrangle free, taking several comforting steps back.

Kai smiles like he won a game I didn't know we were playing.

"You are welcome at Aloha Amour anytime, Reece Dare."

I'm already backing toward the exit. "Cool, man. Thanks. I mean it. But I gotta go."

Outside, Blaze has somehow talked the valet into letting him drive my rental Porsche. I slide into the passenger seat.

"To the airport," I say, buckling up as Blaze revs the engine. "Let's go get Cam."

"DareDuo is back!" Blaze howls, cranking the radio to ear-splitting volume and peeling out of the resort.

We fishtail onto the main road, palm trees blurring on both sides, and adrenaline is pumping through me. For the first time since this whole mess started, I'm not running away.

I'm running toward something.

Someone.

The girl I love.

Cam.

CHAPTER TWENTY

REECE

"Sir, I can't give out passenger flight information. It's against the law."

The ticket counter woman refuses to make eye contact, fingers clacking against the keyboard with the rhythm of someone both underpaid and over this conversation. Her blue uniform vest strains across her chest, the name tag "Olina" pinned at a defiant angle, as if daring anyone to challenge her authority.

"Right, okay, sure, but what if—hypothetically—you accidentally let it slip? Maybe a sneeze that sounds like 'Gate 12' or a casual stretch that ends with you turning your monitor?"

She doesn't dignify that with a response.

"Can you just tell me if Camila Morales is on a plane to LA? Please?"

"As I said, sir," Olina says, slipping back into customer service monotone, "we cannot disclose passenger information. It's a violation of privacy laws."

"What if I bought a ticket? To every possible flight she could be on?"

"That would be both expensive and impractical," she states with robotic efficiency. "Also, TSA would likely flag your behavior as suspicious."

Fuck. She's right. Running through an airport screaming Cam's name like some unhinged romcom hero would land me in hand-cuffs, no doubt. Not the reunion I'm hoping for.

"Next in line."

Shit. Shit shit shit.

I spin in a circle, scanning the terminal as if a tuxedo-wearing welcome agent is going to pop up with a sign that says: CAMILA IS ON FLIGHT 1207. GO GET HER DUMBASS.

Nothing.

Not one heroic airline employee ready to break FAA regulations in the name of love.

I stare at the departure board, panic clawing up my throat. There are too many damn departures to Los Angeles. My brain is frantic, flipping through options. I could call every airline. Hack into the security cameras. Maybe bribe one of the bag handlers—

"OH MY GOD! It's really *you!*"

The squeal hits my eardrums like an ice pick. I spin to find a teenage girl with braces, phone aimed at me. "You're Reece Dare! *THE* Reece Dare!" She bounces on her toes, sparkly phone case catching the fluorescent lighting.

I force a smile. "Hey there."

"AND BLAZE TATE TOO!" Her shriek reaches a pitch only dogs should be able to hear.

I glance at Blaze, who's wandered back from his snack-finding expedition with an armful of chips and candy. His blonde hair is hidden under a backwards cap that says, BEACH PLEASE, and he's wearing sunglasses indoors, which he proudly calls *Incognito Mode*. He notices the fans and hastily grins, bringing his full-on party boy energy.

"Sup, DareSquad!" he shouts.

Then, like shark bait in open water, one excited fan quickly attracts others. Within seconds, we're surrounded—teens, twenty-somethings, moms with their kids, an overly smiley dude with my face on his sweatshirt.

Cameras flash. Questions fly from all directions.

"Can we get a selfie?"

"Will you sign my boarding pass?"

"Reece! I just donated to the Lahaina fund, man!"

"My aunt lost everything in the fires. Thank you for helping!"

"You're actually a good person?! I'm shook!"

More people join the crowd. More phones. More questions.

I pause, taking in the faces of my followers. These aren't just admirers asking for stunts or selfies. They're genuinely moved. I see it in their eyes—a connection deeper than viral videos and merch.

I should be grateful. *I am grateful.* These fans are helping raise millions for Lahaina's recovery. They saw what Cam saw. They believed in something real.

And all I can think is—this is Camila's moment. She should know that her work mattered. *That she matters.*

But right now, I don't have time.

"Guys," I say, raising my hands, instantly commanding the crowd. "I can't tell you how much it means to me that you supported

Lahaina. Seriously. Every donation, every share—you made a differ-ence. And I will be matching those funds dollar for dollar. But I gotta find Cam ASAP. Have any of you seen her?"

Everyone shakes their heads.

The teen girl with braces pipes up. "Go live! Ask the whole DareSquad!"

"I was gonna think of that!" Blaze says.

I pull out my phone, open the YouTube app, and hit the *Go Live* button.

The second the stream starts, the numbers climb. Ten thousand viewers. Fifty thousand. Four hundred thousand—no sign of stop-ping.

"DareSquad. I know this is a long shot, but I need you." My own face stares back at me—rumpled, desperate, the most unfiltered I've ever been on camera. "I'm at the Maui airport, and I have to locate Camila. But I have no idea where she is. If anyone has any clue where she might be—please, drop it in the chat."

The comments flood in immediately:

HI REECE!

Bro doesn't deserve Cam.

Why are you guys fake dating when it's obvious you're in love?

I hold my breath, eyes scanning the comments and looking for clues:

Try CPK like the video.

Ask security.

Call her maybe????

Bro check Instagram!

And then:

@DareDonut78 I caught her boarding her flight. She was crying :(

My heart stops. "DareDonut78, you saw Cam? What flight was she on? Where was she headed?"

I wait, each second stretching into eternity, until:

@DareDonut78 Her flight to LA left like 20 mins ago.

LA. That's helpful. But it means she's gone.

@DareDonut78 She was talking to the gate agent about booking a red eye to New York after LA.

I exhale sharply. She's not just leaving Hawaii; she's leaving *me*. She's going home.

"Are you absolutely sure it was New York?" I ask, desperation bleeding into every syllable.

@DareDonut78 YES! 100% SURE! Delta. Gate 24. I heard the whole convo!

I wrap up the livestream with a hasty thank you, my mind racing. I spot her plane info on the departure board—if it took off twenty minutes ago, she'll touch down at LAX by seven p.m. I might have a tiny window to catch her prior to her boarding for New York. It's slim, but it's something.

I need a plane. And then it hits me—I know a pilot.

I pull up my contacts, scrolling frantically until I find it—"Captain Love." I hit *Call*, circling anxiously as it rings.

"Cupid's Cockpit, where love takes flight. Captain Mitchell speaking."

"This is Reece Dare. I need to get to LA. Right now. Are you in Maui?"

"Sorry, I just got off the ground and I'm heading back to Cali," he says.

A pause, then... a proposition.

"But there's no further charters on the schedule. I can turn around, Mr. Dare, but jet fuel's expensive."

"How's a hundred grand sound?"

"Sold! Wow, love must be in the air."

"How soon can we leave?"

"I'll be back, fueled, and ready to go in twenty minutes."

Relief floods me, making my knees weak. "I'll be there. With a friend."

"The more the merrier," he purrs. "I'll be waiting at the private terminal."

"Blaze!" I shout. "We're leaving."

He's halfway through signing someone's forehead with a Sharpie and stops. "Like, right now?"

"Yes. Right fucking now."

Twenty minutes later, we bolt up the stairs to the private jet, skidding to a stop inside the cabin.

Oh, for fuck's sake.

This. Fucking. Plane.

The honeymoon jet.

The one with no seats, the single, king-sized bed, and the fresh shower of rose petals resembling a goddamn Valentine's explosion.

The romance tray is still there, in all its inappropriate glory, and why the fuck are there even more flavored condoms? Blaze takes one look, and his tiny brain is blown.

"Dude. Duuuuude. Is this an orgy plane?"

Before I can answer, the cockpit door swings open, revealing the pilot in all his creepy glory—Captain Mitchell, aka "Captain Love." His handlebar mustache has been freshly waxed, the ends curling like villainous whiskers.

"Mr. Dare! Welcome back! And you brought a friend! How adventurous!"

"We're not together," I clarify immediately, throwing Blaze a warning glance.

Blaze, clueless as ever, flops onto the bed and defends our friendship. "He's joking. Me and this guy go deep. Like, we've been going at it since we were kids."

The pilot chuckles. "No judgment. Love is love, lust is lust, and my plane has seen it all." He taps his nose knowingly. "There's lots of kinks on my plane, but none that stop her from flying." He whistles.

"Can we just focus on getting to LA as fast as humanly possible?"

"Ah, the urgency of love!" He clasps his hands together. "Fear not, I can have you in Los Angeles in five hours flat. We've got tailwinds on our side today."

"Get us there before seven p.m., and you'll be looking at another hundred grand."

He nods. "One quickie coming right up! Buckle up, gentlemen. Well, there aren't actually seatbelts, so... better hold on to something firm." He winks again before closing the door.

The engines surge with a roar that vibrates through the floor, up my legs, settling in my chest alongside the knot of anxiety that's taken up permanent residence there. The plane lurches forward, beginning its taxi down the runway. Outside the small oval window,

Maui's paradise whirs past us, palm trees and mountains giving way to the massive expanse of blue ocean.

"This is the life, bro!" Blaze gestures at the cabin. "No TSA feeling up my junk! A bed instead of those fake chairs that lean, like, two little inches! No wonder you wanna get Cam back on your sex plane!"

"It's not my sex plane," I growl. The memory of Cam on this same bed a mere two weeks ago slams into me—her guarded expression, the way she'd held herself so carefully apart from me, how I'd deliberately been an asshole and kept my distance.

Now I'd give anything to close that distance.

I need more information. I need eyes on the ground. I need help.

My fingers find my phone and once again I press *Go Live*.

"DareSquad. Quick update: we're airborne. Should land at LAX around sevenish." I flip the camera to show Blaze, who immediately throws up devil horns and sticks out his tongue.

"I'm trying to find Cam before she boards her connection to New York. If anyone's at LAX tonight and spots her, please let me know which terminal, which gate. Any details at all."

I squint at the scrolling text, searching for actual information among the digital screaming:

OMG I SHIP THIS SO HARD.

FIND HER KING!!!!!

I'M CRYING THIS IS SO ROMANTIC.

My sister works for Delta, I'll text her!

Check American terminals first, more red-eyes.

I'M LITERALLY AT LAX RIGHT NOW. I'll hang here and wait.

Blaze leans in, his face filling most of the screen. "Let's spice up this long plane ride, bros and bro-ettes!" He holds up a fistful of foil packets. "Who dares me to try these flavored condoms?"

He rips open a silver one with his teeth, pulling out a slippery latex circle. He pops it into his mouth, chewing thoughtfully. "Yo. Marshmallow. Like, I could actually snack on these."

"This is so disturbing," I mutter. His chaos is somehow comforting in the eye of my emotional storm. And yeah, I end up laughing.

Another rip, another taste.

"This one says fried pickles, but I dunno, dudes." He licks then immediately makes a face as if he's swallowed battery acid. "Gross! Not pickles. More like piss. Wait, no! That's cat piss!

Trust me, he knows the difference. I pulled that prank.

The comments are coming in so fast they're a stream of screaming capital letters and cry-laughing emojis.

"Oh, hell no. That is straight-up bacon." He spits it into his hand, shaking his head. "Man, if I wore this and some chick started chewing on my dick, honestly, I wouldn't blame her."

As Blaze hijacks the livestream with his increasingly theatrical taste test, my mind's back on the problem at hand. Finding Cam.

"I *would've* said yes." Her last words play over and over in my head—like a cruel Spotify playlist I can't turn off. Would've. Past tense. As in, she *would* have before I accused her of using me, before I let Gordon fire her, before I failed to defend her against Astrid's bullshit smear campaign.

I pull at the scrunchie on my wrist.

What if I can't find her at LAX?

What if she's already on a plane to New York when we land?

What if she sees me coming and deliberately goes the other way?

What if she's made up her mind that I'm not worth the heartache?

Worse—what if she's not just visiting New York, but moving there permanently? Panic floods in. I'm gonna be sick. I can't follow her, not with my employees depending on me and a company in the middle of a major overhaul. I'm so tied to Los Angeles I might as well be chained to the Hollywood sign.

But without her, none of it matters.

I'm so fucking in love with her. There's a Cam-shaped hole in my chest, and nothing else will ever fill it. Not fame, not money, not success.

She's it for me. The one.

***

WE **LAND FIVE MINUTES** after her plane does.

For one glorious moment, I think I have a shot. That I can make it to her before she leaves for New York. And then the bitter truth bitch-slaps me in the face.

We are at the wrong fucking terminal.

Private jets don't land where commercial flights do. Cam is on the opposite side of LAX, probably the busiest, most aggressively chaotic airport in the world.

"Dude." Blaze appears at my shoulder, his breath smelling like the banana condom he's currently chewing like bubblegum. "What do we do? Get a car, like an Uber?"

LAX sprawls out like an overgrown concrete monster—parking structures and terminals tangle together in a circular maze of roads choked with gridlocked traffic. Blinking red taillights stretch out in a sea of "you're screwed" as far as the eye can see.

"We don't have time to wait for an Uber."

I stop thinking and do the only thing I can.

I run.

I take off, legs pumping, arms driving, every muscle firing in perfect coordination.

Blaze is shouting at me to slow down, sprinting like hell. As soon as he catches up, I toss him my phone. "Go live!"

"OH, SHIT!" he yells, hauling ass alongside me, phone in hand, and starts the livestream.

"Yo, DareSquad. Check it! My bro, doing the Tom Cruise! That's sick!"

I barely hear him. My heart is slamming. My pulse is a goddamn drum solo. My feet pound the pavement.

I've never run this hard in my life.

I have to get to her.

I have to tell her I'm sorry.

Blaze is behind me, yelling updates from the chat like an auction-eer.

"BRO! Chat says she's heading to baggage claim. WAIT! A fancy driver had her name on a sign."

Driver? Did she cancel her trip to New York?

I push harder.

Faster.

I round the corner to the main loop of the airport. A massive concrete horseshoe that reeks of jet fuel and car exhaust. Horns blare. Brake lights flare crimson in bumper-to-bumper traffic.

The sidewalks aren't any better—exhausted travelers wheeling oversized luggage, families herding children like cats, businesspeople barking into phones, and tourists stopping dead in their tracks to read signs.

I dodge a family of four, nearly taking out the dad pushing a stroller the size of a small refrigerator, and jump over a rogue backpack.

Blaze is struggling. Wheezing. "BRO—" He coughs. "WAIT UP, I'M DYING. CARDIO… KILLING ME."

I turn, grab the phone from his sweaty hands, and keep running. "GO GET YOUR GIRL, BRO!"

I don't look back.

"DareSquad," I pant into the livestream, my breath coming in sharp bursts. "Where is she?"

The chat whizzes past, a blur of words, as my shaking hand struggles to keep the phone steady enough to read:

SOMEONE GIVE THIS MAN A STUNT CONTRACT!
TOM CRUISE IS SWEATING!
WHO ELSE HEARS THE MISSION IMPOSSIBLE SOUNDTRACK PLAYING?
Are those turtles banging on his shirt?
SHE GOT INTO A BLACK SEDAN!

She's already leaving the airport? *Fuck!*

My heart plummets into my stomach. Black sedans. Everywhere. Dozens of them.

Every muscle in my body begs for mercy. Every breath feels like inhaling fire. Every step sends shockwaves of pain up my spine.

But I don't stop.

I won't stop.

If Tom Cruise can run with a broken ankle, I can run through this pain. I can't lose her.

My body moves before my brain fully forms the plan. I launch myself into the traffic lane, narrowly avoiding a shuttle bus that lays on its horn, vibrating my skull. The driver's middle finger shoots up, and yeah—fair. If I saw me doing this, I'd flip me off twice.

"CAM!" I shout, my voice lost in the cacophony of airport noise. "CAMILA!"

I peek into one black sedan.

Not her.

I sprint to the next car, slamming my hands against the tinted glass. "CAM?"

An elderly woman screams.

"Sorry!"

My body moves on reflex, years of performing stunts taking over as I flip, jump, slide, and weave my way through the crowded pickup area. The phone still clutched in my hand, livestream still rolling.

My eyes dart from window to window, searching for her.

"Cam, baby… if you're watching this, please stop!" My voice cracks with desperation. "I know you're upset. You have every right to be. But please—give me five minutes. That's all I'm asking. Five minutes to explain!"

A horn blares, and I whip around to see a Mustang bearing down on me faster than the surrounding traffic. No time to move—my body makes the split-second decision that would make a stunt coordinator proud. I dive across the hood, my palms slick with sweat as they connect with the warm metal.

"Sorry!" I slide off, rolling to absorb the impact.

"What the hell, man?" the driver yells, but I'm already gone, parkour-ing my way into the next automotive challenge.

Phones are out. People are filming. A group of tourists are literally cheering.

A guy yells, "YO, IS THIS A PRANK OR A MOVIE?"

I leap onto a garbage can to get a better view.

And then—

I spot her. Sitting in the back seat of a black sedan. Only two cars up.

"CAM!" I shout, reaching out.

I jump to the ground—

And trip over a goddamn suitcase.

WHAM! I hit the pavement hard, my phone flying from my hand, skidding across the sidewalk.

Pain explodes in my knee, my hands scraping raw against the asphalt. Then survival instinct kicks in. I scramble to my feet, head whipping around frantically, searching for my phone.

"Crap, you're Reece Dare!" says a teenage boy, his eyes wide with recognition. He hands me the still-livestreaming device. "Sorry, man."

I snatch it from his hand with a quick nod of thanks, spinning back toward the sedan, only to see it merging onto the exit ramp that leads away from LAX. The brake lights flash once then grow smaller as the car picks up speed, leaving the congested airport loop behind.

Stealing Cam away.

"What can I do to help?" the kid asks.

"You got a car?" I pant.

The kid blinks. "Dude, I'm in middle school."

Right. I scan our surroundings, desperate for anything—anything—that could help me chase down that car. My eyes land on the kid's luggage—sleek, hard-shell, and by the shine of it, made of titanium. *Oh, hell yes.*

I grab it. "Can I have this?"

"Yeah, sure. Whatever you want."

I rip it open, dump his stuff into his arms—

Socks. A PlayStation controller. A box of Pop-Tarts.

Then I drop the open, empty suitcase on the pavement, hard-shell side down, slam my feet into it like it's a snowboard, and crouch low.

A delivery truck is pulling away from the curb next to me. Do or die time.

I lunge forward, using my legs to propel the suitcase-sled, and grab on to the back of the truck with my free hand. The sudden acceleration nearly rips my arm from its socket as the suitcase catches against the pavement. But I hold on, white-knuckling the truck's metal edge as my impromptu transportation device begins to glide, picking up speed.

I'm skitching. Behind a truck. On a suitcase. In the LAX arrivals lane.

I've done plenty of skitching stunts for the channel—hanging on to moving vehicles with bikes, skateboards, even a shopping cart once. But never with a piece of luggage. The metal shell skims over the asphalt, the wheels completely useless in this position but providing just enough structure for the shell not to crack under my weight.

The truck picks up speed, completely unaware that I'm a goddamn lunatic surfing behind it. Wind roars past my ears, the rush of speed sending adrenaline surging through my veins like rocket fuel. Sparks fly as the hardshell scrapes against the street.

SKRRRRT! SKRRRRT!

I lift the phone, keeping one hand death-gripped to the truck while the other aims the camera at my face. The livestream is still broadcasting, comments flying in.

"Kids, seriously. Don't ever do this. This is the dumbest stunt I've ever pulled in my life." The suitcase wobbles underneath me, threatening to slip out from under my feet. "But you do stupid things when you're in love."

The word hangs in the air like a confession. Love. Not *like*. Not *lust. Love.*

The chat is losing it:

SOMEONE STOP THIS MAN.

REECE, YOU ARE GOING TO DIE ON LIVE.

This is so stupidly romantic I don't know if I wanna cry or call 911.

Ahead, I catch sight of the black sedan, its brake lights flashing as traffic slows near the ramp onto the freeway. I'm gaining on it. Beneath me, the suitcase is heating up fast against the pavement. A sharp, burning stench fills the air. Something's about to give.

The sedan signals and starts to change lanes. *Shit.* They're veering off.

It's now or never.

I shove my phone into my mouth, freeing both hands. Summoning every ounce of strength from muscles already pushed beyond their limits—

I push off the truck.

The suitcase wobbles beneath me as I shift my weight, navigating toward the sedan like an absolute psycho.

I reach out—

My fingers graze the bumper—

SCREECH! The car slams the brakes.

I fly forward, crash onto the trunk with a brutal thud, roll once, twice—

SLAM! I hit the asphalt hard, like a bag of bricks.

For a moment, I lie there, the world tilting and spinning around me. Every part of my body registers a different complaint, from my scraped palms to my burning thighs to what's gotta be three broken ribs.

Then the car door flies open. Cam bolts out of the back seat.

"¡Ay, Dios mío! Reece!" Panic surges in her gaze as she scans my road-rashed body, sprawled across the asphalt. "Are you okay? Did you just...? A suitcase...? What the hell?!"

Words are hard right now. Breathing is harder. Moving? Off the table. She drops to her knees beside me, her hands hovering over my body as if she's afraid to touch me in case something's broken.

"I—" A groan escapes as I struggle to sit up. "Lahaina... Tom Cruise... run... got you."

"Oh my God, he's brain damaged," she mutters, sliding a warm arm under my shoulders. "How many fingers am I holding up? What year is it? Who's the president? Can you feel your extremities? All of them? Even Little Reece?"

Despite the severe pain, her touch has my dick trying to raise its hand.

Around us, traffic has ground to a halt. Horns blare an angry symphony. Drivers shout colorful suggestions about where we can relocate ourselves. Pedestrians stop to film the spectacle.

"Phone," I manage to wheeze, pointing weakly at my device, which skidded about ten feet away during my spectacular dismount.

Cam grabs it then freezes when her eyes land on the screen. "You're livestreaming this? Seriously? What, the seventy million views of me being publicly humiliated weren't enough? Going for an even hundred?"

I shake my head, wincing at the movement. "Not why I'm here," I rasp, reaching for the phone. "DareSquad," I croak, "execution: six out of ten. Landing: negative twelve. But I found her. Mission accomplished. Wish me luck. Signing off." I hit *End*, cutting the stream.

"You're bleeding," she says, her voice gentle as she brushes a thumb near a gash on my forehead. "And I'm pretty sure that's not where your elbow is supposed to bend. You need a hospital."

"Not until you hear me out."

"If it's 'I've always wanted to die in traffic,' you can save it."

I take a breath so painful I might as well be inhaling broken glass. "I'm sorry, Cam. I'm so fucking sorry I didn't trust you."

"Reece—"

"Let me finish. Please." I reach out, catching her fingers between mine. The contact is a defibrillator to my heart, sending a jolt through my system. "I pulled the same bullshit I always do—shut down, assume the worst, run for the hills. Because that's my go-to move when shit gets real."

She doesn't pull away, which I interpret as promising *(or a lack of blood flow)*.

"You're nothing like them—Astrid, Gordon, all the users and takers. You see me. Not the brand or the bank account, but... me. The real me. The one who's terrified of letting anyone close enough to know all my broken parts."

For once, she doesn't shoot back some sarcastic remark.

"Cam, I saw the video."

"And?"

"And it was fucking incredible," I say, voice rough. "You took my channel—my shallow, look-at-me-jump-off-shit channel—and did something *real*. Something *good*. And I don't just mean the money raised. I mean, you made people *care*. You made *me* care."

She glances down at our joined hands, then back up at me. "I *was* going to ask you to promote my channel," she admits. "That part was true. But all that other stuff, Astrid twisted..."

"I know."

"No, you don't." She shakes her head. "I'm not cut out for this. The scrutiny. The comments. The way people picked me apart—it's like being thrown into a woodchipper."

My chest constricts painfully, and not from the probable broken ribs. "Cam—"

"I was so naive," she continues. "I thought I could just make my documentaries, and that would be it. But now I get it—there's no separating the content from the creator. I'd be signing up for all of it. The hate, the obsession, the constant judgment."

A single tear trails down her cheek, and I softly wipe it away with my thumb. My hand cradles her face, and for a half second, she leans into the touch, her eyes fluttering closed.

That's when I notice she's wearing my shirt. The ridiculous rhino one with the animals getting frisky. Memories flood in of that night in the tent when I couldn't hold back my feelings any longer.

It's a sign.

I'm an idiot. Two years—two freaking years—with this insanely brilliant, talented woman right in front of me. A heart the size of the fucking Pacific, and what did I do? Pushed her away because I was too scared to admit how much I wanted her.

No more.

Her lips part slightly, her breath catching.

"I love you, Camila Morales. Not for what you can do for me or my channel or my fucking brand. I love you because you call me on my crap, you see through my walls, and you make the most obscene noises when I go down on you."

"Reece—"

"I love the way you mutter in Spanish when you're pissed. I love knowing when you wear those cargo pants, you mean business. I love that you care more about telling stories that matter than getting famous for it."

Another tear escapes, but this time she doesn't try to hide it.

"I understand you're terrified of the influencer life," I continue. "But you don't have to do any of it. Not the comments, not the meet-and-greets, not the merch, not the fucking TikTok dances. You can make your documentaries, and I'll build a fortress around you so thick that not even the thirstiest internet trolls can get through."

"You can't protect me from the whole world."

"Watch me try." The intensity in my voice surprises us both.

The ambulance pulls up alongside us, red and blue lights painting Cam's face in alternating colors, like she's caught between two worlds.

"How do I know you won't run again?" she asks, voice barely above a whisper. "The next time you get scared or somebody makes you doubt me—why should I believe you won't shut me out?"

I take her hand and place it over my heart, letting her feel the wild, erratic beat that's all for her.

"Because for the first time in my life, I didn't run away from something—I ran *to* someone. I flew across an ocean, jumped onto a moving vehicle, and turned myself into a human toboggan in order to reach you." I gesture at the chaos around us, the flashing lights, the stopped traffic, the gathering crowd. "This isn't a stunt, Cam. This is me, terrified but showing up anyway. Because losing you would hurt worse than every fall, crash, and burn I've ever taken on camera combined."

EMTs push through the crowd, medical bags in hand, expressions caught between concern and confusion as they take in the scene.

"Sir, we need to check you out," a man says, kneeling beside me. "Possible concussion, lacerations—"

"One minute," I reply, not taking my eyes off Cam. "Your video... the Lahaina fundraiser, already hit two million dollars. The DareSquad showed up in force. They listened to *you*."

She blinks in surprise. "Really?"

"They saw what I see—someone who actually cares about others, about causes worth fighting for." I clasp her hand again, pushing off the EMT's attempt to wrap a blood pressure cuff around my arm.

"Mr. Dare, please," he says, "your injuries—"

"I fired Gordon. I'm changing the whole company, the content—all of it. No more empty stunts or superficial bullshit."

"That's... good," she says carefully. "But that's not why I—"

"I know," I say, cutting her off. "That's not why you should be with me. I don't want you to love me because I'm finally doing the right thing. I want you to love me because... well, just because."

A small smile plays at the corners of her mouth. "I do, you know."

"Do what?"

"Love you." She says it simply, like stating a fact about the weather. "I've been fighting it because I thought it would compromise the life I wanted. But it turns out, loving you *is* what I want."

The EMT sighs loudly.

"I want you to help shape whatever comes next," I say, ignoring the growing crowd. "Not as my employee or my fake girlfriend, but as my partner. In everything."

"Your partner? But then who would you argue with about being the boss?"

There she is. My Cam.

"Oh, I'm definitely still the boss," I tell her, my lips curving into a smirk despite the pain radiating through my body. "But I'm willing to accept your frequent strongly voiced objections."

"How generous of you." But she's smiling now, really smiling.

I reach up, ignoring the EMT's frustrated groan, and slide my hand behind her head, pulling her toward me until our foreheads touch.

"Be my girlfriend, Morales. For real this time. No contracts, no cameras, no audience. Just you and me figuring it out together."

"Hmm." She pulls slightly away to study my face. "I suppose somebody has to keep you from killing yourself."

"Is that a yes?"

"Yes, you reckless YouTube lunatic." She kisses me again, softer this time. "I love you too much to let you face the internet alone."

"In that case," I announce, loud enough for our audience to hear, "I think I'm ready for the hospital now."

The crowd erupts in cheers as the EMTs help me onto a stretcher. Cam never lets go of my hand, not when they load me into the ambulance, not when they hook me up to monitors, not even when they start cutting away my shirt.

"Gift from Kai?" she asks, eyeing the turtles with a smirk. "Very on-brand. Nothing screams 'I'm a mature adult in a serious relationship' like fornicating reptiles."

"Says the woman wearing rhinos going at it."

She looks down, realizing what she has on, and a flush creeps up her neck. "Guess we're good for each other."

"Good?" I draw her hand to my lips and kiss her knuckles. "Nah, we're fucking great together."

"Oh my God," she says, pulling the hot pink scrunchie off my wrist. "Did you literally fly across an ocean and almost get killed surfing on luggage just to fuck my tits?"

"Can you blame me? They're perfect fucking tits."

Her smile—that sunshine smile that broke through my walls—is the last thing I see before the pain meds kick in, sending me floating into blissful darkness.

But even then, I don't let go of her hand.

Because I'm never letting her go again.

EPILOGUE

CAM

ONE YEAR LATER

I STARTLE AWAKE, DISORIENTED. My pulse is racing as my body's built-in alert system tells me I'm about to roll right off whatever I'm sleeping on. I blink into the gloom, my brain working overtime to figure out where in the world I am.

This isn't our house in LA.

Or that castle hotel near Paris where Reece surprised me for my birthday last month.

Or the Airbnb in Costa Rica where we filmed the sea turtle conservation series.

My hands slide across unfamiliar silk sheets, definitely not the organic cotton ones Reece insists on buying because "they're better for the environment, Cam." I squint, making out a distinct outline of jungle plants against dark walls. And—*¡Ay, Dios mío!*—is that a sex swing in the corner?

Maui. We're back at the Aloha Amour Resort.

A shiver races down my spine as I realize I'm completely naked. Again. I swear I went to bed wearing the cute matching set from that boutique in Tokyo, but Reece must have some kind of sleep-stripping superpower. The man's magic fingers can remove lingerie without disturbing my REM cycle. I'd be impressed if I weren't freezing my tits off right now.

Because once more, he's stolen every single blanket.

I glare at the Reece-shaped burrito next to me. Somehow the guy's wrapped himself in all the available bedding, as if he's burrowing in for the winter. Only his face is visible, his dark hair sticking up in tufts on the pillow.

HNRFFF-zzzthbt. Mmmrrph. Hhhnkshhpoo…. Snkxxkchh…!

The snoring. Dear God, the snoring—imagine evil scientists crossbred a motorcycle with a congested walrus. How can somebody so ridiculously gorgeous sound like he's crunching rocks with his teeth?

Still, my heart totally flips watching him sleep, enjoying that sweet, secret smile he used to hide behind scowls and barked orders.

Now? It's mine—when he wakes up, when he finds me editing in his T-shirt, when he catches me dancing in the kitchen on FaceTime with my besties Petra and Katie… and especially after nights like last night, when he starred in a kinky, unholy smutshow that'll have me walking funny for a week.

See, that boy wasn't kidding about never wanting to leave once he got inside me. A year later, we've christened more hotel rooms than I can count. It's gotten so out of hand, we had to institute a weekly NO SEX DAY so that my lady bits don't riot. Our favorite *let's behave* activity? Couch marathons of Tom Cruise movies—though we rarely make it halfway through *Mission Impossible* before one of us caves. What can I say? Tom's running scenes do things to Reece, and Reece's fanboy enthusiasm flows right into me *(pun intended)*.

I shiver all over, goosebumps spreading across my bare skin. Punishment is definitely in order.

I slide off the mattress with ninja-like stealth, my feet making contact with the floor in the one blind spot I've learned doesn't trigger the rotating bed sensors. Rummaging through Reece's suitcase, I find what I'm searching for—the neon eyesore he calls his "lucky shirt."

Save the Rhinos—One Ride at a Time!

Those rhinos still look entirely too happy being caught on camera in a mid rump bump. Their enthusiastic expressions have faded after countless cleanings, but Reece refuses to let it go. He wore it the first night we made love, and I had it on the day I agreed to be his real girlfriend. He claims it has "powers." That it's "part of our love story."

The big softie.

When I pull it over my head, his familiar spicy ginger scent washes over me. I step into my discarded pajama shorts from the tile, the silky material sliding over my thighs.

My phone sits charging on the dresser. I unplug it, open YouTube, and hit *Go Live*.

"Psst! DareSquad! Rise and shine, my beautiful chaos enablers!" I whisper, keeping my voice low. "We're back in the sex dungeon—I mean, the Aloha Amour Resort—and I need your help waking up The Beast." I flip the camera, revealing Reece in his blanket cocoon, his snores reaching seismic levels. "Isn't he adorable? A hibernating grizzly with incredible abs."

The comments start flooding in immediately:

OMG! the snoring.
BLAST THE AIRHORN CAM!!
The Blanket Bandit STRIKES Again.
THE RHINO SHIRT LIVES!!!

"Today's a super important day, which means I was supposed to get my beauty sleep," I whisper to the audience, "but your boy over there *stole* my blankets. I was a human ice cube reenacting the Titanic last night while he slept like a baby, practicing his whale calls."

I tiptoe over to the shower area—still no walls, still no privacy, still ridiculous—and turn on the water. The familiar cascade begins flowing over the volcanic rock, steam rising in delicate curls. I reach behind the stones for the shower wand, memories of my first disastrous encounter with it making me bite back a laugh.

I carefully pull it from its new home—a special holster Kai had installed after numerous guests complained about "Happy Button Mishaps."

"See this switch?" I position for a close-up. "It says 'Volcanic.' That's not false advertising, folks. Don't ask me how I know."

I press it and quickly return the wand to its holster, the water already beginning to pulse with increasing intensity. Red lights flicker to life along the stone walls, transforming the water into streams of artificial lava. I back away quickly, knowing exactly what's coming.

"T-minus ten seconds until tropical eruption," I whisper gleefully, backing away to a strategic position.

The DareSquad is living for this moment:

**This is why I have NOTIFICATIONS ON.
REVENGE IS A DISH BEST SERVED WET.
Wake him with the power of love Camila!!!
EVERYBODY TAKE COVER!**

I hold my finger to my lips, suppressing giggles as I position myself at a safe distance, camera trained on Reece's sleeping form.

"Wake-up call in three... two... one..."

I flash the lens with my most diabolical smirk as the first rumbles of the jungle show begin. The water pressure builds to critical mass, and—

CRACK! BOOOOOOM!

Thunder blasts through the room as if Zeus himself is DJing. Lightning shreds across the ceiling in electric veins, throwing the room into a rave with strobing white flashes. Right on cue, I slap the motion sensor beside a snoozing Reece.

The bed lurches to life, spinning maniacally like an evil Bond villain trap. Reece, still tucked up as a human Hot Pocket, starts rolling to the edge.

"WHAT THE FU—AAAHH!"

Reece tumbles off the bed in spectacular fashion, arms flailing from inside his fabric prison, legs kicking at nothing. He hits the ground with a *THUD*—probably fine, but I'm too busy cry-laughing to check.

"EARTHQUAKE!" he shouts, thrashing inside the blankets. "CAM! GRAB THE GO-BAG!"

"Good morning!" I sing-song over the thunderous soundtrack and escalating shower sounds. "Sleep well?"

"What's happening?" His head emerges from the tangled bedding, hair defying gravity, eyes wild with confusion.

Before he understands what's happening—the birds descend.

A platoon of animatronic parrots, toucans, and macaws drops from concealed ceiling panels, wings flapping in jerky mechanical movements. They open their plastic beaks in perfect synchronization and belt out a surprisingly high-quality rendition of "Sexual Healing."

"They remember us!" I shriek with delight, aiming the lens at the feathered choir. "And I think they missed you!"

Reece groans, running a hand through his sleep-disheveled hair. "Great. The sex birds are back. I need coffee."

Some things never change. For all his growth and tenderness, Reece Dare will forever be a grumpy morning monster until caffeine enters his system.

We've been inseparable since that fateful day at LAX when he skitched? Skated? Sledded? Whatever the fuck he did in that suitcase to chase me down. After they released him from the hospital *(three cracked ribs, severe road rash, and a mild concussion—all worth it, according to him)*, we spent an entire weekend wrecking each other in his ridiculous mansion.

When Monday rolled around and I mentioned going back to my apartment to grab clothes, he literally pouted—I shit you not. Then he called professional movers, who showed up two hours later with a truck. By dinnertime, my entire life had been relocated to his place.

When I asked if that was presumptuous, he simply stated, "I'm not letting you out of my sight ever again, Morales."

And he's been my biggest cheerleader ever since.

With a shockingly swift movement for someone who was dead asleep thirty seconds ago, Reece rolls me into the blanket with him, creating a two-person burrito. His morning stubble scratches my cheek deliciously as he smothers me with kisses—my forehead, my nose, my chin, the corner of my mouth.

"Let me see that," he grumbles, plucking the phone from my hand. "Guys, we gotta go gear up for today's big—"

I slap my hand over his mouth. "Don't spoil it!"

He licks my palm like a child, making me yank my hand away with a *you're-ridiculous-but-I-kind-of-love-it* look. "—adventure," he finishes smoothly. "But we'll be back later with something really special."

He ends the livestream, powers down the phone, and tosses the device onto the rotating bed.

His lips find mine in a deeper kiss, instantly turning my insides to molten lava, way more potent than Kai's fake version pouring down the rocks.

"How long does this jungle storm last?" he asks in a dangerous octave that makes my toes curl.

"Until the shower stops," I gasp as his teeth graze my lower lip.

"Well, we don't want to waste water, but..." Mischief sparks in his eyes as he stretches out an arm, groping around until he grabs the resort welcome bag triumphantly and empties its contents everywhere.

Among the scattered brochures, pineapple-flavored popcorn, and tiny bottles of sunscreen, a familiar palm-sized penguin with a bowtie rolls into view.

Reece's face lights up with unholy glee. "Well, well, well. Hello there, little guy." He picks up the vibrator, examining it as if he's reconnecting with an old friend. Then his gaze shifts to me, the corners of his mouth lifting in that panty-melting smirk. "Think you can make my girl scream louder than this thunder?"

"No, Reece, we need to get ready for the..." My protest dissolves into a whimper as his hand slides beneath my pajama bottoms, the vibrator making contact with exactly where I'm already embarrassingly wet for him.

The penguin starts to buzz against my clit.

"I dare you to come all over my hand, baby. And then I'm going to fuck you... hard. The way I did our very first time in that tent."

I play hard to get—"You don't know what I want"—and fail. My back arches as the vibrator hits exactly the right spot, thrumming with spiraling pleasure pulses. "Fuck yes, I want that."

"See?" Reece's voice is pure smugness wrapped in sex. "Your pussy likes it when I take control."

A breathy laugh escapes me, even as my body feels ready to burst into flames. "Who says you're in control?"

His answering grin is pure wickedness. Without warning, he cranks the penguin to HIGH.

"¡Ay, Dios mío!" The cry rips from my throat as satisfaction rushes through me, unstoppable and overwhelming.

White light bursts behind my eyelids—From my orgasm? From the lightning flashing overhead? Who the hell knows. All that matters is the way pleasure swallows me whole, slamming into me so hard I'm screaming Reece's name. My body writhes against his hand, every pulse wrecking me from the inside out. Teasing, wicked vibrations ripple through my system.

"God, you're so fucking hot," Reece growls, his eyes dark with hunger as he watches me come apart. "Tell me you want my dick."

"Please," I pant, still trembling with aftershocks. "Now. I need you now."

"I want you so bad. Every day. Every minute."

With impressive strength, Reece flips our positions so I'm straddling him, the blanket pooling around our hips. His hands grip my waist fiercely, thumbs pressing into my hipbones.

"Come on, baby. Show me those perfect tits," he commands, voice rough with need. "I wanna watch them bounce."

I rip off the rhino shirt, ready to play. Reece's eyes rake over my naked chest, his Adam's apple bobbing with a hard swallow. I reach for his wrist, where—as always—a brightly colored sex scrunchie sits 24/7.

Sliding it off, I pull my hair into a messy ponytail, knowing exactly how much the visual affects him. "You sure you don't want to fuck my tits?"

His eyes roll back momentarily, as if the mere suggestion short-circuits his brain. "Hell yeah," he manages, "but tonight when I can take my time."

His hand searches the bed, finds a foil packet, and he tears it open with his teeth. The distinctive aroma hits me instantly and I laugh. It's the unmistakable scent of bacon from the flavored condom.

"Okay, now I don't know if I want sex or breakfast."

"Dick first, bacon after."

I lean down, my ponytail tickling his cheek as I repeat the words I said to him that very first time: "Shut your gorgeous face up and fuck me."

Pulling my pajama bottoms to the side, I position myself over him, gripping his impressive length with one hand. Without hesitation, I slam down onto his shaft with a single thrust that steals the breath from both our lungs.

"Fuckkkkk, baby!" Reece groans, his fingers digging into my hips hard enough to leave marks I'll cherish later.

"Harder!" I demand, rotating my hips in a tight circle that makes his eyes cross. "Don't be a pussy to my pussy."

"What did I do to deserve you?" he asks, genuine wonder breaking through the haze of lust.

We find our rhythm. His upward snaps meet my downward thrusts, our bodies moving together with the practiced synchronicity of partners who know how to please each other.

The eye contact is what undoes me. Through it all—the frantic pace, our animalistic slapping sounds, the mechanical bird chorus hitting an impressive key change overhead—his gaze never leaves mine. The intimacy is devastating, like I'm standing naked in a storm—bare, vulnerable, completely seen, wrapped in the force of him as his love holds every raw piece of me.

Our frenzied tension reaches a fever pitch, and finally the coiling pressure explodes.

Release hits me—hard, fast, everywhere.

Reece breaks with a roar—loud enough to make a lion jealous—before I collapse onto his chest, boneless and trembling, our skin slick with sweat, our breaths ragged and desperate.

His arms lock around me like he's afraid to let go, our hearts pounding so hard I can't tell which one is mine.

"I love you," he says between gasps.

"I love you more."

He tilts my chin up, his eyes serious despite his sex-disheveled appearance. "Not fucking possible, Morales."

His lips claim mine again.

MWAAARP! MWAAARP! MWAAARP!

It's my alarm, blaring from the bed.

"Shit!" I bolt upright. "We gotta get ready. We can't be late!"

I scramble off him, planting a quick kiss on his lips that he immediately tries to deepen. I pull away with reluctance, pointing a stern finger. "No... later."

His pouty expression almost makes me reconsider, but we're on a schedule. I grab the Pleasure Penguin vibrator from where it tumbled onto the floor and toss it to him with a wink. "But we're taking the little guy home with us. He's officially a member of the family now."

***

It's been precisely one year since Reece and I stood in this very spot—back then, this place felt hollow. The sun had been just as warm, the sky just as blue, Maui as beautiful as ever—but the brightness didn't reach here. The air had felt thick with loss, heavy with the echoes of what had been.

But today, wearing a Dare4Change T-shirt, it carries a different weight. The same sun shines, but now it radiates a quiet hum of renewal. The breeze moves, alive with something new. A pulse. A spark of possibility.

New walls stand where rubble once lay, businesses shine with fresh windows, and kids laugh with dripping shaved ice. Lahaina isn't whole yet—not by a long shot—but pulse points of life have returned. The famous banyan tree, once scorched and skeletal, now boasts patches of bright-green leaves sprouting defiantly from its twisted limbs. A symbol of resilience that perfectly captures the town's spirit.

The street has transformed into a festival. As far as I can see, there are families, kids, volunteers carrying boxes of decorations, and workers putting finishing touches on colorful banners that stretch across the street. Photographers and press teams swarm the crowd, and there's a drone zipping overhead getting aerial shots.

"Can you believe it's been a year since you brought me here?" I ask, squinting through my viewfinder at the transformed landscape.

"You mean since you launched that video and created a movement," Reece says, slipping his arm around my waist.

"I was ugly crying in an airport CPK, not exactly planning to raise millions."

But that's what happened.

Twenty million in public donations. And because Reece Dare has a heart the size of Maui itself, he matched that amount dollar for dollar, bringing the total to forty million.

All because I decided to post a raw, unfiltered video defending the man I loved ... before boarding a plane to forget him forever.

The money was a total game changer—not only for Lahaina, but for us. Our careers. Our purpose. Our whole freaking lives.

"Camera angle looks off," Reece says, peering over my shoulder.

"Excuse me? Who's the videography expert here?" I challenge, hip-checking him.

"I'm just saying—"

"Nuh-uh. This is my area of expertise. You stick to jumping off tall objects and making ridiculous Tom Cruise faces."

His mock-wounded expression makes me laugh.

We're standing in front of Paradise Burger Hut, the Akana family's beloved restaurant that's finally—FINALLY—ready to reopen. The building gleams in the sunlight, its fresh blue paint exactly matching the original shade *(Pono insisted)*. The smell of grilling burgers is wafting through the air.

All around us, volunteers in Dare4Change shirts *(our signature red tees with the heart hands logo)* hustle to set up chairs, hang banners, and wrangle the press to their places. Each one represents another person who decided to show up—to be part of something bigger than themselves.

Behind me, someone yells, "Cam! Where do you want the flower wall?"

"Over by the stage," I call back, slipping into Boss Mode Camila, which is honestly still a weird title to get used to. Because I'm officially the head of Dare4Change. Yeah. *Me.* The girl who used to hide behind the camera, now running a nonprofit that—not to brag—has had one hell of a first year.

We've rebuilt Paradise Burger Hut, constructed a dozen homes—including a new one for the Akanas—and launched more than fifty community-led initiatives around the world.

But don't give me the credit. Or even Reece. It's everyone.

Because this was never just about us.

Gone are the days of empty stunts and mindless pranks. Whatever crazy thing we do now is for a cause. If Reece is swimming with sharks, we're raising money to rebuild schools in underprivileged neighborhoods. If I'm dangling off a cliff, we're raising awareness for mental health.

Our most popular videos?

We Adopted All the Animals in a Shelter (And Found Them Homes!).

We Sent Every Teacher in This District on a Paid Cruise—Here's Why.

Cliff Jumping for Cancer Research (You Helped Us Raise Millions!).

And let me tell you—nothing makes Reece happier than risking his life for a cause.

Even the merch line has changed. The Dare4Change apparel is now our best seller, and the two of us are never caught without it. It's practically our uniform *(when we're wearing clothes)*.

And I won't lie. I love that we get to wear our mission on our sleeves—literally—and show people that making a difference is the coolest thing you can do.

I glance out at the growing crowd, and there's a familiar swell in my chest. *This is where I belong. Here. With these people. Doing this work.*

Reece and I remain the "it couple" the world loves to watch—though let's be real, half of them are only there to see me call him names like "Captain Mood Swing" and "Mr. Broody Pants," and the other half just want to see if he'll toss me over his shoulder caveman style mid-livestream. *Spoiler: both happen. Usually within the first five minutes.*

But the best part? The part that still makes me pinch myself? *We're making a real difference.*

According to Gordon, Reece changing his content from *look-at-me-almost-die-for-clicks* to *look-at-me-almost-die-for-charity* was career suicide. Except Reece Dare now has over 300 million subscribers. The same guy who once dangled off a Ferris wheel wearing a thong for a prank video is now the face of compassion. Turns out, in a world of trending nonsense, people are starving for authenticity.

And—get this—he is *Time Magazine's* Person of the Year. Yeah. THE MOST POPULAR YouTuber EVER. Suck it, Gordon.

Speaking of G-Thorne, last I heard, he and Astrid are now living in Miami, trying to make her "big" on OnlyFans while she waitresses at Hooters.

Oh, how the mighty have fallen.

Once upon a time, Astrid dreamed of a beauty empire. Now? Her biggest brand collab is with Bedazzled Butt Stuff. And don't worry, I checked—#AstridShines is no longer about her "glow up journey" but literally about whatever new rhinestone she's slapped on her hoo-ha for the week.

I'm not saying karma is real... but this town has a banyan tree that survived literal fire, and Astrid couldn't even survive a PR scandal. So, yeah. Universe: 1. Astrid: 0.

"Camila, dear!" I hear from behind me, and I spin to find Mama V, Reece's mother Vera, waving excitedly from her mobility scooter. "We've got everything ready for the families, sweetheart. Once the ribbon's cut, we'll show them their new homes."

My chest warms—because Reece's moms Helen and Vera have been living here in Maui all year to make this happen. Helen—a retired architect turned house-building warrior queen—oversaw the entire framework, from the first beam to the last nail. And Mama started a community arts program for the kids in Lahaina, including Keoni and Nalani, who I see running around in Dare4Change shirts, acting as if they own the place.

Swear to God, the way Keoni's been talking about becoming a YouTuber like Reece? I'm about to start offering *So You Wanna Be a Good Human on YouTube* seminars. These kids want more than fame. They want to change the world. That's what Reece has done—what *we've* done.

Helen beams at me. "You need anything? I've got a clipboard and a mean stink-eye for anybody messing with the schedule."

I laugh, but before I can answer, hands loop at my waist and spin me. "Hey!" I yelp as Reece plants a kiss on me that has my heart cartwheeling.

"Mom, Mama," Reece calls over my head. "Can you please tell my gorgeous girlfriend to stop working so hard?"

Without missing a beat, Helen crosses her arms and smirks. "No can do, son. Maybe you need to work harder."

Vera winks. "She's doing just fine without you slowing her down."

"Wow. Betrayed by my own mothers."

"Someone needs to keep you humble," Helen says with a cheeky smile.

"Oh, I know who the boss is," Reece replies.

"Well," I say. "Technically I work for you, so you're still the boss."

"Only on paper," he says, smiling. "We both know who really runs this operation."

"The Blazeinator has arrived!"

Blaze charges in, a Golden Retriever on two legs, rocking his usual over-the-top ensemble. He's got on a neon-purple pineapple button-down that's both too tight and too bright, paired with hot-pink board shorts and a backward trucker hat proudly declaring, BLAZE

Mode: Engaged. He doesn't need a Dare4Change shirt because he got the logo tattooed on his forearm.

"Yo, my dudes! Let's get started. I need two double cheeseburgers. Stat! Cam, did you tell Reece the surp—"

I grab the front of his shirt and yank him toward me, nose to nose. "Blaze. Stop talking."

Too late. Reece is laser-focused on me. "What surprise? What's going on?"

I shrug innocently. "You'll have to wait and see."

He stares me down, but I'm immune to the Reece Dare Glare now. I reach up and give his pouty lips a quick peck. "You'll find out soon enough. But right now, I need your talented fingers to cut a ribbon."

The crowd is gathered outside Paradise Burger Hut. Families are lined up with excited kids, volunteers are hustling, handing out water bottles, while the media focus their cameras on us as if we're the returning King and Queen of Hawaii. I lift the livestreaming phone, angling for the perfect shot, to show our global viewers all the burger-fueled magic.

I scan the crowd and wish Katie and Petra were here. My besties. My hype squad. The ones who encouraged me to go for my documentary dreams.

But they're cheering me on from the livestream, rapid-fire commenting inside jokes and inappropriate emojis while off living their own ridiculously exciting lives. We may not be standing side by side, but they're here, in every all-caps text, every unhinged voice memo, every *holy crap, I'm so proud of you* message flooding my screen. *God, I love them so much.*

"Welcome, beautiful spirits!" Kai steps forward, raising his hands, and suddenly everyone falls silent—because when Kai speaks, the whole island listens. Or maybe they're admiring his glistening abs, which are fully on display in a sarong that's riding so low on his hips, I'm worried his python is the only thing holding up the fabric.

"Today, we celebrate the rebirth of Paradise, both the restaurant and the community spirit that binds us. Family and community are the threads that weave our lives. Without them, we drift aimlessly; with them, we stand strong, our roots intertwined and unbreakable in ways no storm or flame can ever truly erase."

I feel a lump form in my throat at the unexpected depth of his words. Beside me, Reece squeezes my hand, and I know he's feeling it too.

"And so"—Kai's voice rises dramatically—"after this sacred ribbon-cutting ceremony, I invite you all to join me and my fellow warriors on the beach for a special performance we call 'Rising Wood: Erecting New Foundations for Tomorrow's Pleasure.'"

Aaaand we're back to standard Kai programming.

"Did he just—" Reece whispers.

"Make rebuilding homes sound like a euphemism for group sex? Yes, yes he did."

"The man is nothing if not consistent."

The scissors close, the ribbon falls, and the crowd erupts in cheers. Confetti cannons explode, showering us all in blue paper *(biodegradable, I might add).*

As the applause begins to die down, I step forward, heart hammering with excitement. I hold up the livestreaming phone. "But we're not done! We're looking for international support to expand our cause."

I glance at Reece, who's nodding knowingly, as if he understands what I'm saying. He doesn't. Not even close.

"And to launch this campaign," I continue, vibrating with anticipation over the stunt I've spent months—*literally MONTHS*—orchestrating, "Reece will be re-creating his epic LAX Tom Cruise run on a special course throughout Lahaina, highlighting areas still in need of rebuilding."

Reece's expression shifts… Polite agreement. Genuine confusion. Dawning excitement.

"Did you set up a parkour course through town?"

"Something better." I grin, unable to contain myself any longer. "You'll be running alongside—"

Okay, so here's the thing about planning surprises for Reece Dare—you think you're ready for how it'll play out, but nothing really prepares you for Tom Cruise BASE JUMPING OUT OF A FREAKING HELICOPTER over a rebuilt Lahaina like we're suddenly starring in *Mission Impossible: Maui Edition.*

The second that helicopter comes flying in low, the whole crowd loses its collective mind. I mean, even Blaze's jaw is on the floor, and that man once held a live snake for a Will It Bite Me? video.

And then, BOOM—there he is. Tom Fucking Cruise. He lands with his signature smirk, his parachute billowing perfectly behind him as if it's contractually obligated to behave. He's dressed in a Dare4Change shirt and running shoes and jogs directly up to us with the high-energy enthusiasm of a man half his age.

Tom Cruise, the legend himself, sticks out his hand. "Thanks for raising money for a good cause, man."

Reece finally manages to blink and shakes his hand. "Uh, no, thank you, Mr. Cruise."

"Let's see if you can keep up."

And just like that, Tom Cruise takes off RUNNING—arms pumping in that perfect, high-knee, straight-backed, action-hero way—and for about half a second, Reece appears to be deciding whether to cry or chase him.

"GO!" I shout, laughing as Reece bolts after him, falling into that long-legged sprint I know way too well. All determination with muscular thighs that make me swoon.

Blaze revs the four-wheeler, exactly how we planned, grinning like a lunatic.

"Hop on, DareGirl!" he yells, and yes, that nickname has stuck.

I vault onto the back, twisting around so I'm sitting backwards, one hand gripping the roll bar and the other holding the filming phone steady.

Blaze takes off, wheels spitting dust as we barrel down the street after Tom and my boyfriend—who, let's face it, is doing a damn good job of keeping up right now.

As we zip around the town, the course we designed comes to life—each checkpoint marked with banners showing areas still needing donations. Kids wave, volunteers cheer, and the donations ticker on my phone screen is spinning out of control:

OMG IS THAT REALLY TOM CRUISE???

If Reece beats Tom, I'm tattooing 'Dare4Change' on my forehead.

Best collab of the year, hands down.

$500 if Reece outruns Tom.

As Reece dashes by, he glances at me—for a split second—and there it is. That smile that says, "You're crazy, but I can't get enough of you."

So, Hawaii doesn't suck after all. *Who knew?* It's the place where I found my voice, my purpose, and the love of my life.

Me and my DareBoy.

His one and only DareGirl.

And if this is what forever looks like? I'll take it.

***

Want more hilarious enemies-to-lovers vacation romance? Read all about Cam's bestie Katie in her story: **Italy Can Bite Me**

melisaryun.com/books

hey there, lovely!

Sun. Sand. Wedded bliss. Camila and Reece's honeymoon is supposed to be smooth sailing—but paradise is about to throw a few unexpected surprises their way.

Don't miss the steamy laughs in this FREE BONUS EPILOGUE!

melisaryun.com/bonus

MORE BOOKS BY MÉLISA RYUN

STAND-ALONE TITLES

Fake It 'Til You Sleigh It

a Holiday Romantic Comedy

Live From New York... It's Love

Short Story

HOT MESS SUMMER SERIES

Italy Can Bite Me

Hawaii Can Suck It

Mexico Can Choke On It

THE DENTON SISTERS SERIES

The Love Startup

a Raunchy, Geeky RomCom

AUTHORS' NOTE

Hey Lovelies!

So, let's start with the obvious: this book is a little over the top. But before you roll your eyes and say, "Come on, an army of animatronic parrots belting out 'Sexual Healing,' be honest... you've wondered what would happen if the Rainforest Café got a little freaky.

Now for some backstory: For over a decade, we were full-time YouTubers with our daughters, running a wildly successful family comedy channel called GEM Sisters. We lived and breathed the influencer world, and let us tell you—if you think Camila, Reece, and the rest of the content creators are extreme, you should've seen some of the wild stuff we witnessed behind the scenes.

Boom! Didn't see that coming, did you?

But here's the real reason we wrote this book: for every influencer chasing clout, there are many more using their platforms to make a real difference. We've met them. We've worked with them. And we've seen how one viral video can change lives. That's the heart of this story—what if influencers used their platform for something bigger than themselves?

In *Hawaii Can Suck It,* Camila is Latina, just like our daughters, and representation matters. When we were on YouTube, one of our biggest missions—alongside making people laugh—was to show kids that they could be the hero of their own stories. That's why we partnered with organizations like Boys & Girls Club, literacy programs, Women in STEM, and environmental initiatives—because making people laugh is great, but *making a difference*? Even better.

This story isn't just about romance and viral disasters. It's about using your voice, standing up for what matters, and learning that sometimes the biggest risks lead to the best rewards.

And speaking of making a difference, if you loved this book, help us spread the word and... **LEAVE US AN AMAZON REVIEW!**

Tell your friends, and let's keep proving that a little romance, some mischief, and a whole lot of heart can make the world a better place.

With love, laughter, and the firm promise that no animatronic birds have ever serenaded us in our own bedroom (yet),

MéLisa & Ryun
www.melisaryun.com

Leave a Review

ACKNOWLEDGMENTS

To our readers—thank you for strapping in for this wild influencer-filled ride through Hawaii. You are why we do what we love, and every review, social post, and *"OMG, I laughed so much!"* makes our hearts do a happy little hula dance.

To the incredible people who've supported, inspired, and kept us sane through it all—we're beyond grateful to have you in our corner.

- Happily Booked PR

- Literary Media Tours

- Author Ever After

To the one and only Meghan Quinn—you were the first book we read on our journey to becoming romance authors, and still our ultimate inspiration. Your talent, hustle, and perfect mix of heart and hilarity continue to inspire us. You'll always have two of your biggest fans in us, and one day—one day—we hope to meet in real life for the ultimate sunshine vs. grumpy showdown: MéLisa & Ryun vs. Meghan & Steph. Until then, we'll be here, reading, writing, and forever bowing down to the romcom queen.

SUPPORT LAHAINA

HELP FAMILIES IMPACTED BY MAUI WILDFIRES

As longtime professionals in media, we've seen how quickly the world moves on. News cycles change, trends shift—but for those directly impacted by disaster, the need for help continues long after the headlines fade.

The wildfires that devastated Lahaina, Maui, left behind more than ashes. Families lost homes, local businesses were destroyed, and entire communities were displaced. Rebuilding takes time and support.

If you've fallen in love with the characters and setting of this story, we invite you to make a difference for the real families and small businesses in Hawaii that inspired them. Every size donation helps.

Lahaina's story is far from over. To support the town's rich cultural heritage, learn more at: www.lahainarestoration.org.

From the bottom of our hearts, mahalo for reading—and for standing with those still rebuilding.

DONATE HERE:
https://www.hawaiicommunityfoundation.org

ABOUT THE AUTHORS

MéLisa Ryun is our combined pen name, and we're a husband-wife duo who've been finishing each other's sentences (and steamy scenes) for nearly 30 years. We left the glitz of Hollywood for the glitter of Vegas. Despite calling Sin City home, we say what happens in Vegas should definitely not stay in Vegas—not with our scorching hot romcoms.

We spend our days in a death match of yoga and joke-writing. Living out our happily-ever-after while making silly social media videos together. **Snark. Swoon. Spice!**

VISIT MELISARYUN.COM
FIND US ON SOCIAL MEDIA @MELISARYUN